*PRAISE FOR NANCY VARIAN BERBERICK
and her breathtaking novels of
epic fantasy and adventure . . .*

SHADOW OF THE SEVENTH MOON
A tale of the last dwarf, the songmaker Garroc . . .

"For lovers of ancient lore . . . Berberick has woven
a beautiful novel."

—**Knoxville News-Sentinel**

"Quite obviously the author knows her stuff, both the
history and the legends. This book is definitely worth
reading."

—**Fosfax**

THE JEWELS OF ELVISH
"Deception works within deception to thwart all efforts
to defend the kingdoms against the dark forces of evil.
Lots of action and lively description."

—**Inside Books**

A CHILD OF ELVISH
"Berberick makes a special effort to interest the reader
in her characters' emotional lives, taking the novel a
step beyond an action narrative."

—**Charlotte Observer**

Ace Books By
Nancy Varian Berberick

A CHILD OF ELVISH
SHADOW OF THE SEVENTH MOON
THE PANTHER'S HOARD

The Panther's Hoard

Nancy Varian Berberick

ACE BOOKS, NEW YORK

This book is an Ace original edition,
and has never been previously published.

THE PANTHER'S HOARD

An Ace Book / published by arrangement with
the author

PRINTING HISTORY
Ace edition/February 1994

ISBN: 0-441-00009-6

ACE®
Ace Books are published by The Berkley Publishing Group,
200 Madison Avenue, New York, NY 10016.
ACE and the "A" design
are trademarks belonging to Charter Communications, Inc.

PRINTED IN THE UNITED STATES OF AMERICA

10 9 8 7 6 5 4 3 2 1

To the memory of Henrietta Berberick.
I think of you always when I'm in my garden.

ACKNOWLEDGMENTS

As ever, I thank my husband, Bruce, and—as ever—for too many things to name here.

And I take great pleasure once again in thanking my dear friend Douglas W. Clark, a staunch way-friend and a storyteller whose work always delights me. This tale, like so many of mine, was told to Doug first.

The Panther's Hoard

PART ONE

Sif

Ellisif Hinthan's daughter stood in the doorway of the cottage and she was talking to her father, the old soldier these seven years dead. In the northern sky, witch-light blazed like red lightning, snuffed out all the stars. Very close, that blood-hued light; only across the Rill and north where three small farms lay in the arm of the river-bend. Or had lain before the battle and the storm of witch-fire.

"I'm afraid," Ellisif whispered to the ghost.

Her father wasn't a ghost to see; he was a ghost to hear, and he said:

That's because you've got good sense.

A cold breeze groaned through the apple-garth, naked branches clacked together. Ellisif smelled the last snow of winter padding near. In usual times she'd welcome that snow, for it would soak the ground and loosen up the soil so that she could plant her kitchen garden. But now she didn't welcome the chance of snow, for she was thinking about fleeing here.

The feud between the folk of Welshland and King Aethelred

Penda's son had flared again after three peaceful years. All along the western borderland the Welshmen of Powys came down into Mercia, bent on taking cattle and lands and slaves. The first raids fell on Yule-night, on the feast of Jesu's birth. Witch-lords led the raiders, and those dire witches could run like fire-pelted wolves and some could fly like flame-winged eagles.

But King Aethelred wouldn't cower before witches. He was a son of Penda, the old heathen king some folk knew as Wotan's Blade and others as the Golden Panther. Aethelred was the youngest of Pendas's sons, late-got after all the rest of that brave and storied brood, but he wasn't the least bold. He didn't care that winter is the enemy of all armies, with its snow and ice and whipping winds. He called his war-lord *cynings* to him, and the first to answer had been Haethcyn Erich's son, the lord of the Marches and all the lands around the Rill. Haethcyn Dwarf-Lord, people called him. Up and down the Isle folk say that if you're looking for a Dwarf you must go into Wales where the people are wrong-headed about everything, or into Mercia where King Aethelred lets Haethcyn Erich's son flout the laws of the Church and keep the heathen *dvergr* about him.

"Father," Ellisif whispered to the ghost. "I don't want to take the children and flee. I want to stay." She looked around at the homefield where soon rye and wheat and hay must be planted, at the byre where chickens slept in the rafters and the cow and the pig and the goats in the stalls. "Here there's food, and shelter. But I don't know how long I can keep it if armies come through."

She shuddered at the thought of any army, friend or foe, coming near. Each must eat, and either would take all she had.

Let your eldfather advise you, my girl, said ghost-Hinthan.

Ellisif's throat closed up tight around another fear. She didn't know if Eldfather was alive. Neither did she know if her husband, Arnulf, was alive. The *cyning* had claimed Arnulf for the fighting a long time ago in mid-winter, and no one had seen the Dwarf Garroc since summer's end when he'd gone away to his winter-home, as each year he did. But surely he'd come down from the hills when he heard about the fighting. Surely he was with the Haethcyn's army now.

Out in the night the Rill ran racing past the farm, fat with snow-melt. Yesterday Ellisif had found a broken-boned corpse in the shallows, fallen into the river in the north and fetched up here. She'd seen at once that he was a Dwarf, and for an endless moment she'd been too terrified to look closely at that poor broken body, dreading to see that here was Eldfather come home at last. But it wasn't Garroc, and she'd sent up prayers of thanks to Jesu and his Holy Mother. She didn't barrow the body, she didn't bury it. She'd sent it back to the river and prayed for the soul that used to live in the broken house, the lifeless corpse. Priests would say she did no good there, praying for a Dwarf. Some would even say she'd sinned, and that *dvergr*, like beasts of the wildwood, have no souls. Ellisif knew better than that, and so she'd prayed.

"Father," she said. "Tell me if he's dead."

I've told you, said ghost-Hinthan. And he said no more, went away back to his barrow, across the river where once Erich War Hawk, Haethcyn's father, used to have his hall. Hinthan's barrow was made from the hearth-stones of that hall.

Footsteps sounded behind Ellisif; her eldest son stood near.

"Come in, Mother," Iohann said.

"I will. Are the children asleep?"

"Blithe is. Leofsunu's in the loft and he's got half the thatch off the roof to see out better."

The sky flared again, a silent storm of light beyond the trees. Iohann quickened, his face flushed in the witchy glow. Ellisif put an arm round his shoulder, held him tight to her. He permitted it, but he didn't lean into her arm as he used to when he was a child. Iohann was fifteen now.

"Father's there," Iohann said, eyes on the witch-light.

Ellisif nodded. Arnulf was there. He was no soldier, though, her Arnulf. He was a farmer who knew how to hunt, one who had a keen eye for flying an arrow. Please God, that would be enough.

"And Eldfather."

And him. No kin of Ellisif's, Garroc was yet her beloved eldfather and it was him who'd taught her not to fear the voice of her dead father, how to listen to ghost-Hinthan speaking. He was wise in many things, and he could claim one hundred and twenty-two years for himself, though he looked like one in his middle years. He wasn't the youngest Dwarf in all the Isle, nor the oldest, but he was among the Last. He'd been a soldier all his life, and he served Haethcyn as he'd served Haethcyn's father and Erich's father before. Soldier and skald, he belonged to the Marcher *cynings,* heart and hand. And Garroc had been Hinthan's own foster-father in the days before people here had ever heard of the Christ, before there were priests to say that a foster-father must also be a child's christened god-father. No Dwarf lived who bent the knee to the Christ; they knew older gods—Wotan and

Thunor and Loki. But there was yet a Dwarf who stood, quietly, as foster-father to a child of *mann-cynn*.

Now the secret foster-son said, "I wish I was with them."

Ellisif was glad he wasn't. She'd fought hard for Iohann this year, and in the end it was agreed that he wouldn't go with his father when the *cyning* called the muster. Arnulf had agreed to that reluctantly. Iohann hadn't agreed at all.

Came a cry from within the cottage, little Blithe awake and wailing, terrified of the red-glaring night. Ellisif went swiftly inside. Too late, she remembered to call Iohann from the door. When she turned back, she saw that Iohann was gone. And she nearly choked on her heart leaping suddenly halfway up her throat when—with not even a sound—Garroc stepped into the light, his blue eyes hard as the glint of moonlight on iron. Bruised and bleeding, his face dark with soot, all of him—clothes and hair and wheat-gold beard—smelled of iron and smoke and blood.

"Don't worry about Iohann," he whispered. "Go inside, and ready bandages and food."

"Arnulf!"

"Hush, child. He's all right. You'll have company in just a moment. Do as I say now." Just a little he smiled. "And get that blue jug of whisky Arnulf keeps under the thatching in the back of the loft. Hurry!"

Ellisif ran and did as she was told. She called Leofsunu to tend Blithe, and she wondered, as she flew around the cottage gathering what was needed, where and when and what Arnulf had traded for whisky from over the border in Scotland.

A tall and golden man came into the cottage, a stranger bleeding and too hurt to walk on his own. He leaned on Iohann's shoulder and Garroc's; he could take only small shuffling steps. His high-boned handsome face shone white beneath the grime of battle. Behind came Arnulf, bow in hand, arrow nocked.

Mud and blood matted Arnulf's red hair and beard; his green eyes glittered. No one could see his hard and wary eyes now and say he was no soldier. Blithe stared at her father, sucking hard on her thumb. Leofsunu didn't look at him but from under lowered lids. This man who stood with strung bow and his back to the bolted door looked like their father, but he didn't seem like him. Wary as her children, Ellisif found something to do but stare. She took charge of her hearth and home, told Iohann and Garroc to lay the wounded one down close to the hearth, then told Iohann to bring the bandages, to mix the boiling kettle-water with the cold from the bucket by the door.

"And take Leofsunu and Blithe to my bed. Hurry!"

Ellisif knelt beside the wounded man. She stripped him as easily as though he were a babe, washed him and cleaned his wounds, an arrow's one-toothed bite, a long burn-mark winding the length of his right arm. Witch-burn. The stranger endured her painful work and didn't make a sound, not even to groan. Soon he lay very still, eyes closed, breathing in short, shallow gasps. Ellisif pressed her wrist to his forehead, felt the first of fever's fire.

"Who is he?"

Neither Arnulf nor Garroc answered with a name, but Garroc said he was a man worthy of help. Ellisif looked to the ruddy glow of witch-light seeped under the crack beneath the door where Arnulf stood, and her husband smiled at her to encourage. He looked like himself now, like a goodman farmer come to say to his wife: Girl, we've got us a guest. Have 'ee anything to feed him with, a place to rest him in?

Ellisif pulled the blanket up over the stranger's shoulders, tucked him tight. Outside, the wind sighed round the eaves, ghost-Hinthan came back from his barrow. He whispered soft, and Garroc sat down by the hearth, unstoppered the blue whisky jug and took a long pull.

"Boy mine," he said, low. "Here you are."

He said no more, not aloud; but Ellisif knew that skald and ghost were speaking together. She left them to be private with each other, those two who wouldn't let even death keep them separate from each other for long.

And Arnulf leaned his yewen bow against the door, whispered his son to him, Iohann who looked like Ellisif's father, tall and dark-haired and grey-eyed. Golden light etched both faces in profile as Arnulf took his boy in his arms, hugged him hard, and kissed him. With no word, he unbolted the door and sent Iohann out into the night, out to where witches wore the shape of fire-pelted wolves.

Ellisif's heart raced, sounded like thunder in her own ears. She drew breath to cry out, and a strong hand closed warmly round her wrist and stilled the cry.

"Let it be, Sif," said Garroc, very gently. "Tonight we need our Iohann."

"Where is he going?"

Firelight glinted along Garroc's mail-shirt, spun webs of gleam in iron rings. "To do what his father asks him to do."

Ellisif's throat closed tight, and ached with the need to weep over all the fears of the winter, over tonight's fear, and all the uncertainty. Garroc didn't try to tease away her dread, and he didn't say that everything would be all right.

Time crept by like a wounded thing and made no mark on the night. Stars hung in the sky again. The red glow of witch-light was gone for tonight. Arnulf sat at the table, staring numbly at a long and broad-bladed sword; the wounded stranger's. The look of him, so white and weary, made Ellisif's heart ache.

"Arnulf, go to bed," she said. "I'll send Leof and Blithe to the loft."

He looked up, past her, to Garroc. He got a nod, and got to his feet. "But don't chase the children, my girl. Let me have 'em by me for a while, ay?"

"Ay," she said, and saying, also agreed to keep the watch he'd have kept through the night—over their hearth, for their son. She did that, pacing and restless, clearing the table, storing food, trimming candles, feeding the fire, until—soft—Garroc said:

"Come here, Sif. Sit by the fire and be warm."

He said that smiling, though Ellisif couldn't imagine what he had to smile about.

"I've enough to smile over," he said, as though he'd heard her thought. "A warm fire, a roof overhead."

Ellisif went and sat beside him, within reach of the sick man, close to the fire. "And the sight of home again?"

"That, too. I'd not reckoned to come here this year, caught away even from winter-home before winter was done." He held out his hand. "I've missed you, my Sif."

"Oh, I missed you too, Eldfather. I worried. And I prayed to the Holy Mother for you."

Garroc touched her cheek. "Thank you."

They sat in silence for a long time, and after a while Ellisif began to hear ghosts again, but not her father's. These were the ghosts of older times, the memories of when she was a little girl and all the world was a safe place because it held her mother and her father and *dvergr* Garroc. She remembered how easy it was to become enspelled by the gold and black weavings of fire and shadow, how easily she'd say to Skald Garroc—him honored by kings for his tales and his songs; him her own dear eldfather— Please, will you tell me a tale?

And now Garroc said, "What tale?"

He was like magic; he was all the magic in her life, even now, on this night when fear stood darkly outside her door, grim and cold-eyed and scratching at her window.

"Should I tell you why yon wounded one said he'd not be taken to the house of the outlaw-kin?"

The outlaw-kin! "Eldfather—who?"

"The kin of Hinthan Cenred's son." Garroc laughed, a low warm sound. "Girl mine, have you never heard that your father used to be named Hinthan Twice-Outlawed?"

Ellisif said nothing, not knowing what to say. She'd never heard even a whisper of that.

"The boy never told you about that? Ay well, he's always leaving the larger tellings to me, isn't he? 'What's the use having a skald for a foster-father if I've got to do all the talking?' But maybe I shouldn't tell that tale now." He took another sip from the jug. "Maybe this is the time to tell how Hinthan and I went into an enemy land and found a treasure for Penda Pybba's son who was king before Aethelred was ever born."

The wounded stranger stirred, opened eyes as blue as the jug under Garroc's elbow. Fever whitened his cheek. Ellisif soothed him as though he were one of her boys.

"Or maybe," Garroc said, "I could tell you both those tales, and add into the bargain the story of a promise that bound two witches across the years, even past death."

Ellisif smiled, for this moment forgot her fear. "Eldfather, even Skald Garroc couldn't weave those wild threads into one night's tale."

"Do you think so? Let's see what Skald Garroc can and can't do." Garroc unstoppered the blue jug with his thumb, tasted the whisky again. When he spoke, his voice was so quiet it sounded like part of the night, the fire, the wind, the sigh of a sleeper dreaming.

"It's a tale of old times, Sif, of when your father was fourteen, of when Penda was our king, and folk here in the Marches didn't know more about your god-Jesu but that he was a foreigner from southern lands. And this tale starts in a wondrous place, in the Welshland wildwood."

Ellisif caught her breath, and let it go with a sigh.

"Gardd Seren," she said, and it seemed that all the light in the cottage came now to be with them, to light the tale-telling.

"Gardd Seren. Far-travelled I am, my Sif. And I have seen wonders. The wonder I love best is Gardd Seren, and those words *gardd* and *seren* mean Star Garden in the Welsh language. The garden is a place of magic and earth-craft, of hope and healing. And you're not a stranger to tales of the place, ay? You've heard of my winter-home before now, and of the Dwarf-witch who lives there."

She was no stranger to the tales, the warm stories of childhood. But now, even the word 'witch' made her shudder. And Garroc saw that. He took her hands in his own two, chafed them as to warm.

"Girl mine, not everyone who studies the ways of witch-craft uses those skills in darkness and hatred. The witch of Gardd Seren, this dear Lydi of mine, has nothing of that blackness about her. She's sunlight and starlight and every clean breeze of spring made into the shape of a fair and lovely *dvergr* woman. And she makes everyone welcome in her garden, Dwarf or Man or—" Garroc stopped, frowned a little, over a secret. "Well, well. She welcomes all who come to her for help."

Ellisif's heart quickened, yearned to the story. She moved closer to Garroc, to the fire, to warmth. And Garroc nodded, silent approval. Wordlessly they agreed to put aside fear for a time.

"My Sif, many promises have been made in witch-Lydi's garden, and one—an old one!—was woven to stretch even across the dark sea of death. The net of that promise caught me up in its strong strands, and your father with me. . . ."

◄1►

I hear ghosts. Always. And that's not magic, that's a gift from god-Wotan to some of us in the middle-world. Sometimes the ghost-voices are like the voices a man hears when he walks past a crowded hall. No one is calling him. Sometimes one or another voice comes very close. *Garroc, do you remember . . . ?* Most often these close ghosts are friends, Dwarfs and Men I knew in life.

At the time I'm telling of, my Sif, a ghost came close and he was no one I knew.

I first heard the stranger-ghost on Midwinter Night. He didn't come often after that, and he only had one word to speak. He whispered that word to me when I was in the borderland between sleeping and waking. *Skald!* he called. *Skald . . .* He never said more, and at first the calling troubled me, but soon I reckoned that if he had more to say, he'd come and say it. I wasn't going to lie awake waiting for the ghost to learn another word.

Skald! Skald . . .

The ghost woke me from eager dreams of battle on the first day of spring. I dreamed that dream in a witch's bed in far Welshland, dreamed of fire and iron and a young *cyning* whose courage dressed him as sunlight dresses a sword shining aloft in the sun. War Hawk, we named that *cyning,* for he was golden as the wide-winged eagle, bold and deadly in battle.

Waking, I no longer heard the ghost crying. And the dream faded as I gathered Lydi close in my arms. She yet slept, warm and soft and lovely in rest, and I watched her sleeping, watched the light change as darkness softened toward dawn. As bright as the sky would become, no one of night's stars would vanish, or even fade. In Gardd Seren the sky knows magic. Far away a farm dog barked. Nearer, across the garden, red Werrehund growled. In younger days the dog had gone into battles beside brave men. He didn't like to be waked from dreams of those times to bark at a mere change in the wind.

Yet asleep, Lydi sighed against my shoulder, a warm and wordless farewell.

Beyond the mist-mantled Welsh hills, in Saxon lands, kings

were riding out to enjoy the hospitality of the war-lords who owed them loyalty, taking count of the armies, making new plans to carry on an old war. A deep oath bound me to one of those war-lords; I was his soldier and his scout. I'd put my hands in his, my life, my honor, even my death should he need it. I'd said to him: "Erich Halfdan's son, I was your father's man and I'm yours." I never regretted the oath, my Sif, but every spring I thought it came calling too soon.

I kissed Lydi lightly, careful not to wake her. I dressed quickly in the cold, and she curled into the warm place where I'd been. In the hearth-room I stirred the banked fire, fed the first small flames, and hung the kettle to boil. Two fat scrips sat on the table, filled with meat pies and cheese, winter apples and new-baked loaves, for Hinthan and me on our way to Rilling. From the garden came a low whistle, two dropping notes and one rising. Hinthan was home from wherever he'd gone last night so that Lydi and I could have our private farewell. I left the cottage, quiet as a shadow gliding.

In Gardd Seren are two gardens, one filled with herbs and flowers; some for healing and magic, some for joy and beauty. Agrimony grows brightly yellow beside red dog-rose and dark mountain-mint. Hart's-tongue twines among misty rosemay, all weaving together to make a tapestry as lovely as any of wool and thread. Small magics live there, gentle as breeze-riding scents, as memories, and they linger in every corner whispering about time and how it passes, about spring and summer, and the falling toward winter, the waking again.

The second garden hasn't to do with the mother-earth. That garden is sown in the sky, and Lydi tends it with the arts of magic learned from her mother, Meredydd, who was the witch of Gardd Seren before her. In that sky-garden the flowers are stars and they blossom sweetly to shine as brightly in day's blue sky as on a moonless midnight.

Hinthan stood outside the cottage, in one garden, under the other, with the reins of two horses in hand, my boy in the mist and the morning on the first day of spring. He was fourteen that year, and most people—Welsh or Saxon—would reckon him man-grown. Too, most would reckon him well-off, a freeman's son with his father's good farm for his heritage. But Hinthan had no love for the place. He was a farmer's boy, but he was no farmer. The love of land didn't hold him to the place where he'd seen his father and mother die, war-killed. Was he running from those fiery memories? He'd have liked to, but I wouldn't let him.

You know how it was with me, Sif, in the days when folk used to name me Garroc Silent Skald, in the time before your father came to be my foster-son. I am like all the *dvergr* of my generation, born knowing that I am among the Last, that I will have no child to follow me. You know the tale.

After long life lusted   Dwarf-kings and lawless witches.
Greed tempted them   teased from them schemes and spells
to steal the far-famed   fruit, a god's undying yield.
Thieves padding   proud Dwarf-kings went prowling.
Like webs, the spells   their witches wove.

But the thieves were caught, and the thieves were cursed with a fate to fit the crime—the long lives our eldest fathers sought. My life's span is three times the length of a Man's, and so was my father's and his, back for six generations. We Dwarfs who live now are the Last, and no one of us will ever get a child to follow. Yet it was one thing for me to be taught that my kindred is doomed to die. It was another thing to barrow my father and know it.

I was man-grown then and a skald, taught by Stane Saewulf's son who was my foster-father. I cast away everything Stane taught me when my father died. Skald-craft, history-keeping, song-weaving—that is, hope. What did I have to do with hope, a man at the end of the world? All was ice and ash with me then, and most of the company I kept was with ghosts who'd come to whisper to me even in the moment I fitted the last stone on my father's barrow, even as I turned my back on skald-craft. I fled those ghosts down the cold road that leads to berserker-madness.

At the farthest end of that icy way I found Hinthan, the orphaned Man-child on the edge of a battle-ground. War had stolen his parents from him. He'd grown careless of his life; it was little matter to him if he lived or if he died. But I found a way to make it matter, and he found a way to touch my own cold heart. About then I stopped fleeing ghosts, and turned to stand and listen to them.

I became Hinthan's hope, and he became mine. And I swore I'd never let him taste that untamed grieving again. When he must mourn for his dead, I saw to it that he did. I never let him sit secret with his sorrow, for fear it would become ravening grief-sickness. And soon I learned a thing about Hinthan that surely Cenred his father had always known—this boy was a storm-lover. On hot summer nights he'd eagerly climb to the top of a hill to watch the lightning and god-Thunor fighting giants in some other world.

Hinthan said he could feel that fighting in his belly, like fire in him, and only the day after he first came to me he begged me to teach him war-craft. He was ten then, and he told me he wouldn't be left behind each spring in Gardd Seren. Squaring his shoulders, firming his stubborn jaw, he swore he'd follow me so I might as well take him. I gave him what he must have, and he learned fast and well. These four years past he'd proven a fine scout. Quick-witted and trusty, Hinthan was well-regarded by the canny men who ran into dangerous places to sniff out an enemy's camp and take the count of foemen.

But I'd not set him free to fly into battle, and each year he asked me—When, Garroc? Each year I said only—Soon. He accepted that answer, but less patiently each time.

I wondered now, on the first morning of spring, whether he'd say, "Garroc, now I'm man-grown. Let me go into battle with you this year." But he didn't say that, and he greeted me only in his usual easy way, then looked past me to the cottage.

"Where's Lydi?"

"Sleeping still," I said.

His grey eyes glinted with laughter. "And you're probably still warm from the bed, ay?"

I growled fondly and told him to go away and wait. He did that, but not till he asked the question he always asked on the first morning of spring. He knew which of us had the hardest time leaving.

"Are you all right, Garroc?"

"I remember my promises," I said.

He nodded gravely, then whistled up the red dog and took our horses up the hill to the oak grove that overlooks the river.

Alone, I stood in the garden, in the place between the cottage and the road away, waiting for the friend who liked to take morning walks with me. He didn't keep me long.

First I heard the high voices of his troop of followers, the cheeping of newly hatched ducklings. Soon I saw Aelfgar himself, the tall shape of him unclear as he came through the misty garden. I heard him speaking softly to his downy babies, hurrying them along. And they followed right after him as though they didn't think it was strange to have this tall young man for their mother. He'd hatched them, hadn't he? He'd warmed the eggs

in his large and gentle hands all night after the cat got the duck,
until the shells cracked and broke and gave up the golden treasure
in each, live and hungry. Who else could Aelfgar be but their
mother?

"Garroc," Aelfgar called softly. "Are you there?"

I smiled. "I'm here."

"Come and walk to the river with me."

I went gladly. We were old friends, Aelfgar Ulfhere's son and
me, and I liked his company. Behind, in a straight line of footed
yellow fluff, his ducklings followed us through the mist and to
the river.

As there are two gardens in Gardd Seren, there were in those
days two healers. One was Lydi, the witch who by herb-craft and
wonder-craft gave help to the farmers and villagers of Seintwar,
Dwarfs and Men alike. The other healer was Aelfgar, into whose
care the furred and the feathered found their way. He had only a
very small magic about him, a way of whistling birds and beasts
to him and letting them know he was a friend. Lydi said he'd
taught that to himself. Always generous, Aelfgar soon taught the
whistling song to Hinthan. Try as they did, those two were never
able to teach me.

Aelfgar was an outlaw, an exile, a *wraecca*. He lived in Wales
but he was no Welshman. He was a Saxon, a soldier born in
Rilling and from Rilling exiled by the *cyning*. Child-minded, our
Aelfgar, and so Erich hadn't hung him for the breaking of heavy
laws; Aelfgar had served him well till bad friends took him astray.
Lydi had welcomed the exile gladly, and now Aelfgar lived in the
thatch-roofed stone cottage that he and Hinthan and I had built in
a shady glade at the wildwood's edge.

Aelfgar was no Dwarf. He was *mann-cynn*, wide-shouldered,
long-boned and—by the account of one young woman in the
valley—good to look at. She didn't care that he was an outlaw,
and it mattered not at all to honey-haired Branwen that he was
child-minded. Her kin had something to say about that. They
didn't like her man, and they didn't like it that she went to live
in Gardd Seren to learn magic from the witch. There lived no one
in Seintwar valley who didn't honor the witch of Gardd Seren—
even *Cristens*, though more quietly than the Dwarfs there, who
were used to old gods and old ways. But only a few would give
up a daughter or a sister to the witch's schooling. It didn't matter
to Branwen that her kin were not among the few. She learned
where she would and loved as she wished.

And so my friend Aelfgar didn't have too much to worry about these days, and the poet who tells us that no one is more wretched than the lorn and lonesome exile might have spoken differently if he'd ever met the exile of Gardd Seren.

"It'll be a fine day, Garroc," Aelfgar said, gathering a duckling back from the verge of spring-swift waters. "See, the mist's thinning already. That's good, ay?"

I agreed that it was and accepted the rescued duckling from him, held it gently in my two hands. Aelfgar looked up the hill to where Hinthan sat talking to red Werrehund, his arm around the dog's thick neck, their heads close as though they were telling each other secrets.

"Do you ever wonder, Garroc, how we know that spring's here, even though the morning's so cold?"

"Maybe it's the color of the sky," I said. "Or the smell of the wind and the slant of the sun. Or maybe it's just in our bones to know."

Aelfgar nodded. "Branwen says everything I really need to know is in my bones and—"

On the hill Werrehund sprang up, barking. Hinthan, seeing who the dog saw, shouted a glad good-morning and ran loping down the path to the road. I couldn't see beyond the shoulder of the hill, but I knew who was coming up the road. Werrehund could bark to welcome a visitor or to warn one off. Mostly it was one thing or the other, but with this one coming now up the road, the dog never seemed to be able to make up his mind which was needed—welcome or warning off.

Me, I was never unsure about whether or not to welcome this visitor.

Owain Dwarf-Smith, they called him in Seintwar; come from somewhere two years before, no one knew from where. "I won't stay forever," he liked to say. "Just a while, and then I'm gone." His idea of a while was somewhat longer than mine.

He was a strong young Dwarf. His eyes were dark, his hair black, and his skin pale. He was a skilled smith, and people went to his forge readily. They said that it was good to have a Dwarf to do the smithing again, and they said that old Hywel ap Huw had never done such fine work as Owain. But me, I always thought Hywel did good work for all that he was no Dwarf. I was sorry when he went away to live with his daughter in far Kynlleith, and I didn't see why folk had to speak ill of the old smith's craft in order to praise the new.

"Ah," they said, "awd smith, he was gettin' on, not strong as he once was. And he did never tell such fine tales as t' new 'un does. That Owain, he knows a tale or two."

The people of Seintwar had a lot to say about things, and the most of it was gossip that grew fatter from mouth to mouth. But what they said about Owain's tales was true. He did know good ones, and he liked to come up the road to Gardd Seren of a winter's night to sit by the hearth and weave his stories. Lydi always welcomed him as a friend, and he would pay for that welcome with a tale, speaking well, as Welshmen do, and filling up his stories with wonders and magic and deep passions. Yet they were always odd tellings, as though some thread of each was left unwoven, some question unanswered.

To hear Owain tell it, he'd been to far Rome, to the country of the dark Saracens, and beyond to the land of the Grecas. He'd been to see the cold northlands where the bold whalemen hunt the icy seas; to Daneland and to Ireland; to Francland in the country of the Gauls. But he never did speak of the journeying, only of the lands at the journey's end. And he was word-crafty. He spoke Welsh, of course, and he liked to make noises that he claimed were five or six other languages. Yet, for all the languages he knew, he spoke of little except his tales of foreign places. Anything I knew about Owain Dwarf-Smith I had to guess at, and so I didn't know much about him.

Sometimes I thought he'd been a seaman, for his was a rolling gait. He squinted as a man does when he is used to looking at wide, high skies that never end. I fancied that he even smelled of the sea, of salt and wind. But he'd never admit to seafaring.

"*Na, na,*" he'd said once. "I'm a smith. What do I know about ships and sailing?"

"So then," I'd asked, "how is it you got to all those far places? Did you swim, Owain?"

He laughed, and he winked at my Lydi as if to say to her: *We two know all about how I got to where I went*. But Lydi had regarded him coolly, her eyes blue-grey as a storm-sky. She wasn't amused to be made part of his private joke.

I wasn't comfortable around Owain, and one reason was that he had a sharp-edged feel about him, like a man who fears his fate is closer these days than it used to be. People like that—with fate gathering round them like storm clouds rising—are dangerous to be near. But in the mind of anyone I talked to about my uneasiness, a second reason made the first suspect: It wasn't a secret that Owain wished the witch of Gardd Seren would love him.

And so I could talk about dangerous fate gathering till my mouth ran dry; it all sounded like a lover's jealousy no matter what I said.

"Wi' a touch o' poet's wildness into the pot," they'd say in the valley.

And after all, I thought as I watched Owain come up the road with Hinthan, is he more than another wanderer come to fulfill the promise of Gardd Seren—that all may rest in safety who are weary and hungry and hurt?

At the waterside, Owain pointed to Werrehund shaking off among the reeds. He said something to Hinthan to make him laugh. The duckling in my hands stretched his neck, complained about hunger. I set him down to join his brothers. Beneath the trees the mist was moving, gathering, making ready to ride the sunlight back to the sky.

Aelfgar said that he reckoned it was time for me to go.

A dove alighted on the wooden bench near the cottage door, where my war-axe lay waiting for me to take it up. Gentle grey dove and bitter-edged Harm, they were an ill-matched pair. Maybe the dove thought so, too. She took wing again, sailed into the wildwood. Lydi's lips parted to smile as she watched the dove away. She loves the birds, stonechat and linnet, hawk and sparrow, kingfisher and the little golden finch. Most, though, she loves the grey wood dove. Sometimes she will wear that form and fly up to the sky for the joy of feeling the sun's warmth on her wings.

And often I have lifted my hand to call down a dove, held it gently, felt swift heart in feathered breast beating against my palms. Then—in an eye's blink—I'd find Lydi, slender and strong, filling my arms. And softly, half in her magic and half out of it, she'd say, "You're the steady stone. You're the unshakable ground. The trusted place . . ."

Now I whispered, "Lydi."

She turned quickly, a little catch in her breath, as though I'd not whispered her name but cried out. She came to wrap herself in the folds of my mantle. She stands a head shorter than I, and she can rest her cheek against my shoulder with ease. She did that now, all of her pressing warm against me. Like a blind man who needs to use other senses to remember, I traced the curve of her cheek, of her throat, the firm straight line of of her back. I lifted up her hair, dark as midnight, long and thick and soft as down against my cheek. I filled myself with the scent of her, of morning mist and wind, of earth and gardens and the herbs that have always smelled like magic to me.

"Lydi, will you dream when I'm gone?"

"Listen when you sleep," she said.

I would know her dreams and feel them in the heart of me. Waking, the dreams would become mine. It would be, sometimes and nearly, like being with her.

"I love you, my Lydi."

Ten springs I'd said that, going away from her; ten springs she'd answered by whispering echo to my pledge. So she did now.

The pealing cry of an impatient horse rang out. Hinthan came down from the hill, Owain a half-step behind. They were still talking, and I heard Owain say, "Maybe this year, boy. Might be this is the year I go."

Maybe I'll go, maybe I'll stay—Owain had been saying that for two years. I wished he'd do more than talk about it.

Hinthan listened gravely to what else Owain had to say, and they spoke quietly together until Owain embraced my boy.

"Be well, Hinthan. Be well, my friend." And he turned and went down the hill and around the shoulder. I heard him talking to Aelfgar, their voices twining with the rush of the river, as Hinthan came to get his farewell from Lydi. He hugged her hard and bent to kiss her cheek. I saw it then that he'd grown over the winter. Now he was as tall as me. *Mann-cynn*, he'd grow taller soon. Maybe by year's end I'd be cocking my head to see him eye to eye.

I left them to their farewells and went to the gardens to walk among the little magics, to take the first flowers of the season. Cowslips, primroses, one early sprig of white wood sorrel—I left these on Lydi's bed, the promise we understood as well as we understood the promise of the seasons.

I would come back. I would come home.

◄2►

My Sif, it has always been known that the Saxon kings are the kinsmen of a god. Their eldest fathers were brothers, and those brothers were sons of the Raven-god, children of Wotan. And in that truth is the seed from which a war sprang. The kings of Cent were the first to forswear their godly kin for the White Christ, yet the Aesir blood is true. In the Centish kings you still see a shadow of Witta Wotan's son. The high-boned face, the iron-glinting eyes of Whitlaeg are echoed in the Mercian kings. The twins, Baeldaeg and Waegdaeg, are remembered in the Northumbrian kings.

As Hinthan and I rode out from Gardd Seren, two of these *god-cynn* kings were getting ready to go to war against each other—one who kept faith with the god who was his kinsman, and another who broke that faith and shamed the bonds of kinship. The faith-breaker was Eadwine of Northumbria. The faith-fast was Penda of Mercia, him we named Wotan's Blade. Erich War Hawk owed Penda his loyalty. As my *cyning* did, so did I.

Sometimes you'll hear it said of Penda that land-hunger was the only reason he had for making war on Eadwine. None who knew our king would deny it. Penda liked the power that comes with ruling wide lands, and he liked it well enough so that for the last three years of his war against Eadwine he'd made alliance with the Welshman Cadwalla, the fierce witch-king of Gwynedd. They weren't friends, those two, but they had the same enemy. And Cadwalla had good reasons of his own to hate Eadwine, for they'd been closer than foster-kin; as babes they'd shared the same milk. Boy and man, Cadwalla had loved Eadwine well until his breast-brother began to cast greedy eyes on Gwynedd. Cadwalla didn't mind sharing his mother, but he had no plans to share his kingdom. Like Penda, Cadwalla would make alliance anywhere if it would help him defeat his enemy.

This weaponed wedding of kings was not well-loved among Cadwalla's Welshmen, nor was it too much praised among Penda's Saxons, but that didn't bother Cadwalla or Penda very much. Those two agreed well enough on all questions but one: When Eadwine was dead, which of them would rule Northumbria? Cadwalla had an idea, and Penda had another.

Ay, land-hungry, King Penda, but that's not the deepest truth in the matter between him and faithless Eadwine. The deepest truth is this: For the sake of an alliance with Eadbald, who was in those days the King of Cent—some said to please Eadbald's young sister, fair Aethelburgh, who came with the treaty—Eadwine of Northumbria learned to abase himself before the White Christ. He bent his knee to a stranger-god. As though he had no god's blood in his own veins, he broke the bonds of kinship. No greater shame can befall a family than that one forswears the rest. The man who wishes to keep his honor is obliged to wipe out that worst of shames with blood.

It was to this blood-feud of *god-cynn* kings that Hinthan and I returned on the first day of spring. My boy went eagerly, and I lingered at the crest of each hill to look back to Gardd Seren and magic Lydi. There lay all the summer between us, and you might think I'd have worried somewhat about that. Twenty years a soldier, I had some idea about how fast a battle can end for the unlucky. But I didn't think about that. I worried about how much time handsome Owain Dwarf-Smith would spend at his forge and how much he'd spend in Gardd Seren. I didn't trust him, who smelled of the sea and felt like a thieving pirate.

The young moon rose pale behind dark clouds, the first of spring, which Men name Seed Moon and Dwarfs call the Ghost. Hinthan and I stopped to pass the night in an old broken building, a place of burst walls, fallen roofs, and shattered tile floors. Roman-made, this place, like many another that lies crumbling half-hidden in Welsh forests, sprawling on a wind-racked hill in Northumbria. We left the horses outside the broken walls, slipped the iron bits from their mouths and hobbled them near a small stream where pale winter grass gave way to tender new shoots. In deeper dark beyond the walls, an owl made hollow sounds of hunger. Bare branches clattered in a cool rising wind, their shadows like dark bony fingers, reaching.

Hinthan passed beneath a broken arch to a long, unroofed room. In the moon's thin light piles of rubble looked like shadows; shadows seemed like deep well-pits. We went carefully until we stood in the center of the ruin. The tallest wall left standing was only as high as I could reach. Hinthan traced the shape of a window opening, and the first shy scents of lovage and mint hung on the damp night air, ghosts in an old garden. A drift of pale grey mortar whispered down from between the stones.

No Dwarf had put his hand to making this place. We don't imprison stone with mortar, never fill cracks with limestone paste to leave a wall looking like it's held together with so much dirty bandaging. Dwarfs have another way of building. We know the ancient voices of rock and stone, our earth-kin; voices felt deep in our bones. When we fit one stone to another, we take time to learn the names of each and take care to know that each wants to be where it is set, and so will be content to stay. Some have wrongly called this magic.

Hinthan leaned far out the window, looked away to where the ground sloped down to the stream. "Garroc, this must have been a king's hall when the Romans lived here."

"No, I don't think so. They had kings, those Roman Men, but they lived far across the sea and down in southern lands. The ones who lived here were soldiers and farmers, like us."

"And then they left. Why?"

"I don't know for certain, youngling. People say that many hundreds of years ago the Romans had a great kingdom, and the heartland of it was attacked by enemies. And they were so fierce that the King of Rome must call back his people from every land in his kingdom. Once this whole isle was a part of that kingdom, and all the Romans who lived here went back to defend their king. They never came back."

"And now there's only old houses and towns and streets."

"Only those."

The wind came gusting cold. I pulled my mantle close around me and said I wouldn't mind a fire before we ate. Hinthan forgot about Romans and walls, and went looking for wood and kindling amid the litter of ruin. Soon flames crackled, and their ruddy light shone to cheer us. We split a loaf of brown bread and the fattest of the meat pies, and Hinthan ate while he roamed around the ruin, poking into corners, exploring the shadows. He'd not got far when I heard him call.

"Garroc! Look at this!"

He knelt beyond the fire, his face night-shadowed, the red light gleaming like copper in his dark hair as he brushed dirt and crisp brown oak leaves away from the tiles on the floor to show me what he'd found. Old colors, old patterns. A cross of gold, and a white dove winging. *Cristen* symbols.

Hinthan sat back on his heels. "These people of Rome were Christ-worshipers. Like the people of Seintwar. Well, all the people but Dwarfs . . . And Eadwine's Christ-priests are Roman too. There's not one of them would ever be a good friend to Dwarfs."

He traced the cross with his long-knife's sharp tip. He traced idly at first, as he was thinking. But soon iron glinted in firelight as he dug harder, chipped away the crumbling mortar of a small yellow tile meant to be gold. He didn't work carefully; the tile chipped and white cracks spidered across it.

In the silence between us, remembered rumors whispered. Like dark ghosts, we recalled tales we'd heard from across the Northumbrian border, tales of how Christ-priests had taught Men in Eadwine's kingdom more than how to kneel and beg favors from their god. Lately they'd been teaching that to be other than *mann-cynn* was to be evil, as though Dwarfs were not more than some scattered clan of night-alfs.

We'd heard it that Men there didn't do much to dispute those lies, and we didn't know what to make of those grim tales, for in Penda's kingdom Men had nothing to do with god-Christ, and in Wales and even in *Cristen* Cent, *mann-cynn* still remembered how to treat friends. Not kind or kin, Dwarfs and Men are two races whose histories twine one round the other, like the briar-rose round and through an old stone wall. Eadwine's folk were learning how to forget that.

Hinthan chipped a tile from the cross.

"Youngling," I said. "Stop."

He looked around at me, his eyes like heatless lightning, flash and warning.

"Why?"

"Because breaking is a cold thing to do." I held out my hand. "Come and sit by the fire now."

It was a long moment before he did that, and he took great care to step around the pictures on the floor. He stoked the fire, then wrapped himself in his mantle and sat close beside me. We listened to the night, to owls and the wind in the branches.

After a time Hinthan said, "It's harder for you to leave Gardd Seren this year, isn't it?"

I agreed that it was, and he looked at me sideways, read my heart as easily as monks read books.

"Garroc, Owain's just a visitor, no matter how long he stays. You're real, Foster-father. Lydi knows it."

Owain looked real enough to me but I didn't say anything about that, and Hinthan huddled down into his mantle and another thoughtful silence. Now I waited, thinking he'd ask about whether I'd let him go into battle this year. But he didn't, though by now he should have asked at least ten times. I put my arm around him as the wind blew colder. Soon he fell asleep.

I sat waking for a while, listening to the ancient wall-stones at my back as they spoke in voices deep, or soft as slipping shale; voices rough, or smooth as a honed edge. They spoke one to the other, each to itself. They remembered the touch of frost from winters past. They recalled the hard way wind dealt with them, the soft way a hundred spring rains had loved them into new shapes. Those old stones never minded that I was near to over-hear, and soon one sang me to sleep, an ancient song a-hum in my bones, a song that faded only when the witch-dream came.

• • •

In dream, I saw my Lydi find the gift I'd left on her bed. Tenderly, she lifted the primroses and the springs of coltsfoot and the cowslips. She sat for a long time in the middle of the bed, and the sunlight from the window shone on her dark hair, called out the blue-black gleams. The golden sun shone on tears and smiles.

In dream, I saw Aelfgar come to admire the gift, and to reach down a small blue pot from a high shelf. The pot was marked with a rune, with one sigil only. This mark meant my name—it was *gifu* who means gift and partnership and a soldier's blood-sacrifice.

Lydi thanked him, and she put the flowers back on the bed, right where she'd found them. She'd leave them there all day, and before she went to bed she'd place them in the small blue pot, where they would grow old and, at last, shed seed.

Aelfgar sat down at the table, dipped his finger into a pot of honey. Lydi sat down with him and they shared the sweet while they talked about what work must be done that day—a fence to mend, a bed to dig, plants they must fetch from the wood and bring to live here, small magics to make. And when the day was done, Lydi and Aelfgar and Branwen shared a meal in the stone house at the edge of the wildwood. Afterwards, Lydi came back alone to the cottage and took the faded flowers up from the bed. She put them in the small blue pot, and she stood for a long time at the door, looking away east to where the stars only shine at night.

When she went at last to bed, Lydi fell asleep thinking about the falling season when she'd bring out the seed of the flowers I'd left her. We would take them out to the garden on the day after I returned home, and we'd plant those seeds together.

At the edge of sleep and dream, Lydi whispered, "We'll show each other again how the seasons turn between us, my Garroc. . . ."

Lydi's wasn't the last voice I heard in dream, my Sif. The last voice was the whisper of a stranger-ghost. *Skald! Skald* . . . In me, I said: Ghost, who are you? I got no answer.

• • •

I woke in the grey half-light before sunrise, stiff and cold. The fire was but damp ash; I saw no sign of Hinthan. Wind sent leaves whirling across the stone-pictures, the cross and the dove. Then I felt an echo in the ground, Hinthan's light tread as he walked around a low wall and through the crumbling arch. He stopped when he saw me awake. He had our leather water-flasks in his right hand, fat and dripping. His left hand he held closed.

"The horses are ready and the gear's packed. Do you want a fire, or will we eat riding?"

I told him we'd eat riding, and he came and showed me what he had in his left hand. New sun winked on a mantle-clasp, a polished red agate set in worked gold, the pin a little bent but still useful. The workmanship was good, the stone itself marked with bands in all the shades of red, from palest to blood-dark. He'd found it in a corner of the old garden, outside the window.

"Frost heaved the ground last night; I saw the pin sticking out of the dirt." He rubbed his thumb against the polished stone. "The gold needs cleaning, but I got the inset looking good."

I admired it, and said it would look fine on his mantle.

"Not mine. This is for you, Foster-father." He gave me the brooch, then covered my hand with his. *Mann-cynn*, he couldn't hear the stone, and yet he always did that, hoping that one day he'd touch me and hear. "Who is it?"

I asked, silently, and got an answer. The wild rock is shy and doesn't easily give a name, but proud-minded gemstones love to talk about themselves.

"The stone is Way-friend."

"Wotan's stone."

It was. And Wotan is the soldier's god, the skald's god, the god of all wanderers.

Hinthan took the clasp and fastened my mantle with it, his gift of old stone and gold. And the wool mantle was thicker than he'd thought, or the pin more bent, for he had trouble with the clasp and cut his finger, only a little and enough to bring one fat drop of blood springing. It wasn't anything to feel, his finger callused from the bowstring as it was, and he didn't see the blood until it dropped onto the agate. Nor was he troubled by that. He cocked a grin and said this must mean we were on some fated journey now, blood-bound to the end of the road.

He laughed about it, as boys do who expect that every adventure has treasure or fame at the end. But I didn't laugh, and I didn't like to see my boy's blood on the Raven-god's stone.

Hinthan and I were another day riding before we came out of the wildwood and into the gentler hills of the Marches; once there, we were only three days from Rilling. We rode in the sunny morning of young spring. Bluebells nodded in sunny patches in the oak woods, swifts and swallows sailed the high blue sky, early-come from their winter-homes. In woodland, on hillside, in meadow, the wind carried the rich scent of the waking earth. At the end of the day, Hinthan looked back over his shoulder to the high stony ridge between Powys and the Marches, the place Welshmen name Cefn Arth, the Bear's Ridge. Marcher-Saxons still call it the Barrow Ridge, for the cross-marked graves of Welsh raiders and the barrows of Saxon defenders can be found there. Now five men rode along that ridge, dark against the sky.

"Raiders," Hinthan said.

His brown mare snorted and sidled, and he hushed her with a whisper, held the reins tight in one hand. With his other hand he told over the arrows in the quiver at his side. But when he slipped an arrow from the quiver, I gripped his wrist and held him still.

"Look again, youngling."

He did, squinting, and now he saw what I did—the red light of day's end glinting sharply from the iron tip of an ashwood spear, from helm, from mail-shirts. Cattle-thieves and slave-makers aren't so finely fitted out.

"Those are men of Gwynedd," I said. "Likely they're Cadwalla's outriders."

So it was. After the scouts came the army, a great darkness of horsemen. The riders filled the ridge, and the earth rang with their passing—I heard the song even here below—and the last sunlight leaped from iron-tipped spear to sword to helm. From the shadows beneath the ridge we watched the long line of them out of sight.

Soon after Cadwalla Witch-king was gone we found a good place to camp in the sheltering shadow of Cefn Arth, in the lee of a tall pile of fallen stone. Behind us rose the ridge, before us a wide meadow filled with springing hares. Hinthan took his bow and quiver, changed some of those hares into supper, and we stuffed them with the last of Lydi's apples, roasted them, and reckoned the meal a good one.

• • •

Late in the night, when there was no moonlight, I woke to
hear Hinthan get up and walk away from the fire. Horses snorted
to hear him coming, and he hushed them—then suddenly fell
silent himself. I reached for Harm, gripped the axe's haft; ready.
Swift, he came back to me, and so quietly that I had to feel the
earth-echo to know he was moving. An iron glint shone in his
eyes when he gestured me to come with him.

We went a little south under the ridge, never leaving the safe
shadows. The sky shone with stars like diamonds spilled out; frost
glittered in whispered echo. Grass crunched faintly underfoot; our
breath plumed on the air. From the meadow came a night-hawk's
high *keee!* and Hinthan pointed to a low place on the ridge. We
saw two men there, each holding a horse's reins as they stood
talking. I took Hinthan's arm, brought him back a pace into the
shadow of the stone when one lifted his hand high, as you do
when you're holding a torch.

Light sprang suddenly between the two, a red witch-gleam,
heatless to touch unless the wielder wills. That light might have
benefited them, but it didn't show us any more than starlight
had. Still, I knew one of those men. I was too far away to
see his face, but the shape of him, the proud lift of his head,
his back like straightest iron—I knew him. I took Hinthan back
another step.

Peada Penda's son was a hoarder of secrets, and he warded
his trove like a dragon crouched atop its holy treasure-mound.
Like the blood-hungry dragon, you didn't want him to find you
soft-footing around his hoard.

In silence Hinthan and I watched our king's son and the witch
talking, and we watched as they parted. Now I saw that the witch
limped, and remembered that Bran, Cadwalla's nephew, limped.
The Welshman rode away north after his king, and we saw him
for a while, for the ridge ran straight and did not curve for a
mile or more. But our king's son rode south and we didn't see
him long, for the ridge dropped down, curved around, and he
was gone behind its shoulder. There he'd come to the road that
would take him to Rilling if he didn't leave it, or to Tomeworthig
and his father's hall if he went far enough.

I grounded Harm, though I didn't remember raising her. Hinthan
said, "What do you think he was doing here, Garroc?"

"I don't know."

He came and stood beside me, and he didn't watch the empty
ridge. He watched me. "But you'd like to know."

I told him that I would like to know, and then I sent him to check the horses.

I stood with Harm cradled in my arms, watching frost-bright Cefn Arth, the Barrow Ridge. I wondered what Peada Penda's son had to say to a witch in the middle of the night; I didn't waste any time thinking he was carrying a message to Cadwalla for his father. Penda's eldest son would never be so helpful as that.

◄3►

The river-road on the west side of the Rill was a long stretch of deep-sucking mud the day Hinthan and I came home. The mud grew thicker the closer we got to the village, churned up by the passage of horses and heavy-laden wains, as always is the case in spring when winter loosens its cold grip and people go back and forth between the farms and the village again. This year the passage of the *fyrds,* the levies of soldiers his *thegns* owed to Erich, those Erich owed to Penda, worsened the usual mire. Noon was well past when we reached the wide place in the road where the high hill overhangs the Rill on the eastern side. Today, my Sif, you call that high place Godshill, but when Penda was king— before Christ-priests had anything to say about how places should be named—we of Rilling knew it as Rafenscylf. For Wotan, we named that hill Raven's Shelf.

When Hinthan and I passed through the shadow of the hill and rode round the last bend, we saw the wood walls of Rilling. Those were good and stout walls, but not so tall that we couldn't see the *cyning's* hall rising above. This place too, this Rilling, was home to Hinthan and me. And as to welcome us, high on the watch-walk of the wall glinted a sun-struck brightness—a shining of light on an old mail-shirt, a silvery gleam from a sword's blade as the wall-ward raised his weapon in greeting. Faint, but clear, we heard a glad cry of welcome.

"That's Aescwine," Hinthan said, and he put heels to horse, left me behind to duck flying mud and hope he didn't kill horse and self in the reckless ride.

Me, I didn't ride as carelessly, but I did ride eagerly. I'd not left Gardd Seren gladly, but I was no exile cast out onto the road. I'd left home to go home, and my heart lifted to know I'd find a good welcome here.

• • •

It's truly said, my Sif, that there aren't many old soldiers. My friend Aescwine was one, and he was as old as my father would have been were Grimwulf then living. He wore the many marks of war proudly, even the knife-scar twisting from just below his right eye to his upper lip. That livid battle-rune gave his gentlest smile the seeming of a scornful sneer, but people who knew him understood how to look past that and listen to his voice to know what he was truly feeling.

I'd but put foot to ground and handed my horse to Hinthan when Aescwine came to hug me hard and give the father's kiss he'd taken to offering since his son's death. Then he poked a finger into my ribs and told me that he reckoned I went to den in a land of generous cooks and master-brewers. Hinthan laughed at that, and I didn't quarrel with Aescwine's reckoning. He'd been in little danger of bruising his finger on bone.

"But this one—" He roughed Hinthan's chin. "Boy, they must forget to call you to supper five days out of six. Where've you been all winter? Surely not with our well-fed friend."

Hinthan offered no explanation. He knew Aescwine had never met a Welsh witch but on war-grounds, and wouldn't be glad now to hear that we'd been keeping the winter with one. And Aescwine, who'd wondered about our winter-home before now and gotten no answer, saw that he wouldn't get one this year either.

"Well then, boy, get those horses to the stable and get yourself to the hall. There's a pig roasting, and you'd have better use for the meat on his bones than he has."

Hinthan needed no more urging than that to take our mounts and make off through the crowded street.

Watching him away, Aescwine said: "This year, a battle for him?"

"Maybe."

He eyed me keenly, who'd seen me train youngsters to scout-craft and battle before now. "You'll have to let him go sooner or later. What are you waiting for?"

"Me," I said, for I never but answered this old friend honestly. "I'm waiting for me to be ready."

"Ach, well. Then you'd better go and tell him he's got to be a farmer or a cooper or such. You'll never be ready."

From behind, a growl, a brutal snarl. We turned to look, and saw men draw back as from something dark and deadly—a ber-serker feeling crowded in a street filled with soldiers and horses and wains trundling through the mud.

"Every *thegn* in the Marches is here with his levy," Aescwine said. "A lot of them have the *wulf-cynn* with them. I've heard that Erich's father-in-law can barely feed all the soldiers his *thegns* have gathered, and they say it's the same all through the kingdom." He nodded to a small group of Dwarfs and Men, quiet amidst the jostling crowd and listening to one who was speaking. He cocked his thumb at the speaker. "That one's got 'em all believing that the matter of Eadwine Faith-Breaker will be settled this year."

Ah, that one. A tall Man—wide-shouldered, golden-haired, tossing and catching a small throwing-axe as he walked. His wary companions eyed the flashing iron overhead, but Penda Pybba's son didn't notice that. He trusted his hand to know where the weapon would come down. And that was a good axe he had, the blade keen and the wooden haft rune-carved, marked just so:

with *eoh* for defense, *tir* for victory, and *haegl* for the war-storm. The axe was a gift to the king from Cynewise, his wife, and she'd carved the runes with her own hand on an earlier day when they didn't hate each other.

"Aescwine, is Peada with his father?"

He shook his head. "Only Merewal, and he's in the hall with Erich. I heard Peada was up north at Ceastir with his mother and her kin." He eyed me narrowly. "Why're you asking?"

I'd have told him what Hinthan and I saw on the Barrow Ridge, but the king gave me no chance. Maybe he heard my voice, though I'd spoken quietly. Maybe he felt me watching him. However it was, Penda turned from his listeners. Eyes glinting with his sudden humor, he tossed the axe high, caught it, and then threw it to me. It was a good throw, the arc high, the spin tight, the fall easily gauged.

As I caught it, Aescwine grinned—not a sight for the faint-hearted—and returned to the watch-walk.

"So," said the king when I returned his axe. "I thought it was Hinthan I saw in the stable. *Wil-cuman, dvergr.* Well come, indeed. Erich's been looking for you."

He was in high humor that day. He glittered like iron in the sun, strong and bright. It took no more than being near all that crackling eagerness of his to get the blood rising in me, warm and livening, as it does when thunder rolls down the sky and gods come to watch war-play.

"Come along," the king said. With a look, he dismissed the others. "We've some war-crafting to do, Erich and me, and we'd like the company of a trusty mapper."

He thrust the axe into his broad leather belt, and I followed him to the hall.

Erich's hall was wide and long and tall, for a *cyning* must be able to feed and house the friends he claims, the soldiers he needs, the king he serves. Oaken columns soared to hold up the raftered roof, windows were set high in each of the wide walls to let sunlight stream in by day and moonlight by night. A long board and benches ran the length of the hall; tapestries hung on the walls, wondrous woven colors rippling in the least breeze. The round shields of each *thegn* in the Marches hung between, proud linden-wood, silver-bossed, gold-adorned, glinting brightly. Even the columns, old and smoke-blackened, breathed in the sunlight, the moonlight, like dark jewels. Men named the hall Hordstede. Treasure-House.

There was no great crowd of war-crafters in Hordstede that day. Besides Erich, there was only Hinthan—come to eat—and a thick-chested, red-bearded young man whose eyes were flinty grey, whose fingers drummed a restless beat on the table. Here was Merewal Penda's son. As the king's mood was the lightning before a storm, so was his son's the thunder.

Aescwine had been right about the pig roasting in the hearth, but he hadn't mentioned the geese baking over glowing coals raked to one side of the spit, or the loaves of bread warming on the stones. Nor had he mentioned the just-breached keg of ale in the cool north corner of the hall. The hearth and the good smells of roasting and baking set hunger rolling in me. But Hinthan had better luck than I did, for as I entered the hall with Penda, Erich glanced up from the table all strewn with maps, and gestured for me to join him.

I did that, laid Harm on the board, the axe's blade to me in friendly fashion. But Hinthan didn't let me go hungry. He broke a loaf of bread and gave me half with a slab of cheese and an earthenware cup filled to dripping with frothy ale. Then he found himself a seat where he could eat and watch and listen. No one minded that. Like Aescwine—and Cynnere Brihtwulf's

son and Pearroc Thurstane's son, like *dvergr* Eldgrim and his
brother Dunwulf—Hinthan was a scout of mine.

Erich pushed a map toward me. I hadn't seen that map in a
while, but I had no need to study it. I'd made it the year before,
burned it into a thin-scraped hide with the sooty tip of a dagger.
It showed all of the Isle, and some of it was trusty beyond the
border Erich shared with Eadwine of Northumbria.

I'd not been in Eadwine's country for three years. The Faith-
Breaker had brought the war to Mercia those years and kept us
at home defending our borders. But I'd done some ranging round
Northumbria last time the army was there. I knew better than most
what lay beyond the Roman roads we'd travelled, the old ruined
fortresses we'd sheltered in or fought from. There were villages,
farms, and some *Cristen* monasteries in the north and west part
of Eadwine's country, all fed by bounty of woodland and river-
valley. In the middle of the kingdom lay more farmland, and the
high moorlands, wide places of stone and wind. Higher than the
moors rose a tall and wide hill. I'd never seen this place and knew
only its name: Deorcdun, the Dark Down. When seen on a map,
Deorcdun looked like it sat in the middle-most part of the Isle.

"Cyning," I said. "What is it you need?"

It wasn't Erich who answered, though he drew breath to. It was
Penda. His rune-worked axe soared high, flashed red in the light
from the hearth. It came down blade first to bite into map and
table-wood, fast on the border between two kingdoms.

"We need to change this map, *dvergr*. And this year we're
going to Eoferwic to talk to the King of Northumbria about that."

No sound drew me to look at Hinthan. He was keeping quiet as
he watched and listened. But I did look, and I saw his eyes narrow. We remembered—each at the same time—the dark rumors
of how things were in Northumbria.

"Garroc," Erich said, "what have you heard about Eoferwic?"

What I'd heard wasn't much, only a little more weighty than
rumors and tales. My map showed the place as no more than
a thin mark in the east, close to the River Deorwente where it
broadens and runs to the sea.

"It's a river-town," I said. "And they say Eadwine mounts his
wars from Eoferwic since his nephew took away his northern hall
in Yeavering."

Erich's blue eyes glinted. "The Outlaw presses his grudges
hard."

He did indeed. Folk named Eadwine's nephew Outlawed Osric,

but few used the name to sneer. He'd been a few years in Scotland, fled there as a child when Eadwine murdered his father. He stayed in Scotland because Eadwine had made him an outlaw, free game if he ever crossed the border to home. Not for nothing did people name Eadwine Aelle's son Faith-Breaker.

These days Outlawed Osric was no stripling boy in hiding. He was eighteen and well-grown. And he had a good and strong army made up of his murdered father's faithful men, Dwarfs and Men who'd followed their lord's son into exile. Osric made life hard for his uncle, always pressing him from the north, pushing him south. As we heard it these days, Osric had a fisted grasp on the north of Eadwine's kingdom. And Eadwine spent his winters in Eoferwic now, hating the young kinsman he'd doomed to exile and seeking to enlarge his kingdom by adding Penda's lands and Cadwalla's to it.

Penda removed his axe from the map, smoothed the thin hide so that the rent showed only as a dark shadow in the flaring brazier light. He pointed to Eoferwic.

"What more do you know, Garroc?"

"It's a rich town, a fine big *burgstede*, and they guard it close, King. It's kept by a tall, thick wall of wood and stone and I've never heard that anyone's got past it."

Erich cursed under his breath. Drumming, drumming, red Merewal's fingers beat a restless rhythm. But Penda's mood was still eager.

"Then we'll turn this fine, walled town of Eadwine's into a cage, eh? And we'll lock the cage tight with Cadwalla's help."

I drew breath to say that I'd seen Cadwalla's army riding north along the Barrow Ridge, but I got no word spoken. Like thunder, the hall doors banged open.

The king stopped pacing. Near the hearth an old dog roused, growling. Merewal reached for his long-knife, and I took Harm to hand and went to stand by Erich. Peada Penda's son came into the hall, and we didn't stand down. Wise men never did till they knew whether he was drunk or sober.

He was black and white, as Hel is said to be, she who is close kin to god-Loki, both sister and daughter. He was cold in his heart, as that winter-woman is. Hair and beard like a raven's wing, and his face was like snow, even after a summer spent in the hottest sun. He looked like his mother, Cynewise, who hated the king, her husband.

Peada didn't trouble to close the doors behind him, and he

strode down the hall as though only his own concerns were worth his attention. A cool wind followed him, made the fire in the hearth leap. A wide-winged hawk sailed down from the rafters, then cut its wings, arrowed away again, crying harshly as Peada stopped beside Hinthan. He took my boy by the arm, plucked him easily from the bench.

"Fetch me some ale, boy," he growled, and shoved Hinthan toward the hearth and the ale kegs.

Hinthan staggered, swiftly recovered his balance and turned on Peada, tense and tight, grey eyes glinting. He didn't like being shoved—not by anyone. And Peada didn't like being refused. I saw his fist clench, as did Erich, who eyed me like he was expecting trouble. But I wasn't giving any, yet.

Not moving from the *cyning's* side, I said, "Hinthan. Fetch the ale."

Hands fisted, Hinthan stood braced and never turned to look at me, never took his eyes from Peada. Erich stepped clear of the board, bound to defend my boy if Peada struck him. He would be honorless, the hospitality of his hall worthless, otherwise. Merewal stood, his hand close to a weapon. I didn't know who he'd defend.

And the king stood watching, eyes like sun-edged iron. He didn't raise hand or voice to stop what might happen. He was watching fate weave the moment.

"Hinthan," I said. "Do as I tell you."

And I thought, *There are too many weapons in this hall, boy mine! Don't force someone to use one!*

Hinthan turned on his heel, disdainfully put his back to Peada as though the king's son were no one to worry about.

"As you wish, Foster-father," he said to me.

Head up, back stiff, he crossed the quietly dangerous hall to fetch the ale. Peada came to the board, greeted his father and brother with brittle cheer. He shoved the maps aside and sat on the edge of the table; then he took up my cup and drank off the ale. Only then did he nod to the master of the hall.

Better greetings have been given to servants, and the king reached for the board, upended it, spilled his son and the maps to the floor. The maps fell to the rushes; Peada landed on his feet with a cat's grace, the empty cup still in his hand. But he wasn't grinning. Any who hadn't known it before could see it now: The king and his eldest son weren't friends.

Merewal retrieved the maps, and Penda called to Hinthan at the keg, "That ale is for your foster-father. Take it to him."

Hinthan did that, and when I took the cup I thanked him. Then I raised the ale in silent salute to the king as Peada found himself a place to sit—at the table and not on it this time. But it wasn't over between Peada and me.

"Peada," I said. "Tell us how it is with Cadwalla these days."

He grinned, like a cat licking its lips. "I wouldn't know, *dvergr*. I don't spend much time in Welshlands, and surely none out there by the sea-kingdom."

"I've never heard that you do. I was thinking about that man of his—the one you were talking to a few nights ago on Cefn Arth. He had him a limp. Was it Bran? Maybe he had something to say about his king's plans."

Merewal drummed like thunder again, storming; his elder brother smiled, almost gently.

"That was no man of Cadwalla's. That was—"

"Some other witch? Maybe a witch of Powys, or one of the slave-traders and cattle-raiders?"

The look Peada turned on me was like poison, meant to kill.

"Ah, you mean the man on Barrow Ridge," he said. "That was Bran. I met him on the way from Ceastir—" He smiled at his father, a cool and lazy grin. "You do remember that my mother is visiting kinsmen there, don't you? Well, according to Bran, Cadwalla's got a fine big army this year, and three dozen witches besides. They were riding north and east. No doubt he's hunting villages and monasteries to burn. But that shouldn't occupy him all summer, Father. The King of Gwynedd's boasting that he'll be feasting you in Eoferwic when you get there."

It was a strange thing that happened then. Penda couldn't have welcomed this news, for the man who had Eoferwic would have the best hold on Northumbria. Yet I'd have wagered a handful of new-struck silver coin that Penda heard nothing after his son's guess that Cadwalla was looking for villages and monasteries to burn in Northumbria. The King's face had gone a little white.

This wasn't lost on Erich, who watched Penda and his son the way he'd have watched two dogs stalking in stiff-legged, circling challenge. He wasn't sure yet that his hall wouldn't host a brawl between those two.

"Father," Merewal said, still edgy, still drumming.

The king came back from what white-faced sudden fear had claimed him. He pointed to me, and then to the maps.

"We'll be going nowhere if we don't start making plans. Garroc, tell us what you know about Eoferwic and how to get there. Make your best guesses about the rest."

I did that, though most of what I told him amounted to guesses, reckonings about Roman roads for fast moving, and river valleys where we'd be mostly likely to find the food an army on the march would need. I'd seen some of these places, others I'd only heard about. Guesses like the ones I made that day make wagers interesting, and war-crafting dangerous. Penda was willing to take the risk, and Erich and Merewal stood staunchly by him, listening and offering their own suggestions. These two, red-bearded king's son and gold-haired *cyning,* were of an age, the sons of fathers who had trained them to be hard-handed soldiers. They didn't flinch from war-wagers.

But Peada sat with his back to us all. He had his long-knife in hand, sat paring his fingernails with a sharp blade and watching the fire in the hearth. Brooding and silent, Hinthan sat watching the king's dark-haired son.

The work of war-planning went on all afternoon, and all afternoon Peada kept quiet and Hinthan kept watching him as you'd watch an adder got into the house—ready for whatever the snake would choose to do, slither out again or turn suddenly to strike.

◄4►

A great fire roared in Hordstede's deep hearth, feasting flames crackled. In that hall, my Sif, no man felt the frosty cold of early spring, and none of Erich's guests went hungry. His young wife, fair Gled Golden Hair, made sure that the board groaned beneath the weight of herb-stuffed fowl and fish, fine stews, and a bounty of bread. Braziers burned, and torches on the wall wove shining and shadow together. Beeswax candles lighted the board, and these were as long as my arm and thick as my wrist. Their clear light gleamed in the glassware, made the cups and beakers—amber and green and blue—sparkle like dancing gems. Our *cyning* had good reason to be proud of his wife.

Gled yet seemed more girl than woman, for all that she had given her husband a strong son three years before, a fine daughter since. This night they had their eyes on each other often as he greeted guests and she took care to see that cup and horn were never empty of whatever was wanted—clear wine, strong beer, or *twybrowen,* the rich, twice-brewed ale for which we Saxons are yet famed. And golden Gled offered mead, warm stone pitchers

of thick sweet honey-wine that was the favorite of my friend
Aescwine, who thought there was no better taste than honey. He
filled his cup often and drank deeply, and he watched storm-eyed
Penda in the high seat at the head of the board.

"This is not good. Not good at all, young skald."

He wasn't talking about the mead. He'd properly praised the
brew by drinking cup after cup. He was talking about Penda.

"A king—" He paused to drink. "A king shouldn't be looking
so grim on the battle-eve."

I thought he was right about that. Since the afternoon, nothing
had changed the king's mood but to worsen it. Tonight Peada
spurned Erich's hospitality with his absence, and added to the
insult by feasting his own friends on Erich's bounty and in the
fine house the *cyning* had given him for guesting's sake. These
friends of Peada's were powerful men, *thegns* who had rich
holdings around Ceastir; many were kinsmen to the queen. And
though Merewal was with the king, he was in no better mood
than his father. He had things on his mind, did Merewal. I was
curious, but I didn't trouble to guess—no one could reckon out
what that red son of Penda's didn't want known.

And so, pale of face, dark of eye, Penda sat in the best seat in
the hall, the tall-backed chair at the head of the board. He had
the first cuts of meat, and a fast cup-bearer—Hinthan. "Because,"
Erich had said to my boy with a grim smile, "you've proven
that you can do the work well." But though the king sat with
a silver-chased horn of *twybrowen* at hand, and more to come at
his call, he wasn't happy.

Aescwine wasn't the only one thinking about that. Cynnere
Brihtwulf's son came to talk about it. Long and broad-shouldered,
gold-bearded and blue-eyed was Cynnere. Like many Saxon Men
he made you think of giants. Tonight he looked like a worried one.

"*God-cynn,*" he said, gesturing to Penda. "The family likeness
is clear tonight."

It was. All that was needed to make a man think that Wotan
Battle-Father had come to feast among us were two ravens brooding on the king's shoulders and a hoar, grey wolf a-growl at his
feet. That wasn't good to think on, for the Raven-god, Wotan, in
his great and golden Valholl, broods over a grim fate: the terrible
war among gods which he will not be able to stop, and which he
will not win.

After yet more mead, Aescwine said that he reckoned he'd
better do something to change things. Cynnere snorted, and I

laughed, but Aescwine wasn't daunted by un-believers. He sat waiting until Hinthan again filled the king's drinking-horn. Then he got awkwardly to his feet and shouted loud enough to be heard above the din of feasting:

"Ay! Hinthan!"

Hinthan stopped where he was, and the king looked down the board to where Aescwine stood lurching for balance.

"Hinthan, boy, you're doing fine service for our king there. But you forgot to tell him about the best of the good things Erich War Hawk has to give a guest."

Hinthan shot me a quick look, but I shrugged, knowing no better than he what Aescwine was talking about. Erich, standing halfway down the hall with a group of Dwarfs and Men, turned to see what Aescwine was up to. Gled looked around with a little worried frown. But this was no test for Hinthan, nor any slighting of Gled's generosity; only a word on the way to others.

"The mead is good," Aescwine said. "The *twybrowen* even better, I hear."

That, in politeness, required answer. Penda agreed that Aescwine was right about the mead and the ale.

"King, there's a brew better than these, and there's someone here who's tasted the best of that good drink."

He swallowed more of the honey-wine and wiped his mouth with the back of his hand. That looked very much like a poet's pause, the quiet to draw a listener close. Now I was getting an idea about what Aescwine was up to; as was Erich, who smiled and motioned a questioner to silence. When the king asked what brew had been tasted but not offered to him, I wasn't surprised to hear Aescwine's answer.

"Dwarf's Ale, King! The best of Wotan's own drink!"

The Dwarf's Ale, which elders say makes a song-crafter of any who tastes it; that strong drink was made by *dvergr* in a distant world, an ancient time. The oldest tales teach that the first skalds came to be after sipping the brew. Still, that's only half the tale, and I hoped Penda wouldn't remember the part that tells how the poet's brew became Wotan's only because he stole it from the makers.

But if he recalled the whole tale, Penda chose to ignore the awkward parts. He laughed with more cheer than we'd heard all night. He'd been handily led to ask a question and he liked the answer he got.

"*Dvergr*, who in this hall has tasted that Ale?"

"The skald's right here, King." Aescwine cocked his thumb at me and grinned broadly, terribly.

Penda put a hand on Hinthan's shoulder, gave him a little push. "Go ask your foster-father if he remembers how that Ale tastes, boy."

Hinthan—who knew the difference between a kindly meant push and a scornful shove—went to do the king's bidding.

My Sif, I was a wordless poet for many long years—unless you reckon it skald-craft to go out onto the blood-soaked war-grounds after battle is ended and ask each fleeing ghost his name so I could bring those names to my *cyning*. I did that cold work for Halfdan, who knew me as Silent Skald. I did it for Erich even after I found my words again. That's a needful reckoning. And though some years had passed since anyone had a reason to name me Silent Skald, that night in Hordstede I didn't have a new name.

And so, known but nameless, I went and gave Penda what he wanted. I told old tales, sang new songs, the way such things have always been done: one man standing beside the board, the poet among his friends as the hearth-fire leaps and falls. I wove the songs of lightning and thunder, spun the tales from the last defiant shouts of good men, the first quiet whispers of ghosts.

I told of brave soldiers, Dwarfs and Men whose courage had shone bright on dark battle-grounds. I sang about Halfdan Skuli's son, who built Hordstede, and of the kings who were his friends— Penda and his father. I gave them songs about such brave soldiers as Godwig, who was Aescwine's son. That fearless young Dwarf is barrowed on the Welshland border, on the far ridge called Cefn Arth. I told of *dvergr* Haestan who'd died there as well. Like me, those two were of the Last. Like me, like all the Last, they bore no father-name, but they won't be forgotten.

I sang of *mann-cynn,* of tall Ecgwulf, the bold sword wolf; of one-eyed Dyfed, him who was a riddle-crafter, a ghost-footed scout, and my steadfast friend.

I hear the Battle-Father   hail the faith-fast home,
hear on the wind   the *Waelcyrgies* wild.
on steeds of storm   I see Thunor's sisters
ride to raise the dead   the Raven-god's daughters
stoop to lift   our long-loved friends. . . .

Such songs pleased the king and the soldiers who would soon be going into the battle-storm.

When the last tale was told, and men sat in silence over their drinks, I got a new name.

The king left the high seat to stand at the head of the board. The hall lay still and dark now, for the fire was low, the candles guttered. What light there was went to settle on Penda, a bright cloak for the king. He spoke a word to Hinthan, sent his cup-bearer to bring me ale.

"Garroc," Penda said when the cup was in my hand. "You're a good friend to the ghosts. No one who hears you will forget those who have died." Then, his eyes like the warm blue edges of fire, "*Waes hael, gaests-skald!*"

The cry went down the hall like a long, rolling echo of thunder and grew as other voices took up the king's shout. But they were mostly the Men among us who did that shouting, and Aescwine looked at me, then looked away, reached for more to drink. Close beside me, Hinthan paled as he recognized the grim weight my new name carried, the reminder that the time will come when Dwarfs will be the ghosts in the songs Men sing.

But Penda had meant to praise, not to wound. Nor did any who cheered now mean to offend. The oldest Man there could have told a tale about some Dwarf his own eldfather had known, and maybe he'd be talking about a person who even then sat across the board from him. It's easy to forget about a god's curse when every day you see people who look as though they'll live forever.

Hinthan filled my cup again, now with sweet honey-wine. Ghosts-Skald drank deeply, then spoke his best words of thanks for the king's gift of a new name.

The last log in the hearth broke; the two pieces fell onto heaped embers. Sundered, they still had each his own glowing heart, and they twined their light together to make red and gold raids against darkness.

I walked watch on the wall in the middle-night with only the moon and trusty Harm for company. A thin curl of smoke rose from the bake-house at the far end of the street. Soon the crisp air would fill with the scent of baking loaves, but now I smelled only wood smoke. The street lay still under the stars, owned by cats hunting river rats. In the hall and the guest-houses all was settled to night-quiet. So sharp the air that I heard horses stamping and shuffling in the stable. Behind me one of the great wooden doors to the hall opened, then closed.

I turned away from the river and saw Hinthan leaving the hall. In just that moment I heard gagging and a choked curse as an ale-sotted man came lurching out of the dark alley between two guest-houses. Moonlight glinted on iron buckles, on jewels and a polished silver wrist-bracer. The white light shone on raven-black hair and a beard all matted and fouled with sickness. Peada went staggering down the empty street.

Hinthan stopped where he was, and Peada saw him.

Legs braced wide for balance, Peada stared, head cocked as though trying to remember if he knew him. I was down the ladder, when his sodden wits started working.

"Ay, it is you," he snarled. "The boy who's too fine to fetch the ale but to skalds and kings!"

Moonlight flashed on iron, on two knives drawn suddenly, Peada's sooner than Hinthan's. With a rumbling, roaring shout, Peada lurched forward and drove Hinthan down before him. Came another glint of light on a sharp-honed edge, like ice to freeze the blood in me. I ran for them, and behind Hinthan one of the broad wooden doors opened. Golden torch-light spilled into the night. Erich War Hawk stood in the doorway, a flaring brand held high.

He shouted "Hold!" but by then the brawl had come to its own end.

The hot smell of blood lay heavy on the cold air. Hinthan got to his feet, but Peada never moved; he lay in the mud, blood on his hands where he clutched his belly. Hinthan stood over him, his face sheeted with blood from a thin cut. He had no other hurt, and this wasn't one to worry about.

Then, suddenly, I began to shake—right to the knees—and I thought, *He's killed the king's son.*

"Hinthan, come here."

He jerked a little, for I'd startled him, and he raised a hand to wipe the blood from his face, never minding that he roughed the cut scoring his cheek.

"Hinthan," I said again, "come here now."

He never moved, even when Erich came into the moonlight to poke at the drunk with his foot and turn him belly up. That belly was whole; it was Peada's hand and forearm that bled, and no one ever died of wounds so small as those. As to prove it, Peada rolled onto his side, groaning. He curled up a little, too drunk to know he was hurt, or to know that he was getting comfortable in the mud. Hinthan let his breath go in a long, ragged sigh.

"Boy," Erich said, "from now on you'd better stay out of Peada's way."

"I'm not afraid of him, *cyning*."

Erich laughed, a short sharp bark. "Then you're a fool. If you don't know it, Garroc will tell you that Peada's a miser with his grudges. If he remembers this night, he's probably going to want to kill you. Now if Peada does kill you, you know I'll have to get the man-price for it; I owe your foster-father at least that much."

In the mud, Peada gagged, coughed, and fell still. Erich nudged him again, then shrugged.

"Now I've known Garroc all my life, Hinthan, and so I know he wouldn't take the *wer-gild* for you even if it was ten times the twelve hundred and two a freeman's son is worth. That means I'd have to hang the king's son if I wanted to keep my honor and this good friend of mine. I'm sure you understand why I wouldn't want to do that."

Hinthan said he understood, and Erich nodded grimly. He had no more to say, and he went back into the hall. Soon we heard him shout for men to fetch Peada out of the street.

That night, my Sif, the stranger-ghost whispered *Skald! Skald* . . . as I fell asleep. He whispered again when I got up and went stumbling, half-sleeping, to use the midden. I heard him as I woke in the morning. *Skald! Skald* . . . But the next night I didn't hear him, and the night after, he was silent. After that he abandoned the borderland of my dreaming, and I didn't hear him again for a long while.

But other whispers came. Lydi's dreams never forsook me, and these were close and warm and welcomed.

The king's army set out from Rilling after the spring rains, and early in the war-season it became clear that Cadwalla forgot his boast to take Eoferwic. Undefended monasteries and farmsteads, fat villages—these promised the easy kills the witch-king liked best. By spring's end no one thought Cadwalla would make good his boast to feast Penda in Eadwine's hall.

Peada, the king's black and white son, didn't take care to hide his disappointment.

Our king was no better pleased, for reasons no one knew but him. Times were, on a late night-watch, when I'd see him standing alone and looking north at the witchy proofs of Cadwalla's war-work—fire-red skies, long back columns of smoke. Once I surprised a yearning look in his eyes; another time, fear. I saw these things and remembered the look I'd seen on him when Peada told him that Cadwalla was minded to do his burning and killing in the northern part of Eadwine's kingdom this year.

Yet, whatever Penda dreaded, he didn't let it get in the way of his warfare.

Cadwalla burned and looted in the north, and Osric, the exile come home, fought his own war against Eadwine. He forced the Northumbrian to send two of his sons and a strong force to defend the western borders. Northumbria was cut into three pieces and Faith-Breaker himself chose to defend his southern borders against Penda. But the meetings between Penda and Eadwine were bitter, brutal contests fought to no end; a clash of armies, the din of war-storm, and all of it receding again like the dark waves of the sea which, for all their terrible fury, must abandon the land at last.

All through that spring and into summer I kept Hinthan from war-grounds. He was one of my keenest scouts, but when time came for battle he waited behind with the other boys, the young kinsmen of soldiers come out to learn war-craft. He hated waiting, but I kept him back. I wouldn't let him fly.

In the end, it wasn't me who chose the first battle-ground for him. The choice was made on the night Hinthan fought drunken Peada in the mud outside Erich's hall, the boy against the man.

PART TWO

◄►

Stone and Tree

Stane Saewulf's son, who was my own foster-father, told me that before any of the Nine Worlds were made there was a giant, and the giant was kin to gods.

He told me this on the night my father brought me to live with him. I didn't have much to say that night. I was angry with Grimwulf because he'd doomed me to a life of learning skald-craft, the hundred on hundred old lays, the tales, the stories of gods and their doings. I didn't think there was any reason to make things easier for Stane. But Stane never did like silence with his supper, and so he talked.

"The giant," he said, "was a reaver; a breaker, a foul destroyer. His name was Ymir."

Ymir's kinsmen did not love him, and Ymir had no kindly feeling for them. They made war on each other, the giant and the gods. They fought in the great dark emptiness that existed before the Nine Worlds were. Ymir found his fate at the hands of the gods; the reaver could not gainsay his *wyrd*: life and death and life again; bright strand and dark strand and bright, woven.

Of Ymir, the gods made this middle-world of ours. His blood is the salt sea; his flesh the soil. His bones are the mountains; from his teeth gods made rocks and stone. His skull is the sky, set over all the world, a great and heavy roof.

"I will tell you soon who holds up that roof," Stane said as he filled up my bowl once more with the good stew we shared for our supper. "But now I expect you will ask: How is it that we say the earth is our mother when our world is made of the blood and bones of this warrior-giant?"

I wanted to know, but I wouldn't ask. I had to nurse my anger. And so Stane said:

"It is thus—as a body must have a spirit, so must the world. Into the world, made from the body of the reaver came a soul, a mother-spirit, and her name is Eard, she who is the daughter of Night. And it came to be that one of the gods, one of the giant-killers, the world-crafters, saw Eard's beauty and loved her. That god was Wotan, and he was about the earning of his name, All-Father.

"Eard quickened to the god's love. In her warding womb life grew—Dwarfs, the Firstborn, the true sons.

"So it is," said Stane, "that all folk say that Dwarfs are earth-kin, for your eldest mother is Eard, who loved god-Wotan. And your mother speaks to you always, youngling. Your hear the voices of stone."

Then Stane told me that four of the Firstborn went to the corners of the sky, strong sons to reach up and hold the shining roof, to shelter her and all kin and kinds. Nothri and Suthri, Austri and Vestri, stand at the four points of the world.

"As they are the first of your kindred, Garroc, they will be the last. Wotan's curse may not harm these. They are outside fate, untouched by any doom but one: to hold up the sky until it need be held no more."

That is the tale of Stone.

"Youngling," said my foster-father on that long-ago night. "The Stone has foster-kin, and that kin is the Tree."

Stane said that the All-Father went a second time to the mother-earth and got himself a bright, strong son. Red-bearded that son, and his nature is stormy, made of rain and wind and lightning. When he fights his father's enemies, the blows from his great war-hammer make the sky roar. His name is Thunor.

When first Thunor brought rain, his mother the earth decked herself in green grass and tall trees, for she was proud of her mighty son and honored him by showing off all her best. Soon after this wonder of grass and tree was seen, Wotan went walking with two of his kinsmen. They found standing tall and lovely upon the sea strand two trees, one stout and strong, the other slender and supple. Of the first tree the gods made a man; of the second a woman. Fair, these two, not yet fated, without spirit. To the man these gods gave soul and sense and being. They named him Ash. The woman they named Elm, and they saw to it that she had all they granted Ash, and great beauty as well.

So was *mann-cynn* born, said my foster-father.

"Like the ash and the elm, we grow tall; and we are your foster-kin, youngling. Not born of Eard, we hear nothing of her secret speech; but nurtured at her breast we know that we must love her as good sons love the woman who has shown them generous care and kindness. Men and Dwarfs, we are *wer-cynn*.

"I am a skald, youngling," said Stane Saewulf's son when his story ended. "I know many tales, and as many I'll never know. I'm not like you. I'm earth-deaf. I'll never hear my foster-mother speak. And so—you and me—we have things to teach each other. Will you stay with me, Garroc? Will you teach me the songs stones sing?"

I got up from my place by the fire, filled a cup with ale for Skald Stane. The telling of tales is thirsty work.

"I'll stay with you," I said, when he was done drinking.

And I did. I learned to love him, and he taught me word-craft while I taught him the songs that stones sing.

My Sif, I thought of Stane often in the long months of Penda's war against Eadwine Faith-Breaker, often as spring grew into summer. I thought of him when I walked watch and saw the lights of the enemy's camp and knew that the dark tales out of Northumbria were true: Only *mann-cynn* fought for Faith-Breaker now. For reasons of their own or because of some *Cristen* edict, Dwarfs were not part of Eadwine's army.

And I learned some new words that spring. Devil-wolf, shadow-kin, hel-ghost . . . These words the Northumbrians used against Dwarfs. Walking watch, I'd think: Wise as he was, my foster-father never foresaw a time when any of Men would forget the meaning of the word *wer-cynn*.

Nor would Stane have understood the strangest of *Cristen* ideas—that there is only one world, not nine; and that the One was made by your god and given to *mann-cynn*. A garden to tend, say the *Cristens* of Wales and Ireland. Welshmen and Irelanders love gardens and beauty. A kingdom to rule, say the *Cristens* of

Rome. The people of that country don't forget that they once ruled most of the world, and they still count their riches by counting their slaves. It's said they were that way long before they ever heard of god-Jesu.

"In Cent the *Cristens* think like Welshmen," said Aescwine, who was from there. "But these Northumbrians must have fallen under the spell of the Roman folk."

When I asked him why he thought so, he laughed bitterly.

"Once a woman is made a slave, no man wants her sons for foster-kin. I'm right—you'll see."

But we found no Dwarf in Eadwine Faith-Breaker's land—not at the roadside, not in villages, not living wild on the heath—to say if Aescwine's reckoning was right. Four months into Penda's great war, when Thunor's Moon, the battle-moon, rose up in the sky, that changed.

‹5›

In the last hour before sunrise the stone-paved Roman road looked like the picked bones of a dragon, a naked spine of broken stone and crumbling wall snaking along the curve of a steep hill. The road had a mate on the east hill; between lay Winwaed Vale and Eadwine Faith-Breaker's army of ten hundred. All night I'd watched that valley from the shadow of the wall, with Cynnere and Aescwine for company.

To the north and east, beyond Eoferwic and out by the sea, the red flash of Cadwalla's magic-craft glared like a storm come over a country so blood-soaked that the blood must tint the lightning. We were used to tracking Cadwalla by that terrible light, and we reckoned he was at least twenty miles north of Eoferwic now. That rich town lay only a few miles beyond Winwaed Vale.

A dark-winged raven came from that quarter of the sky, wheeling low over the valley, circling down and down. Another joined it.

"Not good," Cynnere said. He pounded his fist against the stone wall. Grey mortar drifted to shroud a lone stalk of harebells. "When the storm-crows come early, it's not good."

Aescwine twisted his face into the squint-eyed snarl we knew for a cheerful smile. "Boy, you worry too much."

I thought so, too. Last night Eadwine had gone to sleep sure he'd win the day's fighting. To the north beyond the valley's narrow mouth Penda's army waited, five hundred soldiers, some mounted, more afoot. In the south Peada had three hundred camped where the River Winwaed spread its branches like the fingers of a grasping hand. These two were the armies Eadwine knew about last night, and the odds must have looked good to him then. But this morning he'd waked to find that Penda had been joined by friends. Merewal's army camped beneath the eastern crest. Erich and his father-in-law Cynewulf waited below the western hill. After a long summer of wild chasing and hard fighting, Eoferwic was at last in reach, ready for taking once Penda got Eadwine out of his way.

Dark wings gleamed black in the new day, more ravens come to hang in the sky and wait. In the earth I felt a familiar echo as Hinthan slipped through the pale shadows of first-light to join our watch. He was dusty and streaked with sweat, for he'd spent the night riding for Erich—to Cynewulf, to Penda, to Merewal, and back again. He had a look on him like he'd been burdened with bad news all night. He came and sat close to me, shoulder to shoulder. His arm trembled against mine; he was that weary.

"Let's hear it," Aescwine said. He never liked to wait for bad news.

Hinthan stretched out his long legs, pressed his back to the wall. His eyes closed, he said, "Peada's pulled his army back and put the swamp between him and Eadwine. And he'll be glad to pick off whoever the swamp doesn't get once the fighting starts, but he doesn't see any reason to rush in and fight where he's not needed. So says the *aetheling*."

He twisted that word like he was saying 'thief.' He wouldn't be mis-speaking if he did. Peada had lately got in the habit of naming himself *aetheling,* the king's heir, though no one but him and his friends believed that Penda would choose this untrusty son of his to be king after him. Merewal didn't do more than growl over Peada's grasping, but no one knew if that was because his brother had snatched what he'd like to have. That was the way of red Merewal; you only knew what he wanted you to know. Others—men like Erich and Cynewulf—made no secret of not liking Peada's claim to what the king hadn't granted.

The king himself said nothing about his over-reaching son.

Cynnere spat. "He's a coward, that Peada."

"Ah, now," Aescwine said. "We can say better than that about him, can't we? We can hope ravens will pluck out his eyes. Or we can hope that wolves feast on his liver." His face wrenched into a leering grin, his most benign smile. "For that matter, we could ask Hel if she'd mind freezing his balls to ice."

I laughed at that, and Cynnere at last found a reason to smile. But Hinthan didn't smile; he had something more on his mind. I nudged him, easily with my elbow, and he glanced at me, then lowered his eyes to say we'd talk about it later. I didn't press him. I knew what we'd be talking about.

From beyond the hill came the rising sound of an army making ready for battle—the silver song of bridle iron, the rattle of spear and linden-shield. We backed away from the wall, careful not to show ourselves against the sky. We didn't say much but to wish each other luck, and soon Cynnere and Aescwine went to ready their horses. Those two friends would ride side by side into battle, as they always did.

"Now tell me, boy mine."

"The king says he needs all the men he can find now. I was with him when the runner came with the news, Garroc. I saw him when he heard that his son abandoned him. I saw his face . . ."

In Hinthan's own face I saw the shadow of what the king must have looked like, skin white and tight-drawn, eyes glittering with anger. Beneath all, almost hidden, the pain of betrayal.

"Foster-father, I'm riding with you today."

He had more courage that day than I had.

"No," I said, and quickly. I was still afraid.

I expected him to argue, Sif, but he didn't, and we walked the rest of the way to the camp in silence.

He never asked again if he could ride into battle with me.

Foot soldiers made a loose half-circle behind the horsemen. Bright, a shining of new sun on yellow hair and beard, a leaping of light on golden arm-rings, Erich Halfdan's son rode among his army. All around us the songs of war rang out—bridle iron chiming, voices of Dwarfs and Men raised in boast or challenge. A berserker howled among the foot soldiers. Like winter wind racing down the sky, another of the wild *wulf-cynn* answered.

My grey gelding shied and pulled at the rein. Hinthan slid his hand up to the cheek-strap, gripped right where the agate mantle-clasp was pinned to the leather till I should need a mantle against cold again. He whispered soft words learned from Aelfgar in Gardd Seren. When the grey quieted, Hinthan gave the reins to me.

"Stay alive, Garroc."

I gripped his hand hard to answer, to seal a promise, and his face shone very pale. Erich shouted and the army surged forward, horsemen before foot soldiers. Hinthan let go of my hand only when he had to.

It's a loud thing, my Sif, the wave of battle rushing, horses thundering and men shouting, berserkers howling to match the moan of wolves. You can't hold a thought in your head, and you can't hear the man riding beside you even if he's shouting at you. So I don't know what made me look behind just as I reached the crest of the hill, but it was like I'd been called.

I saw Hinthan, with the last of the horsemen, my boy on a long-legged red mare. He had two quivers filled with arrows, one at his hip, one slung across his shoulder. He gripped his strung bow to nock an arrow. Just as I saw him, he saw me.

He had no look of apology on him for going against my word.

And, in truth, if ever there was a time for that, it was past. We knew it, and now we each wanted the same thing—to ride knee to knee into the battle. But we couldn't have that. Even as I tried to turn the grey to cross the line of horsemen to him, the foot soldiers swept between us.

"Stay alive!" I cried.

But I didn't know if he heard me, and I saw his face turn suddenly to ashy-grey beneath summer's brown. We were apart and alone.

No sooner did I reach the valley floor than my horse went down, screaming, belly-ripped. I flung myself from its back, hit the ground and rolled to get away from the thrashing beast. Above me, around me, in me, the roar of armies, the flash of sunlight on iron, and a great swelling of voices; men cursing, bellowing war-cries. Penda's split forces hit Eadwine's in killing waves.

Slipping in blood-stinking mud, I lurched to my feet. The horsemen were past me, battering at Eadwine's line of defense, making a way for the foot soldiers and howling berserkers. I saw Hinthan among those riders, saw him wheel the red mare around and try to come back for me.

I shouted, "No! Go on!" and in a breath's time the whole battle got between us.

The Northumbrians found their mounts and some of them saw that we had no defense on the southern flank. The strutting young peacock who named himself *aetheling* hadn't come to defend us. We lay open and helpless before the line of horsemen come to drive us under the trampling hoofs of our own riders.

They didn't find that easy to do. We held them; afoot, we didn't let them herd us to our deaths beneath slashing hoofs. And red Merewal, the king's faith-fast son, saw our plight, rode to help his friends. But, like a thrown spear, another line of Eadwine's horsemen thrust between us. The two lines met, swords aloft, red-gleaming. I heard Merewal cursing, and he cursed his brother as often as his enemy.

Black ravens wheeled low; the great cloud of them looked no different than the smoke of Eadwine's broken campfires. I couldn't tell a berserker's howl from those of the grey wolves come to pace on the hills. But I knew there was a god nearby.

Like the ravens and the wolves, Wotan Battle-Father waited. With him waited the Valkyries, his nine daughters, Thunor's sisters three times three. On their lips stirred the names of the fated, the Dwarfs and Men who would die on the bloody war-ground.

• • •

There was a shield-wall, a braced line of foot soldiers to keep the Northumbrians from advancing while the rest of our friends found ways past our own horsemen. I was a piece of that wall, with only painted linden-wood borrowed from a dead man to turn a rain of iron. With Harm I slashed at the belly of every horse that came at me and hacked the fallen riders. Beside me, friends made good use of their own iron. We stopped many of the Northumbrians, hewed great bleeding gaps in their line. But some got through, and soon others. The shield-wall shattered.

High above the blood-mire and the smoke, ravens screamed. A wild wind raged down the hot sky. Valkyries stretched out their hands; the battle-maids cried Wotan's greeting to the dead: *Wil-cuman!*

Closer, a boy's voice howled in wild raging.

Iron belled on iron, scraped sparks, metal from metal. The Northumbrian boy dropped back, staggered for his footing in the mud and came at me again. He was a mindless force, desperate to live, desperate to kill. He was like me in all of that, except he was *mann-cynn* and so he had the better reach. But he didn't know how to use the advantage; he kept stepping in closer than he had to. He struck blow after blow, and they went wild when they met Harm's iron haft. Some cut him rebounding. Bleeding and hurt, he howled, "Hel-ghost! Devil-wolf!" and he kept on, battering at the axe's haft until my hands began to numb.

The next blow would break my grip, leave me weaponless. I stepped back. To the side. Made him turn to find me. Then I swung Harm with all my strength and killed the terrified boy. The light died away from his eyes while he yet screamed.

Behind the dead boy a black horse reared and—bright as a sword shining!—Erich War Hawk reached down to pull me up behind him, out of the slaughter-reek. I grasped his wrist, he mine—and an arrow caught him. He fell back and, falling, dragged me to my knees. The archer drew again and aimed for me.

Behind the archer, another rose up; again, a boy. My boy, a tall lean bowman with his dark hair blowing back. Blood covered him, as everyone on that battle-ground, living and dead. Some blood was his, some stained him like sea-splash. Hinthan had one arrow, and one chance at the archer. In the space between heartbeats he reckoned and he aimed. He sped that one and last arrow, and the Northumbrian dropped to his knees with blood pouring from his mouth and nose.

Between Hinthan and me, this unspoken: What if I didn't come with you today, Foster-father? What if I'd not been here now?

I'd be dead. We knew it.

His triumph was a shining thing, and the arrow he'd spent for me was his last. I thought the sudden dread, the leaping fear in him came with that understanding. Too late I realized he wasn't looking at me, but past me. The horse hit me hard, drove me to the ground. A sharp hoof struck my shoulder, another my head. Sight burst into knife-edged shards. Dark shattered light. Iron belled on iron. The dying screamed, the dead whispered.

Last, I heard Hinthan shouting—in rage, or fear. Maybe in terrible pain.

The man in the water had no face. He had no features that I could see, only eyes over-brimming with weariness and tears. All the rest was a mask of red blood and black mud. I found him after a long walk, a limping journey across stone-floored Winwaed Vale, searching for Hinthan. Thunor's Moon hung on the horizon, old now and too weak to help me search. But I had other light—the first leaping flames of funeral pyres, the blood-glare as Cadwalla's witches began another night of burning in the north where people thought the world was breaking apart in fire.

I found Hinthan nowhere.

Once I saw Erich, the *cyning* with his arm bound up. He told me that Eadwine no longer held the valley, that in the end Faith-Breaker got through Penda's line and flew north to Eoferwic. And he told me that we'd be staying here with the king for a time, but that red Merewal would take his own army to Eoferwic. Cynewulf's men and most of Penda's would go with him.

"Pearroc and Eldgrim and Cynnere are going too," he said. "You and Dunwulf and Aescwine stay here with me. No one's expecting Merewal to catch Eadwine now." His blue eyes glinted coldly. "And Peada's not going to have an enjoyable night."

I heard him through, but fixed on one thing only. He'd named all my scouts but one.

"*Cyning,* have you seen Hinthan?"

He looked away, Sif; down and away. He thought Hinthan was dead.

I walked away from him. Hinthan wasn't dead. The battle-ground was loud with ghosts; none was his. Hinthan was alive, maybe hurt and helpless in this blood-mire where black ravens quarreled over the feast and the pale Night Maidens sighed on a cooling breeze.

I walked till the flat stony floor of the valley closed in, changed to thickets of purple heather. There I fell to my knees beside the little stream, some small brother of the blood-running Winwaed. That's when I saw the red-masked, faceless man in the water.

Skald! Skald . . .

And that's when the stranger-ghost of winter came back, whispering to me where I knelt at the edge of dread, in the borderland between sense and fancy.

A cricket piped a thin reedy song, fire-flies winked, light at the edge of sight. Beneath the bank a bullfrog gulped, and I leaned closer to see the face in the water.

Skald! Skald . . .

I recognized my reflection.

I didn't feel the footstep echoing in the earth, didn't hear the leaves rustle, the heather whisper. But, cold to my bones, I did see another face swim up out of the water, a face wide-eyed with fear.

A dead boy's face.

Hel-ghost! he'd screamed at me.

I grabbed bloody Harm, turned and rose all at once. I raised the axe to kill, and the boy lunged at me. He prisoned my two wrists in iron grip, braced and held hard to check the blade's fall. He knew how to do that because I'd taught him how.

Hinthan held the axe, and he held me in locked gaze. His face shone white where it wasn't bruised and stained with mud and blood. Silently, he begged me to see him and know him.

Dry-mouthed, I let the axe fall.

I felt his hands shaking just before he loosed his grip on my wrists. I didn't let him go. I took him by the shoulders and held him at arm's length to see him. He bled from a shallow leg wound. In his eyes I saw bone-deep weariness, the ashy dregs of the brew of fear and rage that carries a soldier through to the battle's end. But he stood straight and tall. Wotan's stone, the blood-red agate mantle-clasp glittered on his shirt.

"I found your horse," Hinthan said. "And the clasp on the bridle."

He took the journey-stone from his shirt and carefully cleaned it of blood. The gold pin gleamed in starlight. The agate, called Way-friend, sat shining on his palm. Silently, he held out his hand in offering, and I took the clasp and pinned it to my own shirt.

Wolves and ravens prowled the battle-ground. The air stank of pyre smoke. A dying man groaned and another man shouted in voice-broken gratitude. A brother had found a brother yet alive, a friend had found a friend.

Here by the stream, Hinthan and I stood quietly for a long time. The battle-ground was behind us both, and today he'd made a crossing into the company of men. Now he must forever stand or fall by his own choices. He was both proud and afraid, and he couldn't un-do what he'd done.

"Boy mine." I gave him a father's kiss. "I hope the luck you had today likes being near you."

And him, newly come from battle-grounds, newly proved a man to all who'd judge him on his skill at killing, he hugged me warmly.

"Foster-father, for your teaching, my thanks. Know that I am at your back. Always."

Never think I didn't know what his promise was worth, Sif; he'd proven the value that day. And—I'll not lie—I loved the feel of his words, the weight of them, heavy as though they knew a hundred hundred boys had spoken them to a hundred hundred men down the long years. But they were, too, the beginning of a farewell. Hinthan was leaving boyhood behind, whether I was ready for that or no.

We were quiet when we went out to the wide valley, the dark hall where wolves and ravens feasted beneath the distant red witch-light. But for those beasts of battle, all I heard were ghosts whispering as Hinthan and I walked across the valley to Erich's camp atop the hill by the old Roman road and the long, twisting wall that looks like the spine of a dragon.

Erich War Hawk had lost good soldiers that day at Winwaed Vale, and I gave him all the names of the Dwarfs and Men of his marcher lands who were dead. We mourned them, lord and skald, privately together. This rite his father taught us. And that night I gave him Hinthan to replace one of the lost.

The brazier light flared and fell and sent shadows scrambling up the walls of his tent, and Erich said, "Are you proud of him, Garroc?"

"I am."

"Your boy," he said, low. He knew what treasure of hope I'd found in Hinthan. "Are you afraid for him?"

Maybe he was thinking about his own son, the small boy who was years away from crossing to manhood. Or maybe he spoke from what all soldiers know—there's pride to be found on war-grounds, just as skalds say; but there's also fear and sorrow and bitter regret found there.

"There's not much I can do about it, *cyning*. Boys grow, no matter if you think they're ready or you don't."

He told me to bring his soldier to him, and I did. And when Hinthan put his hands in the *cyning's*, I felt it as if they were my hands holding, and my hands held. His eyes shone like clean iron, and his voice shook a little under the weight of the words when he spoke the sword-oath.

"Lord, I am yours, a weapon to use and to spend as you will."

When Halfdan's son accepted him I was very proud.

In the night, when there was little to be heard but the hiss of fallen campfires, I came from watch and saw Hinthan standing outside the light of our fire, just the dark lean shape of him against the stars and the fading witch-light.

"Hinthan," I said, soft so as not to wake Aescwine, who slept nearby.

He turned, and I saw tears on his face, a silvery trace. There was a hollowed look on him, for he was feeling everything he'd done that day, every wound he'd given, every man he'd killed. I took him away, out to the dragon-back hill. We sat there for a long time, him sorrowing for what he'd done and me keeping him company while he did. He'd not expected this last lesson in war-work. I let him cry, and when the hard sorrow passed I told him I was glad to know that he could kill if he had to, but that he was no killer.

And so it was that we were sitting the west side of the wall when two men came walking up from the battle-field. They walked in anger, but only one spoke. He spoke of trust and treachery. In low and bitter whispers, he spoke of good men killed in battle and the shame of the coward who hung back from the fight. In a flat and pitiless voice, the king spoke of outlawry, of exile.

Penda told his son that he himself would do the banishing, name him outlaw before kin and friends. But he said that with no heart to do it. This was his firstborn, and once he loved him. And so Penda cursed his son, and in rage and helplessness struck him down. We heard the blow, Hinthan and I, silent on the other side of the wall. We heard the king walk away and leave his son to lie where he'd felled him.

Soon dark-eyed Peada got to his feet and vaulted the wall, the old dragon-back. His father had hit him in the mouth; blood ran down his chin. But his pale face was as still as though he'd not felt the king's blow or heard his curse.

I reached for Hinthan too late.

He rose smoothly to his feet, and they stood face to face, one who'd wept for the foes he'd killed, one who cared nothing about the friends he let die. Peada went suddenly white in the face to know we'd overheard his father's shaming words. But he recovered swiftly, and he laughed to see Hinthan's hands fisted.

"What, boy? Are you looking for a fight again?"

Then he looked away as though to say that Hinthan was no one to worry about. He didn't dismiss me so easily, and his eyes were cold and reckoning until I rested Harm against the wall. Without words I let him know that if Hinthan chose to fight, not me nor my war-axe would enter in.

Hinthan chose, and he struck with arrow-speed, tore into Peada as though he didn't know he'd not have even the smallest chance of winning. He stood up under Peada's harder blows, and he had reason—for a while—to think that his quickness would lend balance to the fight. But only for a while. Peada stopped the brawl when it stopped being amusing. Hands clasped to make one hard fist, starlight running on his broad silver wrist-bracer, he dropped Hinthan with one swift hammer-blow, and turned quickly on me, long-knife in hand.

"Now I'll fight you," he said. "If that's what you want."

I took up my war-axe, made sure he saw starlight running on the keen-edged blade.

"Boy," I said. "You come at me with that knife and I'll cut you in two. You come at me with your fists and I'll beat you senseless. Now hear me: This is the second time you've fought my foster-son. The first time you didn't make out so well, but then you were drunk. Now you've beaten him when he's fresh-come from the battle you refused. How does your victory taste?"

Could he go whiter, that pale man? He could; to the lips he blanched. Then, suddenly, he laughed, a wild and hopeless sound, like glass shattering. He spat, and walked away down the hill.

I got Hinthan to his feet, and when he could stand alone, I said, "The fight was yours, boy mine. But I don't think you made a good choice."

He agreed, and said there'd be another time and then we'd see how things turned out.

◂6▸

On the night between Thunor's Moon and the Witch's, I sat in the lee of broken church walls, near a meadow that was a sheep-graze only two days ago when there was still a monastery called Maed Jesu. Built on a square, all its buildings facing inward, the monastery had been like a village, with grain-stores and cottages, byres and barns, smithies and sheep-grazes and planted fields. But Maed Jesu had been on the wrong side of Eoferwic's walls. Now only this small stone church had a wall or two staggering erect.

Church, monks, and treasures, Eadwine had abandoned them all. After the battle in the Winwaed Vale, he'd driven his army straight up the Roman road. He didn't stop to warn the monastery-folk that danger was near before he shut tight the gates of Eoferwic. Faith-Breaker left Maed Jesu to Merewal, and Penda's red-bearded son didn't treat the monks gently. Now the dead were buried, the ghosts had gone wailing away, and nothing remained but the litter of burning. Beyond the church, Eoferwic's wood and limestone walls shone in the starlight. Both banks of the River Deorwente lay outside the walls. They boasted in Eoferwic that they'd drink good ale and fine wine and never miss the river's water, but the crowing rang hollow. Eadwine would have to come out soon and try to get his river back.

By the Deorwente, in a clearing between sparse-growing willows, I saw Hinthan walking watch. Closer, Cynnere lay stretched out before the fire, sleeping noisily. Aescwine sat awake, and bright bits of light challenged the campfire's sparks as he plied whetstone to his short-sword's iron. He worked with a smooth rhythm, stroke and back, stroke and back. Faintly, red light flowed along the edge of that iron, Cadwalla's war-glare. The witch-king was nearer to Eoferwic than he'd been all summer.

After a time Aescwine sheathed the sword and set it aside. He elbowed Cynnere to stop him snoring before he lay down and went to sleep. I watched the fire-flies some more, but I didn't stay long awake. I had no watch, and all the bones and muscles in me didn't much groan from battle and keep me wakeful.

I went soon to sleep, and came a dream where moonlight flowed down the sky like silver, like something to swim in.

• • •

Lydi stood in the doorway of the stone cottage, a hand on the latch, a hand on the doorpost. On the hilltop a warm breeze sighed through the oaks. Beyond the hill and below, the river ran. And here in the garden, all was silver and white and drenched with the moon's light. In the horehound a spider wove a careful web. Netted dew would gleam there in the morning.

Lydi took a long slow breath, tasted the garden, the scents of mint and yarrow and horehound drifting on the air. Breathing, she listened to crickets singing in the wildwood. And she lifted her eyes to the sky and filled with the light of the moon, white and pure and clear. She moved toward her wordless magic, she yearned toward shape-shifting. She would be a kestrel, the small hawk riding the night and the dark places between the stars.

Lydi lifted her hands, cupped the moon till the light spilled over and edged all she saw. In her she felt wind ruffling the edges of wings, wind running out ahead in currents like the river's. In her she felt wind lifting—

Came a sudden step, a shivering in the earth.

The magic spilled away, draining, wasted.

Like a sleeper roughly wakened, Lydi stood dazed and uncertain, dazzled in the moonlight. And Owain stood on the hill, in the oak grove above the river. He was brittle and bright, a broken vessel with the moon's heatless light running through.

"Witch," he said. His black, black eyes were like empty holes in his face. "Do it, witch. Change, girl. Let me see . . ."

Lydi didn't say anything. She didn't move. And Owain knew that he'd broken the magic, trampled it and scattered it. Lydi watched him walk away down the hill to the river road.

Poor wild thing, she thought.

The dream ended suddenly, Sif, a night-wandering not meant for me and caught back like a startled breath. Twined among the torn ends of that dream, the stranger-ghost of winter moaned.

Skald! Skald . . .

In me I cried, Ghost! Who are you?

As usual, he didn't answer.

In the absence of dreams, the silence of ghosts, I heard Hinthan call a sharp challenge. Riders approached the siege-camp by the river-road where he still kept watch. Cynnere woke, his hand on his sword, his eyes glittering blue in the ember-light. I reached for Harm, and didn't let the haft go again till I knew that the riders had halted as they were bid. The newcomers were Welshmen, in that language they greeted Hinthan. In the same, he passed them through.

Cynnere settled, but I didn't sleep for the rest of the night. I'd felt wandering dreams of Lydi's before now. It was like hearing a sleeper whispering part of his private dream aloud. What you hear, you soon forget. But I couldn't forget this dream, or the black emptiness in Owain's eyes, the hunger and the yearning.

‹7›

The first breeze of day gusted around burst stone walls, kicked up ash and dust as Erich and I went walking in the broken church. We walked until we came to a place before the east wall where the floor raised up, three broad steps to where an altar used to stand. Now the altar was a tumble of rose-veined marble stones, and Erich took a large flat one for a seat.

He didn't say anything for a long time, only sat thinking. I grounded Harm and leaned on the haft, ready to wait.

Outside the church campfires snapped, the flames pale against the lightening day. A berserker prowled the edges of the camp, bored and hungry for a fight. In the meadow, the clean place beyond the burnt buildings, Hinthan and Aescwine were dim shapes in the rosy mist. They were hunting bees in the hope that the ones who'd lived in the battle-broken hives would come back to Mead Jesu's ruined gardens. They two liked the sweet honey, and they were hopeful.

"Garroc," Erich said. "I have a tale to tell. And what I tell you is for no one else to know."

"Then no one will."

My Sif, Erich War Hawk was no word-weaver, but his story might have been a skald's best. He'd had the tale from Penda, and it was the story of a boy the king had never seen.

The boy's name was Wulfhere. He lived in Northumbria, and he was ten years old. He was Penda's son, born in the same year Eadwine Faith-Breaker decided to forget he was *god-cynn*.

In those days Eadwine had only just brought his young wife home from Cent, and soon after her marriage, lonely for friends, Queen Aethelburgh sent for a kinswoman to keep her company.

The woman's name was Gytha, and she was like a primrose with her yellow hair and green eyes. Riding north through peaceful Cent in the company of a flock of Christ-priests, Gytha soon went astray in Mercia.

Penda found these wanderers from across the border when he was out hunting with his *thegns* in the hills. To amuse himself, to have her company, Penda left his friends to their hunting and acted as guide to the Centish woman and her party. He brought them to Eadwine's border, and—for the boast—took them boldly beyond. Gytha was not unhappy to have his company. She left Mercia with the king's heart, and more besides.

"Penda was wed to Cynewise then," Erich said. A late owl, white as moonlight, sailed low over the unroofed church. Erich watched it fly. "But if things had been different, there'd be another woman offering the guest-cup in Penda's hall today."

That stopped me to wonder. I wasn't so much surprised to hear that the king had gone to play at love across the borders. There are other reasons people knew Penda as Wotan's Blade besides his skill at war-craft. And I knew—just about everyone could reckon it out—that if there was a good enough reason, Penda would break his marriage ties and make a generous settlement with his wife and her kin. If the settlement was to her liking, Cynewise wouldn't have spent even one tear on the ending. But I'd never heard it said that Penda did more than play at love, or that he would consider heart's love a good enough reason to risk putting Cynewise away.

As it was, Penda got himself no new wife. He left his Gytha in Northumbria.

Erich said, "She wouldn't go to live with a man who didn't bend his knee to the White Christ. And Penda would have given up his wife for Gytha and risked war with Cynewise's brothers—make no mistake, he'd have had to fight them sooner or later. But he couldn't do what Gytha asked. They let each other go, and he didn't know that he'd got her with child."

He learned that later. Gytha found a way to send the news to him, and Penda to promise her that though things were worsening between Mercia and Northumbria, she and his son would never suffer at his hands.

"That's a big promise," I said.

Erich smiled, a little in understanding, a little for pity.

"He was in love. But in the end no promise he made would have saved Gytha. She died seven years ago of sickness, but before she died she got word to Penda that she was sending their son to a monastery to be raised up by monks. The place is called Haligstane, and she reckoned it was a haven for the boy."

I nodded. "It's somewhere in the north country."

Erich's blue eyes narrowed, looked like glinting ice in the shadows where he sat. Nor did they warm again until I told him that I'd spied out no secret. I'd seen Penda watching, night and night as Cadwalla's war-light flared in the north.

"Always before, Cadwalla fought beside us," I said. "And then it was Penda who said what got burned and where. It's not that way this year." In the meadow, Hinthan said something to make Aescwine laugh, and I said, "*Cyning*, why didn't Penda send for his boy before now?"

"His reasons are his own," Erich said. "And he used to think they were good. Peada's making him think again—his men make up more of the army than they once did and they're getting comfortable with their new habit of naming him *aetheling*. The king's not minded to let his son make choices for him. His heir won't be Peada."

"Nor Merewal?"

Erich drew a short breath, let it out in a gusty sigh. "Nor Merewal."

"Why?"

"I don't know. You never know with Merewal. If I was betting—and I am, I guess—I'd say he's not interested in kingship. He's the spear, not the arm that casts. He likes things that way. Me, I'd rather have him for a half-hearted king than a *Cristen* for any kind of king."

But he wasn't the one who was choosing.

"*Cyning*, what does Merewal know?"

"Nothing of this. But that could change."

So it could; by bad luck or the king's own choice to trust his second son with the news that he had a young brother who would rule after their father's death.

"Garroc," Erich said. "The king's heard that Haligstane is still unharmed. Now he wants Gytha's boy out of there." He pointed to Eoferwic, the tall walls rising. "Eadwine's queen is gone."

I'd heard that. The news was the kernel of a dozen wild tales. Some said that Aethelburgh had abandoned her husband and children to flee doomed Eoferwic, taking only a Christ-priest and a great and wondrous treasure for company. Others had it that she'd vanished into the air by means of some terrible *Cristen* magic— babes, priest, treasure, and all. These stories and others got good tellings at the fire at night, but I was fair sure that Aescwine was the one to have the truth of the matter.

"I say Eadwine's got tired of the siege and advised the girl to take her children and take ship to Cent," my old friend said. "As for treasure—how much of that could she have? Eadwine'll be lucky if he's got a cup to go with a plate tonight. You don't get to have fine big wars like this for nothing."

I said to the *cyning,* "Whatever the rumor, most men are wagering that Eadwine won't stay in this trap much longer."

Erich nodded shortly. "Penda's spoken with two of Cadwalla's scouts; the King of Gwynedd is coming to help his dear friend and ally end the siege." His lean smile let me know how much weight he placed on the dearness of the friendship between those two kings. "Garroc, the knowledge of Wulfhere's fathering is in Eoferwic. At least one man was in Gytha's confidence not long ago. When those walls break, some secrets might come spilling out. I wouldn't expect the boy to live long after that. I don't think Merewal would harm him. If he learns about the boy, he's as likely to leave well enough alone. Peada's another matter. Him, I'd worry about."

I said I'd worry about Merewal, too, if it was up to me to do the worrying.

Erich sat quietly for a while, thinking and listening to the day rise. Then he looked at me eye to eye, and he said that he'd promised Penda to find a trusty man to fetch the *aetheling* to a safe place and good foster-kin.

"What foster-kin?" I asked.

"The folk you choose, Father's-friend. Will you do that, and keep my promise to the king?"

I didn't hesitate to say that I'd do whatever he asked. He was my *cyning,* he trusted me because he knew he could. And I thought we would talk about safe places to bring the young *aetheling,* which good lord or *thegn* would best care for a king's son, but we didn't. Erich put the matter in my hands, told me that he trusted me to find a haven for Wulfhere.

"If you've an idea about where that haven is, Garroc, don't tell me. Don't tell anyone who it is you choose to foster the boy until he's safely hidden and you come back to tell his father."

"And the boy? Will he be expecting word from his father?"

"No."

Then he took a small leather pouch from his belt, loosed the strings and shook something bright and glittering, gold and a flash of green gems, into my hand. Half of a golden arm-ring.

I turned the ring over, watched new sunlight leap on metal and stone, shining gold and green darts. The ring-maker had set emeralds of perfect roundness in the band, etched slender patterns of twining leaves to cradle the gems, the glistening buds whose only language is joy and hope. Like hearing laughter, all that green sparkle.

"When it was whole," Erich said, "the arm-ring belonged to Gytha. She had it halved and sent this to Penda as a token. The other is with the boy. Show this at Haligstane and the monks will know you've come from Wulfhere's kin—though they'll be thinking about his mother, not his father."

"Maybe these monks of Haligstane won't like handing over a *Cristen* child to a Dwarf."

"Maybe they won't," Erich said. "Find a way to do what you have to."

In the meadow, Hinthan shouted a laughing warning to Aescwine. And then his laughter changed suddenly to shouting. "Run to the water! To the water! Run!" The new sun spilled light down the sky, shone golden on the ruined church. Hinthan and Aescwine ran for the river, arms flailing, legs pumping, laughing again as they went diving into the water for haven from a dark swarm of angry bees.

That day, I studied my maps and tried to weave what little Erich could tell me about Haligstane into what I knew. The place was away north and a long ride from Eoferwic. I reckoned there must be some fine Roman roads between here and there; all the summer I'd seen Cadwalla and his witches make speed between one strike and the next. I'd have liked to take those roads, but I had no interest in meeting the witch-king and his army. And so I decided that our journey to Haligstane would take us first east to the sea, then north along the coast and, at last, inland.

When I knew that much, I went to find some friends to take with me.

I found Hinthan at the river, shirtless and sitting in the dappled shade of a willow. He'd not got too many bee-stings, and I guessed that Aescwine had made out better. I saw no sign of him.

"He caught some fish and he's back at the fire," Hinthan said, yawning and sleepy in the sun. He set his back to the willow, then suddenly sat up again, quickening like a hound on a sharp scent. "What?"

"Get a good horse and pack your gear," I said. "But do it quietly. We're leaving here and it'll be better if no one knows."

He filled up with questions at once, and I stopped him at once. "I'd have already told you about it if I could, youngling. I'm sworn not to."

Hinthan held his questions, and he didn't forget them.

I found Aescwine and Cynnere at our campfire, ready to eat a good catch of trout. I sat down with them and while we ate I told them I had some work I needed help with. Aescwine stopped eating to listen, still and silent. Cynnere's eyes lighted when I said this work would take us away from the siege.

"But all I can tell you is that it'll be a while before we're finished."

Cynnere said I could count on him. "Just tell me what to do when it needs doing."

Aescwine didn't say anything. He poked at the fire and watched the flinders fly up and north on the breeze. They were like fiery little stars, and he squinted to watch every one away. When the last was gone, he said, "Young skald, it's going to be hard and strange when we're on our own, ay?"

A chill touched me, a cold finger on the back of my neck. Rumors and dark tales became real this summer. Nowhere had we seen one of the *dvergr* kin in Faith-Breaker's land, not alive and not dead. It was a lonely, empty thing, that not-seeing. I didn't think all the Dwarfs were fled or killed or vanished, but I didn't know where they were. Dwarf and Man, few of us in Erich's army talked about that. We saw, and we wondered, but it was as though we'd made a silent pact to be silent around the emptiness.

I didn't know what to say to Aescwine about aloneness, and it was Cynnere who answered him.

"Old 'un, you and Garroc won't be alone." Soft-sad, his voice, and—a little—reproachful. "How can you say you'll be alone when you'll have Hinthan and me with you?"

Aescwine smiled, but absently, to hear that. He was looking away north again, into the dark beyond the fire.

After sunset, I went to the picket for a horse. I met the king there, came upon him as he was parting from the Welsh scouts. I went about my business as he bade the two farewell and gifted each with a horse and sturdy saddle gear. He knew how to reward service, my king, and surely those two hadn't come so particularly to talk about the condition of Haligstane, but no matter what else they'd had to say, word that the monastery yet stood—a word surely only chance-spoken—was what had earned them these good gifts. They thanked Penda for horses and gear, used fair words as Welshmen know how to do. Wotan's Blade, we called our king, but the Welsh had another name for him. They called him Golden Panther for his yellow hair and beard, for his deadly grace and swift-striking ways. Cadwalla's scouts used the name when they gave their thanks.

I busied myself among the horses, and when I led my mount away I saw Penda standing near. The last red fall of sunlight shone on his golden hair, flashed from the iron head of his rune-writ throwing-axe as he tossed and caught and tossed again. He sent the weapon spinning across the distance between us. I caught it, as I'd done once before.

"Keep it," the king said. "Might be you'll need it."

I waited to see if he'd say more, but he didn't. He turned away from me, looked across the River Deorwente and the last sunlight changing the white limestone of Eoferwic's walls to red. I took my time about stowing the axe, but the king said nothing more, and so I bade him good night and led the horse away.

"Ghosts-Skald," he said when there was distance and deepening shadow between us.

I looked back and saw only the shape of him, tall and wide-shouldered in the dimming. Then he moved, reached a hand or took a step, and stray glints of light shone on the buckle of a sword-belt. He was the son of kings who were the sons of a god and he was always darkly lovely, as a weapon is. And he was a man caught between sons—one who bared his teeth now in the threat he'd been making for a long time, one who might show his fangs and might not, the third hidden away and not thought of till he was needed.

"Ghosts-Skald," the king said, "speak of me to my son."

I said that I would. He turned back to watching the walls of Eoferwic change colors.

◄8►

My friend Aescwine was a Centishman in his young days, and he'd only left that country after *mann-cynn* let themselves be led by Christ-priests, the Romans returning. He'd not made that decision hastily, Sif, as some Dwarfs had. The people of Rome wanted the Centish king to make all his folk abandon the gods, but Aethelbriht thought it was a laughable idea that the matter of men's souls could have anything to do with him. Nor would he abandon his friends, though the people of Rome had no love for Dwarfs. And so when King Aethelbriht went over to the *Cristens,* Aescwine stayed to serve him. After Aethelbriht's death, his son Eadbald ruled—him who gave his sister to Eadwine Faith-Breaker—and he turned his back on the Aesir-gods for a while. Then he changed his mind, and changed it again a few times more. Dwarfs didn't suffer during these sea-changes, but Aescwine thought things were getting confusing. He left Cent and he left no bad feelings behind. He found a good home in the Marches, and later he found a good woman to love. They two made a strong son together, and that son is Godwig who sleeps in the barrow on Cefn Arth. Not till his boy's death did Aescwine know what it was to be among the Last.

Here's another thing to know about Aescwine, Sif: He wasn't born in Cent. He was a dragonship-rider come to the Isle to fight in the wars against Welsh Arthur. He was, like my own father, one of the wild pirates Arthur cursed for sea-wolves. All the tall stone forts you still find on the eastern shore were built against those pirates, and people still call that coast the Saxon Shore because the forts and the soldiers couldn't stand against the sea-wolves.

"I've been a long time away from the sea," Aescwine said on the night we left for Haligstane. "I'm glad to be getting a look at it again."

Truth to tell, Sif, I looked forward to coming to the sea as much as Aescwine did, but for another reason. In those days, when I was young, I couldn't boast of any knowledge of the sea not gained from tales. When we came to the coast, I would look out on East Sea for the first time, the great grey whale-road my own father knew. Almost, I could feel it drawing me.

We four rode east, fast over rising ground and windy lands scored with deep dales. We'd have thought we were the only people in all the middle-world if we didn't see, from time to time, a farm or a gathering of little stone houses folded in a steep-sided dale. We knew them only by a stray gleam of light from a hearth-fire seen as we rode along a ridge. If anyone saw us, he saw no more than shadows running across the night. We weren't too worried about meeting any patrol of Eadwine's, for he'd taken all his fighting men into Eoferwic with him. And we saw no sign of Cadwalla, not in burnt farms, not in burning sky.

Well before we came to the sea, we heard its voice, a low rumbling like thunder rolling down the sky. The wind took on a salty smell and beneath that lay the reek of dead things washed up on the shore, fishes abandoned in tidal pools, unlucky sea-birds snared in nets of kelp. Cynnere said he never smelled anything so awful. Soon we came to the edge of the land, a steep drop with only one narrow trail down through ever-growing heights of stone walls. Beyond, the star-glittering sky arched up from a great and heaving darkness. That restless glittering darkness was the sea.

I stood word-reft on the shingled shore where water and sky and land all rushed to meet. Above, sleepless gulls cried endlessly. Salt-spray rained from vaulting waves; the rumbling we'd heard on the moor was a roaring now, a wordless song with no beginning and no end. When I saw the sea leaping, the wind and the moonlight running on its hurling crests, I felt like the ground beneath me was moving. My belly turned sick, but I didn't look away. I couldn't have. Awe stilled me.

Awe didn't still Hinthan. He ran to the water, then stopped suddenly, checked by the great black and silver vastness. He stood there, braced, and made the sea come to him. It did, and eagerly. Frothy breakers dashed against his legs, leaping, and ran out again. He laughed for the wonder of all the great wide sea, and the sound of his young pleasure echoed among the cliffs.

Aescwine drew a long breath and let it out slowly. "Isn't it the biggest, loveliest thing you've ever seen?"

"It's big," I said, still uneasy in my belly.

I wasn't alone in the feeling. Cynnere took one long and unhappy look at all the water and walked away, back to the shadow of the moor-cliff. He found a pile of stone to sit on and kept his back firmly to the sea. Aescwine, his eyes a-gleam, asked whether we'd camp here tonight, and I told him that I planned to, but I wondered where we'd find wood for fire and fresh water for the horses.

"Ach," he said, smiling his terrible smile. "I'll find some wood, don't you worry about that. There'll be fresh water running down the cliff, and a bit of grass near that. The tide's right, and Hinthan'll use his nets to catch us sea-bass and maybe some herring from the rock-pools. You'll never want here, Garroc, if you know how to look for what you need."

He left me to get Hinthan's help in the search for wood, and I was a while watching the waves, their tossing moon-gleaming manes the whitest things in the darkness. Of Ran, elders say that she is the grasping wife of the greedy sea-god, Aegor. She is the mother of the waves and the wind. In her hall she guests sea-alfs, but worse than those un-souled wights live there. Water-grimmings make their home in Ran's hall, grey, scaled sea-trolls, and they feast on the flesh of the drowned. Ran is Loki's sister and his daughter, both. She's Hel's kinswoman, and she delights in casting her treacherous nets to drag down ships and luckless men to her hall.

And standing there at the water's edge, it seemed that I heard not one voice thundering up from Ran's un-still hall, but many voices, cold and lorn and all twined together. Ghosts or grimmings, alfs or trolls, they made a terrible sound.

Late in the night, Hinthan went out to the water's edge. I watched him standing there, and he looked like he was working at something, maybe honing a blade. But I didn't hear the high song of whetstone on iron, and after a while I got up and went to see what he was doing. He was working, but not on iron. He used his long-knife on driftwood, whittling. I'd never seen him whittle before then, but it was clear that he'd been skilled at the work for a while.

The sea came in and went out, and Hinthan said, "Garroc, what's fate?"

I told him what skalds know. I said, "Fate is a journey."

He looked away from the water, frowning. His hands kept at their work, and starlight shone on his blade.

"Fate is this," I said. "Each step you take fathers the one to follow. What will be, you've already made happen, though you may not know that. And elders say that many journeys don't end as we'd like them to, or fear that they will."

Starlight gleamed on his blade and on the curling waves. The silvery driftwood rested easily in his hand. "Then why do you say the Norns are fate-weavers, when we walk our own fate?"

"Because the Norns are all-seeing. They know what will be because they see all the steps being taken, by everyone in all the Nine Worlds. They see the patterns we make and weave them on their looms. But it's us, who make the patterns."

The sea rushed in, and sighed out. Hinthan waited for more.

Low, I said, "While Dwarf-kings and witches were wondering what it would be like to have a god's long life, the Norns knew what curse Wotan would make for the theft. Before even that, the Norns saw the *aelfen* at their schemes to steal the gods' golden fruit, and they knew that Wotan would take souls for the fee. And so for an alf, life is the search for what he lost."

"That's his fate," he said.

"That's it."

Hinthan came and stood closer, shoulder to shoulder with me against the cold breeze. The waves rushed in and fell back to leave small treasures behind, driftwood, dark stone, glittering shells.

"It's a wonder," I said, watching the coming and going.

Hinthan cocked a crooked smile. "You've got to know a better word, skald."

"A few," I said. "*Hronrade*, poets call it, the whale-road."

"And Ymir's Blood," he said.

"That. Dwarfs call it the Deep, and I've heard that sea-alfs say Foam-Weaver."

He stood quiet for a while, hands stilled.

"Boy mine, when did you learn to whittle?"

"Owain taught me in the winter."

I said nothing, and he no more. We didn't talk about Owain together, him and me.

After a moment Hinthan held his wood-working up to the starlight to judge it. At first sight it seemed he'd not done much to the wood, but when I looked closer I saw that he'd worked wisely. With care and skill he finished what the sea had started. The salt-silvered driftwood, smoothed by wind and wave and shaped by Hinthan's hand, was the head and neck of a horse, strong and proud, stretching eagerly in the joy of running. Small, at the edge of the wood, were graven runes. One was the journey-mark *rad*. The other was the sign of war-storm, his own sign, *haegl*.

ᚱ ᚺ

Hinthan put his work into my hands, and I stroked it as you would a living thing. He looked at it for a long time there in my hands, and then he took it back, walked a little away out into the water where the white-maned waves broke against his knees. He braced against the undertow and threw the driftwood back into the sea. When he came wading back he saw my stricken look, and was surprised.

"It's all right, Garroc. It's sea-wood. It gave up the land a long time ago. All I did was send it back with a wish for a good journey."

When he said that, his clear grey eyes shone, wide and honest and sure. His hands knew what his work wanted, but I wondered if the wood might come back, riding in to shore on the back of a grey wave.

Like Owain, I thought, as we walked back to the fire. Always threatening to leave, and never quite keeping his promise. I hadn't forgotten the dream of the night before. I didn't forget that Owain had stood watching my Lydi with such starved yearning.

I fell asleep watching the sea and the wave-play. I fell asleep thinking of the rune-marked driftwood riding there under the black-arched sky. I wished Owain would leave Gardd Seren. I even wished him a good journey. I'd wish him a hundred times that if he'd only be gone when I got home at summer's end.

That night Lydi didn't dream for me. I didn't dream for myself, good or ill. And the stranger-ghost kept quiet and away.

The sun rose red in the morning, an angry copper disk heaving up from flint-grey water, glaring. The tide crept landward and then withdrew, slow and groaning. Even sea-birds sounded weary, their once-bright cries now only rusty creaking. At noon the sky hung low, dull as unloved iron. The sun's glare faded to hot watery paleness. It was only at the far end of the day that a wind came from the sea to stir the air and wake the waves. Aescwine warned that a storm was coming and here was not the place to be when it broke.

"When Ran hears all that roaring, she's going to want to come and see what she can snatch for her own."

Cynnere, who showed no sign of getting used to the sea, swallowed hard and went a little green in the face. But Hinthan said he wouldn't mind seeing that.

Aescwine snorted. "You'd mind, young Hinthan. You're no curlew to perch comfortably halfway up the cliff—and that's where you'll have to be when the storm breaks if you don't want to find yourself turned into supper for *aelfen* and water-grimmings. The sea's going to come in screaming tonight."

His warning didn't daunt Hinthan, but it turned Cynnere's face greener. I studied the coast, the narrow strip of shale and shingle. The waking sea stirred on our right; the tall, dark moor-cliff glowered on our left. Ahead, dim in distance, a line of grey rose darker than sea and sky where an arm of land reached out from the moor and sloped down to the water, curving a little north to embrace a small inlet. If we followed that headland in and up to the moor, we'd be no drier when the storm hit, but we'd be safe from the sea.

"Maybe we can see if witch-Cadwalla has left a village or two standing yet," Aescwine said when I told them my thinking. "I wouldn't mind sleeping dry." He looked away, out to the waking sea. "I don't expect you or me will get good welcome if we have to ask *Cristens* for it, but Cynnere and Hinthan might do well."

"Not without you, Old 'un," Cynnere said. "I take what my friends are offered."

Aescwine took his eyes from the sea. "Boy, that's foolish." He twisted a smile and slapped Cynnere's knee. "As I long as I don't have to sleep in a pig-run, I'll be all right."

I had no more eagerness than Aescwine to sleep cold and wet on the moor, and so I said we'd see what we could find for shelter.

"You'll speak for the hospitality, Cynnere, if the time comes to speak. No one will know you and Hinthan aren't Northumbrians if you're careful. As for Aescwine and me, we'll take what we get. And we'll all be peaceful, whether it's good fare or not."

Cynnere agreed grimly, and Hinthan only a moment after.

We found the village just before storm-break, when heavy grey twilight spread over the moor. Cynnere heeled his horse and rode ahead of Aescwine and me. When I told him to, Hinthan left my side to ride with him.

Villages then were like they are today, Sif. This one had a street, short and somewhat more than a comfortably worn path through the cottages, kitchen gardens, and the outbuildings of trade—a potter's kiln, a net-maker's shop, a boat-wright's yard, a bake-house. Pigs rooted by the brookside; ducks and snowy geese, chickens and goats, roamed the street, squawked and bleated in the dooryards. All the air was filled with the sound of them, and the boom and hiss of the sea beyond the ness. Many of the buildings were made of stone, the tight-fitted, sturdy kind of dry stone-work Dwarfs do.

At the end of the street stood a tall house, wide and lofted, with more of stone to it than wood. In these moments before the storm, stout wooden doors stood open to the cooling breeze. Torch-glare and hearth-light spilled out to where men stood drinking and talking. We rode quietly through the village, passed along the street to the ale house, keeping hands well away from weapons.

The first fat drops of rain fell, pocking the dusty road as a young woman came round the corner of a small cottage. She had a child by the hand, a pretty yellow-haired girl. When the little one saw us she reached out a chubby hand, the way children do when they are curious. Her blue eyes widened, a smile blossoming—and her mother tugged her back, hid her behind skirts of brown homespun as though the sight of me would do the child harm.

The woman snarled, "Devil-wolf!"

Ahead of me, Hinthan stiffened, his back rigid, his shoulders a hard line. Behind me, sweetly laughing, the pretty child lisped the word her mother had spoken, repeated the lesson.

"Devil-wolf! Devil-wolf! Devil-wolf!"

Rain fell harder. Thunder rolled across the moor, echoed against the ness as villagers came out of their houses to stare. *Mann-cynn,* all, and some touched forehead, breast, and each shoulder, hastily made the *Cristen* sign against evil. We were like an ill wind blowing, and dogs ran barking beside us.

Someone let fly a handful of dung. Stiff-backed, Aescwine wouldn't duck aside. He'd rather be splattered than be seen to care. I ducked. I had no such idea of soldier's pride as my friend did. Hinthan turned to look back at me and someone cried out, mocking.

"Eh, boy! Watch your back! There's shadow-kin behind you!"

Lightning flashed, sudden and sharp. Hinthan's eyes glittered with rage. Cynnere caught him by the arm, forced him to keep quiet and keep pace. The little girl, skipping behind and laughing, crowed a new lesson.

"Shadow-kin! Shadow-kin!"

Rain was falling in wind-whipped sheets when we reached the ale-house. The men who'd stood drinking hadn't gone within, and those who'd been lining the street pressed close behind us, torches in hand. Black oily smoke curled up from the brands. The smell twined round the odors of wet homespun, of ale and food, of horses and dogs and fowl and pigs. A cold fear settled in my belly. Everywhere I looked I saw no Dwarfs but Aescwine and me.

‹9›

Devil-wolf . . . shadow-kin!

Hinthan turned in the saddle, trying to keep his eyes on me as the crowd shifted and moved. By chance or choice they separated Aescwine and me from our friends as a yellow-bearded man of common height stepped forward from among his fellows. He wasn't much to see, balding and thin, but the crowd stilled as though they were used to attending him. He held his torch high, the better to see us. A careful man, he kept the other hand near the long-knife at his belt.

"*God-aefn,*" he said to Cynnere. Nothing in his thin, reedy voice carried the usual warmth of that greeting. "What brings you to Saefast and my ale-house?"

"I wish you good evening, too," Cynnere said. "Though I don't expect either of us're about having our wish unless we're both keen for rain. I'm Cynnere Brihtwulf's son. I'm a kingsman, and I'm looking for a dry place for my friends and me."

Muttering followed his words, like thunder rumbling. Far back in the crowd someone snapped a whip-crack of laughter.

"There's news! Our King Eadwine's found a sudden fondness for pig-stinking Dwarfs!"

Aescwine paled as others took up the jeer and bandied it from one to the other. He shifted his hold on the reins to have his sword arm free. I leaned close to restrain him, and an old woman, weathered and thin, stepped up to the master of the ale-house. Bright-eyed, head tilted to one side, she went up on her toes to whisper. The man heard her out, then eyed Cynnere again.

"Are ye a *Cristen* man, Cynnere Brihtwulf's son?"

Cynnere lifted his head and spoke haughtily. "I'm a kingsman. Should you ask?"

The yellow-beard decided that, after all, he shouldn't ask. But he had another question and he asked that.

"What about these Hel-ghosts ye've got wi' you? Does the king know about the filthy company his man keeps?"

Cynnere allowed a small, cool smile. "The king knows a lot of things. Now you tell me," he said, suddenly dark and dangerous, "do you have a place for me and my friends to sleep dry? Or do I have to spend the night in the storm, reckoning which words'll suit best when I tell the king how well folk here treat a soldier who's fought witches—ay, and stood on the same war-ground as blood-handed Penda himself and no one knowing where the battle-light from his sword began and that from mine ended?"

Penda!

The name ran round the crowd like a ripple of fear, and in that moment god-Thunor bellowed, lit the rain-swept sky with a bolt so bright that the orange torches paled. In the breathless silence after, a child began to wail.

"You fought that king?"

Cynnere smiled coolly. "We'll know each other when we meet again, Penda and me. And I'll tell you he's everything men say he is—and more besides. Or I would tell you, if I had a dry place to do it and some hot food to warm me and my friends."

The yellow-beard grunted, but he was impressed. In the pale glare of lightning, I saw the old woman whisper to him again.

"I'll feed you," he said. "An' hear yer news and tales. Yer boy, too. Come within. But I'll tell you," he warned, as Cynnere put foot to ground, "I'll not be housin' those devil-kin 'neath my roof—no matter who you know. I'm a *Cristen* man an' I allow none such as them at my board. Send the Dwarfs to sleep in the byre—if the horses an' the pigs'll have 'em."

The insult fell heavily into silence. The crowd fell back, parting to leave me and Aescwine in the clear. Pig-stinking devil-kin we might be, but we were weaponed pig-stinking devil-kin. Wind swept torch-light forth and back; rain hissed in the flames—and Hinthan was foot to ground before Cynnere could stop him, fists clenched, ready to fight.

Thunder roared again. Lightning flashed, a long bolt streaking across the dark sky. I drove my heel into my mount's off side. As though frightened by the storm, the beast snorted and lurched forward into Hinthan and sent him sprawling face-down in the mud. One of the torch-bearers shouted. People in the crowd cursed me as I backed my horse away again. And Cynnere hauled Hinthan to his feet and kept good and tight hold, as if he were supporting him and not squeezing the breath out of him to keep him quiet. For show, he snarled at me and jerked his head at Aescwine.

"You and him get off, and take the horses with you."

We offered no argument and no one barred our way, for Aescwine smiled so that his face twisted fearsomely in the running torch-light—worse when the lightning flared. He unsheathed his sword and laid it across his horse's withers.

I looked back only once, swiftly over my shoulder for a sight of Hinthan. His face was white where it wasn't mud-covered, and he stood tight and quivering, a bow ready to be drawn. I lifted my hand, a gesture to calm him, but he didn't see. Cynnere called him and he turned on his heel to follow.

"Everyone around here is crazy, young skald. Pig-stinking? If you aren't forced to sleep with pigs, you don't stink of 'em. These people don't have the sense they were born with—shadow-kin!" Aescwine thumped a fist against a wall. "Devil-wolf and Hel-ghost!"

I didn't look up from the lamp I was trying to light with flint and striker, a stone bowl filled with rancid fat and a stubby wick. I'd dashed my fingers with the stone too many times already.

Out of the darkness, Aescwine said, "And what is a devil, anyway? Sounds like a night-alf, the way they say it. Do the fools think we've come to steal the life out of them, sucking all their blood in search of their soul?"

"I don't know what they think, Aescwine." Sparks leaped, the wick caught, guttered, then settled. "Or even if they think."

By the lamp's weak glow we saw two narrow stalls which four horses must share. And for us, piles of hay shoved against the walls where the roof didn't leak too badly. Chickens roosted in the rafters and piglings rooted round the bracken-covered floor. Somewhere—unseen in the darkness, but known to us by her smell—their mother grunted. Together we stalled the horses, and filled the mangers with hay, and we didn't have much to say until Aescwine wondered what we'd have to eat and drink.

"Someone will remember us," I said.

He grunted and filled up the last manger. "I hope it's Cynnere who remembers us. Or Hinthan. The master of the ale-house might be willing to have us for Cynnere's sake, but I'm not sure his neighbors are so broad-minded about who gets to sleep among these pigs. Maybe we should keep watch, ay?"

I thought that was a good idea. "I'll take the first watch if you like."

"Yes," he said. He yawned. "I'd like that very much. But wake me if any food comes."

I went to sit with my back to the stall closest to the door and laid my war-axe across my knee. The lamp guttered again, and fell dark. I heard Aescwine rustling around as he piled up some hay and folded himself into his scratchy bed, burrowing deep to avoid the worst of the leaking roof. For a long time after, I heard only thunder growling and rain drumming, horses snuffling and the greedy sucking of piglings taking their evening meal. Then, after I thought he was asleep, Aescwine said:

"I don't like it here, Garroc. They've got a thin hospitality."

Grimly, I smiled into the darkness. "They do."

"And . . ." He took a breath, let it go slowly, carefully, testing his resolve before he set out on a strange road. "And we don't talk much about it, do we?"

"Me and you? No."

"Me and you, and anyone else. We're quiet around it, this strange hate. I know how it is when they hate you across a border—Welshman to Saxon, Northumbrian to Mercian. I know that. It mostly has to do with what your king's doing, or not doing. But this . . . this about hating a man for being who he is— how do you talk about that?"

Came a clap of thunder, a flash of lightning. At the door of the byre something rustled, a scuffing that might have been a footstep. I let my pent breath go—knowing only then that I'd held it—and I reached for Harm. A pigling shrilled and scampered past, brushing my knee as it ran howling to its mother.

"Pigs," Aescwine growled. "Nothing here but pigs and chickens. And us."

I settled back against the stall, but carefully, the way you do when you're not sure about how steady or trusty something is. And Aescwine continued on his way down the aching, strange road.

"Garroc, where do you think all the Dwarfs are? Do you think they're all dead? Killed, maybe?"

"No."

"How can you say that, like you know?"

The rain tapped softly on the roof. "Wouldn't I hear the ghosts? Some of them . . . somewhere about?"

"You would, youngster," he said heavily. "And only you and the gods know how you stand it."

I smiled, and I wasn't feeling so grim-minded now. "I don't think it's a matter of liking or not. And I don't listen all the time. Mostly we nod and go our ways, me and the ghosts."

"Sounds like witch-work," he rumbled, snugging into the hay.

"It's not any kind of work. It's just in me. Now go to sleep because I *will* call you for next watch."

He was already snoring.

• • •

A long time later, my Sif, when the storm stilled, the old woman I'd seen standing before the ale-house, she who'd spoken to the master of the place, came into the byre. Wet and wind-blown, she carried a basket filled with food. Jugged hare, and the rich scent of ale and thyme and meat stewed to tenderness put my belly to growling. The old woman didn't seem to be afflicted by her neighbors' loathing of Dwarfs. She greeted me courteously, and set the basket down in front of me. She said her name was Hild Aldhere's daughter and, hands on her hips, she asked whether I'd come looking for the girl.

‹10›

"The girl," Hild said again when I—surprised by the question—gave no answer. "The girl. Have you come lookin' for her?" She gestured to the basket. "Go on, now. Eat. You can do that and talk, can't ye?"

"I can." I set aside my war-axe. Behind me, Aescwine never stirred, but I knew by the sound of his breathing that he was awake and listening. "But I'm not sure I can tell you what you want to know, mother."

"Mother, is it?" She laughed, a girl's laughter, never aged. "Have y'never wondered, *dvergr*—from time to time—whether you need to be naming me 'mother' so courteously when it's likely that I've got not many more years than you?"

I'd never wondered, before then.

"Ay, well," Hild said before I could answer. "I reckon it I'm lucky you've remembered courtesy. There's not much around here to remind a person, is there?"

She sat down with a great groaning for the stiffness of old bones, and urged me again to eat. I tore the loaf of bread in two and offered her some. But she shook her head and told me she'd long ago eaten, and that if people around here remembered a whit of what they'd been taught of hospitality, I'd have done so too.

"Now," she said, "I've told you my name, but you've not told me yours."

I warmed to her, for the food and the kindness. "I'm Garroc. Some people say Garroc Ghosts-Skald, but I don't mind if that last doesn't get over-used."

"Ah, well. It's a drear name, that about ghosts. I won't over-use it. Now then—about the girl. Have you come lookin' for her?"

"I'm not—"

"Not you, exactly. She said naught about Dwarfs, though she didn't take on about the earth-kin the way they do here. All filled up with foreign ideas and this new god's unsensible ways, they are. They forget who are friends an' have been since time out of mind. Shadow-kin, Hel-ghost . . ."

She snorted her disapproval of those names, and I quickly swallowed a mouthful of bread, tried to snatch a chance at getting in a word.

"It's—"

"Shameful." The old woman sighed. "That's what it is."

"The girl—" I said.

"Oh, the poor girl. They weren't well, those babes of hers. One of 'em fevered and coughing, and the other with no taste for her milk. Poor little wights. She should have rested here longer than she did. But the priest must have his way about everything."

"What priest?"

"The one she had with her." Hild gestured to the food again. "*Dvergr,* are ye going to eat, or are ye makin' ready to starve yerself?"

I'd have answered and been grateful to get a chance to, but from behind me, Aescwine shouted:

"Woman! Will you give him time to either eat or answer?"

The horses snorted and stamped, startled piglings shrilled. At last Hild fell silent, and stayed that way for as long as it took Aescwine to rise up from his hay-pile bed. But only that long. She was back to her tale before I could reckon what to say.

"The girl told me that a kingsman would come riding up the coast looking for her. She said he'd be glad for word of her if it could be given, and I promised to give it. I'd've spoken to that young man in the ale-house, but I'd like to know who can get near him now with all the village crowded round to hear him telling tales. And when he's done talking, he'll find there's a girl or two ready to jostle for the warm place beside a handsome kingsman tonight."

She snorted her disapproval of that, and Aescwine, eyeing the basket, said: "What do you have in there? Any honey?"

"No. Our bees're unhappy this year. And I haven't come to talk about them. I've come to talk about the poor child and her babes—"

"So you have," Aescwine said gruffly. "Why didn't this girl of yours wait for her friend? Or don't they like young mothers and sick babes here any better than they like Dwarfs?"

Hild looked down the length of a sharp nose at him. "We like babes fine here, sick or well. But she wasn't minded to fight the priest she had with her. And *he'd* hear naught of waitin'. He said they must leave word here and go on. 'God wills,' he said. 'God shows us the way.' Didn't seem to me that god of theirs was willin' or showin' much but more long roads to travel. The poor girl didn't like that, but you could see she was in the way of steppin' sharp to his word and—"

She stopped talking abruptly, on a quickly caught breath. Now she understood the meaning of Aescwine's question.

"Hild," I said. "We haven't come looking for this girl and her babes."

She looked from one to the other of us, uncertain now, and may-be frightened. "But—your friend said he was Eadwine's man."

"He's a kingsman," I said, careful of Cynnere's story. "But we're on other business."

She sighed, relief and disappointment both. "Then there'll be another comin'?"

So hopeful, she looked; and for the sake of a stranger who'd touched her heart in passing.

"If the girl was expecting him," I said, "he'll come."

Hild sat quiet for a moment; then she got to her feet and shook out her skirts. "If you see this kingsman in your travels, will you give him word of the girl? Rowenna Brand's daughter, her name. She's bound north up the coast and hoping he'll find her."

North. And so the chances were good that we'd have one of Eadwine's men unknowingly on our trail as he searched for young Rowenna.

"I'll look out for him," I said. "But you keep an eye open, too, and I'll be hoping you see him before I do."

That eased her, and she wished us good night and left.

"Come eat," Aescwine said when we two were again alone.

"I'm not hungry."

"Not now maybe, but you will be. Then the stew'll be cold."

He was right about it, and I took some bread and the small stone pot still half filled with stewed hare. I ate standing by the byre door and watching the night.

All was quiet now, and the lights from the ale-house were the brightest thing in the night. Above the sky was clearing. Clouds flowed west and left misty stars behind them. Beyond the ness the sea boomed, and I thought about the man of Eadwine's who was riding to meet a girl whose trail would lead him here. I didn't think he'd be riding alone in this dangerous land.

Soft, a step behind me.

"If I could've slipped a word in," Aescwine said. "I'd have told that old woman to talk to her bees. Bees don't like change and bother. Unhappy bees think more about being unhappy than about making honey, but if you talk to them they usually feel better." He squinted out into the misty night. "I reckon she could manage that."

"Likely she can." With some bread I sopped the juices and shreds of meat from the pot. "I didn't know you're so filled up with bee-lore."

"I'm not. Hinthan told me about it a year or so ago. I've been watching, and it turns out he's right. Do you two spend the winter with farmers, Garroc?"

I smiled, for that about the bees was Aelfgar's advice, and to remember Gardd Seren and gentle Aelfgar in this cold place was to be comforted. I said that we didn't winter with farmers, but I did tell him that some of our winter-friends liked gardens.

He gave me a sideways glance, his face twisting in a smile. "I expect one of 'em at least is a woman, and probably very good to look at."

"Do you think so?"

He nodded thoughtfully. "You can get honey anywhere, but year after year you keep going back there—wherever it is."

So I did.

Soft, Aescwine said, "Young skald, I've been thinking about someone since we got here to this Saefast. He's been haunting me like a ghost."

"A ghost?" I pretended surprise. "Voice and all?"

His face twisted into a grimace, his dear damaged smile. "You've not forgotten Aelfgar Ulfhere's son?"

"I remember him."

And I wasn't much surprised to hear him speak that name in this place where it seemed all of our kind had been cast out as exiles. Those two had been friends before Aelfgar lost his way and was banished from Rilling.

"We don't talk about him much, ay?" Aescwine leaned against the doorpost, stared out at the dripping and the night-mist. "He had a smile like a babe's, and him man-grown. He had a heart like a babe's, too."

He turned away from the night, turned away from me. When he spoke again, his voice was rough and low.

"Tonight, when we came here, I wondered about him. Is he alive? Driven out in winter . . . how could he be alive now? Still, you can't ever tell what happens to the exile, ay? Us who stay behind, we never know."

I squeezed his shoulder, hoped to hearten him. "We don't know, Aescwine. But, I've heard no ghost."

He nodded once, shortly, and then he told me he'd watch the rest of the night.

I gave him the stew pot and the rest of the bread and returned to the byre. I was still worried about having some man of Eadwine's unwittingly on my trail—but Aescwine had shown me a way to solve another problem. Soon I'd be claiming the king's son, his heir, the *aetheling*, from the monks at Haligstane. I still didn't know where I could hide young Wulfhere safely, but I now knew where we'd go so that I could sit for a while in peace and think about it. We'd go to Gardd Seren.

I had no trouble sleeping that night, and that night I dreamed easily.

At first the dream was a memory, my own of how golden sunlight flowed like honey and spilled past the window by Lydi's bed. Light shone warm on the curve of her shoulder; her shoulder felt warm beneath my lips. Bees droned past the window. Aelfgar walked through the garden, whistling on his way home. A dove sighed in the eaves, settling. Slowly, so that I was unaware of the change, the dream became more than what I remembered, and no longer wholly mine. Even in that far village by the sea, Lydi could find me.

Girl, I said sleeping. *Lay down beside me . . .*

In dream, she reached for me. In dream, I reached for her.

Grey dawnlight woke me, and waking scattered my dream. I saw Hinthan standing in the doorway. Aescwine got no greeting from him as he came inside. He tossed me a wallet stuffed with breakfast, new bread and cheese.

"Where's Cynnere?" I said, piling up a comfortable place to eat with the hay that had been my bed.

Hinthan jerked his head toward the doorway, toward outside. Then he said to Aescwine that he wanted to speak to me alone. He was like a storm, dark-eyed, lowering. Aescwine yawned and scratched his jaw, and decided there was no need to brave a storm not meant for him. Outside the day was filling up with morning-song, chickens and dogs and children all a-hunt for breakfast. I heard the murmur of voices as Aescwine told Cynnere about Hild and the girl who was waiting for a kingsman.

To Hinthan, unmoving in the doorway, I said, "Boy mine, I'm in no mood to sit and eat stared at."

Dark and lean, the shape of him against the morning sky. When he came into the byre his stride was long, his hands knotted to fists. He didn't sit beside me, but stood over me, and his face was white, his eyes glittering. When he spoke at last, he spoke a warning.

"Garroc, what you did yesterday—don't ever do it again."

I ate some cheese, and then I said, "What did I do?"

He snorted, as though I should know the answer to that. I took some more cheese and he stood there tall in rage, a-quiver with anger barely checked.

"Now tell me what you mean, youngling. But if you're going to talk about getting knocked down in the mud, we're not going to have much to say to each other. You earned that."

"I'm not talking about that." Now some of the hard-edged anger left him; he came and sat close to me so that we two were eye to eye. "Garroc, when we leave this place I'm riding beside you."

I drew breath to speak, but he stopped me.

"Hear me," he said. Anger cooled, and now I saw that pain lay behind it.

I took another bite of bread and listened.

"I hated being in that ale-house last night. I hated what . . . people said. I hated to hear it, and I hated to keep quiet about it. But I did, and I feel like I've wronged you and Aescwine.

"No," he said when I started to speak. "Don't tell me you wanted me to keep peaceful, like it didn't matter what they said about you, about *dvergr* all. I know you wanted that, and that's why I did it. They can say what they like, these crazy people. I'll bear it if you tell me to. But you are my foster-father, and I won't stay in ale-houses while you stay in byres, and I won't ride ahead of you today looking like I'm ashamed to be with you. I won't— I can't—ever do that again."

He said no more, and he got up to ready the horses and gather gear. Me, I sat at ease with my breakfast. It's not a hard thing to hear how well you are loved.

We left the village in the sun-washed morning, and Hinthan rode beside me as he must. I didn't want to ride out to the coast and find myself between Rowenna and her kingsman, and so I decided that we'd ride across the moors and west a little. I counted that no bad luck, for we'd have to in any case, this day or another. Haligstane didn't lie at the edge of the sea.

We had no more trouble leaving Saefast than we'd found arriving; but no less. The people lining the street were silent now, caught between their belief that Cynnere was indeed one of Eadwine's men, and their hatred of his companions. Their silence was like a wall. Behind it, all the jeers and curses of the night seethed.

And yet, Dwarfs had lived in Saefast once. The stone-work in the village cried it. Aescwine glanced at me, and then away. I knew what he asked so silently. Where are they? Did they go out to live on the wind-haunted moor? Or did they go down to the sea and leave the Isle?

The silent wall broke, and Hild stepped out from among her neighbors to smile brightly at me. She called out, "Good-speed!" and before she could be cried down or elbowed away she waved to us. The old woman bade us farewell as gaily as any girl.

‹11›

Erich had said that Haligstane was hidden in the deeps of a river valley. He said that all around there was nothing to rival, no stead, no village, no *cyning's* fair hall. On the tallest hill above the valley a man would be in sight of the sea, but only just. The great water would be only a shining in the east.

"There's a moor to be crossed before you get there," Erich warned. "And you'll ride eight or ten days before you'll see a hill, or anything that looks like a valley."

I thought the moor would go on forever, Sif; filled up with sky and wind and the piercing cries of hunting merlins. Roman roads of crumbling pave-stone ran straight beneath the wind-racing sky. They never seemed to end. I'd seen no land like this before, not even the high place between Eoferwic and the sea. It's a spreading country, green and grey. The grass is tough and spiky, the bedrock only thinly covered. The few trees we saw were wind-racked, twisted and small, their gnarled roots half-naked to sun and wind. For many miles the sweeping land was broken only by sudden and ancient upthrustings of rock.

It was Aescwine's opinion that these tall stone towers, these stark *torrs*, are the barrows of giants. I don't think all of them are, but it's true that the wind's voice booms and growls when it runs round some of those piles, and the song is a harsh one. I felt it in my bones that if I'd understood the words of that unrestful song, I'd have heard tales about reaving and killing and torment. These are the things giants like best.

And smaller, even older than the barrows and *torrs*, grey stone walls stitched the moor. These still faithfully warded the boundaries of folk who'd died away before the first Romans knew about the Isle; people who left behind only their walls. The Welsh will say that these people were the giant-killers, and some of them were Dwarfs, others Men.

One night the stars shone as a great sweep of brightness across the sky. I was able to work at map-making even outside the light of the fire, and I sat for a while drawing what I'd seen. With a sooty knife-tip I burned lines to show Roman roads, high *torrs* and moaning barrows.

"You're filling up the empty places fast," Hinthan said. He swept his finger round one unmarked place in the middle of Faith-Breaker's kingdom. "Except this one."

His finger smeared some soot, made the circle stormy grey and black. This was Deorcdun, the dark down I'd never seen and had heard little about.

"Do you think we'll see it, Garroc?"

I shook my head, and he smiled. When I asked him what he'd found to smile over, he said, "Now I know more than I knew before about where we're going."

"No. Now you know one place we're not going to. It's a big island, boy mine." I rolled up the map and tossed it to him. "Put this away, and go tell Aescwine his watch is over."

"Who's watching next?"

"You," I said, yawning.

On the seventh day the ground began to fold again, the bedrock settled deeper. Now the hunched hills wore a lushness of soft green grass and sweet purple heather, and the tallest and most distant wore the dark trees of an upland wildwood. Small farmsteads sat in the dales, and sheep and goats roamed the slopes. Times were when we'd see a shepherd out walking among his flock, or a farmer crossing the road from field to field. They offered us no greeting, only stares to chill us.

We never saw even one of the earth-kin. The Dwarfs who once lived in Eadwine Faith-Breaker's kingdom—folk who once and not long ago dwelt side by side with *mann-cynn* in the villages, the soldiers who fought in his armies—were gone. This vanishing didn't happen countless years ago. This had occurred only lately. At night Aescwine would sit by the fire, looking out past the flames to the dark and empty moor. Once he said, "It's an awful emptiness, young skald. This moor is filled up with a terrible quiet." I knew he wasn't talking about the stillness of the desert place.

We were careful on our way to Haligstane. Sometimes we came in sight of empty villages and ruined farmsteads, the ground a fire-black wasteland, the air yet stinking of smoke and dying. Our last word of Osric was that he was fighting in the west, but that could have changed by now. There was no way to know if Osric or Cadwalla had done the work.

We couldn't track Osric, but we tracked Cadwalla as we'd done all summer—by the red war-lightning and the black smoke rising. He kept close to the sea, always moved south and, at last, a little west toward Eoferwic. I wondered if one of the burnings we saw was Saefast. I thought of Hild, and hoped for her. Hoping for her, I remembered Rowenna. When I watched the sky, red-lit, I wondered whether the young mother—or the kingsman who was said to be riding up the coast in search of her—would survive Cadwalla's ride south.

On our tenth night out of Saefast, Hinthan kept watch with me, both of us restless and unable to sleep. Wind moaned low, hissed through brittle grasses, and rose up to keen around the barrows of giants. Hinthan and I stopped walking watch at the same time. In silence, he came and stood beside me to look away south to where the stars paled before the flaring of witch-light. A blood-red dawn sprang up in a quarter of the sky where dawn isn't meant to shine.

"That's Eoferwic," he said. "The siege is over."

It was, at last. Eadwine had gotten hungry or thirsty, or he'd seen the two armies ranged around his walled city and didn't like the idea of being burnt out of his hole like a rat.

"Get the horses ready, youngling. Tell Cynnere and Aescwine we're leaving here."

He ran to do that, and I stood a moment longer to watch the red sky where surely ravens and Valkyries were gathered. Penda's secret, so long locked behind Eoferwic's walls, might lie naked now in those burning streets, a few words more precious than jewels: one of the queen's women bore a son whose father was the King of Mercia.

We rode through the night, our way lighted by the countless stars. The next day we rested on the shady side of a hill, away from the noon sun. When the horses could run again, we were off. From time to time I saw Hinthan cast a swift glance over his shoulder, keeping watch against pursuit.

"Be easy, youngling," I said once, quietly, when we slowed to make a dark and downward road easier for our horses. "We're not being followed."

But he didn't give up his backward-looking, and at moon-set he was the first to see that the fight for Eoferwic was over.

"Or as good as," Cynnere agreed, watching the red witch-light flaring and bursting farther north and east than this time last night. "Cadwalla's heading right up the coast again."

At sunrise we came to Haligstane. From the last tall hill we looked eastward and saw the shining Erich had told me about— new sunlight glinting on the sea's ever-changing waters. I searched the sky all around for witch-light, saw only moon and stars, white and clean and shining coolly in the hot black night. Now I didn't know where Cadwalla was.

The narrow valley lay at the foot of two grassy slopes running down and down. Sheep grazed on the hillsides, their white fleece like clouds come to ground. Young sunlight shone on the sheep-graze and gilded a mortar-bound stone wall winding across the crest of the hill. Seasons of wind and rain had weakened the mortar, corrupted the bandaging. Hinthan climbed atop the wall, and he had only an unchancy footing.

"It's like we're standing above the whole middle-world," he said, careful of his balance.

It was like that. On the valley floor a thin river ran gleaming, bridged by a broad arch of stone. Trees grew in a regular pattern at the northern end of the valley, an orchard. In the south and on the eastern slope, grain-fields ran in the wind, like golden waves. Haligstane sat in the middle of all. The buildings—low and tall and middling—stood close together on a square so that there were only narrow alleys between. One building rose above all others, given a greater sense of height still by the two crossed beams atop: the *Cristen* cross, two dark slashes against the blue sunny sky.

We'd come to Haligstane at last, and they might not welcome me there but I was sure of getting a hearing. In my belt-pouch sat a golden half-ring studded with emeralds. The monks of Haligstane had promised to heed this token. They'd sworn it to Gytha of Northumbria, and she was kinswoman to Aethelburgh, who was the sister of the King of Cent, wife to the Northumbrian king.

My eyes yet on the dark cross, I said, "We're stopping here."

Hinthan turned to look at me. "Here?" He pointed downslope. "You mean there? Garroc, that's a monastery."

"I know. It's called Haligstane, and we're stopping there for a while."

Hinthan and Cynnere traded puzzled glances, but it was Aescwine who asked what made me think we'd get good welcome at a monastery.

"We're not looking for welcome. And now I have some things to talk about before we go down there."

I didn't tell them much, though what I said was the truth; or the bones of truth. I said that we'd come here to fetch a boy away from the monastery and take him to live with foster-parents, that this was a favor to his kinsman who'd lately begun to worry that the boy wasn't safe.

On the hillside, sheep bleated; comfortable sounds. The wind ruffled through tall grasses. And Aescwine spat to show his opinion of the boy's kinsman.

"Lucky thing Cadwalla didn't burn the place to cinders this summer. Who is this thoughtful kinsman?"

I told him that wasn't for me to say, and he tried another question, asked me who the boy's foster-parents were and where they lived. The first part wasn't easy to answer; I still had no idea about that myself. But I answered the second question.

"We'll be in Welshlands before we're done."

Hinthan looked up, and I nodded—but only barely—to let him know that we would indeed be riding to Gardd Seren. Aescwine saw none of that; his mind was still on the matter at hand.

"This boy must have an interesting kinsman," he drawled.

"Do you think so?"

"He's sent Mercian soldiers into Northumbria to fetch the boy to foster-parents in Wales. You don't think that's interesting?"

Cynnere snorted. "He didn't say the foster-parents live in Wales, Old 'un. He said we'd *be* in Wales before we were done. But we're not going to be done anytime soon if we have to sit here all day while you ask questions Garroc can't answer."

"Can't, is it?" Aescwine shook his head, scowling to smile. "Better to say, won't. Our Garroc's the most shut-mouthed skald anyone ever heard of."

And so he accepted that I'd say no more. I reached for my horse's reins, ready to walk away down to Haligstane. But

Aescwine stopped me, a hand on my arm.

"Young skald, I'll wait here for you."

Hinthan looked from Aescwine to me and I thought he'd say something, but Cynnere's hand on his shoulder warned him to silence.

"Or I'll wait anywhere else you tell me to wait, Garroc. But I won't go begging shelter from any monk, or fight his dogs for the table scraps."

The wind picked up, whistling along the wall. Hinthan whispered something to calm a restless horse. Cynnere shifted from foot to foot, uncomfortable suddenly. Aescwine's hand lay warm on me, and I went suddenly dry in the mouth.

I felt loss breathing near, like a wolf in the brush. But what reason did I have to dread loss? Still, it remained: When I looked at Aescwine, my friend standing braced and stubborn before me, I felt loss breathing near.

"Aescwine," I said, "I'd rather have you with me."

"And I'd rather be with you—anywhere else." He pointed down the hill to Haligstane. "But there's the well that poisoned the country hereabout. I don't want to go there."

But he'd go if I ordered him. We two were standing eye to eye, close, and I saw it in him. He'd go, if I ordered him to go. I wouldn't do that. And so, silently, the matter was decided: Aescwine could stay here and I wouldn't argue.

Hinthan took his horse and mine and walked the path at the top of the hill. He squeezed Aescwine's shoulder as he passed, to hearten. And Cynnere said, "We'll miss you, Old 'un."

Just a little, Aescwine smiled. You'd think it was a wince of pain unless you saw the light in his blue eyes. "No you won't, because I'll be here watching. Just you remember to come and fetch me when it's time to leave."

We said no more about it, and we left him alone on the hilltop gathering wood for a campfire. Hinthan looked back often, unhappily. Cynnere looked back only once. If I'd but said the word, Cynnere would have bounded back up the hill to keep Aescwine company. I didn't say anything, and I never looked back. I didn't want to see Aescwine standing alone, for fear that I'd have to admit to feeling as lonely as he'd look—suddenly alone even in the company of Hinthan and Cynnere.

I'd not ever felt this way before, and nor ever noticed if I was the only Dwarf in the company of *mann-cynn*. I noticed now, and the separateness felt like a betrayal.

PART THREE

◆◆

The Gift
of the Runes

One day Stane Saewulf's son said to me: "Wotan is a bold fellow. He is war's father—the god who must search for ways to win the final war, terrible Ragnarok to come."

All the world outside my foster-father's cottage was still and silent but for snow hissing at the window, drifting like whispers under the door. I sat near the fire, honing the blade of a broad-headed war-axe and thinking about Grimwulf, my father. The axe was his, or had been once. He'd left it with Stane on the day he'd left me for fosterage, and it was the only thing of my father's I saw day to day. I saw, but I didn't have much to do with it. I reckoned the axe was a gift to Stane, and in those days I knew more about words than weapons. But now winter blew outside the door and my father hadn't come back from the war-season; the old soldier hadn't returned as he always did and I didn't know if he was dead. I must hold his axe and do something with it. Each year of the past five he'd come back to Stane and me well before the snow fell. Not this year.

"Youngling," said Stane, watching me work. "It was war-need

made Wotan pay a witch the fee of his right eye to learn what his fate will be."

I listened, but I didn't stop my work. And Stane said, "The god needed only one sip from the deep waters that spring from under the third root of the World Tree. That water, icy and clear, comes up from Giant Home, and only a sip will show a man—or a god—his patterned fate, his woven *wyrd*. Wotan paid the fee, gave up his right eye, and the witch at that well granted him what he wanted."

And with that wondrous water on his lips Wotan learned about Ragnarok. With the icy drops on his tongue the god learned that he will never win that war at the worlds' end. And he learned why he still must try with all his heart and his might not to lose.

"That was a bitter learning," said Stane as white sparks leaped from the blade of Grimwulf's axe. "But Wotan wasn't put off by it, didn't try to ignore it or hide from it. He swore that he'd fight the Last Fight, and he went home and built him a high hall, Valholl. He told his nine daughters, his Valkyries, that they must go out to all the worlds and bring the bravest of the battle-slain to Valholl. These will be the Last Army."

And the Raven-god wasn't content to sit around in his golden hall and count his army. He swore a deep oath that he'd search through all the Nine Worlds for the knowledge and wisdom and magic that would help him when Ragnarok came. He went down to the World Tree a second time, and now he didn't speak with the witch at the spring, but with Eard, the mother-earth, the world-spirit. He said to her that he wanted all the wisdom of the world.

They are lovers, the god and Eard. But they are not always friends. When Eard saw Wotan—one-eyed, his beauty ruined to pay a witch's fee—she grew jealous and angry. She said that she'd grant him what he wanted, but he must give her more than he'd given the witch, and he must share all the wisdom he won with her children, her true sons and her foster-sons.

Give me your life, she said. Die for me.

Wotan swore he would do that.

Stane said, "Wotan hung for nine days on the World Tree. He hungered and he hurt. Wind-whipped, he thirsted. And he bled from a terrible spear-wound. Bleeding, emptying, he hung there and saw into all the Nine Worlds, spied every treasure, every hidden thing, even those that magic-craft renders unseen. When he was near to dying, nearer still to madness, Wotan found the runes, the holy-stones, the graven signs.

"He reached for them," Stane whispered.

Snow hissed, the wind mourned round the eaves of the cottage. I leaned closer to hear, let stone and axe be silent.

"Wotan reached for the runes, and he grabbed them up as he died."

And, dead, god-Wotan learned this: One rune heals, another helps. One rune will hold back floods of enemies, and his brother will break fetters. Still another will turn back weapons.

The Raven-god learned of the rune named Fire Quencher, and the one that withers hatred. He took up the rune that quiets sea-rage, and the one that is known as Witch Bane. He learned the way of the rune that lets a man hear ghosts, and at his rare whim he whispers the name of that ghost-rune to one of his choosing.

There is a rune that knows the name of every god and mortal wight, even the secret names of the un-souled *aelfen*. Another rune was made by Dwarfs, and it gives war-might to gods. There is a rune to whisper in love-play; another to speak after those warm games if you want your lover to love you always.

Last is the unmarked stone, the wordless rune of secrets. The name of that is made up of the names of every unrevealed and hidden thing.

While snow fell, Stane told me that each rune is the mark of a promise kept. For when Wotan died on the World Tree he learned all there was to know about runes. When he understood their wisdom well, Eard gave him back his life.

"They kept their promises," Stane said to me. "And this must be remembered, youngling—no rune comes to you by chance. Runes are holy-stones, and some people are confused about what the word *halig* means. They think 'holy' is another word for 'good.' That isn't so. Holy isn't good or bad. Holy is a promise made and a promise kept."

Stane took the war-axe from my hands, turned the wood haft up to the light. "See," he said, running his finger over a small mark graven in the wood. "This rune is *thorn*."

"Now some say *thorn* means 'wolf'; others say it means 'win-ter.' There are folk who say it's the soldier's mark, for it is Thunor's war-hammer. In the far north where our fathers are from, they say *thorn* is a gateway from one place to another."

He put the weapon back into my hands, and he smiled into my eyes, saw all my fear and hope.

"This is your father's weapon, my Garroc, and *thorn* is the rune he chooses for his own. This axe is a promise that he'll come back in winter."

Stane was right to have faith in his old friend, Sif. My father didn't fail his promise, for he'd written it with a rune to make it holy. The next day Grimwulf came home.

I thought of that tale, that promise, those holy-stones Wotan had paid so dearly to have, as I walked down the hill to Haligstane to keep my own promise to Erich War Hawk and my king.

‹12›

No one guarded the old stone bridge across the river to Haligstane. No one challenged us, though we were three weaponed strangers and one a Dwarf. Beyond the bridge the square lay empty, and from the church we heard a voice lifted in a language we didn't know. After that cry, followed the toneless bleating of many voices. These made their plea in our own Saxon.

Be, Lord God, a noble friend! Look, Lord, upon me and shelter me in my need!

Hinthan glanced over his shoulder, eastward at the absence of witch-light. "Do you think they're worried about Cadwalla?"

Cynnere said they'd do better to look to the count of their weapons if they were so worried. But he said no more, for from round the corner of the church, from a shadowed alley, came a brown-robed monk.

Round and red-bearded, the monk was as young as Cynnere. He stopped when he came into the sunlight, still as a hare caught by a warning scent. He was blind, eyes cauled white, and so maybe something in what he smelled did warn him—horses where there'd been none before, the rank smell of sweat, the tang of iron.

"God to you, friends. Who goes?" His voice was warm and soft, the words as round-sounding as he appeared. That's how Irelanders shape Saxon words.

"Travellers," I said. "Come to talk to the head of this place."

His face lighted all over with a smile. "Welcome, then. I'm Brother Raighne, and I—" He stopped, suddenly on a caught breath. "Ah! Have you come for Rowenna Brand's daughter, then? Now 'tis a shame if you have, for she's two days gone from here, and sad-sorry to be missing you again."

Cynnere and Hinthan exchanged glances. We were still behind her.

I said to the monk, "We're here on another matter."

Raighne's smile dimmed a little when he heard that news. He came forward, using the church wall as guide, and I went to meet him. When I was in reach he touched me, hand and arm and face, as blind men do. He traced the form of my face, and his questing touch was a little like the way a Dwarf touches stone. If he'd told me he could know the color of my hair, know my beard for yellow, I'd have believed him.

Low, for only us to hear, he said, "Have y' had a hard journey, earth-kin? Have y' heard hateful words from *Cristen* men?"

I said nothing, and he stepped back—from me, and from his close question. He'd got his answer in my untrusting silence.

"Raighne," I said stiffly, "I thank you for your welcome. My friend is Cynnere Brihtwulf's son, and the boy is Hinthan Cenred's son, who is my foster-son. We have another friend waiting on the hill above here, and he's no threat to you. He's Aescwine Ivaldi's son, and he's *dvergr* like me. I am Garroc. Ghosts-Skald, some say."

"Garroc Ghosts-Skald." He rumbled the name, made it sound like deep thunder. "There's a fine brave name. 'Tis been a long time since we've had your like to guest, Garroc Ghosts-Skald." He turned his face east, toward the hill, and so I knew he'd not been born blind. He hadn't got out of the habit of seeing yet. "Your friend is welcome here."

"He's happier where he is."

"Well, well. He'd know best about that, wouldn't he?" A shadow of sadness touched him, then left him. "Make no doubt—this place'll buzz to hear the news we've even one of the earth-kin among us now. But for me, anyone who comes here in peace is welcome. Poets are three times welcome. It's the abbot you're wanting to see?"

"If he's the head of this place."

"He is."

The air stirred under the weight of deep voices from the church. *In your hallowed name, make me whole, O God; free me from foes by the might of your love!*

And I said, "He's probably in there . . . ?"

Raighne smiled. "He should be. Now, near the river's a byre. Have your foster-son take the horses there and fill the mangers— and fill them again if the good beasts need it."

I waited to see what else he'd say about the byre, and behind me Cynnere shifted from foot to foot. Out the corner of my eye I saw Hinthan stand straighter, a little braced. In Saefast they'd taught us about how Dwarfs are guested among *Cristens*. But Raighne said no more about the byre, and so I sent Hinthan and Cynnere to tend our horses.

"Now come with me," Raighne said. "I'll show you to the guest-house."

We went past the church, from which prayers still drifted, past a long stone building with many and tall windows. Raighne said this was a scriptorium. The word had a foreign sound, and when I asked him the meaning he said that I'd like to see what it was all about better than being told.

"But not now. Later, when there's time to savor."

We went slowly the rest of the way. Raighne took no step for granted, and he clutched my arm to steady himself when he stepped wrong. I trusted him only a little, and he trusted me wholly. I covered his hand, told him thus silently that he could have my arm the rest of the way.

The guest-house sat in the middle of a walled garden, and I sat on a bench outside the door watching doves fly to and from the dovecote behind the house. We'd had a good meal of bread and cheese and small beer. Now, in the warmth of the afternoon, Cynnere and Hinthan were sleeping off the food and the days and nights of long riding. And I sat outside the house, honing the blade of Penda's rune-writ hand-axe and keeping the soldier's careful habit to watch and ward while low sweet dove-song filled the garden.

That was an over-neat garden, Sif. Tall mint grew at the outer bounds, and meadowsweet with its flowers floating like clouds against the sun-blest walls. Larkspur and white-starred stonecrop grew closer in. Tidy clumps of ground-hugging thyme, yellow loosestrife and soft, grey-green lamb's-ear filled the center. The fierce neatness of the place was nothing like the free-growing tapestry of Lydi's garden, but when I closed my eyes and had only the doves and the bees to hear, the twining scents to smell, I felt her near. I was doing that when the boy came into the garden and banged the gate shut behind him.

He was thin, and he walked barefoot in the warm day. He wore a faded red shirt and trews of grey homespun. I knew him, though he didn't look like his brothers, neither red-haired like Merewal nor dark like Peada. Wulfhere Penda's son had hair like white-gold flax, cut short in Roman fashion, much shorter than is the custom here where winters are as cold as Hel's hall. His eyes were darkest blue, like shadows on snow. He came marching into the quiet garden like a soldier. The stiff straight line of his back, the set of his shoulders, made me think of Penda.

He saw me and he stopped. Wulfhere and I watched each other in careful silence.

"Brother Raighne wants to see you," he said at last, sullenly and without addressing me. As rudely do people speak to servants or slaves.

"Boy," I said. "Has no one told you my name?"

"Brother Raighne says your name is Garroc Ghosts-Skald."

Bees hung flower-drunk in the sunny air between us, and I said, "Would it hurt you to use it?"

Haughty, he told me that it wouldn't hurt him at all.

I held his father's axe up to the sun to see the keen edge. Wulfhere never looked at the shining; he had eyes only for the rune-writ handle. He looked from under lowered lids, not wanting to be seen at it.

"Boy," I said. "You've got my name, but I don't have yours."

"Wulfhere." He ground a clump of thyme beneath his heel, filled the garden with sweet scent. "Wulfhere Gytha's son."

If Erich had never said it, I'd have understood that the *aetheling* didn't know who his father was. He must have known that his mother wasn't ashamed of his birth, for she'd proudly given him her own name. Just as plainly, he would have done better for knowing who'd helped make him. I softened a bit toward the surly boy. I reckoned it must be hard not to know fully half of what a person should know about himself.

I told him to wait where he was and went inside. He did wait, but not patiently. The garden, even the cottage, filled with the sweetness of crushed thyme while I roused Cynnere to tell him where I'd be. I returned to find the *aetheling* stripping a stalk of mint.

"Be easy on the plants, Wulf," I said mildly. "They'll be happier for it."

"Wulfhere," he said flatly, correcting me as he brushed past to open the gate. Then he stopped, hand on the latch, making up his mind about something. He turned to me and asked why I was called Garroc Ghosts-Skald.

"A king named me Ghosts-Skald," I said carefully.

Again, his scorn flashed—and a cold kind of triumph, as though he'd proven something.

"You lie, shadow-kin. Our King Eadwine is a *Cristen* man. He has nothing to do with your kind."

He said that—shadow-kin—like he was spitting. The name rankled, but I let it go. I told myself that if a boy has no manners it's because no one bothered to teach him. And I stepped wide around the matter of which king had given me the name.

"Not now, he doesn't. But he used to. As for why I've been given the name—I can hear ghosts speaking. And ghosts can hear me answering."

Eyes wide, Wulfhere crossed himself, then did it again for good measure. I smiled, and tried to do it in kindly fashion.

"Ghosts-Skald is a new name. I had another before, and I might get some others before it's all done. But I'll always be Garroc."

Now he kindled with the same curiosity I'd seen when he secretly looked at the runes on his father's hand-axe. "Garroc. The spear and the word. Because you're a soldier and a poet?"

He was a word-lover. For that, I warmed to him a little more.

"I've been each, and now I'm both. My father couldn't have known that's how it would be with me when he chose my name, but it seems he made a good choice."

Bees droned in the garden, their humming soft as the wind wandering through the plantings. And the *aetheling* said, "I didn't know your kind had fathers and mothers."

I stared at him and almost laughed. "Young Wulfhere, where do you think Dwarfs come from, if not from fathers and mothers?"

He shrugged, and he never took his eyes from me. They were clear and blue as lakes, those eyes of his.

"Some say you were made in the fiery pit, in the Wasteland that is Gehenna where Beelzebub and his god-forsaken devils live."

A chill crept along my spine, and I should have heeded the warning. I shouldn't have asked further.

"Really, boy? Who's this Beelzebub?"

Wulfhere answered flatly, repeating a lesson. "He is the Outlaw, the Betrayer. He's the Thief of Souls, the King of Devils and the maker of all things evil." Again, he shrugged. "That's what priests say, but I always reckoned you didn't have fathers and mothers because everyone knows Dwarfs are *geldr*."

Geldr, he said. Geldings.

The word cut like a whip, and the pain of it burned past mind and heart to places where no thinking gets done. I'd have struck him down, child though he was, if Cynnere's hand, his sudden grip on my shoulder, hadn't held me.

"Who's this, Garroc?" His voice was quiet and his grip on me hard as stone. He knew me, and he knew that no matter how I burned now, I'd not want to remember later that I'd beaten a child.

Dry-mouthed, I had to swallow before I could speak. My words, even then, were like dust falling.

"He brought the message from Raighne."

Cynnere took a step to put himself between me and Wulfhere. "Right then, boy. You've delivered your message, and puked up some lies along with it. Now get out of here."

Wulfhere balled up his fists, bristling. But he thought better of it and left us. He was well gone before Cynnere let go of my shoulder.

"That wouldn't be the boy we've come for, would it?"

"He is."

"Then I'm sorry for his foster-parents. They're going to have to do a lot of un-teaching before that boy can even begin to reckon what's true and what's not. And that's only if he's not killed along the road to his new home." He nudged me. "You'll be sure to let me know if you need someone to do that, won't you?"

I didn't smile at the hard jest, and Cynnere went to sit on the bench by the door. He watched me leave the garden. We two were long-time friends, and I could feel it that he was thinking about me for a while after I was gone.

Raighne waited at the door of the scriptorium, head cocked and listening to the song from the church, the voices lifting and falling in deep and densely woven harmonies. I saw him hear me coming, and I saw him hear Wulfhere's absence.

"Now where's the boy?"

I told him Wulfhere had delivered his message and gone. And it's a wonder what blind men can know though they are sightless.

"Has the boy been speaking his pain to you, Ghosts-Skald? Has he been lashing out and hurting you?"

I was in no mood to answer that, in none to delay getting Wulfhere out of this place and quickly off my hands.

"Raighne, I thank you for wanting to show me this scriptorium, but I don't have time. Now I will talk to the abbot."

He smiled—ay, more a grin all full of mischief—and he told me that I was talking to the abbot. He couldn't have seen my surprise, but maybe he was used to hearing it from others.

"I'm thinking you're not wondering why so young a man is abbot here, are you, Garroc Ghosts-Skald? Well, well, I can't see anymore, but I'm still good at ordering things—and ordering people around when that's what's needed. It's one of an abbot's best skills. Now be sure I'm not minded to order you, for in my homeland even kings dare not take the high hand with poets, and I'll not be forgetting the right of things, though I'm far from there. But I think you'll like what you find in our scriptorium.

"Come on, poet. Come inside with me and see if you don't feel better for being there."

I went, and the deep singing from the church rose up, a swelling of sound to follow.

The scriptorium was about words, Sif, and about the monkish passion for orderliness. Row upon row of small tables filled up the long stone building, marched from the doorway to the far wall with only a narrow aisle between. On each table was a ledge, on each ledge—braced in small holes—stood ranks of feathered quills, writing tools like plumage. Under the ledges sat stone pots, and these held inks of many colors. Raighne counted up the rows till we came to the tenth. Then he stepped in past three tables and stopped at the fourth.

"Now," he said, "if Wulfhere's been neat about his work—and he isn't always!—he'll have left his manuscript rolled and a little to the left-hand side. Do you see it?"

I did and, at his word, unrolled the sheet. The vellum was creamy white and soft as down to touch. It shone a-light with color at the top corner, an emerald drawn to form the first letter of the first word. Bold straight lines of dark writing marked the upper third of the page; the rest was white and clean.

Raighne took a seat on the edge of the desk, to be eye to eye with me. There is no reason for a blind man to do that but from courteous habit. "Can you read, Garroc?"

"No."

"But I'd be lucky bettin' you know the runes, wouldn't I?"

I smiled to answer, then remembered he couldn't see that. I said, "You'd be lucky betting I know some of what's to be known. No one but the one-eyed god knows it all."

The many-voiced song from the church rose up louder. It sounded like the sea—running and cresting and falling.

"Ah, it'd be a blessing to be able to gift a poet with the reading art," Raighne said. "Think of it! Each mark on the page is a letter, and each letter means a sound. Words are made from sounds, ay? If you know the sound the letters stand for, you can fit them together to make words."

He reached to touch the page I yet held, then drew back. Here, his fingers couldn't tell him what he wanted to know.

"Garroc, what's the gem on the page?"

I told him it was an emerald.

"Then Wulfhere's been writing the story of the angel Muriel. The emerald is Muriel's talisman, and his is a hopeful stone."

"So I hear."

Raighne threw back his head and laughed like I'd made a good joke. Echoes of his laughing rolled around the writing-hall like gleeful thunder. And I smiled again. I couldn't help it.

"Aren't you a poet rich in luck and blessing!" Then, suddenly, his mood turned sad. "What else but a blessing the wonder-songs your kin have heard? The voices of stone and gem and the earth herself. And those told to us, the earth-deaf, for no fee but the asking . . . They are poor fools here in this Northumbria, Garroc, and madly driving out friends they won't miss till it's too late."

The deep-song from the church fell, and in that moment of silence I trusted the monk enough to ask a question.

"Raighne, where are my kindred?"

He turned his head, like a sighted man looking away. "Gone. The earth-kin are gone. Some are dead, surely some are. And the rest . . . I don't know. Maybe they're fled away."

He said that sorrowfully, and that sorrow tapped the new and raw loneliness in me. He grieved for my lost kin, *Cristen* though he was. Song swelled again out of silence, rolling like waves from the church. Raighne sighed, taking comfort from the singing.

But I found no comfort there in those woven voices. In that singing I heard a gathering sea rising up to flood the land.

I returned the vellum sheet to the desk, and when the page curled at the edges, wanting to spring back into the roll again, I reached for something to weight it still. My fingers closed on half of a golden arm-ring, tucked away in the shadows beneath the ledge. The ring was the mate to the one I carried, and the emeralds glinted and laughed lightly in the sunshine streaming in the windows, and they sang of every hopeful thing, the song not failing to touch the heart of me, like a promise kept, a trust fulfilled.

I glanced at Raighne, but he couldn't have known what I'd found, or understood that it had meaning for me if he had known. I set the half-ring to weight the sheet, and stayed quiet about it for the moment.

"Raighne, this writing looks like something only the well-skilled could do. Yet you tell me this is a boy's work."

"It's Wulfhere's work, and he's a well-skilled boy. He was very young when he came to Haligstane. We came here about the same time, him to live in peace and learning, and I to teach the art of writing. I could still see then, and so when Wulfhere was ready to learn his letters, I taught him. This work used to be my greatest joy." He ran a finger along the edge of the page, very gently caressed the vellum. "He's not a bad boy, Garroc. Only filled up with bad ideas and pain. It's lies that hurt him."

"Ay, well, he's learned a few," I said flatly.

"He has, and not all of them are about Dwarfs. He's learned a few lies about himself, too. These Roman-minded monks here say that he's *il bastardo*. There's no word to match in your language. It means his mother wasn't married to his father. In a Roman's mind that kind of birth is shameful."

"That's senseless," I said. "A son is a treasure wherever you get him."

He shrugged as though this were an old fight he knew he wouldn't win.

"Not all *Cristens* believe it. But the people of Rome do, and it's them who want to order what all must believe. In my own Eire we learned differently about our Jesu God, and we know he loves all of us and would shame none who are blameless. But here in Haligstane they all believe what the people of Rome believe. Wulfhere's been taught to accept a shame he hasn't earned, and I've never been able to un-teach that idea, or ever to ease the pain it's caused.

"In pain," said Raighne, "the lad clings to the idea that there are others who are less than him. You've heard the namings, Garroc, and the lies and the hatred. He's been taught that because Dwarfs are different from Men you are ill-made and evil. The tale of your beginnings, the deep tale of Stone, is twisted into a lie. What we know of the great sorrow of your ending they've torn full of holes and changed into more lies. These lies give Wulfhere someone to hate for being worse than himself. It's a mean comfort. Pity him, Garroc."

"Instead of pitying myself, ay?"

He smiled ruefully, caught giving advice before it was asked. "You'd know best about that, my friend."

I did know best, and I wasn't going to talk more about it. I didn't want to come anywhere near the pain of the word *geldr* again. I took up the half-ring, the sun-glinting gold and the singing emeralds, and put it in Raighne's hand. He ran his fingers along the gold, the delicately etched vines. I couldn't read writing, but I could read his face. His love for Wulfhere shone.

"He's been using it for a model, hasn't he? But it's his to use. It was his mother's, and I remember the loveliness of it. Someday the other half'll come here to call him away from Haligstane."

"Does he know about that?"

"Yes. But I don't think he hopes for it. He likes it here."

"Even though people shame him?"

Raighne ran a thumb along the face of an emerald, a small stone leaf. "Haligstane is his home; he bears what he must to stay here."

This was Penda's son he spoke of with such love and pity, the next King of Mercia. Penda shouldn't have left his boy in the hands of wrong-headed *Cristens,* to hurt him with lies and strange teachings. Still, the *aetheling* had one true friend among these people of Haligstane. That one would miss him when he was gone.

I was sorry when I closed Raighne's fingers around the half-ring and placed the mate in his other hand. He knew it after only the briefest of searching touches.

"You've come from his mother."

I could have said that, and I'd planned to. But my heart moved me to give him the truth about this boy he loved. Or some of the truth.

"His mother is dead," I said. "A kinsman sent me to take him to live with foster-parents."

"A kinsman . . . and a friend of yours, I think. A friend you love well enough to come to a place where you had no reason to expect welcome."

"One I love well."

In the church, one voice rose up and soared over all, giving wings to words in a language I didn't know.

"I'll tell him," Raighne said. "Tonight, I'll tell him."

He put both halves of the arm-ring into my hands, gently, as though he were already giving me Wulfhere to care for.

‹13›

They have long summer twilights in Northumbria, my Sif. The dimming goes on for hours after the sun sets. Darkness comes as a deepening of blue to rosy grey, grey to purple and, at last, to star-washed black. I went walking in that long twilight, after the monks of Haligstane had all gone to bed. The cloister was still and empty. The monks kept no watch, as if the war raging across the Isle was nothing to concern them. I couldn't rest so easily.

I walked once around the place and then went out behind the church, to look up at the hill. There I saw a spark of light, so small and distant it might have been a fire-fly winking. But it held steady, and I knew it for the gleam of Aescwine's fire. I looked beyond, to the east, toward the sea. I saw no sign of Cadwalla, and I wasn't much comforted.

What if he'd gone around Haligstane, past the monastery by some swift Roman road? What if we rode out in the morning only to find him ahead of us, burning and looting somewhere west of here? Once again I thought of Rowenna and wondered if Cadwalla's army had chanced upon the young mother with her ailing babes. Her one friend wouldn't stand against an army, and there'd be some hard and deadly sport on the moor then.

I looked around me for some cheer, a sheen of brazier-light at a window, the soft glow of a hearth-fire. Haligstane was dark as a tight-shut byre but for a shadow of gold breathing out past the wide-flung doors of the church. Drawn by the light, I crossed the cloister. But I didn't go into the church, for I heard someone speaking, and knew the gentle voice for Raighne's. And then—suddenly—a sob, a sharp breath drawn and let out raggedly on weeping.

Wulfhere cried, "Raighne, no! Don't make me leave! Oh, please!" His breath caught in his throat, a sob so wrenched it hurt to hear. "Please . . ."

Please, sighed the little exile who would tomorrow be sent out into the wild moorland with me. Don't send me away!

These prayers weren't for me to hear. I walked away, across the cloister to the guest-house. There, I left the gate open so I could see out, and I sat in the garden and the shining moonlight for a long while before I saw Raighne and Wulfhere walking across the cloister, the monk with his hand on the boy's shoulder. They spoke together; I saw it, but I didn't hear them. A few moments later I heard a door open and close; soon after, I heard another. Now everyone was safe a-bed, and on the hill Aescwine's campfire flared up against the darkness, then settled, well-fed for the night. I went in to the guest-house and I went to sleep.

At the end of the night, in the still and darkest hour, a dream came to me. Swift-flown on the wings of magic, it was a cry and a prayer and a telling.

Lydi looked up from the table where all the scented sweep of herbs to be hung and dried lay spread out around her. The cottage door stood wide open so she could see the last light on the garden while she worked, but she didn't look out; she

looked to where Owain sat in the shadowed corner of the room.
He'd been there all evening, leaning back so that the chair was
braced in uneasy balance on two legs. Now the sight of him,
testing his balance and darkly brooding, spurred a small start
of fear in her. He was like a storm, and the cold little clench
of dread Lydi felt was just like the storm-fright she seldom
admitted to.

Owain had come up the hill with no tale to tell tonight, though
usually he offered at least one.

"I've got none in me tonight," he said. "Though that's how
poets pay for their meals around here, and whatever else they get,
ay? Well, I'm no poet, and I'm no storyteller tonight, witch. Feed
me or send me away."

Owain had said that leering, but that was the fling and thrash
of a man caught in his own stormy pain. That pain of his was
like a burden he carried around with him always. Like a miser,
he checked it from time to time to make sure none of it was lost.
Lydi knew how to keep separate from that.

Now the first night-breeze drifted through the doorway, and
Owain turned suddenly restless. He never moved, wasn't even
seen to blink, but Lydi felt the change in him. She waited for him
to say something, and when he didn't, she returned to her work,
gathering grey-green horehound into thick bunches. Absently she
pinched off a sprig and chewed it for the sweetness and the
sudden small tang that followed. Lydi never tasted horehound
without thinking of her mother.

"You've a liking for the bite and the sweet," witch-Meredydd
used to say. "But you should leave something for the harvest,
my girl." Then she'd laugh and give her girl another sprig. The
soft, warm voice of memory was yet speaking when Owain
said:

"I have to go now."

Out in the garden Aelfgar said something to Branwen to make
her laugh. Lydi barely heard. Owain's eyes were like empty
midnight, and they held her. She remembered the look from
a night in spring when he'd come to see a magic. Poor wild
thing, she'd thought then. Now she didn't think that. His words,
so bleakly spoken, touched a place in her where a promise waited
to be kept.

With the taste of horehound still on her lips, Lydi remembered
a thing her mother had told her. "With the garden and the magic,
my girl, come promises you must keep. Most you know. One I
must tell you about now."

So she must, for Meredydd had died young, and the dying hadn't been a surprise to the witch who, with only her lightest touch, could know whether a sickness or wound was mortal or able to be healed. One night at the end of a long sweet summer Meredydd had laid out all her promises, and asked Lydi, one by one, to keep them. One promise had to do with Owain.

In that telling, Meredydd said that Owain was a poor wild thing. "You'll know that when you see him. He's come to me for help before and not been able to accept it. I think he'll come again. If he's ready to accept it, Lydi, help him for my sake." And then, gravely, Meredydd warned her daughter to be careful of Owain. "Remember what he is, always. Don't ever forget."

Poor wild thing . . .

Lydi never forgot, and the first time she saw Owain coming up the hill to Gardd Seren she knew him before ever he spoke a word.

Now, a storm ready to fall, Owain left the hearth-nook. His steps were like thunder in the earth. He reached a hand to touch her, and she pulled back. Between them the table jarred, and a bunch of horehound tumbled off the edge. Owain caught her wrist. He was a smith, with broad strong hands. His fingers went round her wrist with no strain to meet.

"Lydi, it's time to go." All the bones of his face seemed sharper; he was like a fevered man fading from sickness. The flesh sinks, the mask melts, and only the strong bones of the face, innocent of expression, remain. "Witch, on your mother's word—it's time to go."

The forge-smell of him—iron and fire and sweat—fought and whelmed the tangy sweetness of the horehound he crushed underfoot. Outside, in the garden and the golden end of the day, Aelfgar and Branwen stood close. They laughed softly together, thinking about the night.

I could call out, Lydi thought. *Aelfgar would come. If I told him to, he'd drive Owain away.*

Owain saw her glance out to the garden. "You could do that," he whispered, rightly guessing her thought. "But that wouldn't send the promise away."

It wouldn't.

Lydi freed her hand, and she closed her eyes, gathering herself, her strength, her resolve.

"Owain, if you say it is, then the time has come to go. But I'll go only to the promise's end. After that, I'll come home."

He smiled to let her know that he wasn't so sure as she was about that. But he left her with no word, and a moment later Aelfgar put his head in the door to see if all was well.

"Yes," Lydi said. And then, stooping to pick up the bruised bunch of horehound, she changed her answer to the truth. "No, Aelfgar, I don't think things are well. And it's time for me to tell you and Branwen some things."

He stood in the doorway, the light at the end of day shining behind him. And he said, "You're going away, aren't you Lydi?"

Child-minded, they said of him, but Aelfgar had his own wisdom, his own way of seeing and knowing.

"Yes," Lydi said. "I'm going away, and we have to talk about that."

So they did, and much later, when she lay down to sleep, Lydi looked along a shaft of moonlight to the high shelf and the small blue pot filled up with the seeds that were a promise. The mark on it shone a little in the silvery light; the rune that means a gift, a partnership, and a soldier's blood-sacrifice.

More asleep than awake, Lydi whispered, "Garroc, are you ever afraid? When you ride away in spring to tend that promise to your lord, are you ever afraid that you won't come back? I'm afraid. . . ."

I woke in a cold sweat, Sif, soaked with it. And Hinthan's hand closed on my shoulder, gripping.

"Wake up," he whispered. "Garroc, wake up."

Somewhere in the darkness Cynnere snored, and Hinthan gave me another shake, grumbling about how no one could sleep with all the din of people snoring and other people groaning in dreams.

"I should've gone and slept on the hill with—"

"Hinthan she's gone," I said into the darkness. I wasn't sure even then if I was awake or still dreaming. "Lydi's gone."

He caught his breath sharply. The witch-dreaming was no secret between us, and he knew now that he'd waked me from no simple dream.

"Lydi's gone? What do you mean . . . ?"

I sat up, shook my head to clear it. "She's gone. She's left Gardd Seren and gone away with Owain."

He drew breath to ask another question, and then he tensed and stilled. We heard low voices outside, and he turned sharply as the door opened. Raighne stood there, and his face was white as whey.

"Garroc," he said. His voice was strangely calm, and a chill crept down my spine. "A friend of yours has come to tell us that Cadwalla's near."

Hinthan bolted past me and woke Cynnere with a cry. They scrambled for clothes and weapons, and out beyond the open door I saw Aescwine pacing, his hand on his sword, his eyes on the hill beyond the river. There, red lightning flared beneath low clouds that were not really clouds but thick dark smoke.

Cadwalla was very near.

◄14►

"Farmsteads are burning," Raighne said. He spoke quietly. I had to stand still to hear him. "There are a few steads, out there and east. God save them."

And Cynnere put Harm in my hand and said to me, "Those won't even quench his thirst. He'll be here soon, Garroc. Hinthan and I can go to the river with some of the men from here. If we kill a few witches, maybe we'll have a chance."

Outside, Aescwine stopped his pacing. He caught my eye and nodded once. He was with us.

"Go," I said to Cynnere. "Take Aescwine and leave Hinthan here with me to—"

"No!" Raighne lifted his hand, a dark shape against the blood-red sky. "No, Garroc. Maybe you'd kill a few of Cadwalla's men, but the rest would kill you, and they'd do what they came here to do, anyway."

Cynnere's eyes glittered like the keen blue edge of honed iron. "Not until they knew that good men stood against them."

"Good men, indeed." Raighne smiled, very gently. "Ah, and aren't you some of the finest I've seen in a rare while? But in the end it won't matter. We've no weapons here—"

"You've hay-forks," Aescwine said gruffly. "And hoes and wood-axes—"

Raighne turned to where he'd heard the voice. Red light shone on his face, showed an eerie calm. "We've no weapons here, earth-kin. And we won't fight. It's not our way. If this death is what the Good God plans for us, we'd be sinners to resist. When Cadwalla comes, he'll find us in the church, praying."

"Then you're a poor fool, man," Aescwine said, and he went

back to pacing. But Cynnere couldn't let it go.

"Raighne, you'll be slaughtered—Garroc, tell him he's crazy."

I thought he was crazy. Dwarf and Man, every wight must die, later if not sooner. Surely these *Cristen* folk hadn't so far fallen from the right of things that they could believe there's no shame in letting themselves be slaughtered, helpless sheep bleating in the pen.

I almost said that, but Raighne spoke first.

"Garroc, my friend, you don't have a choice."

I didn't. We'd taken Raighne's hospitality and so owed him whatever help we could give him now. But we could give him nothing, for I'd promised my king that I'd get his young son to a safe place.

"I'm sorry," I said.

"Take the boy away and keep him safe." Outside, the sky burned; Raighne was a dark shape against that red glare. "You've nothing to be sorry for, Garroc Ghosts-Skald."

He left us, and soon after, Cynnere and Aescwine went to ready horses. But Hinthan hung back, his grey eyes narrowed as he searched me in the wild red light. He wanted to ask about Lydi. And—I saw it in him—he wanted to ask if we'd still run to Gardd Seren though Lydi was gone.

"Go," I said. "We'll talk about it later. Go!"

Hoofs clattered in the cloister: bridle-iron chimed, echoed in the unnatural stillness. The walls of the church shone with witch-light as though the stone-work bled through the mortar bandages. The voices of monks at helpless prayer drifted out from the church, words I'd heard before.

"Be, Lord God, a noble friend; look, Lord, upon me, and shelter me in my need!"

I'd seen few of those monks the short while I'd stayed here; they were only voices to me, or shadows flitting from here to there, men in robes of brown homespun who'd taken good care to keep away from the shadow-kin and the friends of devils. And now, as he'd been the sole one to greet us, only blind Raighne stood outside the church to see us away.

The morning had a tight, stretched feel to it, as though something big pressed down against the sky, something heavy and hot and very dangerous. The fiery witch-work was close now, and Hinthan kept an eye to the east, not sure whether we'd get away from Haligstane before Cadwalla fell upon the place, a tide of burning and killing.

I wasn't sure either. The *aetheling* was refusing to leave.

Wulfhere wouldn't mount to ride, wouldn't be reasoned with, and didn't cease his objections even after Cynnere scooped him right off his feet and thumped him down hard on the horse's back.

"Cowards," Wulfhere hissed. "*Nithings!* Run and hide if you want to—I won't leave!"

Aescwine growled to hear that; my friend paled at the insult no soldier bears easily. Cynnere grabbed the *aetheling* by the shirt, yanked him hard and down so that they were eye to eye.

"Do you remember me, boy?" Like an iron edge, his voice. "We've still got some matters need talking about. Don't make me have to do it now, because I haven't got time to do it gently."

Wulfhere still struggled, though he had only defiance to offer, and in the end his red rage stood him in no good stead. Cynnere's threat didn't still him; Raighne's touch did.

"Raighne!" I could hear the boy's heart breaking in that cry. "Don't make me leave you!"

"Wulfhere, make the hard choice. Make it for me if you can't for yourself."

Strangely brilliant their every expression, etched boldly in the red light. On each face I saw love and the dread of loss. After another word, softly spoken, Raighne pressed a small scrip into Wulfhere's hand.

"Remember, the Good God goes with you."

Tears shone on Wulfhere's face, gold in the red witch-light. Hinthan took his horse close, till they were knee to knee. He said something to Wulfhere, but I didn't hear what.

And Raighne spoke to me, his words threaded through with the pleading from the church.

"I'm asking a favor, poet. If you see her out there in your running—if you see Rowenna Brand's daughter—tell her we didn't forget her, and we remember her always in our prayers."

"I'll tell her, if I have the chance."

He took my hand in his own two, gripping hard as friends do in farewell. When he withdrew I wasn't empty-handed.

"That's an old stone," he said. "A friend gave it to me when I took ship from home. No Gael, him. He's Saxon, like you. And he's earth-kin, like you. Maybe this stone would like to travel with a Dwarf again, ay?

"Go now," he said before I could look to see the stone-gift. "*Dia dhuit,* poet. God to you, Garroc Ghosts-Skald."

I put his gift into my belt-pouch, with the two halves of the emerald studded arm-ring. A great singing rose up from the church. Over it rang the harsher song of iron-shod hoofs as we rode away.

West beyond Haligstane there are no Roman roads, only narrow sheep tracks, shadowy sketches on the land that follow the curves of the rising moor. The most sure-footed horse couldn't be urged to speed. We rode hard from Haligstane but not fast. All the while Wulfhere never looked back. He rode in brooding silence, and no one tried to talk to him. Mid-morning, with not even five hard miles past, we stopped to rest our horses. Hinthan kept watch at the crest. Aescwine and Cynnere were glad to stretch their legs, and they kept an eye on Wulfhere while he did the same. Alone, I sat with my back to the east and looked at Raighne's gift.

The stone was pale limestone, flat and no longer than my thumb, but wider; one of Hinthan's arrowheads was thicker. Meant to be worn, it had a hole at the top and a leather plait run through. A graven rune marked this gift, so:

Ing is the name of that rune, my Sif, and Ing is the name of the god no one knows. There aren't many tales of this god's doings, but Stane Saewulf's son knew that much, and he knew this: One night, when god-Aegor was gone from the sea, Ing went into the waves and found Ran, Aegor's sea-wife, all alone. They played at love all the night long, but Ing left Ran heartsore and bitter before the sun rose again and Aegor returned.

"That tale and one or two others are all we hear about Sea-Ing," Stane would say. "And what we know is less than that."

I stroked Raighne's gift with my thumb, and heard the small voice of a small stone. It spoke of wind and rain and the great wide moorland; once of the hard tip used to mark it. It didn't offer a name, and I didn't try to tease one from it.

I sat with the stone in my hand until Aescwine whistled low for my attention. He pointed to the hilltop where Hinthan stood watching for Cadwalla. No sign of fire or smoke stained the sky, but I knew Haligstane was burning. Hinthan stood, dark and straight and still against the bright blue sky. Even with the distance between us, I could read him. He was watching a firing. I looked for Wulfhere, and didn't see him till he was halfway up the hill, running and scrambling and stumbling for the top.

I put Raighne's gift into my belt-pouch, and went up the hill after Penda's son.

The moor is a voiced place. The wind blows always, whistling through the grass, booming down the sky, mourning past some giant's barrow. Hinthan and Wulfhere didn't hear me walking. Earth-deaf, like all of *mann-cynn*, they didn't feel it.

I stopped below the crest. In the east war-light leaped, flashing above the low-hanging smoke. Haligstane burned. The gardens and the guest-houses, the fair writing-hall with all its many and wonderful vellum sheets, the church and the byres, the orchards, the fields and the grain-stores, all burned. Raighne and his brothers were dead or dying. I knew how it was. I'd done that kind of work well, and if you don't have a witch to do the burning for you, a torch will do it as well. Another day, it might be me at the sheep-slaughter, red-handed while ravens crowded the sky.

But today I made no ghosts, I could only listen for them. And I did hear them, a great rush of dying. Among those ghosts was red Raighne, his voice low and soft like the sigh of a home-come man.

Hinthan put an arm round Wulfhere's shoulders. "I'm sorry," he said.

Wulfhere nodded, but no more. Mind and heart, his were on the burning so terrible he could see it from here.

Hinthan said, "I never knew how fast buildings could burn until I saw my father's house and byre go."

He'd been—to the year—the same age as Wulfhere; a farmer's boy, brown with seasons of sun, not so tall as now or even showing promise to be. The first time I saw him he was limping and ragged, his long face thin and smoke-stained. He'd escaped the killing and the burning; his father had sent him away in time, over the fields and into the woods. But he'd seen it all, helpless.

Wulfhere trembled, just like he was standing face to a cold, cold wind. Hinthan held him closer.

"You can't save anything," Hinthan said, telling the boy what he needed to know. "By the time you even know it's happening, it's too late. The chickens, the cow, the goat, everything's dead. The fields are burning, the rye and the wheat and the barley. And then you know that your mother's dead, and your father— and you're not even sure that you're alive. Or that you want to be."

Raggedly, Wulfhere sobbed. Choking, he said, "Were you all alone?"

"All alone. I wandered around for a few days—" He stopped on a small bitter laugh. "I was lost, is what I was. I was so . . . lost."

"What happened to you then?"

Then he found Erich War Hawk's battle-ground camp, then he found me, just as though I'd been waiting for him. I suppose I had been, waiting all the son-reft years.

Wind rose and blew harder, carrying smoke. Hinthan lifted his head, smelled the dying and the memories.

"Garroc found me. I'm his foster-son now."

Wulfhere drew a tight, frightened breath. Raighne hadn't told him that. And no one had told him anything but lies about Dwarfs.

"You can't be! He's shadow-kin—"

Hinthan turned, swift, his grey eyes a-blaze. He grabbed Wulfhere's shoulders, and the boy flinched under his white-knuckled grip.

"Don't ever say that about my foster-father." Wulfhere hissed against the pain of the grip. If Hinthan heard, he didn't care. "And don't say any of the other things you *Cristens* like to say about the earth-kin. They're lies."

Cold sorrow turned suddenly to hot anger. Gripped and held, helpless, Wulfhere demanded to know why he mustn't say what everyone knew for true.

Hinthan stood very still. Then, with sudden gentleness, he loosed his hold, let Wulfhere go.

"Wulf, did monk-Raighne teach you to say those things?"

Shaking, but never so far giving in as to even rub shoulders where bruises would show, Wulfhere whispered, "No."

"I didn't think so."

Wulfhere stared at the ground, tears running down his dusty cheeks. He was friend-reft and without hope for another until Hinthan gathered him close, held him warmly and hugged him safe.

"You'll be all right, Wulf. Be sad for Raighne, and miss him. But you don't have to be afraid."

It was then Hinthan saw me out the corner of his eye. I'd heard it all and I couldn't have walked away from any of it. He was surprised, but not angry or unhappy to have been overheard. He said nothing, and I went away down the hill. I took red Raighne's gift and wore the rune-stone round my neck, inside my shirt. Nearest my heart now were two gifts—Ing's stone and Wotan's agate, the journey-stone pinned to my shirt.

• • •

We rode all through the day and long after the sun set. At the end of the day, the moor changed suddenly and became wide and stony again, flat ground and low-hanging sky. Now we saw little dales, gaps in the flatness of stone; some no more than water-cut gorges, others broad enough to nestle a stead. Sheep grazed on the hillside, and once we saw a lone man walking beside a heavy-laden, ox-drawn wain. In the last hour of the half-light, Aescwine and Hinthan went to find a place to camp. They weren't long gone before Hinthan returned to tell of a high-sided, narrow dale through which a clear fresh beck ran.

"There's plenty of brown trout in that beck and we'll eat well tonight."

It was as he said.

Silver-edged black clouds ran in front of the moon, galloping before an east wind. The distant thunder was like an army riding, the lightning like flint-fire flashing from iron-shod hoofs. Aescwine and I kept watch while the wind changed, running from the north, higher and cooler. When Aescwine saw rain coming across the moor in dark and distant sweeps, he said, "It's about time to turn over the watch, don't you think?"

I thought it was time, but he didn't go to wake Cynnere or Hinthan. He stood with his arms folded tight across his chest, still watching the storm coming.

"It's like old Wotan's curse has finally run out," he said. "It's like all of 'em are gone, every last one of our kin."

"Don't, Aescwine," I said, low and quickly. "Don't say that. It's not like that."

But it was like that, he was right.

Now the storm was so close we could feel the breath of the lightning prickling the back of the neck.

"That red monk was a friend, wasn't he, young skald?"

In his way, for the small span we had together, the Irelander had been a friend. I didn't deny him. I said, "Yes, Raighne was a friend."

"I hope this boy is worth it."

Eyes on the storm, I said, "He is."

And he didn't say more. He went away down the hill to wake Cynnere and Hinthan.

The wind blew harder, sobbing across the moor. I turned my back to it and looked south and west to Wales, to a long blue line of mountains, those western heights we call the Pennines. Beyond lay Lydi's wildwood, the forest nestled between the Pennines and the Cambrian mountains that are the western border against the sea.

In dream, she'd said: Garroc, are you ever afraid that you won't come back?

Came a sudden flash of lightning, and Cynnere cried, "The horses! Stop him!"

In the darkness after the lightning I smelled blood on the heavy air, the faint coppery scent of pain.

◄15►

By the pale pulse of lightning, in the glow of the dying campfire, I saw Cynnere on his knees, blood on his hands and glistening darkly on the breast of his shirt. He held Hinthan close in his arms, and my boy lay limp and still, his face sheeted with blood.

Rain fell, sudden and hard, hissing on fire's embers.

By the beck a horse whinnied, the cry heard over a crack of thunder. Aescwine roared a withering curse, Wulfhere shouted in rage.

"Devil! Demon! Fiend!"

I knelt down, reaching to feel Hinthan's heart. The very skin of my palm cringed in dread till I felt the strong steady beat.

Cynnere sighed for relief in the moment I did, and gently he set Hinthan on the ground. Rain washed some blood from Hinthan's face, showed me the swelling bruise and the ragged cut above his eye. The wound was deep enough to bleed freely, and all that blood was an aching thing to see. While he lay senseless I searched to see if he was worse hurt, or if his head was broken.

"Cynnere, what happened?"

"That whelp hit Hinthan with a rock and he was going for me when Old 'un came down the hill and caught him at it. I'm not liking this boy much, Garroc."

Hinthan started, stung awake while I was cleaning mud from the cut. He tried to sit, and managed it with help.

"Where's Wulf?"

Cynnere answered, his voice low and growling. "Aescwine's taking care of it."

Groaning, Hinthan tried to get his legs under him. He had no luck, and Cynnere hoisted him to stand. He shook his head to clear away the daze, but soon found out that was a bad idea.

Came a near flash of lighting, and Wulfhere's shrill cursing. Aescwine hauled him from the beck in iron grip and never let go till the boy was standing before me. White-faced as Hinthan, Wulfhere clutched the scrip Raighne had given him when we left Haligstane. He was muddy and wet, his shirt was torn at the neck and ripped in the sleeve. Not once did he look at Hinthan.

"He's lost us a horse, Garroc." Aescwine shook the boy hard enough to rattle his teeth. "My horse. So if you don't mind, I'd like to hang him for a thieving little killer."

Wulfhere lifted his head and never took his eyes from me. He looked like he was going to spit.

"Let him go, Aescwine," I said. And coldly I said to the king's son: "Boy, now you'd better tell me what you think you were doing."

"You're scarelings, shadow-kin!" The boy quivered with the force of his loathing. "You ran away and left Haligstane—you left Raighne!—but you can't hold me. I'll find a way back to them if it's only to bury them decently. *Nithings!* Cowards!"

And then, for me only, his icy smile, for me only the one word mouthed in the after-glare of lightning. *Geldr*, he said silently. Gelding.

Thunder roared down the sky. Hinthan shouted—"Garroc, no!"—as he caught and held my wrist.

I saw it in his eyes that he didn't know what word passed between Wulfhere and me. But he didn't doubt it was a harder one than *nithing*.

"Don't," he said, low for only us to hear. "He's afraid, Garroc. It's all because he's afraid."

I opened my fist, but I didn't break Hinthan's grip or even try to.

And so he had his hand on me when Cynnere shouted, "Down!" We dropped to the mud and took Wulfhere down between us as an arrow buzzed overhead, and another. I flung an arm around Hinthan, pulled him tight to me, half under me. He had Wulfhere by the wrist; I sheltered both. But I didn't understand that a witch stood on the hill until Cynnere shouted it.

Tall and broad, no Dwarf, but a Man, the witch wore fire like a cloak. The fey fire leaped all around him, up from the soaked ground; lapped at the night, fiery plumage. And in the heart of the fire, darkness; the witch himself, unharmed by the flames.

In a wild and skirling voice, he cried: "Wulfhere Gytha's son! I've named you, boy!"

So a Welshman shouts in battle when he wants to find a single hated foe amid the bloody mob of armies. Wulfhere moaned softly, in terror spoke a name he'd taught me: *Beelzebub*—and swift on the heels of that name, a prayer I'd heard before.

Be, Lord God, a noble friend . . .

Another arrow flew, and this one was flame-fletched. It stuck burning and hissing in the ground close between Aescwine and Cynnere. They scrambled away from the fire, and Cynnere rolled close to me.

"Your hand-axe, Garroc. Get ready when I run."

"Go," I said. I elbowed Hinthan. "Hold tight to Wulfhere. Don't let him break and run, or he's dead."

Lightning flashed. Cynnere jumped up, bellowing a blood-freezing war-cry. Sword aloft, the iron shining, he ran to the left and up the hill. I saw him as no more than a shadow in the driving rain, a dark thing howling. The witch saw him as a wild berserker and changed his aim. Streaking across the darkness like tailed stars, red in blackness, the witch's arrows hunted Cynnere.

And I rose up, let Penda's axe fly for the dark heart of the fire. The witch died with the king's axe in his breast.

It was a while before the fey flames faded, and though the fiery cloak the witch wore had no power to hurt him while he was alive, it didn't deal so gently with him after he was dead, all his wonder-craft unknotted. The stench of burnt flesh hung on the rain-soaked air as the fire and the magic, unleashed, turned against its maker.

Cynnere came loping back to us, his grin the brightest thing in the rain and the dark, and Aescwine got to his feet, wiping rain from his face, spitting mud. He allowed as how he didn't mind that the witch burned, but he minded the reek of it.

I looked around for Hinthan and found him kneeling in the mud and the rain, his back to us all, holding Wulfhere while the *aetheling* spewed his supper.

"Wulfhere Gytha's son," Aescwine said. "I'm wondering why that witch was chasing him—though I expect you'll say something like there's no time for the whole story now."

I smiled—he could always make me do that—even after such a night as this one.

"That's just what I'd say."

"All right, then. But someday, Garroc my friend, you're going to sit yourself down with a keg of ale between us and tell me just exactly what kind of tale I've been part of." His face twisted into a grisly grimace, his dear smile. "And not a drop of that ale for you until you're done the telling."

I promised him I'd do that when the tale was mine to tell, and I went up the hill to fetch Penda's hand-axe.

I didn't go alone, for Hinthan came running after me. The last breath of the witch's magic, the final traces of power, raced like cold tingling on my arms as I walked. Hinthan shivered from it.

Hinthan stopped well short of the burnt witch. Only a few last flashes of lightning remained of the storm. One showed me my boy's face waxy and white before he turned away from the body hissing and steaming. The witch didn't burn now, and not as much of him as you'd think had been lost of flame. I put my foot on the dead man and wrenched Penda's hand-axe from his breast. From a long reach away, Hinthan took it and wiped the blade clean in the soaking grass while I knelt beside the body.

Wind mourned and sighed, thunder growled far away. I stilled myself and listened to the ghost rising up and going away. I heard only the torn ends of bewildered prayers to several gods, among them the White Christ.

Lightning flickered, and Hinthan came a little closer. His breath hissed, suddenly caught.

"Garroc! I know him!"

In the next flicker of light I saw him and knew him too. This was one of the scouts who'd brought word to Penda that Cadwalla would join him for the breaking of Eoferwic. Hinthan had passed him through in the night. Later, I'd seen him thanking Penda for his good gift of horses.

Hinthan went down on his heels beside me and, braced, he reached for the man's burnt arm. He slipped a wrist-bracer over seared flesh and naked bone. It was handsome work, beaten silver inlaid with red enamel shaped like ravens. The blood-hued storm-crows wheeled round one dark onyx.

"It's Peada's," Hinthan said. He dropped the bracer into the mud and wiped his hands on his shirt. "Why is one of Cadwalla's scouts wearing it?"

Cold in my belly, I knew why. This bracer was part of a hireling's fee. Peada had learned about his father's secret son, even to the boy's name, and this hunter had known who to look for, and where.

And Hinthan said, "You know, don't you?"

"I know."

He had the king's rune-writ axe in his hand, and he picked up the wrist-bracer again. He hefted each while he weighed what he knew against what he guessed. And he was my foster-son, Sif; he'd been around the king and his kin enough to reckon out the biggest part of the truth.

"Wulf is Penda's son," he whispered, his grey eyes wide and on me to see the truth of his guess. Then, quickly, "There'll be more than one hunter, won't there?"

"We can be sure of it. And we can't count on all of them being Peada's men. No one knows how Merewal might feel about suddenly being one brother richer."

I got to my feet and went to look out over the moor. West lay Wales and Gardd Seren. No one in that part of the Isle failed to respect the witch's haven. Who was welcomed there could stay in safety. I looked north where only storm-dark lay, south along the line of *torrs* and barrows to where forestland rose up from the moor, a wildwood. I looked east to where I'd become used to seeing signs of Cadwalla's doings.

Where could I run from enemies whose faces I didn't know, hunters I wouldn't recognize until they were on us?

"We have to go to Gardd Seren, Garroc. Even if Lydi's gone."

I closed my eyes, trying to catch back some of Lydi's dream. I saw only the shaft of moonlight leading her to look at the rune-marked blue pot on the high shelf above the hearth. There were all our promises, and Lydi had filled her eyes with it like it was a talisman to bring her home again.

Hinthan came and stood by me. He was quiet for a moment, his hand on my shoulder, and then he said, "Owain's gone, and Lydi went with him. Garroc, tell me what happened."

I told him what I knew, about Lydi and her mother's promise, about how Owain came to claim it. I told him about Meredydd's warning—*Don't ever forget what he is*.

"That makes him sound dangerous," Hinthan said. "I don't think he's . . ."

But he didn't finish that thought and say that he didn't think Owain was dangerous. Of we two, he knew Owain best, but he was finding out that someone else knew him better and would surely not warn without good reason.

And I remembered a night-wandering dream that had found me outside the walls of Eoferwic on the very night Hinthan had passed this dead Welshman through the watch. In that dream Owain had watched my Lydi with dark and deep hunger.

"Garroc, what are you going to do?"

He asked as though I had a choice, as though I could weigh one need against the other and choose between my promise to safeguard Wulfhere's life and my need to find Lydi.

I had no choice. The boy I'd sworn to protect was here, down in the hollow in the wreck of our night camp. I didn't know where Lydi was, and I knew it then—standing there on the hill in the wind with the storm riding away—that she'd chosen not to let me know where she was bound. All unwilling, I had to leave her to her choice and keep my own promise.

"We're going to take Wulfhere to Gardd Seren," I said bitterly.

"Straight west?"

I said we'd go south for a while, to the forest beyond the barrows and the hills. We'd not be so easily spotted under wildwood as on the moor. "And we'll find fast roads the farther south we get. We'll cross home into Mercia and then head for Gardd Seren."

Hinthan nodded grimly.

Stars shone between clouds now, and in the dark hollow their light glinted on bridles and bits. Cynnere had the horses ready, and it was time for us to go.

We rode away through the night and through most of the morning before we had to stop and rest our horses. In the days after, we saw no sign that anyone followed us, but I didn't slow our flight or ever stop looking back. We'd not seen that hireling-witch until we'd seen his arrows first.

We fled across the moorland under the brazen skies of summer, and each day grew hotter and more windy than the one before till it seemed we were spitting dust. Sometimes in the north we saw the dark smudge of smoke on the sky, and we thought that might be Outlawed Osric pressing his claim to this dark Northumbria. More often we saw the track of burning in the east, smoke and the red flare of witch-work. None of us doubted that was Cadwalla's mark.

Wulfhere rode up with Hinthan, the two boys a light load for the red mare. He was very quiet, and he didn't complain about the heat or the dust or the company. He kept himself away from everyone, and though he rode with Hinthan, Wulfhere seldom spoke or noted if Hinthan spoke to him. But often at night, he would wake from nightmares of burning and witches, cold-sweating and shaking. Then Hinthan would go and sit by him, and I would hear them whispering, two boys together against the night-fear. Come the morning, Wulfhere would have nothing to say again, but that didn't seem to bother Hinthan.

On the sixth day away from Haligstane, we came to the wild-wood and I decided that we'd get half a day's ride into the cool shadows, then stop to rest for a day and a night.

In all that time I learned no more about where Lydi was bound, or why. And Hinthan never asked me more about it, never prodded to know if I'd dreamed, but he was always near to watch as I woke. Watching, he'd read the answer to his unspoken question on my face. Once, as he was walking away, I heard him mutter curses under his breath, and all of them were flung at Owain Dwarf-Smith.

The first night we spent in the sheltered forest, my sleep was disturbed by the sound of Cynnere and Aescwine talking together. In the moment of waking I heard their voices. In the moment after, just before falling back to sleep, I heard a familiar stranger whisper.

Skald! Skald . . .

The ghost I'd first heard in mid-winter was back with me. I'd all but forgotten about him. This time, I told Hinthan about him.

◄16►

Hinthan said, "Garroc, who is this ghost?" and I told him that I didn't know.

It was a day of sun and moon. The ageing Witch, the last silver curve, had reached his height at noon and was stooping now for the west to set with the sun. The dark undersides of oak leaves danced with bending light, reflections from the near-by water.

"You don't know who the ghost is even though you've been hearing him all year?"

"Even though."

Hinthan stood leaning against an oak, whittling. I lay on my back beside the stream-fed, sunlit pool, listening to Cynnere and Wulfhere splashing in the water. Those two bore each other's company only grudgingly as they got clean of a week of moorland mud and dust. Above, a woodlark went skipping from branch to branch. Jays scolded and woodpeckers hammered. We would stay over here to rest our tired horses, to rest ourselves.

"He doesn't say anything but 'skald, skald'?"

"That's all. Not much to learn from it."

Hinthan made a close cut on the wood, and then another. "Don't you wonder?"

"No. He'll say something when he's ready. Or he'll go away and say nothing."

The horses on long tethers cropped lush grass, blowing and snuffing together, content. Aescwine sat with his back against an old, old oak at the other end of the glade, sleeping in sun-dappled shade beneath spreading branches.

"Is it never quiet in you, Garroc?"

I yawned, sleepy in the sunlight and the sweet-smelling day. "Most times it's quieter in me than it is around me."

Out in the middle of the pool Cynnere floated on his back, arms outspread, enjoying the warmth and the water. Nearer, Aescwine stirred, soon to wake. Wulfhere came out of the water, scurrying to dress quickly in the sudden chill of the shade.

"Skald, skald," Hinthan said, grinning. "I'm going fishing for supper."

He put his knife away and tossed his whittling aside. It hadn't been more than skill-work, a test for new kinds of cuts. I watched him gather up his nets and slip off into the wildwood, and then settled again. In the water, Cynnere startled, snorted, caught sinking and dozing; but he didn't do more than spread out and float again. Aescwine woke, got groaning to his feet. He walked away into the brush by the water downstream. The sun's rays slanted lower now, redder, and shadows deepened. Out the corner of my eye I watched Wulfhere.

Head low, the king's son sat in a falling shaft of sunlight, emptying the scrip he'd taken from Haligstane. Spread out on the ground lay pots of ink and a bunch of quills tied with a strip of green cloth. He took out the vellum sheet Raighne had shown me in the writing-hall, the page with the hopeful emerald at the top. He was very careful not to get the sheet wet; no more than these few remained of Haligstane. Wulfhere wiped his palms on his shirt, spread his hands over the page and closed his eyes. His face smoothed to peaceful, and in that quiet breath he had no likeness to his kinsmen, not to Peada or red Merewal or even Penda.

I watched him without being seen to, and I wondered if—thus peaceful—he looked like fair Gytha who stole away a king's heart.

Wulfhere sat quiet with the tools of his work around him and his hands on the vellum, while the sun and the moon dropped behind the trees. Out in the pond Cynnere still dozed. I drowsed, listening to small creatures scurrying in the brush, and to the mother-earth's voice, the murmur and sigh in the bones of me.

And I woke fully a moment later when I heard Hinthan's step.

Aescwine, coming back from the brush, felt what I did. Like me, he didn't hear much to worry him, no hard thud of running, no sliding shuffle to speak of wounds. But Hinthan wasn't alone, we knew that, too. Aescwine took his short-sword from the sheath. I made sure keen-edged Harm was near to hand.

Wulfhere saw that. The pulse beat hard in his throat. His face drained of all color and his eyes glittered. Witches!

"It's all right," I said. "That's Hinthan coming."

He heard me, even nodded once. But his hand shook as he tried to roll his vellum sheet.

Jays screamed and scolded in the trees as Hinthan came into the glade. He was not alone; a young woman leaned on his arm. Her face and neck were bruised and scratched. Her shift showed white through the small rents in a rusty colored bramble-torn gown; coppery hair fell astray from a thick braid.

Aescwine took his hand from his sword. He put his back to an oak, vanished into the shadows. And Wulfhere, seeing the limping woman, cried out in dismay.

Out in the pond Cynnere heard that cry and jumped to his feet in alarm. He was something to see, my friend Cynnere—big and tall and broad-shouldered, narrow at the waist, thick in arms and legs, with the late sun gleaming on him and the water running off. There weren't many women who wouldn't notice him. This woman didn't seem to see Cynnere—or any of us—until, from the shadows beneath the oak, Aescwine barked:

"Sit down, you!"

Cynnere did, and young woman started, gasped, and all the color ran out of her face. She saw where she was, and she saw herself surrounded by strangers.

I said, "It's all right, girl."

Her eyes widened, she stared at me wordlessly.

"It's all right," I said again. "I'm no devil to hurt you."

Dry-mouthed with fear, she could but whisper. "I know you're no devil, earth-kin."

But she didn't know whether I'd a mind to hurt her, for mortal men know how to do that well enough and most don't need the

skill of devils. She began to tremble, had a look on her like her
knees were going out from under her. But she didn't fall. Hinthan
had an arm around her waist now, and he held Rowenna Brand's
daughter firmly.

Ay, that's who she was, Sif.

I knew it the way you can watch a weaver at her loom and
know where the thread she's lifting will go in the half-made
pattern. I'd been catching sight of Rowenna's thread these several
weeks past, a glimpse out the corner of my eye; a word here and
there from people who'd met her, who'd worried about the young
mother and her babes.

In truth, I'd heard of this woman before ever Hild came to me
in the byre at Saefast, before ever Brother Raighne of Haligstane
asked me to speak to her of his prayers. But I didn't know that
till a long time later.

I sat with Rowenna in the long ending of the day, in the
dimming and through till twilight. We didn't sit alone; Hinthan
was near, working wood with his knife to keep his hands busy.
Cynnere sat to one side, tending our fire. Nor was Aescwine far
off, only walking watch at the bounds of the glade. Of us all,
Wulfhere sat closest to Rowenna, for he remembered her from
Haligstane and watched her now with haunted eyes, trying to see
all the way back to a place that was no more.

But it might only have been we two, Rowenna and me, sitting
there before the fire. I made it that way. In hall or on heath, with
night pressing close and only the fire's light and my voice to
hold it back, I can gather listeners to me, hold them as in my
two hands. That night I held Rowenna, and I told a tale for her
alone; the tale of herself.

"In Saefast," I said, "on the coast by the East Sea, lives an old
woman, and her name is Hild Aldhere's daughter. And Hild came
to me one night, to the byre where I waited a storm through, and
she brought me food and asked me whether I'd come looking for
Rowenna Brand's daughter, who'd fled north along the coast with
her little children and one friend—him a Christ-priest. They were
hoping that another friend would find her. A man of the king's,
Hild said, is looking for the dear girl."

"Bacseg," Rowenna whispered. "Yes. He's Eadwine's man;
heart and hand, he's the king's man. He never found me. He
never came." She clasped her hands hard together; the knuckles showed white. "And later we saw burning, out by the sea
and—"

The trembling came on her again. I gathered her back from that memory of burning with word and voice.

"I saw that, too. My friends and I were bound for Haligstane to fetch Wulfhere Gytha's son and take him to live with foster-kin." I nodded toward Wulfhere. "You remember him, don't you?"

Something sparked in fear-dulled eyes then. Rowenna made a slight move to unclasp her hands, maybe to reach for him, but she couldn't do that. It was like those hands were bound one to the other, gripping.

"We ran the same way, Rowenna; you always a day or two before. Bacseg didn't find you in Haligstane."

Ing's stone, the monk's rune-gift, moved against my skin when I sat a little forward. I remembered my promise to Raighne of Ireland.

"In Haligstane they prayed to Christ for you, Rowenna. And they didn't know what happened to you after you left them, but they hoped that all would be well."

Her hands shook, though she kept them tight clasped, each a fist gripping the other. All had not been well.

Gently, I said, "Rowenna, where are your children?"

Her face shone white as naked bone. Hinthan laid down knife and wood. Wulfhere moved close to him.

"They are dead. I am alone, *dvergr*. I don't know where my friend is. Or Bacseg, or my husband. He sent me away, my husband. I didn't want to leave him, but he said, 'Take our children away to safety.'"

She stopped, and she looked at me, suddenly urgent.

"There's war all over this kingdom, *dvergr*."

"I know," I said.

"And my husband and his sons must fight . . . soldiers must . . . I was to meet Bacseg at the coast where a ship would be waiting. But the ship never came, and Bacseg never came."

Rowenna looked up, but not at me; past me, beyond now to then. What she saw made her shudder. Even the firelight couldn't tint her white face.

"Penda's army kept getting closer from the south."

Wulfhere caught his breath in a hiss of fear, the pulse beat raggedly in his throat. Penda was the father he'd so wanted all his short life, but he knew Penda only as an enemy-king, a storied foeman, and tales of his doings were the nightmares that pounced out of the dark of every Northumbrian boy's sleep.

Rowenna didn't see how the boy changed; she yet lived in her own tale. She said: "And the witch-king came down from the north. We ran up the coast, to Saefast, and then west, for my friend knows—knew the monks of Haligstane. We saw the burning of that place. . . ."

In the woods beyond the fire an owl hooted, a hungry sound.

"There are too many enemies here about, *dvergr*. We fled from witches who burnt Haligstane, and we crossed paths with one of Penda's sons.

"In a small village," she whispered, as to herself.

Hinthan looked up at me, wondering—was it Peada's army, or Merewal's? Would one be worse than the other?

Fire sighed, a log broke in two, fell to ash. Weary sounds.

Rowenna said, "The people of that village fought for a long time, but my friend and I fled before the fighting was over. I didn't want to. I shouldn't have left—but I had the babes.

"And then my babies died." In the firelight, her face was all hollow shadows. "Later, after the village was burnt, we went back and we buried them, and all others we could find, in the churchyard. And once, in the middle of the night, I went to see the little graves again. I stood for a long time, praying. And then I walked away. I didn't . . . I just didn't stop walking."

And she had become lost, in the sorrow and in the wildwood; she'd wandered away and never thought about anything but the need to keep moving, away from the burnt village, the unbearable emptiness of child-loss.

"Rowenna, surely your friend is searching for you."

"If he's alive." She said that whispering, with no hope for it, and when she looked at me her eyes glittered like glass. "What will happen to me now, Garroc Ghosts-Skald?"

"You can stay here tonight, and none of us will harm you. I promise it."

Rowenna unclasped her hands then, and the flesh was all bruised from her gripping. She saw that, and she gasped a little. She'd not felt the pain till then. Cynnere, silent through all her tale, reached for her hands. He took them gently and held them in his own two. Rowenna had told her tale dry-eyed, but now her tears ran, and it was that simple tenderness of Cynnere's that freed them.

I went out to take the watch from Aescwine and I found him standing by the little pool listening to the night, the frogs under the bank, the crickets in the forest. A fire-fly took his eye, and he followed the dancing flight. He didn't move when he heard me walk up behind him, but he said:

"Is the tale all told?"

"Yes."

I waited for him to ask what the tale was, but he didn't. He picked up a small stone and sent it skipping across the smooth face of the pond. All the frogs under the banks fell silent. One darkly glistening bull went jumping into the water, ungainly and smacking hard on the surface before it dove down and swam away.

Aescwine leaned against an oak, his face a little turned from me. "What's she say her name is?"

"Rowenna Brand's daughter. We've heard of her, ay?"

He nodded curtly, but if he was surprised he didn't say anything about it. A kind of haughtiness was settling on him, Sif; he was moving away from me, though he moved not at all.

"Where are her children?"

He asked that sneering, like he was trying to expose a lie. And I, remembering the bleak emptiness in the young mother's eyes, answered him coldly.

"They're dead."

I didn't see his face, but I saw his shoulders move and tighten; I saw him flinch. He'd held a dead son in his arms; he knew what Rowenna felt now. But that didn't stay his cold anger long. He turned, and no warm light shone in his eyes to soften his twisting scowl.

"What're you going to do about her, Garroc?"

I said that Rowenna could come with us if she wanted to.

He shook his head, and I knew him well enough to know that he was thinking I was a poor fool. He pitched another stone. It fell flat. As flat was his voice.

"You'll remember," he said, "that Hild said this Rowenna had a friend with her. A priest, it was. You'll remember that priest wasn't much fond of Dwarfs."

And so he touched, gingerly, the pain.

"Aescwine, she doesn't think like that."

His bitter wrenching smile hurt to see. "Maybe she's like your red Raighne, ay? A wonder on two legs. And maybe she's not."

A kind of frost was blighting him, Sif, and before my eyes. Northumbria, changed by *Cristens* and a faithless king, was changing Aescwine, shaping him the way the battle scars he wore had never done. I reached to grip his shoulder, but he shrugged away.

He had no more to say, and he didn't go to the fire, but sat with his back to an oak by the water. I left him there, walked the watch, paced around the edges of our camp. It was a long time before I saw that he was asleep. He didn't sleep easy, there by the water. His hands moved and twitched on the short-sword across his knees. His dreams weren't good.

‹17›

In the morning, Sif, it was seen that Rowenna Brand's daughter had changed, like a season turned. The grieving mother who'd clung dazed to Hinthan's arm was gone. In her place stood a young woman whose every gesture spoke of resolve. Something must get done, a destination must be reached. Nothing would daunt her. So completely did she change that you could have thought the other, the grieving mother, had never been.

In Cynnere's arms, comfortably before him on his horse, Rowenna drifted through the green and gold morning, sailed on a tide of sun and breeze into the long afternoon. She spoke sometimes, but not often. Once I heard her ask: "Who are you, Cynnere Brihtwulf's son?"

Cynnere smiled, and he sighed for good measure, likely just to hear her voice. Rowenna sat in the strong circle of Cynnere's arms, but it was she who held him, bound and tight.

"I'm a man of the king's," he said, answering as he had in Saefast.

Rowenna heard this and nodded, but there came a careful look on her, like one who senses that she's not being told a lie, and who knows at the same time that she's not being told the truth.

We rode beneath tall oaks, down-water till the stream became a swift-racing beck, tracked the beck till it changed into a deeper, broader river-feeder. For a while Rowenna watched the path ahead as oaks and wych-elms gave way to misty willows, the ground became softer, and stones wore rich green moss, not stingy lichen rags. When we heard a river's rushing, she said:

"You're not a *Cristen* man, Cynnere."

A sweeping willow made him duck and lean close over her in a manner he didn't mind. "How do you know that?"

She didn't answer, though she would have if Aescwine had given her chance to.

"Because," Aescwine said bitterly, "you've two *dvergr* with you, boy. Reckon it out: *Cristens* have nothing to do with us unless they've got some insult needs spitting out, some dung needs throwing. Or have you forgotten?"

Cynnere flushed, his face dusky beneath summer's brown. High up in the trees a jay screamed, scolding, and Rowenna turned in his arms, the better to see Aescwine.

"Father," she said, naming Aescwine respectfully, "did the monks treat you badly in Haligstane?"

"No, girl, I didn't give 'em a chance to. They're dung-throwers in Saefast, though, ay? Someone taught 'em that, and worse."

Rowenna lost some color, went a little white like she was hearing a judgment.

Aescwine smiled coldly, a twisting, a writhing, a bitter grimace. Silently, he dared her not to look away. She didn't, and she didn't flinch. With a curse Aescwine kicked up his horse, cut hard past Hinthan, hard between Cynnere and me.

Perched behind Hinthan, Wulfhere lost balance as the red mare danced and shied. He'd have fallen if I'd not plucked him from the mare's rump and lifted him to ride before me. Hinthan calmed the mare with a steady hand on the reins, and the soft secret words learned from Aelfgar, the half-magic. He had harder words for Aescwine, well-crafted curses.

Rowenna said no more to Cynnere or to anyone. She rode in silence again, her eyes cast down, as a child harshly chided. Like the lie she sensed and the truth she felt, this seeming of a girl rebuked almost fit Rowenna and it almost didn't.

At noon we came to the river. We rode out of the wildwood and crossed into the sun. We rode south along treeless, grassy banks, down reed-fringed paths past faded clumps of tall yellow-flag, the flowers ageing now, the stalks old but still standing bravely. Aescwine, who'd kept well ahead of us, came back to say that farther on the ground became lower and swampy, with sinkholes and sucking mud.

"But that's only here on this side," he said. "It's higher on the east bank, and the woods come close to the water. There's not much shore on that side, but you can see a long shoal reaching into the water."

He reckoned we could cross to the other side on that shoal and so avoid the swamp. It sounded like a good idea, and he and Hinthan rode out often to test likely crossings. Each time, they met the river's deep channel, a swift drop into white-maned water whirling round stubborn stones. Those tall rocks hoarded flotsam like treasure, clutched close the wrack of storms—root-torn bushes drowned, trees broken and black. Late in the afternoon we'd still not found a ford.

• • •

"There's a storm coming," Hinthan said after he'd urged his mare up out of the water, off the sandy shoal one more time. He pointed north to the pale sky, where no cloud hung. "From there, and soon."

Wulfhere, his scrip slung over his shoulder, held tight to my horse with both hands while the beast watered at the river's edge. He tilted his head far back, squinted at the sky, said there wasn't even one cloud to see there.

"Not one," Hinthan agreed. He pointed to the ground, to where the mounded nests of ants were tall and new. "But the ants know rain's coming. See, they're building up their walls."

Wulfhere grunted suspiciously, as though he wasn't sure whether he was in the presence of witchery or a joke.

"How do you know it's coming from the north?"

Rowenna answered that. "Because that's where the wind is coming from. Child, have you never stood out in the fields and felt the wet wind on your face before ever a cloud was seen?"

"Yes." He shifted the scrip so that he could clutch it tight again, one-handed while he held to my horse. "Of course I have."

But he said it in such a way, Sif, that I wondered whether he was lying, whether he'd spent all his young life within-doors, in the glass-windowed church on his knees in prayer, in the writing-hall bent over his desk inking white vellum and reading what others had written.

Hinthan rumpled Wulfhere's hair with a kind of absent affection, and he said to me, "Garroc, if we're crossing, we'd best do it here. The drop is still steep, but we can make it if we're careful. I don't think we'll find a better place before the storm."

I reckoned he was right about that, and told Cynnere and grim-minded Aescwine that we'd leave soon. The one cheerfully nodded, looking forward to getting horse-aback with Rowenna again; the other spat into the river and walked away down-water.

I watched Aescwine away, the straight angry line of his shoulders, the braced defense that was his back. Once I'd walked off a battle-ground with him, we two drunk with exhaustion, with blood-spilling, and he'd looked like that—back straight, hands fisted, pride and heart the means of moving. I'd been but a little hurt that day, Aescwine had almost died of his wounds. He was as full of health today as he'd been yesterday, but he looked like a bleeding man.

"Aescwine, wait—"

He kept walking, never looked back. I wasn't of a mind to let him get away with that anymore, Sif. Now I must know what bled him. I followed, laid a hand on his shoulder to halt him.

"Leave me alone," he said, eyes on the river, shoulder hard and tense beneath my hand.

He drew breath to say more, but stopped suddenly, head up, alert. The air felt hot, and tight, like a fist clenched. Through the earth rose a rumbling—horsemen riding north along this western river-road.

The riders were close; even *mann-cynn* could feel the ground-thunder, the sound of horses hard-ridden.

Up-river, Cynnere reached for his sword.

Wulfhere still held my horse, listening to something Rowenna said, but he let the reins fall when he saw Cynnere's iron glinting. Hinthan strung his bow swiftly, nocked an arrow ready. Sure that Aescwine was behind me, I ran back to them.

By the riverside Wulfhere raised a trembling hand to cross himself, and his scrip slid from his shoulder, fell to the ground. He didn't retrieve it, and came a panicky look on him then. He'd have bolted, but Rowenna gathered him close to her. She held him as a mother might. She saw the riders now—Dwarfs and Men—a war-storm running at us from the south.

A horse of ours whinnied, the sound pealing loud in the still air.

Behind me I heard wild laughter and jeers, Aescwine's challenge to the approaching foremen. He'd not followed me, stood now braced and ready, sword-iron shining in the sun. I was nearly in reach of Rowenna and Wulfhere when I heard one of the riders cry out in triumph.

"There! By the river!" He pointed to Wulfhere, showed the way with an ashwood spear. "Wulfhere Gytha's son! Get him!"

Iron rang on iron, Aescwine bellowed battle-cries, blood-soaked curses. Hinthan was to horse, bow strung, arrow nocked, the hunter with prey in his sight.

I snatched the *aetheling* right out of Rowenna's arms, flung him onto my horse's back and jumped up behind. Wulfhere screamed in high boyish rage, straining down for the scrip left forgotten a moment too long, the last work of Haligstane. I held him motionless, helpless, where he was.

Rowenna cried out, but only once and choked, for Cynnere had her round the waist and used more haste than gentleness getting her on his horse. But he didn't leap up behind; he chose Aescwine's horse instead. He dug his heels into the beast's flanks, went to put himself between Aescwine and the enemies hemming him round.

The man with the spear shouted orders; more riders broke out from the pack, blocked the river-road north and south. Free of his pack, I knew him. He was more than a man of Cadwalla's. He was Bran, the witch-king's nephew. And all at once I understood that the witch who'd attacked on the moor was no man of Cadwalla's. He was Bran's. At once I knew it—Bran and Peada were working together.

Hinthan cried "Heads down!" and I ducked over Wulfhere as from behind us his arrows whistled, one and two and three. Men screamed, one in rage, arrow-stung; another only once before falling dead to the ground.

A terrible howling rose from the swamp, a wintry wolfish cry. Berserker! I bent low over Wulfhere, holding him tight against me. Berserkers cannot be stopped but by death, Sif; we know it.

But it wasn't a berserker came out of that swamp. It was a wolf, and the beast had fire for a pelt. The witch-wolf had eyes like lightning. Flames leaped around it, from it, setting afire the reeds in the swamp, its every step a hissing. I felt it look at me. I felt it see me. In my arms, Wulfhere shook and the fever on him was fear.

The reed-beds burst afire, the flames feeding and racing ahead for more, flung from one clump of reeds to another. Trapped with the king's son, we two between baneful magic and our own bowman, I pulled Wulfhere close, bent low, wheeled my horse round tight looking for a way out. There was none but the water, the unmeasured channel beyond the shoal.

Flew another of Hinthan's arrows, fell another of Bran's men. And the witch-wolf ran for Hinthan, flames streaming from its mouth like slaver.

I turned my mount broadside, kept Wulfhere to the water. And Hinthan cried—*Garroc, get out of here!*—as I snatched Penda's hand-axe from my belt, ready to put it into a witch's heart again. Not heart did I hit, only shoulder, and the wolf-witch fell, blood pouring like pitch afire.

A Welshman screamed in agony, killed by two thrusts, one Cynnere's, the other Aescwine's. In the river, Rowenna's horse snorted and shied, refused to step off the shallows into the channel. And Cynnere reached a hand to Aescwine, pulled him onto the horse. Friend clasping friend, they rode the beast into the river. At the same moment Rowenna forced her mount into the current.

The fire-wolf staggered to its feet. Snarling, mad-eyed, it came on, came for me as Hinthan raised up a wild war-cry to stop the heart, a sound like storms and eerie baying. One arrow flew past me, took the wolf through the eye, dropped it down dead while Bran cried his men on. Hinthan's arrows killed two men even as a third came at me roaring Wulfhere's name. The boy clung hard to me, shaking in terror, both arms round my neck to leave my hands free. In one I held the reins, in the other my keen-edged Harm.

That long-hafted axe swept the sword—and the hand gripping—from a black-bearded Dwarf; on the back-stroke it swept him from this middle-world. My horse slithered in the mud, backward off the bank, staggered on the shoal. Hinthan got himself between me and the witches, loosing bolt and bolt.

Bran howled loud, a long and tearing sound. I hoped it was a death-cry, but it was no more than rage-song. He tore an arrow from his shoulder and he roared, "I know you, boy! I'll be the one to kill you!" And swift on that oath, with his blood still pouring, the witch hurled a cry to summon his own baleful magic.

Came a storm then, and not one Hinthan had foreseen.

The sky rained red hail, biting embers. My shirt caught fire. Wulfhere beat at it, shoulders and arms; his own kindled in small places, and his hair. Though I leaned far over him, I couldn't protect him.

"Run to the water!" Hinthan shouted. "Garroc! I can hold them! Run to the water!"

I saw Rowenna's horse and Cynnere's flinging all their strength against the frothing, galloping river, striving for the shore. Riderless, those horses, and they were losing the race with the river.

Behind me Bran raged; his dire magic flared into flames, fire raining down. Again I heard Hinthan's war-cry rising, loud and laughing challenge as Bran's men closed in round him like a noose hungry to hang.

And I, with the king's son held tight in my arms, had no choice but to take the chance Hinthan gave me and hope luck held for us both. I heeled my horse, kicked hard, forced the screaming beast into the cauldron of the river.

I lost seat fast, didn't try to cling to reins or tie my luck to the horse's, the poor beast caught by the current and shrieking in terror. But I held to Wulfhere, grasped hard the king's son. I had him under the arms, gripped him round his back, would not let the river cleave us apart.

I had my way about that for all of a moment before something panicked the boy—the roar of the water, the screams of a drowning horse. Or maybe it was the fiery rain did it. Like whip-lashing, it burned through clothing to sear skin.

Wulfhere went stiff and, stiff, the water couldn't hold him up. The unyielding weight of him threatened to sink us both like stones roped one to the other. The river pulled at him, tugged with cold hands, unarguable strength. I could do nothing but cling to him and try to keep his head up.

There was never a chance that I could swim to the far wooded bank. Even alone, unburdened, that wasn't possible. Nor could I keep us out of the way of the tall rocks, the rising stones hoarding drowned treasures—bush and branch, a nest of leaves, a luckless young doe with head flung back, neck-broken, dead eyes wide and staring. For amusement, the current spun us past the first of the rocks, hurled us past a second. But there was another, a high thrusting pile of stone. Choking on a mouthful of river, I hit it hard. The blow blasted the breath from me and with it all the water in me.

I lost Wulfhere.

The river reeled him away; the greedy spate stole him, left me behind dazed and pinned against the rock by force of flood. I hadn't even heard him cry out, only saw his eyes go wide in mute terror as he reached for me, desperately lunged, and lost me.

Where does a drowning man find the strength to scream, to rage, to hurl curses at the cold grey foe? Ay, well, it doesn't have to do with courage, be sure of that, Sif. To dying men, nothing is at risk.

So curse I did, spitting water and spewing oaths. And then came the swell, rising under me, lifting me, tearing me from the painful shelter of stone to fling me out into the flood.

At last came the storm Hinthan had foreseen, great sheets of rain pouring down from the sky. I had one glimpse through water-stung eyes before the storm closed around me and the river took me again. One look at the wooded west bank and two boys there, close together astride a soaking horse—Hinthan and Wulfhere.

River and storm, they granted me only that, briefer than the space between heartbeats, before cold hands pulled me all the way down, clasped me to a stony breast.

‹18›

I was very thirsty.

Someone took me by the shoulders and carefully turned me face-up to the sky. All of me burst afire with pain. I had no breath to scream, but the one kneeling beside me saw my face. He didn't touch me again. He gave me a little water and seemed pleased when I swallowed it.

"Can you hear me, Ghosts-Skald?"

I could hear him. Morning sun stabbed my eyes, and I saw Merewal as a darkness against that glare.

"My foster-son?"

Wulfhere's brother leaned close, and when he'd made sense of the harsh groan and gasp that was my voice, he shook his head and said he'd seen no one but me.

"And you look like you've been here at least since the storm."

"When . . . ?"

"The storm? Two days ago. We didn't find Hinthan along here, or anyone besides you. What happened?"

I had no more strength. I closed my eyes, and Merewal laid a hand on my shoulder, gently.

"I'm sorry," he said. "We're going to move you now."

Then he called some of his men and told them that they must carry me away from the river. They did that, Sif, and I don't like to remember more about it.

When next I came back to myself, I lay naked but for the god-rune round my neck, warm and dry on a thick-stuffed mattress, between smooth linen sheets, beneath well-woven blankets. My bed was in a fine airy loft and near a window where stout wooden shutters stood open to the cool air. Outside, the new moon—the Harvester's silver scythe—shone above the branches of a broad oak. By its light I saw my clothes, clean and folded neatly, near to hand. Upon them lay my long-knife. It seemed that no other gear of mine—not long-hafted Harm, not even my belt-pouch with my way-gathered treasures—had survived the flood.

Merewal was near by, and he told me that I'd been sunk in sickness for near to four days, but that things were looking much better for me now. He had some bread and broth, and the king's son handled me carefully when he helped me to sit, to eat and drink. I needed his help; the rocks in the river were kin, but they weren't kind. They'd battered and bruised, peeled away skin as though hungry for bone. They'd broken three of my ribs as though, after all, bone wouldn't do and they must have marrow.

I didn't have much to say to Merewal. I wouldn't mention Hinthan again, or ever speak of Wulfhere. Nor did Merewal press me to talk. He kept me company while I ate, and he told me that I was his guest in a hall that used to belong to a *thegn* of Eadwine's.

"A fine hall," he said. "And mine—larders, byres, and barns. The man who built it is too dead to argue."

When I asked whether he'd be spending much time here, he said he wouldn't. He offered no more, and I didn't ask. We were quiet then, and he watched me with sideways looks, as one full of questions. But Merewal didn't ask his questions, and after a time he bade me good night, said that he slept in a room at the other side of the stairs. I must call if I wanted anything.

I didn't sleep much that night, Sif. And wakeful, I worried about Hinthan and Wulfhere. They were alive, I knew it. So were Cynnere and Aescwine. I'd have heard ghosty voices to tell me otherwise. Beyond that, I knew nothing and feared everything.

It was me trained Hinthan in the arts of scout-craft and war-craft, and so I knew he wouldn't stay long where foemen had attacked. He'd move on, and he'd keep to the course we agreed on—south into Mercia, west into Wales—as long as he could. And if he hoped that I was yet alive, he'd trust me to follow when I could. If hope failed him, he'd do what he must to get Wulfhere safely to Gardd Seren.

If hope failed him . . . I hated to think on that. By now, hope must have failed. How could he think I was still alive?

At noon the next day Merewal came and sat in the window by my bed. He had an earthen cup brimmed with wine, and he had his unasked questions. I pushed myself up to sit. I was slow at that, hindered by tight bandages bound round and round my chest, but I managed without his offered help. When I'd got comfortable, he gave me the wine.

"Ghosts-Skald, we have things to talk about."

I held the cup in both hands, drank watching the sun lay gold on the green-dyed wool blankets. *Now he'll ask his questions*, I thought.

But he didn't, not then. He spoke about the war, how it was when Penda and Cadwalla took Eoferwic. Tales of iron and fire, he told; of fallen towers, and halls aflame, streets running with blood. He told me that walled Eoferwic didn't fall easily. Many died on both sides before Faith-Breaker fled the war-field, the burning city.

"And two of Eadwine's sons are dead of that fighting, his youngest and his eldest. There's only the middle two left, those twin boys of his, and they're still fighting Osric. Penda owns Eoferwic now," Merewal said. "His northern hall, he calls it. Eadwine's fled, but there are others—*Cynings* and *thegns*—who'd like to take Eoferwic back. So my father's got the hall, but he has to fight for it every day."

I turned the cup in my hands, watched the wine rise up and fall back in tiny blood-red waves. "Did Cadwalla have nothing to say about that?"

Merewal laughed, but bitterly. "Cadwalla thought it would be better to go raging around the countryside as he's been doing."

His grey eyes grew dark, gloomy above that red beard of his. I swallowed more wine.

"Garroc, there's not a Welshman will admit that turning berserker is anything but a curse we Saxons have to bear—like it's some sickness our fathers brought from the North. And I've heard a song or two of yours—

Ware the witch-king's battle-play   his war-rage
in fire leaping!

"Witch-king. I'm thinking it's time you changed that name, Garroc. He's a berserker-king, that one. If he could but stay to one course, this war would be over now, Eadwine forgotten by winter."

Then he said no more. Maybe he thought—belatedly—that it wasn't his place to talk of re-making a song to the skald who made it. Maybe he thought, too late, that it wasn't his place to talk about berserkers to a man who'd been one.

Outside, the wind whispered through the oak, rustling leaves, and I drank some more wine. He couldn't stay quiet long, red Merewal. Un-still, he drummed his fingers on the windowsill, a small thunder.

"Or maybe Cadwalla *is* keeping to one course—his own. After he left Eoferwic, he split his force, sent Bran to put everything to sword and flame here in the south while he keeps the east to plunder."

I said I'd heard something about Bran being here, and he nodded grimly.

"It'd be hard not to. And maybe Cadwalla's fighting my father and Eadwine, both. Each farm he burns, each town, each standing field of wheat, is one Penda can't use in the winter. Every man he kills is one less for Eadwine's army. But I don't know what good he thinks he's doing himself by killing all the rest—the old men, the women, the little children."

Never think that red Merewal wasn't a hard-handed soldier, Sif. Fierce in fighting, Penda's son; in battle-rage most deadly, and when rage spilled past the borders of the war-ground, those who met him had no reason to hope for mercy. He taught that lesson to the monks of Maed Jesu. It must have been very bad, what he'd seen of Cadwalla's war-work.

"Merewal," I said. "What about Eadwine? Where's he got to?"

Thunder grew quicker, the drumbeat of his fingers. "He's gone to his wife's brother in Cent, looking for more men. What army he had after Eoferwic he sent to his western border to help the last of his sons. Things aren't going too good there."

"Osric," I said.

"The Outlaw. And that's why your Erich War Hawk is back in his Marches defending the border by Powys. Osric's had it all his own way this year with everyone fighting here in the north and east. Now he's made a few reaches into our Mercia."

My heart beat hard, thickly with fear. Hinthan was running south to Powys even now. And Lydi—where would keeping a promise to Owain take her?

Merewal reached into his shirt, pulled out a pouch, spilled the contents on the bed—agate mantle-clasp, two halves of an emerald-studded golden arm-ring, Peada's silver wrist-bracer.

"We found this pouch when we found you, Garroc. I could hardly pry it from your hand."

Sun winked from the gold-gripped agate as Merewal pushed it toward me. Wotan's stone, the journey-stone, greeted me like an old friend when I touched it.

We travel, dvergr, ay? Alone, together, we journey. And we find our ways back to each other. . . .

I took the clasp and took up my shirt, pinned the journey-stone to the breast.

Merewal poked at the two halves of Gytha's gemmed arm-ring,

made sunlight dance from emerald to hopeful emerald. But he let the gold lie, instead took up Peada's silver wrist-bracer with its enameled red ravens wheeling round a black onyx sun.

"Ghosts-Skald, how'd you come by this of my brother's?"

I told him I'd taken it from a witch, a Welshman. He wasn't happy to hear that.

"Did the witch follow you from Eoferwic?"

I didn't say anything, and he laughed.

"I know you left Eoferwic before the siege, Garroc. And I know you had Hinthan with you. I think you had Cynnere Brihtwulf's son and Aescwine Ivaldi's son with you too. I reckon it you're on some business of my father's."

I admitted to that. And I said, "The witch was dead when I got close enough to be able to ask him his business, and the ghost of him didn't feel like talking to me."

A breeze passed softly through the window, brought the sound of a sheep's flat-voiced bleating from some distant graze. I thought of Haligstane, the quiet cloister, the church spilling prayer-song on the morning we'd left red Raighne and his brothers to Cadwalla's doomsmen. And I remembered what Erich War Hawk had to say about Merewal, that no one knew how he felt about the matter of Wulfhere, whether he resented the boy or would stand by his young kinsman, his father's heir.

"Merewal, why are you here, so far from the king?"

He smiled in such a way that I knew he would let me change the subject, but only for now.

"Peada left us soon after Eoferwic fell. He took all his army with him. My father wasn't happy about that, but he wasn't surprised. And it's true, Garroc—we all felt better without Peada skulking around at our backs." He dropped the wrist-bracer onto the bed. "But we didn't think he'd gone to Cadwalla. Though maybe we should have considered that earlier, ay? In the spring at Hordstede, when you challenged him."

I turned the silver bracer over, once and then again. "I didn't see Peada talking to Cadwalla that day in spring. It was Bran."

Merewal nodded and grimly accepted the difference. He knew his brother, and he was canny enough to know that an alliance between Peada and Bran meant trouble for their kinsmen.

"These are strange times, Ghosts-Skald. Kin abandon kin, and sons hate their fathers so deeply that treachery is nothing to them but a tool." He left the window, paced restlessly. "My father's set me on Peada's trail."

"Are you hunting to kill?"

"Penda's left that up to me. But he'd probably rather I brought him back alive."

The afternoon sunlight fell bright on the bed, sliding along Peada's silver wrist-bracer, his gift to a witch. And Merewal stood looking at me, his hands restless.

"Garroc, you've seen Gytha's boy?"

He spoke the name awkwardly, and I let it hang between us. The last I'd heard, Penda hadn't told anyone but Erich the name of Wulfhere's mother. Maybe that was changed now, but I didn't know. Not knowing, I said nothing.

Merewal turned his back to me, stood at the window looking out. I saw his shoulders twitch in dry, silent laughter.

"Tell me, then—did you get him to a safe place, as you promised my father?"

Again I didn't answer.

Low, Merewal said, "What would I have to do to get you to tell me where the boy is, Garroc?"

"I don't know. No one's tested me yet."

Came a chill creeping into the sunny room. In me, my heart beat harder as it does when danger is near. The set of Merewal's shoulders, the way his two fists hung like weighted weapons at his sides, made me fear he'd be the one to test me. His back was yet to me; I could reach my long-knife. I could fight for a little while if I had to.

Merewal's fists opened, the hard square stance eased. Still, he kept his back to me. A breeze drifted past the window, smelling of river and tree and his sweat.

"Do you think Wulfhere Gytha's son is worth all the hunting and hiding?"

"Wulfhere Penda's son," I said. "As to his worth, I didn't set it, your father did."

And now I was weary, with talking, with this game. I tried to settle more comfortably in the bed, but I moved too quickly and Merewal heard my grunt of pain. He turned from the window to help me. He did that carefully, and he put the pieces of the golden arm-ring and the silver wrist-bracer back into the pouch and set it on my piled clothing. He settled the wool blankets around me, but his eyes were flat, unreadable all the while.

When he was gone I took the long-knife from the pile of my clothing and hid it under the blankets.

I woke in the middle-night, my sleep suddenly broken by streaming red light, the spill from a torch in Merewal's left hand. In his other hand he carried a keen-bladed short-sword. Unseen beneath blankets, I gripped the hilt of my long-knife as, silent, he stood in the doorway. Behind him lay darkness, ahead the ruddy light of his torch, and he stood between one and the other, as a man who hangs between two choices. One of the choices was to force a betrayal on me.

He chose swiftly, with such a wrenched look on him that I knew he hadn't chosen lightly. He upped the sword and showed me something else—a mail-shirt. The iron blade and the woven rings gleamed like gold in the light.

"I've had word that an army's been seen west of here, burning and killing but not with witch-weapons. Sounds like Peada, doesn't it? I'm leaving in the morning. You're welcome to ride with me."

"No." I smiled a liar's smile, and didn't let go my knife. "I'm not able to ride, with you or on my own way. I'd be grateful if you let me stay here a day or two yet."

He nodded as though he'd expected the answer, but he didn't leave. He came into the room, bracketed the torch, and went to sit in the window. The sword and the ring-shirt he rested on his knees, and now I saw that this gear would fit a Dwarf well.

"It's a hard place, this Northumbria, Garroc. It won't be good for you to be alone, a man of Penda's, and *dvergr*."

I said that I reckoned I'd be all right if I didn't go around shouting that I was Penda's. "As for being *dvergr,* there's not much I can do for that. We are what we are, ay?"

"Do you know where your kindred have gone?"

So Aescwine had asked, often and often. The asking had blighted him, chilled the warm heart of him.

"I don't know where my kindred are," I said coldly. "Maybe they've decided not to stay where old friends can be convinced to turn against them for no good reason."

"You don't think a god's a good reason?"

"Not much of one." I let go the long-knife. "And I've got no good opinion of a god who bids folk to turn on friends."

He couldn't let it go. "Is that the god's saying, or the saying of his followers?"

"That seems to depend on which follower you're listening to, and I'm not much interested in sorting over the sayings of a god his own followers don't seem to understand."

Merewal accepted that with a wry grin, and I knew that he wondered why any of it interested him. And then he asked wheth-

er I would accept company, some men of his to ride with me
when I was well enough to leave here.

Maybe he meant that in a kindly way, Sif, offering friends to go
with me into Dwarf-reft Northumbria so that I wouldn't have to
ride alone where *mann-cynn* didn't love my kind. But I felt it that
the matter of Wulfhere still crouched between us, the unanswered
questions. That might be a kinsman's concern, and it might be a
foeman's. I didn't know, and I wouldn't take chances.

"Merewal, I thank you, but I won't deprive you of soldiers you
might need."

Again he smiled wryly, and he said that he hoped his father
knew how well served he was. Then he put the sword and the
byrnie by my clothes. He must have seen that my long-knife
wasn't where he'd left it, but he said nothing about that and left
with no other word.

Now I didn't go back to sleep. I was very careful to stay awake,
to listen till I heard Merewal pass back to the stairs and beyond to
the other loft room. When I heard no noise but the wind and the
crickets and the distant cry of a hunting owl, I dressed silently,
wore the byrnie under my shirt to keep the ringing mail quiet
against skin and bandages. Then I took up my weapons and the
small pouch with its way-gotten treasure, went quietly down to
the hall where Merewal's men lay sleeping.

Not one of those was *dvergr*. I was curious about that, Sif.
Never think I didn't wonder where all the Dwarfs were who used
to be in red Merewal's army. But there was no way to know, and
no time to stop and think about it.

No one so much as stirred as I passed through the hall, and I
saw no guard near the stable. I didn't think—even for a moment—
that Merewal had become careless. But I didn't know whether he
was making things easy for me, or whether he had a man set to
follow me to his brother. Still, I could stay here no longer. I hoped
that his gifts to me were tokens of friendship, and I helped myself
to another. I got a swift horse from the stable, and left Merewal's
Northumbrian hall.

I took no war-horse from Merewal's stable, but a slender mare,
the color of fog and smooth-gaited whether she went at a trot or
at the top of her speed. I rode south, and slowly; I was recovering,
but hadn't yet got all well. I followed the river, the traveller's
natural road, until the wildwood crowded so close against the
edge of the land that I must go inward to find a path, follow the
river by her voice. So would Hinthan have done in his southward

ride. From time to time I had a look over my shoulder, but I never saw Merewal's men riding, heard no whisper of anyone on my trail.

At midday the forest fell away to sudden meadows where *torrs* and the barrows of giants rose up darkly against the bright sky. As on the high windy moors, this row made a straight line pointing south. I was all day going past the hills and the barrows, for soon after I passed the last in the line, I saw another row, and beyond that others. Each marched south, and I beside them. But not close beside; the wind there ever sang dark dirges in languages I didn't know.

That night I lay under countless stars, well away from the barrows. I lit no fire; I didn't want to be so easily seen. And so I had no supper, for though the river was close, I didn't have stomach for eating fish raw. I wished I'd taken some food from Merewal's hall, but I only wished for a while. Hunger didn't keep me awake.

Asleep, I dreamed.

There was a high place, a dark place crowned with ruined buildings. Reft of roofs, the buildings had only sagging stone walls to ward heaved floors. Most of the many doorways led to nowhere. Windows stared blindly. One tower rose up from among the battered floors, the burst walls, like the last broken tooth in an old man's head. In that high and dark place the wind shivered and sobbed.

I heard a stranger's familiar voice beneath that mournful wind. *Skald! Skald . . .*

And I heard other voices, countless cries, rising and falling, swelling and sinking. The ruins were ghost-ridden, but that sea of voices didn't drown the one I knew.

Skald! Skald, find me!

And now there was a hunter in the tower, and he sat in the highest window. As I were within the tower room, I saw only his back, long and lean. He had a strung bow ready and near to hand. If the hunter heard the swelling voices, he gave no sign. I knew, as you know in dreams what can't be known waking, that all his mind and heart were bent upon searching north. I knew, as you know in dreams, that he was looking for me.

Long sunset light shone on the land, red-gold and heavy with age. The purple sky was just showing early stars when a kestrel came winging down the northern sky. In dream I knew that the little hawk had been searching, and that she'd not found me.

She trimmed her wings to bank and turn. She didn't fly to the hunter, and he didn't offer his wrist. He leaned dangerously far out the tower window to watch her come to ground somewhere below.

And the voice of a stranger-ghost whispered, *Skald! Skald, ride south to Tŵr Du and find us!*

I woke suddenly and hard. Hunter and sparrow-hawk, I knew who these were. I'd know Hinthan if I saw only the hand of him reaching from a shadow. I knew Lydi even winged. They were together, somewhere. And with them was a ghost who'd haunted me with very few words since Midwinter Night.

I didn't see the threads of fate's weavings, Sif, so much as feel them knotting in my belly, like a fear I didn't yet know the name of. On my skin a cool dawn breeze chilled sweat. I couldn't call back the dream; behind closed eyes I couldn't see but the last fading images—the hunter in his high window, the kestrel sailing down the purple sky.

And in me, as that image turned to mist and faded, a ghost whispered, *Find us! Skald, find us on Tŵr Du!*

I got to my feet groaning, stiff and missing the soft bed in Merewal's loft. It was no easy thing to get up on the mare's back, and I didn't think her paces were so gentle now. I knew to ride south, for the hunter had been looking north for me. But south is a big place, and I didn't know enough about this Northumbria to know where a place called Tŵr Du might be. I could but trust that the familiar stranger wouldn't let me go astray.

I rode through meadows until I came within sight of a small stead. Old and empty it looked, and nearby were ranked new wooden crosses. Swiftly cut, their ends raw and unworked, the *Cristen* burial signs stood up dark against the sky. War had been here and the last living hadn't stayed but to mark their dead. Still, I took no chance that I'd cross paths with unwelcoming *mann-cynn*. I went wide around the fields and the small cot, went back into the wildwood. There I found apple trees heavy with fruit, the wild sons of orchards planted hundreds of years before by Roman Men.

In the wood I had no barrows to follow, only winding wild-wood paths. I made my way carefully and kept an eye on the sun so that twisty forest ways could not mistake me. At noon I saw the first toothy groundwork of an ancient Roman ruin. Not the dreamed tower, this, only a small fort by the look of it, vine-cloaked now, home to sparrows and hares and squirrels. I found the shadowy etching of an equally ancient Roman street, overgrown by the forest so that only a few pave-stones could be seen here and there, picked out by glint. The ghosty road went southward, and I followed.

At day's end I saw another tumbled fort. This ruin had a few more courses to its walls. It was like to the ruin Hinthan and I had sheltered in the day we'd left Gardd Seren; like in more than shape. Beneath the litter of ages lay a tile floor, shattered by time. Still I could see the pictures made in the floor by tiles that had all but lost their color to age—the cross of gold, and the white dove.

There, as I slept, the ghost found me. In dream he called again.

Skald! Skald, come to Tŵr Du! Find us!

In the misty morning I followed the ghost-road south again, and it ended when the wildwood did, at the edge of a clearing, the foot of a great stony hill rising. Red as the best gold, that hill, for dawnlight shone on each mist-dampened stone, glittering. At the top, like a broken crown, sat the ruins I'd twice dreamed of—curved walls of varying broken height, empty windows like blind eyes staring. And I saw doorways that might once have led to paths down the hill, paved ways going out from the ruin to other *straets,* paths that now ended suddenly at the edge of a drop where the ground had long ago broken away. From the center of the ruin rose an unroofed tower.

Hinthan stood in the highest window, straight-backed, his dark hair blowing back in the morning breeze. He held an arrow loosely against taut bowstring, a watch-ward ready against all comers. And he called me a greeting, gladly but not too much surprised to see me.

"Good morning, Garroc! Stay there, I'll be right down."

I slid down off the mare, took a step onto the path; and Hinthan, his voice a little harder, said, "Stay right there, Garroc. You can't come up here."

I looked up then, saw his arrow nocked at the ready. I took another step, not to gainsay him, but to see him better.

"Don't come closer, Garroc." He widened his stance and raised his drawn bow. "Don't."

The morning breeze touched me coldly, Sif, like a breath out of nightmare where everything warmly familiar twists into the strange and threatening. And maybe I moved, though I only meant to speak. However it was, Hinthan loosed his arrow. The shaft sped whistling to hit and hum in the ground at my feet.

"I mean it, Garroc! Don't move!"

He meant it indeed. Very exactly put, that arrow; like a warning clearly spoken. I heard him running, and cursing someone who'd got in his way. And now—suddenly!—I heard more, the countless voices of ghosts. Not loud, the voices; soft and distant, like the sound of the sea when you're too far away for sight of it.

◄19►

Dawn haze drifted up from the dewy ground, rising around the foot of the crowned hill, grey turning to rosy-gold in the new light. The morning sang with the rowdy challenge of hooded crows, the quicker voices of whinchat and stonechat. Fell once, from the heights, the cry of a golden eagle far from his moorland home.

And ghosts sighed and moaned and whispered, like the far-distant sea, but I didn't hear the familiar voice of the stranger-ghost. Still, he was near. I felt him like a brooding storm-threat, a chill tingling on the skin.

Beyond the hill's shoulder, a cloud of grey doves lifted, wings beating like small thunder. The mare snorted and sidled. I reached for her too quickly, cursed aloud in pain, and lost her as she went dancing away. Then came a low note, a calling-song, the half-magic I'd never been able to learn. Hinthan came round the shoulder of the hill and the mare turned her head, ears cocked. He whistled again and she went to him, picking her way daintily over small stones tumbled from the hill.

"Welcome to Deorcdun, Garroc." Hinthan took the mare's reins, and he looked at me from beyond the warning arrow, smiling a little to say he was sorry. "Or Twr Du, as they say in Wales."

Ay, Deorcdun, Sif. Twr Du. Each name meant the same thing—a dark down, a black tower, a lightless height. Neither name had a good feel to it.

"Hinthan, where's Lydi?"

He glanced over his shoulder at the dark hill. "With Owain."

I looked up at what had till now been an ashy smudge on a map, and I had to crane my neck to see all the way to the dawn-gilded top of the ruin. It hurt to do that, and Hinthan, reaching to pluck back his arrow, saw that pain.

"It's all right," I said. "Some ribs are broken, but I'm healing up."

But he must touch me to know the truth, clasp my hand, grip my shoulders. He must finally hug me to feel my heart beating. That close, I felt his own heart racing in swift dread.

"It's all right," I said again. "I'm all right, Hinthan. Now take back your arrow. I'll stay here and listen to what you have to say."

He plucked the arrow, and said he was sorry to have loosed it. "But I was afraid you wouldn't listen to me. You can't go up to Deorcdun yet."

"So it seems. Tell me why."

"I will, but not here." A little, mischief glinted in his eye. "But you can ask me about Wulfhere if you want."

"No need," I said. "He's been with you, boy mine."

He glowed to hear that praise from me, and then his pleasure faded. "Garroc, we haven't seen Cynnere or Aescwine or Rowenna." He widened his stance, bracing for bad news. "Have you . . . heard them?"

"No, but—"

"You heard the ghost-wind." And when I glanced up at the tower, "It comes from there, but you won't have heard their ghosts on that wind. You haven't heard the ghosts of them in you?"

"No."

He nodded, once and firmly. "Then they're not dead. Now come with me. I've got something you need."

"If it's sight of Lydi, youngling, you're right about the need."

"Oh, well, yes," he said, pleased with himself again. "I've got her too."

The dawn-gold slid away from Deorcdun's broken crown as the day's light spread out across the land to lower places. Now the hill was a dark height against the sky.

"And you've got Owain," I said.

"And him. Wulf and I came here because it looked like a good place to wait out a storm. Lydi and Owain were here already. It looked like chance, Garroc." He laughed a little, grimly. "And I told Wulf that it was only blind luck that I found friends here, but . . . it wasn't chance."

"And what have you told Lydi about Wulfhere?"

"Not much, but it was all the truth."

Now his eyes kindled again with silent laughter. He'd told Lydi the same tale I'd told Cynnere and Aescwine, that we'd been sent to bring this boy home to foster-kin. "And I told her we found him in a *Cristen* monastery, and that he's got some strange ideas about things and people. But you know Lydi—she knows when she's only getting the skimmings of things.

"Now come with me, Garroc. We can talk in a better place than here."

He whistled softly to the mare, and she followed peacefully behind as he took me away from the path up to the ruins, round the shoulder of the hill and behind.

The ghost-wind never calmed, and the ghost who'd called me here never spoke.

There was a wondrous treasure behind the ruin-crowned hill, Sif—a hot-spring. These are rare, more often heard of than seen. Like magic, the hot water comes bubbling up from the earth, and sometimes right in the middle of a deep pool that would otherwise be cold and cramping as the snow-melt that feeds it. Then the icy pool becomes so warm that steam rises up, and anyone who gets into that bath finds it a sorry thing to have to get out again.

There by the pool, grey rock rose in tall walls on three sides and, rising, became the foot of the hill, then flank and shoulder, and at last crowned head. The ruins made a horseshoe shape, the open end to the south so that the dark staring windows of the lower ruins and the high tower overlooked the pool. And all around the pool the ground was stone, hard and black and very warm. Beyond and below, the wildwood fell swiftly away in green slopes unrolling. At the edge of the woods two horses were tethered, grazing on dewy grass in the last of night-dark gathered beneath the trees.

I looked for Lydi, and saw only Wulfhere. The king's son tended a campfire by the stony pool, and he sat among saddles and scrips—his own from Haligstane among them, though I didn't know how he'd got it back. He looked up when he heard us coming.

"Wulf," Hinthan said. "Come take my foster-father's horse."

The *aetheling* did as he was bid, took the reins from Hinthan's hand and led the mare away.

"How is it with him, Hinthan?"

"He's all right. And I'll say this for him, he's no sniveler when things get hard. He knows how to set to and do what needs doing once you tell him what that is."

At the pool's edge Hinthan laid my weapons by, and his grey eyes lighted with interest when I told him how I'd come by the sword and the ring-mail.

"How'd Merewal seem? Friendly?"

"Friendly enough to me, as he's always been. Ay, well. That sells him short of his worth. He found me by the riverside and he took good care of me. But I couldn't reckon him on the matter of Wulfhere. I'm not sure he knows himself how he feels."

"You'd think he would," said my boy, and he showed all his youth with those words, for the young aren't so skilled at seeing what lies between black and white.

Hinthan helped me get my shirt off, and the wink of the gold-edged mantle-clasp caught his eye. He rubbed his thumb on the smooth face of the agate, his good gift, Wotan's map-marked stone, before he tossed the shirt aside. And he whistled low, admiring the mail-shirt as he helped me off with it, but he forgot about that richness of mail when he saw the most of me bandaged and the rest of me bruised almost to black. Very carefully, he loosened the bandages, the sun-bleached wool-cloth once snowy and soft, now turned stiff and grey with sweat.

When the last length was unwound, pain like a storm dropped me to my knees. Hinthan went down on his heels beside me, held me and hushed me till the storm passed.

I could do no more to get myself undressed; strength had run out of me with the pain. What I couldn't do, Hinthan did for me and he soon had me resting against black stone warmed for countless years in the wondrous pool. The water was like a blessing, like a healing hand. By the time Wulfhere returned, pain had retreated to a sullen distance.

The *aetheling* asked if I wanted some water to drink. I said no, and he came and sat closer, right at the edge of the pool.

He reached out to lightly touch a bruise. You'd have thought by the look of simple wonder on him, Sif, that he'd not considered till then that I might bleed or bruise as easily as anyone else.

A breeze sprang up from the south, from the wildwood. It smelled of green and growing things, of darkly sweet earth still damp from the night. I let the water warm and soothe and lull me. Soon I was drifting toward sleep.

"Wulf," Hinthan said, low. "Get your sling; it's time to go find some breakfast."

I tried to wake enough to tell Hinthan that we two had some things to talk about—the stranger-ghost who'd led me, the dream I'd followed, the ghost-wind whispering down from the heights.

But I didn't wake, and I didn't hear whether Wulfhere answered him. I heard only the voice of the mother-earth. In the bones and blood of me, I felt her speak.

Rest you, dvergr *my son . . .*

Before that voice even the ghost-wind, at last, fell silent.

I awoke long hours after Hinthan and Wulfhere went hunting breakfast. The light on the land was old and fading; I'd slept all the day away. In that golden light, I saw Lydi standing at the foot of the road up to Deorcdun. I didn't see her face; she was cloaked and hooded, but what could be seen hinted at her loveliness—the slender back, the whisper of a curved hip as a breeze hugged the cloak to her and plucked it away again.

"My Lydi, have you come to tell me why I can't go up to Deorcdun?"

She caught her breath, startled. I pushed up to sit on the edge of the pool, and that didn't hurt too much. I dressed, but not before she saw the bruises, the dark tracks of pain, and she came swiftly to kneel beside me. She touched me, a light touch bruises never felt, and her hand was warm. It could get warmer; her touch could reach deeper to heal, but I took her hand and held it, stopping her.

There are witches, my Sif, and there are witches. You don't find many among the Saxons, one or two now and then. We fight shy of magic and few of us try to learn the wonder-craft. Most witches are among the Welsh folk, and when tales are told, the most are told about the terrible warrior-witches who are filled with the power-lust and ready to use their magic to have what they must. But they aren't the only witches in the world. There are others, quiet folk who live in quiet places, in glens and gardens, in peaceful corners of the wildwood, laboring silently. They are healers, and in healing they lend strength where it will make a difference, and with magic they do what broken bone or torn flesh can only do over time. It costs to do that, the fee the strength lent, for we who are not witches don't know how to give back what we borrow.

And so I stopped Lydi when she reached to heal, for I'd got well of worse wounds than this.

"Save your magic, my girl. Nothing's broken beyond fixing, and what is broken is nearly healed up now."

Down from the dark hill came the grim-song of a hundred hundred ghosts mourning and moaning. I could tell no one voice from another. Lydi heard none of it, but she knew what I looked like, hearing.

"I came here dream-led, Lydi."

My Sif, I'm no healer like her, to be able to touch and feel if a person is well or in pain, but ten years had taught me how to know her. Lydi said, "It wasn't my dream," and I knew it almost before the words were spoken.

"Hinthan dreamed," she said. "With help."

"From you?"

"From a ghost, a witch. There's only one magic allowed here."

Lydi tried to take her hand from mine, but I held it, kept it, wouldn't let her go even that far away from me as she made her admission.

"Garroc, that ghost-witch is much stronger than me. I can't work any magic in the tower because he won't let me."

As the little kestrel, winging in dream, must alight outside the tall tower though her friend the hunter waited for her within. In that dream was a truth I'd not seen till now. Lydi had been bested at some contest of wills. She's been shown the limits of her strength and the number of her weaknesses. She couldn't hide that from me, even in the hood and the shadows.

"I didn't want Hinthan to do that dreaming, Garroc. But he offered himself, and I couldn't stop him. The ghost took what he needed."

So he'd offered himself at Winwaed, hand and heart to the cause of a king whose son had betrayed him. This was Hinthan, and neither Lydi nor I had cause to be surprised.

A breeze came wandering, smelling of stone and wildwood. It ruffled the water in the rock pool between us, blurring our reflections as I reached for Lydi's hood. She raised her hand to stop me, but when our fingers touched, she changed her mind and let me push the hood back onto her shoulders.

How changed, her face! Brighter, keener, free of the great beauty of her hair. The long spill of gleaming midnight, heavy and thick and soft, was no more. The shearing still looked blunt and new, and Lydi's hair only barely passed her neck, lay in curls along nape and cheek and temple. I stared, wordless, as she leaned a little forward to see into the mirror of the water. Now I could only see her face in reflection, and her eyes were like wide and deep wells, shining like amethysts, softly with hoarded light.

"Lydi—" I stopped, for when she looked up I saw tears on her cheeks.

"I cut it the day I left Gardd Seren. Some of it I plaited and gave to Branwen, some I gave to Aelfgar." She smiled then, remembering. "The thickest braid of it, for he wanted it. The rest I scattered all round the gardens, all round the wildwood, for the birds to find in spring."

She did this in the hope that these tokens would bring her home again, with wish and wonder-craft woven into the strands. So she said, but I felt it that she wasn't sure whether her quiet magic was strong enough to do what she hoped it would. Here on Deorcdun, here at Tŵr Du, my witch had been taught to doubt her strength.

Lydi got to her feet, and now she threw off her cloak, impatiently cast it aside. It was only the hiding hood she'd wanted, but she didn't need that now. She wore an old green-dyed shirt of Hinthan's and trews of tough homespun, clothes that had stopped fitting him two years ago, clothes she liked best for riding. I cupped her face in my two hands. As gently as ever I'd touched anything, I touched those cropped curls. They were soft as down.

"Lydi, tell me what promise of your mother's has you here now—has us both here."

She came into my arms, and she pressed her cheek against my breast and spoke so softly that I could feel her breath warm through my shirt.

"A wanderer came to Gardd Seren when my mother was witch there."

This wanderer was Owain, and a witch's vengeance made him an exile. He could return from exile at any time, but not until he came to the witch and learned what fee he must pay. This, and more, Owain told to Meredydd, and when his tale was done he said, "Witch, I'm cursed. Can you cure me?"

Meredydd couldn't do that. No one could cure Owain of the curse but himself. He must go and learn his fee and his fate; she couldn't do that for him. But Meredydd gave him a promise: When Owain was ready to go home, the witch of Gardd Seren would go to Tŵr Du, to Deorcdun with him. She would help him if she could, and bear him company if she could do no more. This didn't please Owain, and he left Gardd Seren in anger.

"My mother knew he'd come back," Lydi said. "He was angrier with himself than with her, and that anger would fade. But Meredydd died before Owain returned. Now her promise is mine."

The ghost-wind rose higher, then fell to moaning again.

"Owain thought he'd come here to a living place. He says he supposed that if the witch was dead he'd find a kinsman who

would know to say, 'Owain, you must do this or you must do
that, and then you can go home.' There is no kinsman." She
shivered in my arms. "There is only the witch, the ghost. And
that witch-ghost wants no magic but his own here.

She pressed closer to me, and that hurt, but I wrapped my arms
around her, tried to stop her shivering.

"Garroc," she said, "the witch's magic is as strong as any I've
felt. His will is stronger. I could find out what Owain needs to
know if the witch would let me speak to him in magic. But he
won't."

And so she needed me. So Owain needed me. The ghost on
Deorcdun needed me—and he'd been watching me since Midwinter Night, whispering a word now and then to keep my attention,
abiding his time till Owain Dwarf-Smith decided to go home.
There aren't many folk who can hear ghosts speaking. This ghost
had found me and kept near me till he needed my voice.

I wondered, was it on Midwinter Night that Owain began to
think about finding his homeward road again?

Yes. Skald, yes . . .

And now the ghost didn't sound as he had once, a whispering
wanderer going by in the night, crossing the borderland of my
sleep. Now chill touched the voice, and chill touched me. High
up, dark and looming, Deorcdun stood above us, and I heard the
ghost-wind, the rushing sighs of uncounted dead.

"Garroc," Lydi said. "I need your help. If I can't hear what the
ghost has to say, I'll fail my mother's promise. But it's dangerous
there, Garroc. For you . . ." She shuddered. "Hinthan was right
to keep you from going up without knowing that. There are so
many ghosts—and they're all starving to be heard, hungering for
a voice."

And I didn't say, What? Should Ghosts-Skald be afraid of
ghosts? I didn't try to cheer her with swaggering. Lydi doesn't
worry needlessly. But I was willing to take what chance I must
to help her. If I could send Owain Dwarf-Smith on a swift road
home, Lydi's promise would be kept and she would be free to
ride away from this dark place and come home to Gardd Seren
with me.

I gathered her close again, and didn't manage to hide a grimace
of pain when I pressed her to me.

She said, "Please, let me heal you."

This time I didn't stop her. She'd been barred from her magic
on Deorcdun, all her craft banned from there by a jealous ghost.
In the last light of day I took her hands in mine, brought them to

the bruised and broken places, and let her touch me deeply, warm me, and mend me.

When the moon rose, the Harvester's golden scythe glinting, Lydi and I went up the hill to Deorcdun, around rock-spills, fallen mortar-bound stone. And we met Wulfhere coming down the hill, looking grim in the mouth like he'd been sent away against his will. Lydi didn't pass him by till she touched his cheek lightly, to reassure. And—a wonder!—he let her do that.

Soon we came to a gaping hole in a wall, a crumbling doorway. I stepped into the ruin, and I felt Hinthan's hand on me, braced against my chest to hold me back a moment longer. He said something, but I didn't hear it. I was filled up with such a din of wind-rushing cries and sighs and laughter and pain-howling that I couldn't hear the roaring of my own heart, nor even feel it racing against my ribs.

< **20** >

Ghost-wind, high and howling wilder-wind tore round me, through me, a hundred voices times a hundred crying to be heard. Lydi's hand fell from me like some fair and fragile leaf blown away in the gale as ghost-voices, ice-voices, raised up in winter-howling. *Hear me! Give me voice! Hear me!* Like beggars, poor exiles, abandoned outcasts. *Oh, hear me!*

The storm of their lorn howling, the wretched din, would have torn me apart, blown the pieces of me far and wide as all those hundred hundred voices burst out of me. I'd have died there on Deorcdun if I'd not felt hard hands on my arms, fingers digging with bruising strength.

"Garroc!"

I came back from the ghost-storm, for a moment came back to where Hinthan was, my boy holding me as you hold to a stagger-drunk friend, tight to keep him from falling, gently because you love him. We stood in a ring of mortared stone, bandaged rock, Roman-made ruins—

Give me voice! Oh, hear me! Skald, tell my tale!

I tried to see and recognize something of the sharp-edged, feeling, middle-world. Starry gaps breached the ruin's wounded walls, passageways leading nowhere, windows seeing nothing.

Moonlight shone down, shadows looked like old, old blood.

Skald, hear me! Give me voice!

Caught back by the ghost-gale, I hunched over like a man gut-stabbed, head down and howling. Words and words and words pouring out of me like blood.

Someone stood behind me. I heard his voice and I didn't understand his words. But I understood the meaning of the grasp come suddenly from behind, knew another anchor in the storm. Harder this grip, careless of any pain to me. These hands didn't love me.

Owain Dwarf-Smith said, "Hurry, boy! Get him to the well!"

I thought that was a good idea. My throat burned, raw and dry, as though I'd been talking for hours without even the scant courtesy of a dipperful of water. That's no good way to treat a skald.

Maybe I said that aloud, Sif, for Owain laughed, a great and brute booming.

The stairs up to the tower were made of stone, ages-worn, dipped in the center of the treads, long ago polished smooth by the passage of countless folk gone up and gone down. Hinthan led me as though I were blind, his hand on my shoulder to guide me up the winding way to the broken tower.

Owain followed, marching behind like a guard taking the soon-dead to the gallows.

They hung me! moaned the ghost of a murderer.

Burned me! howled a faithless traitor.

They put me to the sword! cried a man wrongly judged, screamed the mis-killed man, screamed I.

Each thought I had, each thing I saw, each sound I heard, called up ghosts. Dwarfs and Men, womankind and mankind, lord and soldier, Welshman, Roman Man, Saxon—I heard them all. Thief and king, witch and weaver and poet and smith and stoneman. Once, like the rushing roar of wildfire, I heard the ghost of a giant.

They were trapped here, ghosts prisoned in the ruins of Deorcdun to keep another ghost company, a well-dweller, a bard-witch who'd condemned himself to wait here till the time of his vengeance—till Owain Dwarf-Smith came to find out what toll must be paid on the road home.

All those caught ghosts battered me, Sif, mind and heart and soul. They howled for a way into me, for a chance at my living voice as I made that fearsome journey in darkness through a place no less cold than the hall of the Woman of the Dead, Ice-Hel herself. Owain Dwarf-Smith kept close behind me, wouldn't let me flee. But it was Hinthan's hand on my shoulder, warm as faith, that gave me the courage to go up to Deorcdun tower.

Lydi sat beside the well in what might once have been the tower's guard-room. She sat most beautiful in the moonlight, cloaked in blue as in shadows, leaning a little over the edge of the well as she were watching her reflection. Her cropped and curling hair was black as the places between the stars, and the skin on the nape of her neck, so white, looked like cream.

"Lydi."

She looked up at me and I saw what I must have looked like in the days when I was called Silent Skald. She was bereft of her magic, and her poverty was like rags on her.

Silence filled up the un-roofed tower. Not even wind sighed past the window where a hunter once sat watching north, trusting and waiting. So perfect was the silence that I thought I'd been struck deaf. Then I heard a nightingale in the wildwood, a leaf scratching across the tiled floor. But that was all.

"I hear no ghost, Lydi," I said hoarsely.

Not even in me did I hear a soft whisper, not even there where I'd become used to hearing ghosts.

"There's only one here," Lydi said. "He's barred those poor trapped others from the tower for now, and any wanderer. Garroc, will you help me?"

Hinthan's hand fell away from my shoulder, but not till he gripped once more, hard, and whispered, "Be careful!"

Owain let me go last, and he said nothing to me.

I crossed the broken tile floor to the well. But I stopped, a reach away, and looked over my shoulder. Hinthan stood in the doorway of the tower, the stars a-shine behind him. Owain was a darker shadow in shadows.

I said to Lydi, "Tell me what to do."

She gestured me closer and told me to kneel and look into the well. I did, and looked into darkness blacker than pitch. I saw nothing on the water's surface, not even my own reflection.

"Look again," Lydi said, her voice like a sweep of fingers 'cross a harp's strings, a chord felt deep in the breast.

Now I saw mist rising from the surface, as when water is warmer than air. I saw the faintest green at the edge of the water, a reflection of the slick moss on the stone well-shaft.

And I saw clouds, though the moon shone over my shoulder. Clouds racing and spinning, dark at the edges, like storm-fleece, lighter toward the center where, whirling, there was an eye of clear space, a tiny tranquil circle. But even in that clear space no moonlight showed.

"Look!" Lydi whispered, her breath warm on my cheek.

He was *dvergr,* the ghost in the well; he would have said *corrach,* for he was one of Lydi's countrymen. It was as if he stood behind me and from there cast his reflection into the water. But there was no one behind me who stood closer than Hinthan, my boy on guard at the top of the stairs.

My heart beat hard and heavy. Lydi touched my wrist, and all quieted in me.

The ghost had a thin face, and hard lines shaped it into a prisoner's face, bitterly hoping for nothing but revenge. In life, that face might have been handsome. In death, in this ghosty well, it was ugly with self-inflicted pain. Vengeance delayed becomes like a ravaging cancer. I saw it in this ghost's eyes.

He'd been no poor man in life, and he showed it even in death. His black, glossy thick beard was braided through with gold and silver wire. His hair hung long past his shoulders. Dark as night his deep-set eyes, the light in them like the glint struck off an eagle's talons when the bird comes diving down. Both bard and witch, this ghost, and his name was Caerau ap Einion.

Ghosts-Skald, he said, his familiar voice away deep inside me. As though he were at the bottom of that well, he reached his hand to me, smiling. *Kind, and kin of the craft.*

I reached my own hand to the water, feeling like I reached for my own reflection. Crying out, Lydi caught my hand back, quickly as though I'd been about to plunge it into fire. I heard it in her cry, in Caerau ap Einion's keen and cold laughter, that to touch that water was to touch a barrier between worlds; to reach into the well was to reach into all the places where the dead are—to Wotan's gold-glittering Valholl, to wild Ran's ever-restless sea-hall, to Hel's dark winterland, and even to the *Cristen* dead-worlds of fire-torn Gehenna and high Heofon.

And I will tell you the truth, Sif: It was luring, the thought that I could reach out one world and into another, touch some other place. I could go there, if go I wished. And I'd spent some time on war-grounds avoiding the worlds of the dead, but I saw it now, here by the well, that something about the dark underside of living drew me. The lightless gnawing cold was like to what grief-ridden berserkers taste.

And you were one of those winter-wolves for a while, skald, weren't you?

I shuddered, cold to the bones, and Lydi said, "Be careful of him, Garroc. He's no friend."

I'm not, whispered the ghost in me, laughing. *But I want something from you. We know you, Ghosts-Skald. All of us who are dead know you.*

I shivered, shaking like a fevered man about to die. Lydi pressed close, warm all along the length of me, and the chill was worse in the withdrawing, like some of my life went out of me.

"Stay alive!" she whispered. "Don't let him test you—that's not why you're here."

And her words warmed me, gathered me back like loving arms.

I said, "Caerau ap Einion, tell me what you want."

Your voice.

I managed a scornful laugh. "You're no different than all the howlers outside of here. I didn't surrender my voice to that army of ghosts, why should I give it to you?"

Them out there, they captured it once, Ghosts-Skald. I heard you spilling words like a drunk puking ale.

"And you hear me now, ghost, owning what's mine."

Soft footsteps sounded. Hinthan came and stood by the well. He put his hand on my shoulder, as often he did when I was listening to stone or earth. I felt it in his tightening grip, he could hear nothing through me.

Caerau ap Einion stared out from his well, his eyes deep and old as the first Roman Men come to the Isle, older than the god-curse that dooms my *dvergr* kin. He wasn't as old as the giants who lay buried in the barrows all round the moors of Northumbria, but if I'd bet that his eldfather had seen the building of those barrows, had known the giant-killer folk who used to live here, I'd not have lost the wager.

Skald, lend what I need. The next word came hard for him, came torn. *Please.*

Wind sighed round the well, cold around me. For no reason I understood, I reached for the rune-stone round my neck, the gift of a *Cristen* monk, the mark of the god no one knows. The Ing-stone grew warm in my hand, and that warmth heartened me. I said:

"Swear to me, Caerau ap Einion, that what you borrow, you'll return."

I swear it.

Hinthan didn't hear the ghost's reply, but he guessed it.

"Ask him what he swears by." He gripped my shoulder hard. "Garroc, ask!"

I did, and came a change over the ghost then. Those dark and deep eyes of his filled, the reflection in the water spilled tears, and the moon's light gave that sign of his sorrow the seeming of liquid silver running. Beside me Lydi caught her breath, let it go again in a barely heard sob.

On my own child's memory, said the ghost, the bard-witch. *I swear on my dear child's memory, for it's her we've come to talk about, Ghosts-Skald. Is it an oath you understand?*

I told him that I would lend him my voice.

Hinthan's grip on me tightened harder—I'd find bruises later. Then his hand fell away, as though flung off me. Cold came on me, rising up from the broken tiles of the floor, falling down from the frosty stars, seeping from the well.

Caerau ap Einion took what I offered, and he helped himself to more—my blood and bone and flesh. And I went . . .

Where did I go?

I don't know, Sif. Even tonight, I don't know. I went somewhere with the nightwind, and from there I watched what happened at the well, in the tower on Deorcdun.

Caerau ap Einion held my hands up to see them, to watch moonlight through spread fingers. He clenched one fist and then the other, rejoicing to feel the strength. He flung arms wide, stretched as to embrace the whole of the tower room, all the night, all the middle-world.

I felt all that, but only numbly. Who felt the most was Caerau ap Einion. For the first time in uncountable years he shivered against the wind chill on skin, thrilled to the beat of heart in breast, the song of blood rushing in veins. He loved the solid, trusty weight of a hale and fit body, and all his feelings ran stronger than mine, swifter, wilder, an undammed spate.

"Tell me now," Lydi said, her eyes like darkest sapphires in the moon's light, as coldly lovely, as hard. "Caerau ap Einion, tell me what I've come here to know."

The bard-witch laughed with my voice, but that bitter, ungiving sound wasn't my laughter. "How much of the tale do you know, impatient girl? What has he told you, that thief, that lurking marauder?"

"All of it but what fee he must pay to learn the way back to home."

Hollowly, the ghost said, "Then he told you about the murder."

Soft, a groan crept from the shadows, from Owain. Lydi stood straighter against that bleak word. And I was as an eavesdropper, trying to piece together words to make up the whole of an overheard tale.

Lydi said, "Owain told me that your daughter died."

"Ah. But he left out the part about the murder. Well, he didn't poison her cup," said Caerau ap Einion. He took a sudden step away from the well, closer to Lydi. "He didn't plunge a knife in her heart."

Hinthan left the well, stopped a short step away from putting himself between the bard-witch and Lydi.

"And the murderer didn't put his hands round her neck and choke," Caerau ap Einion said.

The ghost reached with my hands, touched Lydi's cheek, her lips, traced the smooth line of her neck. She shuddered, and I was helpless to stop what my own hand did. I saw, as Caerau ap Einion saw, the loathing in Lydi's eyes—a terrible moment like forever till Hinthan shouldered between, broke the touch.

Caerau ap Einion snarled, in anger hurled a curse, and Hinthan dropped a hand to the hilt of his long-knife.

Lydi cried, "Hinthan, no!"

And the ghost smiled, a cold peeling back of lips. He took my own knife, laid the moon-whitened edge of iron to my wrist. He pressed only a little. Like a man thinking about self-murder, he brought a small drop of blood springing. Lydi cried out in dread, reached to stop him, but Caerau ap Einion brushed her aside and never even looked at her. He cared only about weaponed Hinthan.

"I've dreamed in you, boy. I know what you love." He laughed, a dark coldness of sound as a drop of blood slid down my wrist and fell to the stone. "Remember: What you do to me, you do to your foster-father."

All the color ran out of Hinthan's face, left him ashy and looking sick. Nightwind blew harder. Old dead leaves scurried across the tower floor. In the wildwood, an owl cried, a cold and pitiless sound. Owain let go a breath in the smallest of sighs.

Caerau ap Einion heard that and he filled up with loathing, with hatred alive beyond death. He turned as on an enemy; he still had my knife in hand.

"You! Finally you've found the courage to come and learn the way home?" He laughed, and his laughter was like a whip-crack, swift and scornful. "It took you long enough. Hear me, you! It's no easy road you'll be taking, but it's an easy one to find. Leave here by the way you entered."

Owain's dark eyes glittered, and I'd seen that starved look on him before. In dream I'd seen his face white as the moon, stark and empty as moorland. Caerau ap Einion laughed again, and a wild pulse beat against Owain's throat, fear-sped.

"Look to where the moon rises," the bard-witch whispered hoarsely. "Look, thief, and follow. And then take that silver road as far as it goes. Do you need more explanation than that?"

Owain came out of the shadows to stand in the tower doorway, a black shape against the countless night stars. Very low, he said:

"You've told me enough." He flung a brittle smile, offered a bitter compliment. "The silver road . . . That's a fine revenge you've crafted, Caerau ap Einion."

"I'm a witch." Like the wind sighing, the ghost said, "I'm a bard. If I were nothing more, I'm her father. You killed her—"

"I never hurt your daughter! She was woman-grown, and she went with me willingly. She was happy while she lived, and I didn't kill her." Cold and sneering, he said, "I only took her away from you, old man."

A great tide of sorrow rose up in the ghost then, Sif, an ancient grief undying. With my eyes, he wept. I felt the unrelieving ache of it even in the far place where he'd sent me.

"You took my child to the edge of the world and beyond, Owain. She died there, where she never should have gone; where she didn't belong. You murdered her."

In sudden blazing anguish, Owain cried *"No!"* and the echoes of that tormented howling rang and ran all around the broken tower, the lover's grief as wild as the father's.

The last echo wasn't gone before I felt myself as myself again—heart and hand and mind. I was safe where I belonged, earth-bound, and Hinthan was on his knees beside me, supporting me again, as he had once before.

"He's gone? Garroc, is he gone?"

"Gone," I said, my voice my own again.

But Caerau ap Einion hadn't returned to his well, for I saw two reflections in the water there, Lydi's and Owain's. She reached for Owain's hand, took it in both her own, and there were tears on her cheek, silvery. And then the ghost whispered in the heart of me, the ages-dead bard, the grieving father.

Ghosts-Skald, hear me! For thanks, I warn you: He knows his way home now—watch him. He's a woman-thief, and he's already thinking how he can steal what you'd hate to lose.

He left me with a hissing of laughter, like the final breath leaking from a dead man's lungs. I leaned far over the well, looked into the water and down to nothing but blackest water.

And all around me I felt a great settling sigh, a weary groaning, an aching of sudden release. All the hundreds of ghosts gathered to Deorcdun, caught to keep the bard-witch company, were gone or going, freed at last, even to the giant whose voice was like rushing wildfire.

It was a long time before Caerau ap Einion spoke to me again.

Starlight poured from the sky, shone like silver as Hinthan and I went down from the ruins on Deorcdun. We went alone, for we'd lagged behind, let Lydi and Owain go before us. We had some things to talk about, my boy and I. Now echoes of our passage leaped from wall to wall, and Hinthan looked at me sideways, ready to smile.

"Skald, skald—"

And those words, spoken in jest, broke fear loose in me like shattering a dam. He'd dreamed with that ghost, that pirate, that vengeful witch, and I might have lost him. How if he'd reached into that well, that dark place between worlds? Before Hinthan could draw breath for the next word, I took him hard by the back of the neck, with both hands gripped him and held him still where he was.

"Hinthan, do you know what risk you took with that ghost?"

The color drained out of him, his cheeks showed white, his lips were a thin angry line. I didn't let him utter even a word.

"Do you understand what could have happened to you?"

And him, he stood stiff as stone, unyielding.

"Lydi couldn't do it," he said. "The ghost wouldn't let her dream to you."

I remembered the ghost's cold tempting and I shifted my grip, held Hinthan hard by the shoulders as if I was holding him back from some high cliff-edge.

"And so you rushed reckless to do something you knew nothing about?"

He laughed, a swift harsh sound. The echo of it bounded round ruined walls and down the passage. He closed his hand around my wrist, with his thumb traced where my own blade had pressed and drawn blood. There was no blood to see now, but the dark blade-rune, the long thin cut, remained.

"You've been a little reckless yourself, Garroc."

Then, suddenly, his hand started to shake, and he couldn't still that. He tried to say something, and it fell apart in ragged breaths before the cold image of self-murder. I didn't let him go.

"It didn't happen, Hinthan. That's nothing I'd ever do."

And he knew it. I felt it in him relaxing, saw it in his grey eyes clearing. After a moment, he broke my grip, but gently.

"Garroc, how else would I have found you if I didn't let the ghost dream in me? And . . . I wanted to know what it was like to dream with a witch." His grey eyes glinted, hard and keen. So he looked when he'd go out into a storm and climb up to a high place to lightning and the thunder. "I couldn't tell who was dreaming and who was guiding. I think the ghost tried to speak to me, but I'm not you. I couldn't hear him. All we had were my dreams and his magic to send them. I could feel the dreams go out flying from the tower. It was like they carried some of me with them. And I *knew* it when you felt the first one. I knew it right in the heart of me."

He was quiet for a moment, and then he looked at me sideways again, smiling a little.

"Skald, skald," he said, mugging the ghost again. "Would you have come here if it was only the ghost calling? Or would you have gone looking for me and Wulf and kept putting the ghost by? Lydi wouldn't have taken that chance if he'd let her use her magic. I didn't take the chance, and I let him use my dreams."

And what was to say, Sif? Nothing. He'd done what he'd done, and it frightened me, but it shouldn't have surprised me. This was Hinthan.

Behind us the whole tall bulk of Deorcdun rose up, and ahead there was light, a campfire's flames to cheer the dark. Like a shadow, Owain stood outside the light, arms folded tight to his chest, brooding. Lydi and Wulfhere sat with heads bent close together, studying dark-writ vellum sheets by firelight.

And I said to Hinthan, "I thought that scrip was lost by the river."

"I fetched it up when the witches came. He's got the thing lined with sail-cloth and the pages locked up in a box with the joints tarred. His pages stayed—mostly—pretty dry. I wish I'd been able to get the king's axe back for you."

"You saved what we needed most, boy mine. Don't worry about the axe."

Wulfhere leaned a little closer to Lydi, pointed to the vellum.

She tilted her head, as when something delightful suddenly surprises her.

"Has she charmed him?" I asked, only half in jest.

Hinthan shrugged. "He'd never seen any of *dvergr* until he saw you in the garden. I think you really did look like some devil to him because he only knew how to see what he'd been taught to see. But when he's with Lydi, he remembers the truth Raighne tried to teach him. And besides, he likes to preen."

So it seemed. Wulfhere's face shone bright as the firelight when Lydi leaned over the page to praise.

The nightwind blew chill, moaning down the twisting path from Deorcdun. We went in silence for a few moments; then Hinthan said, "I learned some things when I dreamed with the ghost—about the curse and about how the ghost thinks Owain's a murderer. But I got the feeling that there's a piece to the story of Owain and the bard-witch that I don't know. But I'll tell you what I do know, Garroc. Owain's a little older than he looks."

He was right about that, Sif. If Owain had known Caerau ap Einion in life, he was near to nine hundred years older than he looked. Curses wait as long as they must, and ghosts can wait forever.

"Hinthan, the ghost thanked me with a warning." And I told him the warning, every word.

He stopped, stood watching Owain, the dark shape in the darkness outside the fire's light. "I used to think I knew him. I don't know anything about him now. But I don't think he's a murderer, and I can't hate him, Garroc."

"I'm not asking you to hate him. I'm telling you I'm not going to let him take Lydi anywhere she doesn't want to go."

He nodded grimly. "You can count on me."

That went without saying.

PART FOUR

◆◆◆

Fire and Stars

Stane Saewulf's son said that the farthest of all the Nine Worlds is called Muspellheim.

"It is also the most terrible of all the worlds, youngling."

I was near to grown when he said that to me, Sif. I'd learned some things other than skald-craft by then. I could use my father's war-axe, knew the ways of weapons. It wasn't Stane taught me that; I didn't give him the chance. I went to learn the first lessons of war-craft on my own.

It was dark-moon night when Stane talked about Muspellheim; a night clear of clouds, and the stars owned the sky. We two stood out in the meadow beyond Stane's small house, waiting for the Wolf, the mid-winter moon. While we waited my foster-father said:

"Muspellheim is a place of fire where god-Surt lives with the trolls who are his many sons, each got on the body of a dead woman. An evil place, Muspellheim; the lakes of it are filled up with flame and they are called fire-baths. The mountains are made of brimstone, and those high places are ever-burning. They are called *byrn-torrs,* the burning hills. From there Surt will ride at the great ending of the Nine Worlds, and he and his troll-sons, the fire-kin, will fight in Loki's army against Wotan and the Aesir gods. But if you think that no good comes from their terrible world, my youngling, you are wrong."

Stane told me that the stars were born in Surt's world, the lovely night-gems, the countless showers of sparks from the fire-world flung out into the darkness when Muspellheim was made. Wotan and his Aesir-kin seized these sparks and put them in the dark sky, fixed some to act as guides for men and set others free to wander the sky-roads.

And Stane said to me on the night we stood watching for the Wolf Moon, "You have heard it said, my youngling, that when comes Ragnarok—the Nine Worlds' Ending—all the stars will vanish from the sky, flee to the fire-land, to Muspellheim. So it must be. For when all the Nine Worlds are destroyed in that last battle, burnt to ash and barren cinder, these stars will live, burn as banked embers. These sparks will warm the frozen ruin, kindle new life, nine new worlds where gods and alfs and giants and Men and Dwarfs will live again. All those gleams that once were stars will be those embers and sparks."

"Foster-father," I said, shivering in the cold night, "do you think all will be then as it is now? Or do you think things will be different, that in these new worlds alfs will not be un-souled, Dwarfs not doomed, and gods will be wiser?"

He'd put an arm round my shoulders, for he saw my shivering.

"Youngling, I don't know how it will be then. The *wyrd* of new worlds hasn't yet been woven. But tonight I stand here looking at the stars hoping that you will remember about the nine new worlds, and that you'll remember even in darkest and most dire times that a skald—be he fleet-lived Man or doomed Dwarf—must fling out his songs and histories just like the stars were flung out from Muspellheim, for word-woven songs and histories are sparks from the fire in a skald's heart. And he must set them out like stars that burn bright for a time, then become embers awaiting the birth of the new worlds.

"Stars and songs," Stane said to me. "They're other words for hope, youngling."

My Sif, I told that tale to Lydi in the shadow of Deorcdun, after moon-set when the stars were brightest in the sky. Hinthan walked watch round the camp, Owain slept outside the light. And Wulfhere sat close to the campfire, awake and at his pen-craft.

I told the story to Lydi because all night through she'd sat
looking up at the sky, yearning. She missed the day stars and
her gardens; I knew it though she never said a word about it.
I'd hoped this tale of stars, this story of life and death and life
again from the fire, would ease her. But when she thanked me,
her voice held a whisper of yearning not eased. In that yearning
I heard a truth I didn't like.

"You're not going back to Gardd Seren, are you, Lydi?"

She shook her head. "We'll go south a while, and then west to
the sea. I'd like to ride with you for as long as we may."

"We're still hunted, girl. I know it. I feel it."

"And that has to do with Wulfhere."

I nodded, and she asked no more about it.

"We'll come with you, Garroc, as far as we may."

In the dark, hunched under his mantle for warmth, Owain lay
very still; too still for sleeping. Soft, Wulfhere's quill whispered
to the vellum, never stopped even when he heard us talking about
him.

"Lydi, walk with me."

Owain stirred then; and Wulfhere looked up, then away to his
work again. Lydi gave me her hand, and we went out beyond the
light of the fire. Hinthan, at watch, saw us and said nothing, only
smiled as we went into deeper dark of the wildwood. There, we
stood listening to the night breeze, to crickets, to owls.

And, after a while, Lydi said, "I'm going with Owain because
my mother would have gone, and it's her promise I'm keeping.
She'd have gone with him right to where he must go, and waited
while he got ready to leave, and stayed to see him away."

"And maybe you're going because you have something to prove
to yourself?"

Her hand was very cold in mine now. "Maybe."

Meredydd was never a ghost who had anything to say to me,
but I didn't forget her warning against Owain, known from Lydi's
dream: *Remember what he is, always. Don't ever forget.*

He's a woman-thief, the ghost on Deorcdun had warned.

"Be careful of him, Lydi."

She drew breath to speak, but I stopped her.

"Don't defend him—you couldn't to me. And don't defend this
promise-keeping—no one should do that. Only be careful." I put
my arm around her and said, "Now come back to the fire, my
girl. It's getting cold here."

She looked at me from wide blue eyes, saw deep into me; and
I began to shiver, cold all to the bones of me. Lydi held out her

hand, and I took it in both of mine.

"*Cariad*," she said. Beloved. "You've been too much among the dead tonight. Come with me."

Shivering, I went with her, and we made a bed of bracken, the thick fern that smells like the whole wildwood. For a cover, we had my mantle, and Lydi settled herself there. I knelt beside her, colder still, shaking now.

Too much among the dead. . . . My witch was right.

All the fire-flies flickered like stars in the deeps of the woods, and I watched as Lydi untied that old green shirt of Hinthan's. I couldn't stay watching long, but when I reached to help she took my hand, turned my wrist up to the starlight.

She kissed the blade-mark, the rune written in her cause. "I can make this go away."

But I said, "Let it heal in its own time, girl dear."

Lydi said no more about it, and she reached for me, silently bade me come and get warm.

‹21›

I woke in the misty hour before dawn, the grey time when all sounds are muffled. The fire had fallen, Wulfhere was a dark shape pacing watch in the shadow of high Deorcdun, the boy with his back straight, his shoulders squared. He made one pass around our small camp, and then another, head up and alert. He carried a sling fitted with a stone the size of his fist. He was a good hand with that sling and Hinthan swore to me that it was Wulfhere fed them more often than not when they two were together.

"I taught him to use it," Hinthan had said. "But he's got a good eye, and he's a fast learner."

The *aetheling* passed by me again—then stopped suddenly, sniffing the air. He didn't like what he smelled, a thin wisp of smoke, a pale wanderer caught in the thicker web of morning mist. This wasn't smoke from our fire. It came on the south wind, faintly.

"Wulfhere."

He turned, dropped his shoulder, ready to let fly. He eased a little when he saw me.

"How long have you smelled the smoke?"

"Only just now, when the wind turned."

I saw it in his eyes that he was remembering the burning of Haligstane.

"Come and eat," I said. "There's some hare from last night. Then get ready to leave."

Ay, leave . . . and go to where? I saw the question in his blue eyes, but he didn't voice it. I got to my feet, walked wide around Owain still sleeping. I nudged Hinthan awake with my foot and bade him come with me. We went to the edge of the wildwood where our horses were hobbled, alone to speak privately.

There in the misty morning I gave him all the news Merewal had given me, of Erich's return to the Marches, of Penda's victory at Eoferwic. As the day lightened I told him how the king had sent one brother to hunt down another. Hinthan's eyes glinted coldly when he learned that Peada had deserted his father's army and run west, maybe to throw in with Bran of Gwynedd and his witches. He didn't forget his feud with the king's eldest son.

And I told Hinthan something else, an idea I'd been thinking about. Penda's wife, unloving Cynewise, had holdings in Ceastir, the town on the border between Mercia and Northumbria. If the queen had little love for her husband, her kinsmen had less. The marriage was no peace-weaving, though it was made to be. I didn't think it unlikely that these kinsmen of hers would be glad to help Peada work against the king if the queen thought they should. I told my thinking to Hinthan, and told him it was another thing to keep in mind.

"But we can't count on guesses. We've got to keep our eyes sharp and get Wulfhere to Gardd Seren. With good speed we can be in Mercia in a day or two. And there we ride east to get wide around Ceastir and the queen before we turn west again."

He glanced past me, to Lydi who was awake and mending the fallen fire. "Lydi and Owain won't go as far as Gardd Seren with us, will they?"

"No."

"Do you know where they're going?"

"South, and then west—but not so far south as Gardd Seren."

No more did we say, and we worked together readying horses.

As I worked, Sif, I thought of the road ahead and wondered how things were with Cynnere and Aescwine. They weren't dead; I'd have known. Maybe they were laying up somewhere, bone-broken from the river, or sick from other wounds. And I wondered, too, was Rowenna with them; or was she lost again, friendless and adrift in the wildwood?

Again I smelled smoke, faint on the southern breeze.

We went south by woodland ways, and the sun shining down through the leaves made light and shadow flow like a dappled river around us. We took the wildwood paths and they often crossed near-hidden Roman roads overgrown and barely seen. These roads led—always—to ruins, tumbled stone ghosts of the forts that used to be. All these ruins made a ring around the heights of Deorcdun. The wildwood paths took us ever downward, and so steeply that I reckoned we'd not even see Deorcdun's lofty head by nightfall. I wouldn't mourn the loss.

That morning Lydi rode a neat-footed little grey mare, one I knew from Gardd Seren, and Hinthan yet had his red mare. He rode beside Lydi, his quiver near to hand, his strung bow at reach across his horse's withers. They talked quietly together, and Owain walked beside them, solitary in silence. He didn't look like a man happy to be going home.

Now, here is something interesting I learned about Owain that day, my Sif, a thing I'd not noticed before. Owain Dwarf-Smith, who'd shod all the horses in Seintwar at one time or another and was known for his firm and gentle hand with even the most ill-tempered beast, didn't like horses. He didn't like it that they let a smith drive nails into their hoofs to hold on iron shoes, didn't like it that they let themselves be saddled and bridled, that they would so far submit to the will of Dwarf or Man as to carry burdens at anyone's behest.

"Be it light or heavy, if a burden's forced it's a burden of shame," he said. "Horses have no more pride than oxen."

That was his answer when I asked him whether he'd like to ride up with Hinthan. He found himself a good walking stick of stout oak and went on his own legs. He had a strong stride, not what you'd expect from a man nine hundred and some years old. He stayed nearer to Lydi and Hinthan than to me, and that left Wulfhere to my company and me to his.

It was quiet company. The king's son had nothing to say to me for a long while. He kept still and quiet as we rode the down-winding path through the wildwood, past glades and round tall piles of stone, the boulders that some say are left over from the making of the giants' barrows. Then, shortly before noon, and for no reason that I could see, Wulfhere was moved to speak.

"Garroc Ghosts-Skald," he said carefully. "Brother Raighne said that you know who my father is."

I answered as carefully. "I know."

"Do you know him—the man, not just the name?"

He asked breathless, like one reaching gingerly to open the lid of a coffer, afraid to know if it is empty or filled up with treasure. And then, on a sudden-caught breath, rushing to pray one last time before the lid is opened, he said, "Garroc Ghosts-Skald, I'm—I'm sorry for the things I've said to you."

Il bastardo they'd named him in Haligstane, all but red Raighne who was his friend and loved him, who knew a gentler way. And that name was like a badge of shame, a charge and a judgment of guilt. What Wulfhere didn't know about his father was an ever-seeping wound in him, Sif. Yet when was the time to tell this Northumbrian boy, this monk-raised *Cristen* child, that his father was Penda of Mercia, the enemy-king?

I knew only that the time wasn't now. And it might have eased him to know who his foster-kin were, but I hadn't the first idea who they might be.

"Boy," I said, and I'd not spoken so gently to him before now. "Wulfhere, I can't tell you what you want to know yet."

He flinched, as though I'd struck him. "I told you I was sorry. I *told* you—"

A new breeze whispered through the wildwood, carrying before it the ghost of smoke. Hinthan lifted his head, frowning over that ghost. A small shudder ran through Wulfhere, and without thinking, I tightened my arms round him as you do when you're holding a child against the cold. He drew a wincing breath.

"I hate you!" he whispered, the words near-silent. "They were right at Haligstane! You *are* devil-kin! *Geldr*—I hate you!"

He did hate, Sif, fiercely as children can. Hating he used a weapon he knew for a keen one. It hurt, that word; it never failed to cut deeply. But this time I was braced for it. I knew how to see the blow coming now. Hinthan, who'd heard the sound of discord if not the words, turned to look back.

"Come take Wulfhere for a while," I said.

Before he could answer, Lydi said, "Garroc, Wulfhere is welcome to ride my mare, if you think that's a good idea."

She'd not finished speaking when Hinthan snatched Wulfhere up. He dropped the king's son swiftly to the ground and hard enough to make the boy grunt. Wulfhere drew breath to protest his handling, but Hinthan bent such a look on him as to make him shut his mouth with a snap of teeth; fast.

I lifted Lydi from her grey mare and settled her in front of me. It made a cold wound, that word *geldr,* even when I was braced for it. I was minded to get warm as best I could.

"He is a strange boy," she said, soft and for only me to hear. "He's full of the seeing-skills—he can read and he can write. But he's been blinded to half the people in the world. And, worse I think, he's been blinded to himself. Who will teach him how to see himself for the treasure he is?"

So said my witch, who would have no such wealth of her own. *Geldr,* Wulfhere said. It was a lie, and it was a kind of racked and twisted truth.

"There was a monk," I said. The Ing-stone moved a little against my skin, the warm token reminding me of a friend unexpectedly found and too soon lost. "His name was Raighne, and he was an Irelander. He was blind, and he was trying to teach the boy to see. Maybe, with more time, he'd have done it."

"Maybe," she said gently, "with more time Wulfhere will remember what his friend taught him."

"About Dwarfs," I said.

She shook her head. "About himself. He's got in the habit of hurting you, man dear, but not because you're who you are. Oh, maybe at first it was that. But now he strikes out at you because you know what he so badly wants to know. And he uses the sharpest weapons he can find against you because he feels so helpless."

Lydi turned in my arms, and she lifted her face in such a way that I couldn't but kiss her. The warmth of that kiss reached to the heart of me, eased the cold pain stirring again.

Ahead, in the dark shade of a tall oak, Owain stopped and looked over his shoulder. The ghost on Deorcdun had said: *He's a woman-thief, and he's already thinking how he can steal what you'd hate to lose.* As if he'd heard that warning then, or knew what I thought now, Owain Woman-Thief's eyes met mine and he smiled as though to say, Enjoy her while you can.

Late in the afternoon Hinthan said to me that there were more songbirds in the wildwood than before, but there were no ravens or even crows. The smell of burning darkly haunted the wildwood all around. No breeze stirred; neither Hinthan nor I could tell where the fire was. Now we rode a little east, and soon the wind dropped. The sun fell full and fair through the wildwood roof and the stench of burning vanished as it had never been. I didn't forget it, nor did the others. Wulfhere studied the sky over every clearing; once he pointed up to a sudden blue patch. Ravens circled darkly.

When shadows reached toward the day's end and the sunlight lay old on the ground and didn't much warm, we passed an overgrown ruin, the only one we'd come upon since those rounding Deorcdun. Wild in the woods, that ancient place. In the south-facing wall there were windows yet blindly staring. Lydi said she remembered tales her mother had told her of the building of these ruins, the ones here and those in Wales.

"In Arthur's time," she said, "these forts were already very old, for the Romans had long before gone away to their homeland. But our king kept the forts in good repair and his soldiers manned them, each keeping care of the lands about for Arthur." She yet sat in my arms, and I felt her straighten a little, proudly. "My father was one of those men, and they say that a woman could walk from one end of the Isle to the other, weaponless with a gold-sack in one hand and her babe in the other and never come to harm."

Hinthan snorted and said that people used to say the same thing about Eadwine of Northumbria for a while, too. "It's a thing they say about kings."

"Yes," Lydi said, "it is. But when they say it about Arthur, they're telling the truth."

Hinthan gave her a long and sober look along his shoulder, and Lydi laughed suddenly to see him mimic her fierce solemnity.

Thinking of Aescwine, I said that I'd often heard a friend of mine talk about the Roman forts and Arthur of Wales, and in his tales my friend used to praise the Roman roads and curse them, depending on whether the story he was telling had to do with how the King of Cent and his army were chasing Arthur and his men, or were being chased by those swift-riding Welshmen.

"And I've heard people say that Arthur was the King of Dwarfs," I said. "But no one ever tells how he got that name. Do you know, Lydi?"

"My father used to say the same thing," she said. "But I don't know why. Dwarfs and Men all served in Arthur's army as Welshmen. There was no difference made between us, even after god-Christ came. Sometimes I think we've lost too many of our tales, and sometimes I think we haven't learned them all yet."

There are few better ways to pass the time riding than at story-telling, and Hinthan pressed Lydi for another tale of her famous king. She gave it gladly, and told about Arthur's raising-up, his hidden boyhood spent fostered with good folk in the wildwood while a witch taught him how to be a king. Wulfhere hung on each word, and I wondered—silently, Sif, and only half in jest— whether that witch had been *dvergr*, whether he yet lived, and if he'd be willing to take another boy to teach.

At sunset a breeze sprang up and we smelled smoke again. Now ravens crowded the sky and Wulfhere asked Hinthan if he thought maybe we'd be going a little more east. He was thinking of the warrior-witch, Bran Hel-Thane. I was, too. But I kept to our course.

In the first hour of the dimming we came out of the wildwood and we found what had burned. We also found Cynnere and Aescwine, but not before we found the madman.

◄22►

Ghosts mourned in the black wasteland where the madman ran.

They were only a few, the last of a great flight, and their cries rose thin as the blue-edged smoke curling up to the twilight sky, private keening. I left it so, didn't try to ask questions of the dead. I didn't need to ask to know what made this blackened wasteland. War had laid a burning hand on the land and the village beyond.

It was a weariness to see, Sif. The crop-fields stretched out in burnt agony before us. Here and there, in strips wide or narrow, some wheat yet stood; unburnt, half-burnt. Here, there'd been a ditch the flames couldn't cross; there, the wind had turned suddenly and driven the fire in a different direction. All the rest was black cinder and grey ash and dying, with a madman running through it.

He was tall and thin, and he ran shouting to the sky. I didn't understand what he shouted; he howled in a language I'd never heard before. But I knew it was word-woven poetry, I heard a pattern. Ravens screamed up from the ground in front of him, black wings like thunder beating. The madman stopped, stared down at the raven-feast. The wind turned, came east, dark with the stink of rotting. The madman took up his rage-song again and ran.

Soft, Owain spoke the lines of the poem after him:

> My God, my God, why have you
>   forsaken me?
> Why are you so far from saving
>   me,
> So far from the words of my
>   groaning?

A stark verse, that. I took up my short-sword, put Lydi foot to ground as Hinthan strung his bow and checked his quiver. Wulfhere sat the grey mare, very still. In the dimming-dark beneath the trees his face shone white, and Owain said:

> All who see me mock me;
> They hurl insults, shaking their
>   heads:
> He trusts in the Lord;
> Let the Lord rescue him!

Owain fell suddenly silent.

Someone else came running across the wasteland, out from the ruined village. Tall and fleet, coppery hair loose and streaming behind in the swiftness of her flight, the skirt of her rusty gown bunched high and clutched in her hands, Rowenna Brand's daughter ran after the madman. She wasn't surprised by the sprawling dead. She leaped over one and another and never broke stride.

But the third—ah, the third body she came to wasn't that of a dead man and Rowenna fell, dragged down by a hand thrust up from the burnt ground, fire-black and blood streaked. Another man leaped up, dark from the ashes. A third showed himself, and a fourth, robbers come to steal the dead naked and come suddenly in sight of better prey. They made a circle round Rowenna and the one who'd dragged her down, filled up with the dark lust, waiting not patiently for what might be left for them.

By then Hinthan and I were halfway across the wasteland. We didn't go alone. Owain jogged behind. With his grip he'd changed his walking stick into a quarterstaff.

There's no need to boast about that whipping-off of curs, Sif. Hinthan shot one cleanly through the heart; Owain clubbed off another who would have plunged a long-knife into Hinthan's leg, torn and maimed. Rowenna got a knee free of the pinning weight of the bloodied man. She thrust up with that knee and he yowled and tried to lurch away. I caught him on my short-sword, killed him with the keen edge.

"Up, girl!"

I grabbed her wrist, she mine, and she scrambled up behind me as Owain broke the arm—and then the head—of the last of the looters. Blood-covered, shaking with terrified laughter and with sobbing, Rowenna pointed to the madman, him who'd run away through the fields.

"Please! Fetch him before he's killed!"

I nodded to Hinthan and he went to do that. All the ravens settled again and Owain cleaned blood and brains off his quarterstaff, knelt to scrub it with grey ash and black dirt. A lone man came running out from the broken village, sword in hand, but low. He had the sun behind him, the red light like an omen of fire all around him. I knew him and was glad to hear his welcome.

"How is it with you, Cynnere?"

"Not so good," he said, gripping my hand. "But things might get better now."

He reached up and lifted Rowenna down, held her and stroked her tangled hair back from her face. He scolded her for being abroad in the burnt night, but he scolded only gently, his words not but sounds against her neck as he held her. Now that I had time to look, I saw that she was thinner than when last we were together, and pale in the face. She'd not been well lately.

Like wind, the black wings rustling all around us; like drunken feasters in the dark hall of an evil king, the ravens at their supper. A terrible cry rose up, wordless and so filled with blackest pain and deepest despair that it chilled me to the heart. I turned to find Hinthan, and saw him just leaping from his red mare. He went down on one knee, reached for something, and then he got up, shaking his head.

"The priest is dead," Cynnere said.

"I think so."

Cynnere held his Rowenna closer, and to me he said that he reckoned the man had died of a guilt-broken heart.

"Why that?"

It was Rowenna who answered me, and her voice broke under the weight of bitter sorrow.

"Because he drove away half of his friends, and doomed the rest to death." Her green eyes glittered, strangely bright. "The will of the queen's priests has reached all the way to here, skald. She brought the best of the Roman-born with her when she married Eadwine. The finest speakers. The fiercest in faith. And now all the old bonds are breaking. . . ."

Cynnere hushed her, held her closer. Somewhere a wolf howled, then another. The night-hounds were gathering and Cynnere cocked his thumb back over his shoulder, to the village beyond the fields, the bones of houses, overthrown stone, black beams and rafters still smoking.

"There's a house still standing in the village, Garroc. We can talk there, ay?"

"We can. Is Aescwine with you?"

He nodded. "We made it out of that river, all of us. We fetched up on the swampy side, though, after all. Took us a while to get out of the marshes, and no way to cross the river afoot. The best we could do is go south, and watch out for you." He smiled then, and he said, "Ay, it's good to see you, Garroc."

As good it was to see him, but the shadow of sorrow on his face put a dread into me.

"Is he well, Cynnere?"

Cynnere didn't answer but to say that I could see for myself how things were with Aescwine.

I looked for Hinthan, and whistled sharply. Ravens screamed, storm-crows lifted up from the wasteland. Hinthan heard, and when I pointed to the village he lifted a hand to say that he understood. He'd follow with Lydi and Wulfhere.

I reached down a hand to Rowenna, but Cynnere wasn't minded to let her go again. I followed them across the burnt fields and, soft-footed as shadows, Owain followed me. He'd said not a word since last he'd spoken the madman's poetry.

Silent, he'd killed; silent, he went with me now.

The house Cynnere had spoken of was no house, but a church. It had no roof—wood and thatch burn easily—but the mortared stone walls had withstood the flames. There were two chambers in the church. One was a little chapel with a very small altar. The larger chamber might once have held all the village in meeting.

In the chapel were signs that folk had been living here—two mantles and a cloak spread to make a bed, saddle-gear neatly piled up in a shadowed corner. Fire flickered in a stone ring in the middle of the earthen floor, cheering the gloom. On the little altar—where rats must scramble for them—turnips and apples and onions lay, unspoiled bounty from a cottage garden. Owain went and plucked a glossy apple from the pile.

"Old 'un's in there." Cynnere pointed to the dark door that led beyond the chapel. Glumly he said, "Yon priest wasn't the only one off his head around here. Old 'un's about as crazy. You should know that before you go talk to him, Garroc."

And so, though I found them here together, things were no better than the last time I'd seen Cynnere and Aescwine.

"I'll keep it in mind, but aren't you coming with me?"

"Not if you wanted to pay me," he said bitterly. "He's—"

Rowenna stopped him with only the lightest touch, and a look passed between them.

"Go," she said. "Please."

Cynnere said he didn't see what good it would do, and he already knew all the harm to be found. But he went with me because she asked him to. Owain, chewing his apple, was two steps behind us.

Aescwine wasn't alone, Sif. Coming from the fire-lighted chamber, my eyes not ready for the shadowy dark, I thought it was a boy with him, they two talking while Aescwine honed an iron edge keen. But when Aescwine stopped honing and gestured his friend aside, I saw no boy.

She was very lovely, the young *dvergr* woman; straight and slender. By the look of her she was not as old as me, maybe some ten years younger, though so small a difference isn't much to Dwarfs and seldom even seen by *mann-cynn*. She stood as tall

as me—heart-high to a Man. Her eyes were large and green, and
her long hair was woven into silvery braids thick as my wrist and
hanging to her waist. Unbound, all that silver would spill to her
knees. She wore grey woolen hose and a Man's long shirt belted
like a tunic, and she didn't bother to tie that shirt, so I saw the
glint of a byrnie beneath. I wondered what she wore under the
war-shirt to keep the ring-mail from nipping.

Her name was Reginleif and when she spoke it she smiled
coolly to say, *Yes, I know it's a Valkyrie's name and I know
what it means.* Wrecker of Plans is what that name means in the
old language of our Northern fathers, Sif.

Behind me, Cynnere towered in silence. Owain chewed his
apple noisily.

"And you," Reginleif said to me. "You're Garroc, aren't you?
They used to call you Silent Skald, but now they say Ghosts-
Skald." Her eyes glinted with a lusty light and you could believe
she was a Valkyrie. "I like that last one."

Before I could answer, Aescwine growled something that
sounded like orders, and Reginleif left him. A twitch of the hips she
granted him as she passed, and he swatted her backside, laughing.
Not fatherly, that swat, and very fond. The wink Reginleif gave
him along her shoulder said she didn't much mind. When she
was gone Aescwine leaned back against the altar. He didn't look
at Cynnere or Owain; it was like we two were alone.

He looked well, Sif. His hair and beard shone very white in the
shadows at the end of day. The battle-rune, the deep scar that
twisted his smiles to sneers, showed livid in the half-light, but I
could read his smile in his keen blue eyes. He seemed fit and hale,
and I reckoned silver Reginleif had something to do with that.
Even by the slow measure of our *dvergr* kin my friend Aescwine
was old, but—by anyone's measure—he wasn't finished.

"Silk," he said.

"What?"

"She's wearing silk under the mail. I know you, young skald.
You were wondering about that. You don't see many sword-girls
around, ay? But she's one." Darkly, he said, "Her father and
brothers were iron-smiths. Her mother was known wide around
here for a good weaver. Eotenfeld, the name of this place. Dwarfs
used to live here, once happily enough. These days her kinsmen's
swords are all Reginleif has left."

In the silence between us I didn't hear Owain chewing his apple;
he'd gone away. But Cynnere had stayed to glower. Outside the
church I heard low voices, Lydi's and Hinthan's.

Aescwine said, "Is that a girl I hear?"

"That's a girl."

"Another wayfarer?"

I nodded, and we were silent for a moment. Then he said, "Is the priest dead?"

"He is."

He shrugged and his eyes were flat and cold, Sif, like we were speaking about a foeman he'd hated for years.

Then, quickly, he put all thought of the priest by and, heartily glad, he said, "But you're not dead, are you? And I hear Hinthan out there. I was afraid you two drowned in the river."

I told him there was a time when I'd thought we'd all drowned in the river. I told him that Hinthan and Wulfhere and I were separated for a while, and that red Merewal's men had found me and that the king's son had taken good care of me when I needed it.

"Ay, him. I heard he's about."

"Peada's around, too, and Merewal thinks he's made a pact against Penda with Bran of Gwynedd."

"Bran, y'say? Not Cadwalla? Ach, the young bucks and the stags!" He laughed grimly. "All the wildwood's going to be filled with the racket of horns rattling, ay?"

"Looks like it. But I don't want to talk about Peada. Some things are going on here that I don't understand. I want to talk about that."

He nodded. "That's reasonable. Come here and sit. I'll tell you what's been going on. But you're going to have to hear about Peada, even if you don't want to talk about him."

He said nothing to Cynnere, and Cynnere stood unmoving, as if he was carved from stone.

I went to sit, put my back against the altar. It had a deep voice, that altar-stone. It remembered strange songs, ones that sounded like the sea-waves coming in and drawing out, like those songs monks used to sing in Haligstane.

Aescwine picked up his whetstone, went to work on his sword again. His wasn't a tale of good tide.

Peada's army came from the south, Aescwine said. And so exactly from the south that you could have thought he'd but the day before crossed the border from Mercia to get here.

"And he wasn't with Bran, for what that's worth. He was with Outlawed Osric. Now, day before yesterday I didn't know that one from anyone else, but that's what they were all shouting here.

'The Outlaw! The Outlaw!' I know him now. He's three years, maybe four, older than Hinthan. But bigger—like an ox, him. And bloody-handed. Peada and him worked well together," Aescwine said bitterly. "They tore this village bone from bone."

Aescwine saw them attacking from the wildwood, the army like a bow bent to killing, and he went to fight beside the folk here against Peada and Osric. I said I thought that was a strange thing for him and Cynnere to do, considering that these folk of Eotenfeld were Northumbrians.

Cynnere looked away from us, and Aescwine sneered, but not like he was trying to smile.

"*Him* and me didn't do anything. Him and that girl were here in the village. She wasn't leaving, and he wasn't going anywhere without her. He's got used to a woman warming his nights now, our Cynnere. Can't be without her."

Low, like the first angry rumble of thunder, Cynnere said, "She was fevered and swamp-sick. Should I have left her alone among strangers?"

Aescwine didn't even look at him, Sif. He picked up his story's thread as if he'd not but taken a breath between one word and the next. "He's lucky Peada and Osric didn't kill him. They would have if it wasn't for me and some friends of mine."

A band of Dwarfs, those friends of Aescwine's. Exiles in their own land, living wild in the woods, unwelcome in their old homes. They weren't the only such in Eadwine Faith-Breaker's lands. Driven off by once-friends, they haunted the wildwood and the hearts of those who'd turned them out at the command of a Christ-priest.

"And you can say: Ach, one of those Christ-worshiper's a Roman Man and the other's an Irelander or a Welshman or whatever and there's a difference between 'em—" He glanced at Cynnere and quickly away. "They're all one faith-breaking tribe to me."

The first stars shone in the blackness outside, gleamed down through the missing roof. Other gleams, the stars born of iron and whetstone, lived and swiftly died in the darkness on the altar as Aescwine finished his tale.

Peada and the Outlaw struck at dawn of the day I spoke for Caerau ap Einion. Like a band of death-born trolls come riding from Muspellheim, they gave out no mercy. Bitterly, Aescwine told me that the band of exiles made little difference in the outcome of that attack but to give women and old ones and children a chance to scurry into the forest and away.

"But we didn't much help the men and boys who stayed to defend the village. We fought hard, but it was too late by the time we started. Most of 'em in the village died right away, in the first wave of horsemen. It wouldn't have happened if every man in the village was here and ready. But half the folk weren't here. Half of 'em—and all of 'em Dwarfs—were banished to the wildwood, *wraecca* in their own homeland."

And in the end the priest who'd done the exiling had lived long enough to know he'd doomed the village, shepherded his halved flock right into the jaws of wolves. He'd died of that grievous understanding.

The altar-stone was silent, and cold against my back now. I got up, walked the length of the church to stretch. I went to the window, saw Hinthan walking along the edge of the wasteland, a tall boy with a strung bow in hand, a quiver filled with arrows over his shoulder. He went to hunt for supper, and I watched him till his path curved away behind the church and into the wood.

In the burnt fields thin wisps of smoke yet rose, and I said, "Aescwine, what about the lurkers among the dead out there?"

He snorted. "Looters come to strip the dead. They belong to no one, not to Peada, not to the Outlaw." He laid aside his whetstone. In the silence my ears yet rang with the song of iron and stone. "And they don't belong to me."

Cynnere put his back to the altar and the two of us, stood looking out into the chapel.

"They don't belong to you, Aescwine? To the exile band? How do the *wraecca* belong to you?"

Cynnere sighed, but quietly for loss. I wasn't supposed to hear that. And Aescwine looked like one carved from snowy marble, so white and still was he in the starlight. Solemnly, as though speaking of a holy thing, he said:

"We belong to each other, my *wraecca* and me; as longship-riders belong to each other, cast out on the sea to live or die by the strength or weakness of all. That's why Cynnere will tell you I'm off my head, but I'm not. We came here together, him and me and that girl. But we didn't get to stay here together. Ah, no. The Christ-priest wouldn't have devil-kin staying in Eotenfeld— ay, not even to sleep in the pig-runs.

He must've been some kind of witch. He managed to change us *dvergr* into soul-reft *aelfen* in the minds of all the folk who heard him. Most of *mann-cynn* here thought the dead god spoke out of his mouth, but some didn't and one of them told me where I could find friends. 'Like-minded folk,' he said. He meant my *wraecca*. They took me in, and Cynnere stayed here.

" 'Old 'un,' he said once. 'How can you say you'll be alone when you'll have me with you?' " Aescwine spat. "Well, I'd've been all alone with that cold promise if there hadn't been *wraecca* to take me in."

Cynnere flinched as under whip-sting. And I wouldn't judge between one man's pain and the other's, Sif, but neither would I watch one hurt the other.

"Cynnere," I said. "Go. Don't stay here. Go."

He didn't look around, or say anything. But he left us and went back to the chapel. Soft, Rowenna's voice lifted in question. I heard no answer.

"Aescwine, you're too hard on him."

"Am I? He made his choice, and he stayed with the girl. I didn't have a choice to make. There's no more to say about it."

There was more to say, but none that he'd hear. And so I asked him which way Peada and Osric went when they were done here.

"Peada went south. Osric went east. Are you still heading south?"

Outside I heard an owl waking, the long, hollow cry. "I have to get home, Aescwine."

"I wish you luck, then."

He sheathed his sword and pouched the whetstone. He came down from the altar and said I should have some supper and a night's sleep before I left.

"Me, I'll come back and say you farewell when it's time."

And he left me, went right out through the chapel and looked not one way or the other.

I said to Cynnere, "Are you coming with me?"

Simply, he said, "I am."

Lydi looked up from the fire she was tending. Only to see me, she knew I'd been hurt somehow. She touched my hand; her fingers closed round mine. Rowenna, sitting with her back to a wall and Wulfhere's head on her knee, regarded me silently. The sleeping boy was as white in the face as she.

"Rowenna, our way's got no easier than before. We're chased and hunted. But you're welcome to come with us, if that's what you want to do."

She put her hand on the *aetheling's* shoulder. "Thank you,

dvergr. This second time, thank you. I will go with you, and maybe I'll end up being worth something to you."

I didn't say anything to that, and when Lydi told me that Hinthan would soon be back with something for supper, I said I wasn't hungry and that I wanted to be alone for a while.

I went walking down all the paths of broken Eotenfeld, the alleys between houses, the ways through the trampled gardens behind burnt cottages, past what might have been an ale-house. Once I stopped to watch Hinthan come out of the woods. Unseen, I watched him walking, the hunter with a brace of hares over his shoulder. They were already gutted and skinned, and the meat steamed in the chilling air. When I saw him safely got back to the church, I went walking again, through the rest of the village and finally out to the edge of the wasteland where the wind ran mourning and the sudden green eyes of a wolf glared. There wasn't much worth picking over now; the ravens had most of the feast.

Far away from the village, close to the dark wildwood, Owain stood. I stopped to watch him, and he heard me or felt my eyes on him. He turned, lifted his hand.

"Poet, come and talk to me."

And that was a dare, for we two hadn't spoken but scant words to each other since I'd done the speaking for a ghost. I took his dare, and went the rest of the way to stand beside him. We were quiet for a while, me reckoning that if he wanted to talk, he'd better start; him smiling into his dark beard and seeing how long I could wait for him to say something.

I could stand there next to him—next to all witch-cursed nine hundred years of him—and wait till the night ended, the day came and went, and he fell over from hunger and thirst. When that became clear, Owain let go a gusty sigh and laughed low.

"It is a long time, poet—nine hundred years. I feel like a stone on the land, one of those tall ones raised up and capped and left like a question in the woods. Who raised it, giants or giant-killers? Why did they leave it just there? And I can't tell you I've learned much in these long years. People come and people go—Romans, Arthur, you Saxons. What's it to me? About what it is to that old stone standing when leaves go racing by in the wind. Not much. One day follows another and they've been a long tally, but I don't know anyone who lays himself down to sleep thinking, 'I've had enough of days and living.' Not even the un-souled *aelfen,* not even them."

I looked uneasily around me, across the wasteland, into the wildwood where fire-flies danced. It wasn't good to stand out in the night and speak so lightly of the un-souled.

Then, sharply, Owain said, "Promises, ay? You've got one to keep, Lydi's got another. What are you going to do, poet, when time comes for me to take her away from you?"

A light sprang out in the front of the church as the door opened. Lydi stood there in the shining gold, one hand on the latch, another on the doorpost. Just as I saw her, she looked back over her shoulder, listening to what someone had to say.

"Owain," I said, watching my witch in the doorway. "When the time comes for Lydi to go and keep her mother's promise, I won't stop her." I turned and met him eye to eye. "But if you try to take her away from me, I'll find you and I'll kill you."

And him, Sif, he laughed, suddenly and wildly.

"Ah, poet!" He slapped my shoulder. "Wouldn't it be something to talk about if it came to that?"

He went away, back to the church and the fire and the light, shaking his head and laughing still.

We were ready to leave burnt Eotenfeld when the eastern sky filled up with ruddy gold light and only late and lonely stars clung to the sky. Last before we left, I went out to the wildwood's edge with Hinthan to say farewell to Aescwine.

We went alone. Cynnere waited for us at the church. He had nothing to say to Aescwine, and Aescwine had nothing to say to him. Yet as hard as things were between them, I wished Aescwine would come away with us. I didn't like to leave him behind, didn't like it that he'd changed himself into an exile when there was no need.

Now, in moonlight and night-chill, Aescwine said, "Skald, what will you have to say about a man who leaves his king so suddenly? Will you say he's shamed himself?"

"I'll say the truth, Aescwine; that sometimes ways part, and no matter if we don't want them to."

He nodded, but only shortly and like he didn't wholly believe in what I said.

Four *wraecca* came out of the wildwood, suddenly, like shadows given life by a witch's magic. Hinthan's hand dropped to his knife, but I gripped his wrist, whispered, "Peace!" and he stilled. One of the *wraecca* was Reginleif, and she came and stood close to me. She lifted a hand, strong and callused like a soldier's, took the leather plait round my neck and drew the stone from within my shirt.

"Ing," she said. "The Unknown." She held the rune-writ stone up to the young light, then tugged a little on the plait. "Are you going to the sea, Ghosts-Skald?"

Hinthan lifted his head; if he were a hound his ears would have been cocked.

Reginleif tapped the agate-mantle clasp with her other hand, then gently caressed the journey-stone. "Are you wandering away over the sea, like Ing?"

"No," I said, suddenly chilled and trying not to shiver.

"That's not what the signs say. We'll see, ay?"

Her hand lingered warmly when she returned the stone to where it had been.

"Ach, girl, you leave him alone now." Aescwine caught Reginleif round the waist, held her tight in the crook of one arm. "He's not got any interest in you. He's got him a garden-girl hidden away somewhere, and come whatever may, he's back to her each winter. And you, you're too wild. Who's ever going to tame you, ay?"

"You will," she said, and she put her arms round him, kissed him well, and took her place in the circle of *wraecca* again.

She loved him, Sif. You could see it in the way she stood at his back, her sword in hand, ready to defend him no matter what she must do or give. She loved him like a soldier and a daughter, a sister and a beloved. She loved him like a Valkyrie loves the man Wotan sends her to find. You could see it in her.

No longer did Aescwine and I stand at farewell now than it took to wish each other luck and him to give me a father's kiss. As warmly did he say farewell to Hinthan, but my boy had things to say before he would let Aescwine go.

"I hate it that you're leaving," he said, low. Then, more boldly, "I hate this Northumbria! Aescwine—don't go."

"Ach, now," my old friend said. He took Hinthan by the shoulders. "It's *wyrd*, youngster; fate. Might be I've been taking this step since first I left the Northlands, Daneland, so far away."

And from Daneland, to Cent, from Cent to Mercia. From Mercia . . . to these outlawed folk, these exiled Dwarfs, these *wraecca*. Whether or not he liked it, Hinthan knew about journeying, about fate.

"Be careful of yourself, boy," Aescwine said, when Hinthan

protested no more. "Be careful of your foster-father, ay?"

"Always," Hinthan said, and they embraced as kinsmen.

One word Aescwine said to his *wraecca,* low and not for Hinthan and me to hear, and they vanished into the wildwood like they were no more than shadows on the burnt ground.

And I stood there, Hinthan beside, and remembered the night I'd left Aescwine to watch on the hill above Haligstane. Then I hadn't turned back even once when I walked away. I'd been afraid that I'd feel as lonely as he looked if I looked back and saw him. Now I watched him and his exile band as far as I could see them, till nothing remained but the small wink of the last starlight shining on a sword, a mail-coat, maybe Aescwine's white, white beard.

Swift in me rose up a longing to go with them, Sif. Suddenly the yearning came and pulled at me, as though it would take me into the woods and the last of the night, under the trees to run with the *wraecca* band, the Lost and the Last of Northumbria.

But I didn't do that. Hinthan said, "They're waiting, Garroc," and across the burnt fields I saw Lydi and Rowenna, Cynnere and Owain and Wulfhere, my own small band of wayfarers ready to leave. And so I went back with Hinthan to all my promises.

‹23›

We were six riders with four horses—Hinthan's red mare and my grey, and two sturdy geldings Cynnere had found running loose after Peada and Osric laid waste to Eotenfeld. We made good speed, but we didn't cross into Mercia that day, though by my reckoning we were but a day's ride from the border. I wanted to go east a while and not cross so close to Ceastir, where surely Peada was keeping himself these days, comfortable among his mother's kin while he searched for his father's heir.

We made a slow progress through the wildwood, beneath the high roof of branches just turning to gold and bronze and copper. Hinthan rode ahead, and Owain, afoot, went with him. From time to time the sound of their voices drifted back, a weaving of talk and no word clear enough to tell me what they were talking about. Rowenna rode with Wulfhere, and she held my king's son before her as warmly as though he were her own. Wulfhere, a boy in exile, on a dangerous road with strangers, welcomed that warmth.

And I, astride that trusty grey I'd borrowed from Merewal, had Lydi up before me. Her eyes were ever on Cynnere, my friend riding close beside Rowenna.

"He's in love with her," Lydi said.

I said that I supposed he was. "But love's brought him no good luck. All it's done is force him to choose between Rowenna and Aescwine. He couldn't have made a good choice, no matter what he did. He was bound to lose one of them."

"You think it was love forced that choice on him?"

"I do." I smiled a little. "But you don't, ay?"

"Not when I look at him."

Cynnere leaned close to say something to Rowenna, and he shone in the sunlight—yellow hair and beard like gold, the light glinting from his sword's grip, from bridle-iron, from one gleaming silver arm-band, a gift got from Erich War Hawk for a good service given. And there was a shadow on him, too; the friend-loss he couldn't prevent.

"But when I look at him I see how a woman would fall in love with him," Lydi said.

"One or two have."

"But he's not ever been in love."

I laughed then, and asked her how she knew all this about a man she'd only just met.

"I watch, and I see. Garroc, I don't think Aescwine wanted Cynnere to choose between him and Rowenna."

"He acts like he did."

"That's how he acts. But I think—if he doesn't know it now— he'll soon see that he's angry because Cynnere had a choice to make, and he didn't."

"Ay, that got taken away, didn't it? These *Cristens* are a blight and a darkness."

"Not all, and none of them are so hard-hearted in Wales. There's more joy in them than in those Roman-taught Men." She smiled and a small dimple danced at the corner of her mouth. "There's even been a priest known to come up the hill to Gardd Seren now and then looking for me or Aelfgar."

I said nothing about that, though I knew it was true.

"Garroc, this pain between your friends doesn't have to do with the god. It has to do with the people who worship the god."

Rowenna looked up to smile at Cynnere, and I said, "It's all one to me."

"But it isn't all one." Lydi turned a little in my arms and she lifted the Ing-stone from out my shirt. "If it's all one, why would Raighne have given you this? This god-rune has nothing to do with the Christ, and yet your friend recognized its value."

Sunlight made the limestone glitter, and the etched rune on the shining stone showed dark and deep. I remembered what Reginleif had asked when she saw the agate mantle-clasp and the Ing-stone.

Are you wandering away over the sea, like Ing?

Lydi traced the mark, gently with her forefinger. "It's like the mark of our little blue pot, the gift-rune."

The gift-rune, the mark of a soldier's blood sacrifice, the mark of a promise. Ing's mark was like *gifu,* but doubled. It could be seen as one promise joined to another.

Are you wandering away over the sea, like Ing?

No, I wasn't. It was Lydi who was going to the sea. On swift impulse, I reached to take the Ing-stone from my neck, for it seemed that of the two of us, Lydi would need it most. But she stopped me.

"No, man dear. This isn't for me." She closed my hand around the stone. "This rune-stone is yours, and runes don't come to us by chance."

Saying that, she echoed words she'd never heard; Stane's words, spoken a long time ago when I was a boy waiting for my father to come home. *No rune comes to you by chance, youngling.* And so I kept the Ing-stone, but I didn't understand what need I'd have of it. I was bound inland, east and south to Mercia, then west to Gardd Seren.

Ahead, brush rustled and Cynnere laid a hand on Rowenna's bridle rein, reached for his short-sword. But he let the weapon go when he saw Owain coming back down the path. Hinthan walked beside him, leading his red mare. They were talking together, but not as they used to when friendship was easy between them. They looked like people who'd just met on the road, strangers who didn't know how to trust each other.

My eyes on Owain, I said, "When will you leave, Lydi?"

She leaned closer into my arms, and her blue eyes were like amethysts, like the color of the dimming. "I can't go much farther south."

And I couldn't do anything but go south, for the sake of my promise, for Wulfhere's sake. One promise and another, Lydi's and mine, these were not joined.

We stopped at noon to rest the horses, and while we did that, something didn't happen.

Owain Woman-Thief—him they knew in Seintwar as Owain Dwarf-Smith—didn't hear the ground-echo, was deaf to the mother-earth when she whispered of someone following quietly behind us. I heard it; I was standing with my mare beside a stream while she drank. Lydi, yet astride the grey, heard nothing, but Owain was foot to ground; he should have felt the soft step whispering in the bones of him. He didn't. I knew that, looking at him.

Owain Dwarf-Smith had been wearing a false name. He was a smith, but he wasn't *dvergr*.

"Or he's a Dwarf, and he's earth-deaf," Hinthan said when I told him what I'd learned.

"I've never heard of that happening but I guess it could, like being born blind. But I don't think that's it."

"Do you think he's *mann-cynn?* A witch who changed his shape for the bard's daughter? Lydi's mother said, 'Never forget what he is.' Maybe she warned like that because he's some witch trapped in a shifted shape."

"Maybe," I said. "Maybe."

He smiled wryly, who knew me well. "But you don't think it's that easy, do you?"

"It hasn't been so far. But I do know we're being followed, and I know that for sure. Go back along the path with Cynnere and see what you can see, ay?"

He did that, and they were gone a while. They came back with four grouse for supper, and no news. But someone was following. Each time I listened, I heard a soft padding in the ground, secret footsteps.

When it came time to find a place to stay the night, Hinthan said he'd ride ahead looking for high ground. He wasn't long gone before he came back to say he'd found an old ruin.

"You get to know how to sight for them along the Roman roads," he said. "This one's sitting high up on a grassy hill and there's no trees but at the foot."

It was no great hall he'd found, or even a fort. It was a small round place where the best of the walls stood nearly as high as

Cynnere's shoulder. Maybe, in a far time, it had been a watch-
tower. If it wasn't, it would be one soon. From the height, we'd
watch carefully against our silent follower.

Hinthan sat whittling, working a twining pattern into Owain's
oaken staff. The cuts weren't deep, nothing to weaken the wood's
strength, only a weaving of slender lines like waves curling. Inside
the larger pattern ran another: *rad* twined round *rad,* the journey-
rune braided into the waves.

Lightning flickered, far away.

I sat with my back against the lowest of the ruin's stone walls,
watching Hinthan and listening to the night and a storm coming down from the north. Outside the wall our hobbled horses
snorted and blew, good friends talking over the day. Cynnere and
Wulfhere walked watch, the man at the foot of the hill, the boy
round the outside of the ruin.

In the ground, in the bone, thunder was a thing to be felt. Like
a whispered echo, I felt a foot treading on the earth. The follower
was coming closer by stealthy steps. Owain, on his knees trying to
keep a fire going in the lee of the wall, heard only the thunder.

I looked to Lydi, standing not far away on the other side of
the wall with Rowenna. There a stream sprang up and ran away
laughing down the hill, a good place to find savory and lovage
to flavor the grouse. Now and again they stopped talking, stood
in listening silence. Like me, Lydi listened to the mother-earth.
Like anyone who'd spent time with *dvergr,* Rowenna knew when
a Dwarf was listening to what *mann-cynn* couldn't hear.

Owain looked up from his work. In the rippling veil of heat
between us the shape of his face seemed to shift, as an image
on water does when a small breeze comes and breathes on it.
When he saw me watching he smiled, white teeth flashing in
dark beard.

"You can feel it," he said. "Can't you?"

"Feel what? The storm?"

"That. And the time pressing close, all filled up with our promises."

A chill crept along the back of my neck. Wulfhere stopped in
his watch-walk; out the corner of my eye I saw him fit a stone
into his sling. Lightning flashed, closer.

"Wulfhere," I said.

He stopped, wild-eyed and trembling, like a yearling colt with
the storm-dread on him. I picked up two stones from the ground,
and took a seat on the wall.

"For your sling." He accepted what I offered. His hand was cold as ice. "It's all right, boy."

The king's son said nothing. Our rickety bridge of words had collapsed on the road from Deorcdun, and neither of us had tried to build another. Hinthan put down his knife, set aside Owain's staff. We were listeners, all of us on that hill, and he'd been listening to Wulfhere and me. He took up bow and quiver, and vaulted the wall. The two boys went together, walking the watch.

I tapped my knife in restless rhythm against the wall. Iron ticked on stone. Thunder rolled, tumbling down the sky. Hobbled horses snorted and stamped. A whisper, quieter than the hushed voices of women, I heard steps on the north side of the hill.

Lydi came and stood close to me. The green shirt was untied at the throat, and a stronger breeze shaped that shirt to her. Her cropped hair danced lightly against her neck and cheek. Not even a reach away from me she stood, looking soft and warm as the grey-winged dove she liked best to be in shape-shifting magic. She smelled of sky and quickening wind. I touched her, lips and chin and the curve of her cheek.

Lightning flashed, and in her eyes I saw the storm-fear she could hide from everyone but me. I took her hands, held them in mine. Without words, I told her we'd be all right.

The earth whispered. Lydi lifted her head. Across the ruin Rowenna saw.

"Go on now," I said, smiling. "She's afraid and she wants a friend."

It was all she needed. Calming Rowenna, Lydi would calm her own fear.

Hinthan came near and I stopped him, spoke a few words, told him to pass them on to Cynnere. One fat drop of rain fell. Another. I said, "Wulfhere, come inside the wall." Hissing, the wind rose, warm and heavy from the south.

Owain cursed the fire and the flinders flying up in the wind. He turned to look for Lydi, and found only me. Even Owain Earth-Deaf knew there was danger near now.

"Don't worry, Ghosts-Skald," he said. "I'll watch out for her." He glanced at Wulfhere. "You just keep an eye on that holy promise of yours."

Long and slow, his smile; as though he'd won something.

Thunder lashed like a whip-crack.

Cynnere shouted: " 'Ware! Behind you, Hinthan!"

An arrow shrilled over the wall, past me. Cynnere cried out in pain—Rowenna screamed—and I dropped behind the wall, yanked Wulfhere down beside me, held him tight in one arm, short-sword ready in my other hand. The boy's heart beat hard; I felt it running under my hand.

Cynnere staggered against the wall and Hinthan heaved him over, came scrambling behind him as another arrow flew. I smelled blood heavy on the night air. Hissed another arrow over the wall, and another. Lydi bent low, ran to Cynnere. She wasn't more than a faint shadow in the night and the rain. A moment later she cried for help, and Wulfhere took a deep breath and broke away from me. On hands and knees he went to her.

Hinthan raised up to loose an arrow and shouted cheer to someone below. Lightning leaped, the heatless glare, and Reginleif vaulted over the wall, all silver shining from iron sword and ringed mail. She dove right into my arms, laughing at my surprise.

"I'm sent by our Aescwine, Ghosts-Skald. He reckoned you'd miss his good sword-arm on your way."

Another arrow whistled over the wall and Reginleif wriggled out of my arms, elbowed me aside to better see down the hill. I pulled her down again as an arrow flew past, tugged at her silvery hair. Came a flock of arrows after that, all screaming high and thinly. And my heart beat hard and heavy in me, banging against ribs. This was not a swordsman's fight, and we had only one bowman.

"Reginleif, what's out there?"

"Welshmen!"

An arrow skittered past my hand, wood clacking on stone. Then there was no arrow, but a long line of blue-edged flame. Like a snake, that fire, hissing, dying in the rain but taking longer to do it than fire should.

"And some witches," said Reginleif, grinning. "Didn't you hear 'em?"

"I heard you," I growled.

"You didn't hear *me,* skald. No one hears me, not even earth-kin." She cocked a thumb over the wall, then ducked another arrow, laughing. "You heard one of them."

Hissed another arrow, and Hinthan ducked. "Could you talk about that later?"

Streaming with rain, his face; and bright, bright as any shining shaft of lightning. I didn't answer, and he didn't wait for one. The night filled up with a terrible high howling, the foemen's battle-song.

Foes ringed us, swiftly got all the way around the bottom of the hill. Arrows flew from every quarter. The night shattered into blood-red light as witch-fire poured down on us to burn us out of our haven. And all around the ruin shadows and red witch-light, night-black and white storm-glare, leaped and wrestled and fought with each other.

Not only warrior-witches came against us, Sif; no Welsh lord ever had more than two or three with him. Always the strength of his army is his wild-hearted soldiers. These, shouting and singing and howling after battle, came up the hill after us in numbers three times our own and more, a few riding, the rest afoot.

Now came a fight that welcomed swordsmen, and even as I lifted iron I heard Cynnere's bellowed rage, the clash of his sword on a foeman's blade. He was hurt, and bleeding, but still on his feet and fighting. Nor did he fight alone; Owain laid about them with his quarterstaff, broke bones and heads with the rune-carved oak, the staff whistling with each mighty swing.

Hinthan loosed shaft and shaft. I tried to stop the tide of foes with keen-edged iron. At my other shoulder Reginleif laughed in wild battle-joy. She who was named for a Valkyrie had a chilling war-song, beat out the rhythm of it with sword on foe's sword. Together we three fought, to hold back foemen surging like sea-swell, for our lives and our friends.

Roared thunder, flared lightning. Leaped a tall man atop the wall, dark-bearded, wild-eyed, and bellowing like the storm-god.

"Wulfhere Gytha's son! I name you!"

Behind me Wulfhere wailed in blood-chilled terror. I thrust hard at the Welshman, gutted him with iron, and his blood poured down, black in the red glare. In the same moment Hinthan let fly a black-fletched bolt and killed a foeman who came scrambling over the dead to get inside the wall.

Reginleif thrust herself between Hinthan and me, slapped his shoulder and pointed to the middle of the ruin. Our night-haven was all afire, and the rain falling looked like a golden curtain shimmering in the wind. Beyond, untouched by even spark or flinder, my Lydi knelt, bent over someone, undefended.

Hinthan ran to Lydi, bow in hand.

Came another horseman over the wall, and another. Soldiers afoot followed, their iron blazing in the firelight, in god-light. Back to back, silver Reginleif and I fought all who came at us. Sweat stung in cuts, blood ran into my eyes. Fire heated our ringed war-shirts, rain fell down on us and rose up from us, steaming. Like a smithy, that small ruined watch-tower, and all the iron in it was red, wild and virgin.

Someone got between Reginleif and me. She cried out and fell

away. Now I had no friend at my back. Swiftly fire circled me
round, the fence ever shifting, felled by rain, kindled up again by
magic, hissing, wind-lashed. And I wasn't alone, hemmed in there.
I couldn't see but the form of my foe—him a Dwarf like me. The
near blaze blinded me to all but shapes. And that was enough for
me. Like it was a war-axe, I lifted my sword, the blood-running
blade—and the witch lunged at me, grasped both my wrists and
held the stroke.

His hands burst suddenly afire and only one of us felt the flame,
his terrible burning grip.

"Wulfhere Gytha's son! Where is he?"

I dropped to my knees, skin searing, blood heat-hissing, dumb
with pain. Flashed lightning, roared thunder. Somewhere beyond
the burning, Lydi cried out in dread and sudden lashing anger.

"Let me go! Hinthan, let me go!"

And when it seemed that all the blood in my hands and arms
steamed away into the rain and the night, that cry became a wild,
high hawk-song. A kestrel dropped screaming down from the
night, flew at the witch, talons flashing red in the firelight. The
little hawk's high cry sounded like words, Welsh-spoken magic—
Bant a thi! Ffwrdd a thi! Dos!

With glinting talons the kestrel tore at the witch's eyes. The
Welshman flung up an arm, stabbed upward and out with a long-
knife, the blade flashing in the firelight. Whistling high, a black-
fletched arrow took him in the neck, through the throat.

Hinthan!

Another arrow bit to the heart, and the witch fell into his own
fire. Now it burnt him, for he was dead and could not keep it from
him. Hard hands closed round mine, dragged me up and past the
fading fire.

Now I could cry out, Sif, and I did, howled at Hinthan to let me
go my burnt hands.

But my hands weren't burnt. They were whole, bore only the
memory of pain, and that soon fled. And it wasn't Hinthan who
pulled me to my feet, but Reginleif, looking like fire herself, her
mail-shirt reflecting flame-light. She had Hinthan's bow in hand,
his quiver slung over her shoulder.

All round me the witch-fire was dying down, steaming in the
last of the rain. The fighting was done, the foemen fled. And
god-Thunor must have seen enough battle to sate him, for he'd
gone away, growling north and westward with the wind. Rain
fell only fitfully now. Even *mann-cynn* could hear the ground
rumbling of horses hard-ridden.

Reginleif said, "They took the boys, Garroc. Riders came and snatched 'em up and flung 'em across their saddles and ran away into the night. It all ended after that, like the boys were all they wanted in the first place." She paused, but only barely. "I don't know where the other two *dvergr* are."

And so Owain Earth-Deaf had felt what I hadn't, the time pressing close, filled up with our promises. He'd taken my Lydi away.

I tucked my hands one under each arm, remembering pain and holding close to myself. Lydi was gone away with Owain, south and west, into Wales and to the sea. About Hinthan, I knew only that he was in the hands of warrior-witches.

◄24►

I walked away from the ruined watch-tower. I walked away from Rowenna's voice lifted in a sudden ragged cry hopeless of an answer. "Wulfhere! Where is he? Hinthan!" And I heard in her cry for those lost boys something of how she'd cried out for her own children.

As though they were but rubble, I stepped over dead foemen, and Reginleif followed me. I had nothing to say and so I said nothing, and she kept as quiet. Only her mail-shirt rang a little as she walked. She wore Hinthan's quiver slung over her shoulder, gripped his bow in hand. A black-fletched arrow nocked and ready, she watched out for me as I searched for sign.

It didn't take long to find what I sought. I had the last flashes of storm-light to see by and I knew what to look for. On the north side of the hill I found churned mud, the mark of horses. Two had taken Hinthan and Wulfhere away. On the south side I saw no sign until I'd gone all the way to the bottom of the hill; then I found two sets of footprints. Rain spread them wide and stretched them long. I had no way to know whether they'd been made by *dvergr* or *mann-cynn* until I found a clear set beneath an arching oak, on drier ground saw Owain's broad print and the mark of Lydi's slender foot. With the help of faint lightning, I followed the marks a little way into the woods, saw that no other set of prints met with them, none joined them. They went alone, south.

Reginleif cleared her throat softly. "You think that's the two of them?"

I nodded.

"Well," she said, standing easier. "Maybe it's just as well they're gone, ay? Those two were Welsh and—"

I turned a cool look on her. "And what?"

She shrugged. "And nothing." Then—sudden as lightning— she grinned. "Why, Ghosts-Skald! Are you hot after that Welsh girl? Oh, faithless! What about your garden-girl—? Oh! This *is* the garden-girl! A Welshwoman, and her a winged witch, too. Well, well. That's something our Aescwine doesn't know, ay?" Swift, surprise fled before a frown. She shook her head ruefully. "Who are you going to chase after, Ghosts-Skald—your foster-son or your garden-girl?"

I stood silent in the weary fall of spent rain from oak leaves onto brush, onto stone, onto earth. And I took the mantle-clasp, the journey-stone, from my shirt, held it up to see the new grey light shine on all the agate's pathways. Round and round those roads went, Sif, and all ended where they started. In new light, I saw my own fingers, unburnt. My hand shook as I remembered pain that left no mark. Belly-sick, I filled up with fear to think of Hinthan in the hands of one of those witches.

In the ruin, on the muddy hilltop, I heard Cynnere's voice, low and troubled. Beside me Reginleif spoke gruffly, said that she supposed I should make up my mind soon.

"Your garden-girl and your foster-son." She sighed over my bad luck. "It's time to choose."

I turned away from the footprints under the oak. Reginleif was wrong; it wasn't time to choose, because I didn't have a choice to make. Lydi had gone away to keep a promise. I must do the same.

Rowenna took up Wulfhere's scrip from the mud and handed it to me. The sail-cloth sack was rain-soaked, but when I reached inside I found the box's tarred seams tight.

"Hold it for him," I said, giving the scrip back to her.

Her eyes lighted, a little with hope. "Do you know where they've been taken?"

I didn't, but Reginleif did. She came and sat by me on the wall to say that Bran of Gwynedd had a stead not far from here.

"It's so close to the borderland that no one can say from one day to the other whether it's in Welshlands or Northumbria." She ran a finger thoughtfully along the black cock-feather of one of Hinthan's arrows. "I'd bet those were his witches here tonight. No horseman'll reach the stead before the dimming. But us afoot could get there well before they do."

"How is that?" Cynnere asked, looking doubtful and not so trusting. "We've not got wings to wear, girl."

He glanced at me, to tell me he'd seen a witch wear wings and fly in this ruin, that witch one I'd come riding with to Eotenfeld. And Aescwine's pretty *wraecca* smiled, her eyes sparkling.

"Now, now, Cynnere; don't be speaking against that little kestrel or our Garroc'll take a bite out of you." She winked broadly. "That's his garden-girl."

Cynnere's eyes widened, but I gave him no time for questions.

"If you're finished with that," I said to Reginleif, "tell me how to get to Bran's stead."

She sobered, quickly became the keen soldier Aescwine knew.

"Sign says the Welshmen went south from here, which is what they'd do if they wanted to take the fastest way back to the stead. The woods west of here are thick and tight and no horseman carrying a boy over his saddle can expect to get far in there. But we could get through afoot, while they'll have to go south and west to the river, where the clear paths are, and then cross at the bend and go north again to the stead by steep paths. Even afoot, we'll get to the stead before 'em. That river's not as easy to cross as some you've seen."

Cynnere grumbled that he hadn't seen any river lately that was easy to cross, and I closed my hand tight round the gold-gripped agate, the clasp pinned to my shirt.

"Now," I said. "Here's what I'll do. I'm going after the boys, and I'm leaving now, though it's not full light. Anyone who wants to come with me is welcome. Anyone who wants to stay behind, or go another way, is welcome to do that."

Cynnere stepped forward. He no longer bled from the arrow wound in his shoulder; the bandage Rowenna had made of his shirt showed clean. But there was another pain, hidden almost out of sight. However much Aescwine had claimed to be hurt, that much pain he'd inflicted on his old friend. Now Cynnere braced. He wouldn't flinch if I doubted him.

"I'm with you, Garroc."

And I said, "No need to tell me what I know."

Rowenna let go a held breath. "Garroc, if you'll have me, I'll go too. Twice you've found me, and twice you haven't left me. Maybe this time I can help you."

She said that as though we had a choice, Sif; as though she could decide not to go with me and yet survive on her own here in the wildwood, as though I could leave her alone in merciless Northumbria. It was a brave courtesy. I told her she was welcome.

And so we three went out in the wildwood, followed Reginleif through the soaking forest, to find the hall of Bran of Gwynedd and take back Hinthan and Wulfhere.

Cynnere and I crouched outside a rusty bracken thicket, in a spill of late sunshine with the last of the wildwood between us and Bran Hel-Thane's hall, waiting for the wide yard to grow quiet. In the brake behind us, Rowenna knelt, clutching Wulfhere's scrip close. Reginleif kept watch at the head of the steep hill-path, watched for Welshmen coming home with prisoners.

"What plan, Garroc?" Cynnere had asked, as we'd followed Reginleif through the woods.

I told him I didn't have one, but I would when I needed it.

"What plan?" he'd asked when we got in sight of the hall.

"None yet," I'd said. "Till we get all round the stead and know the ways of it."

We did that silently, Cynnere and me, and we found that Bran's stead was a fine one. For the distance of two bow-shots around the hall the ground lay clear; no enemy could come sneaking to attack. The hall was wood-framed and thatch-roofed, flanked by byres and hay-stores and barns. Behind it lay bake-houses and one smithy, with the smoke rising from both. We'd seen hall-folk crossing from the byre with baskets of eggs, with yoked buckets of water drawn from a freshet near the bake-house, with cheeses from the cold-house. These were Welsh, as you'd expect in a Welsh lord's hall, and some were Dwarfs and some were not. So, too, you'd expect of a Welsh lord.

And warriors came striding from the ringing forge where weapons were born, gripped gleaming iron. Dwarfs and Men, these soldiers weren't Welshmen. They spoke Saxon and they rounded their words as Irelanders do, but the round was rougher. So do the folk of Scotland speak. So did Outlawed Osric's men speak, for there is where he spent his childhood and these were the faithful men who'd gone into exile with him, his father's friends who'd learned over years to roll their words as the Scots do. Osric was a guest of Bran's, and his men seemed very comfortable about the stead.

In that, Sif, I found my hope. Peada knew Hinthan, and Bran had reason to remember him as the archer who'd killed a man or two of his. But there was no sign of those two around the stead and so Osric would be the one to receive the prize Bran's men would soon be bringing here. The Outlaw wouldn't know Hinthan from anyone, and certainly not from Wulfhere. Peada had set half the

Isle on his brother's trail, showed how valuable he considered his young brother, and so the man would be a fool who didn't hold out for a heavy ransom before he turned the prize over to Peada. I'd never heard that Osric was a fool, and I never heard of a man mounting war who didn't need all the gold he could get. Osric would keep both boys safe till they could be sorted out.

And with hope, Sif, a plan kindled. I would get inside that hall, and I'd do it before the Welshmen arrived.

"That's a thin plan," Cynnere said doubtfully. "What're you going to do—walk up to the door and ask them to let you in?"

"Yes, but not with the yard all crowded with soldiers like it is. Someone's apt to kill me before he thinks to ask why I'm here. I'll wait till I only have to deal with a door-ward."

"And what do you do when you get inside?"

"Wait."

He tugged at his beard. "And how do you get out again?"

It was Reginleif who answered him, her green eyes sparkling with laughter. "Why, I'd think that was easy to reckon out. Once Garroc captures the boys back and kills everyone in the hall, he'll have no trouble at all walking right out the front door."

She didn't think mine was a good plan, but she admitted that—lacking an army to storm the hall and drive everyone out before the Welshmen arrived with their prisoners—there wasn't much else to be done. Rowenna kept quiet through all this, motionless in the fern brake. Cynnere said she was praying, and he said he reckoned that couldn't hurt.

And so Cynnere and I watched in the shadows while Reginleif watched at the head of the hill-path. When at last I saw only a door-ward standing in the yard, I sent Cynnere to bring Reginleif back, for there was no need to watch anymore. He did that, went soft-footed through the woods. He was a while coming back, longer than I liked. Rowenna didn't pray now, but looked away into the woods, waiting for him. And when Cynnere came back at last, he had no good news.

"Reginleif's gone," he said, low and bitterly. "And the sign says someone else was there with her, a Dwarf by the size of the print. They didn't spend too much time standing around, and they went north into the woods." Cold and ice-gleaming, his blue eyes. "She led us into a trap, and now she's gone."

"You don't know she's done that," Rowenna said.

"I don't know she hasn't."

"Aescwine sent her to Garroc, Cynnere." She laid a hand on his arm to soothe. "Do you think he'd sent her to harm?"

He didn't think so, Sif. He'd never think that of Aescwine, no matter what pain lay between them. But he wouldn't say it aloud. Nor did I think Reginleif had planned treachery. For what reason? And I didn't know what else to do now but what I'd planned.

"Cynnere, take Rowenna and go into the woods to wait."

"But you might need help—"

"No doubt about that. But unless you can manage to find me an army to bring with us, you'd best keep to the woods and watch from there. I might need cover coming out again."

And between us, a silent understanding: I might need cover only if I came out again.

"Luck," he said glumly, clasping my hand.

"*Dia dhuit,*" Rowenna whispered. "God to you, Garroc."

The words were the ones Raighne of Haligstane had used when I left him to his god and Haligstane, soft words spoken in the language of the Irelanders. When I whispered her thanks I felt the monk's rune-stone slide a little against my skin.

I walked across the yard, through the blue dusky shadows and into the last light. I never looked right or left, never gave sign that I was but one lone man come to the hall looking for food and drink. So I said to the door-ward, and I told him I was Garroc Ghosts-Skald who was willing to pay for all with what is always welcome in any land, a poet's song or story.

The door-ward laughed in a good-natured way. He saw no threat in one man alone. Like me, he was *dvergr*. He was a young man and he said his name was Ros. He gave no father's name, but I didn't know if that was because he saw no need to be overly polite to an untried skald or because, like Welshfolk and we Saxons, the Last of Scotland don't take father's names.

"Ghosts-Skald, is it? Ay, it's a brave name y'got for y'self. Do y'talk to the dead, then?"

"From time to time," I said.

"An' what do them dead have to say?"

I smiled darkly. "Whatever they want to say."

Came the dimming, at last free of the woods, the dusk like a dog at my heel. Ros gave one swift look across the clear yard, around the edges of the woods. White-eyed, that look; he wanted to be sure I'd brought none of the unliving along with me.

"Well, then," he said, "come in if yer coming."

He opened the door wide, and waved me in. I entered, and laid my short-sword on a bench near the door as all good hall-guests do.

The fire-witch's hall was all bright golden light and feasting, filled up with folk eating and drinking. All of these were Osric's, part of the army Northumbrians and Mercians had learned to fear this summer. They looked very comfortable there in the Welshman's hall. More than one man lifted a laughing girl right off her feet and set her on his knee. Not too many objected, and those who did weren't heard above the din of feasting, the screams of hawks gliding from the rafters to raid the board, the snarling of hounds hunting the rushes for bones.

The forest hall wasn't hearthed, Sif. Fire and warmth and food came from a narrow, stone-sheathed pit stretching full the length of the place. I looked around me for the high seat, but couldn't find one. The table was shaped like a horse's shoe, started at one end of the fire-pit, curved round the other end, and ran back up again. Where was the head and the high seat? Where was the foot, the humbler place for a stranger come wandering in from the night?

"Sit anywhere," said Ros. He pointed to the broad benches filled with feasters. "It's a long fire; there'll be a place. Take what you want of food and drink." His dark eyes gleamed. "But if it's mead or wine or gentle ale you like, you might be disappointed. We've none of that mam's-milk here."

Me, I shrugged and said it had been a while since I'd reckoned it out that there were other reasons to go to a woman than thirst. He laughed at that, a cheerful bellow.

Flames leaped from the pit, and meat hissed and dripped on spits; kettles steamed on iron grates set within, jugs of drink warmed near the edges. I took a wooden trencher from the board and filled it with sliced meat from the whole pig roasting and bread to soak in the drippings. And I filled a stone cup from a warm jug, brimmed it with a drink lovely and clear and colored like amber, and went to sit against the wall, in the shadowed place between two bracketed torches. There I hoped to be alone and unnoticed, able to listen to the talk of the hall.

What I hoped for didn't happen. Ros came to keep me company, him with a jug half-filled with whisky. He sat cross-legged on the floor beside me and waited in easy silence while I ate some meat and bread. Then he took a long drink from his jug, lifted it to me in invitation to drink what I had.

Only the smell of the amber drink set my eyes to watering, Sif, but I had no mind to hear what talk of wet-nurses would surely follow if I didn't taste deeply. I downed half of what was in the cup, and learned that this is not a good way to have your first drink of *usquebaugh*.

I might as well have taken a mouthful of live embers, but I wouldn't spit out the whisky. For pride, I braced and swallowed and sat as still as I could till the fiery drink made its way from mouth to belly, the heat of it spreading all through me and right to my fingers and feet. I did that watching the hawks in the rafters twin themselves.

Ros nudged me. "Not your mother's milk, ay?"

"No," I said, but thinly. "This is somewhat milder."

He let that boasting be, maybe counting it to my favor that I was able to swallow the stuff and yet talk. He took another drink from his jug and wiped his mouth with the back of his hand.

"Tell me, skald, why is a Saxon like yourself lost in these Welsh woods?"

And I, whisky-inspired, became the wandering skald I claimed to be in only a breath's time.

"Welshlands? Is that where I am? Ay, well, I don't know how man's supposed to reckon where he is from day to day anymore. These days you spend most of your time hiding from the *mann-cynn* around here for fear they'll be chucking rocks at you while they're deciding how best to insult you. Might be a wonder to you, my friend, but it's none to me that a man loses his way."

Ros nodded glumly, urged another drink on me. I accepted, and this swallow sat warmly in my belly.

"I hear you, skald. We're all full of Christ-priests where I come from, but they're home-folk and they don't bother anybody. Some of 'em you could even like. These people of Rome, though—"

He clenched a fist and brooded over it for a while. I took another drink.

"Skald, I didn't used to think there was a great lot of difference between me and any Man you see—well, but that they're so lofty for whatever reason pleased the gods who made 'em. But there's no difference in the heart of us. Folk are folk. You can make friends with 'em or enemies of 'em, but none of that has to do with if or not they're Dwarfs or Men." He looked around the hall, at the smoke hanging like a thick pall in the middle of the air, not rising, not settling. "Or it didn't used to. It's a dark age these people of

Rome are bringing to the Isle, and it's Eadwine lets 'em do it. They call him Faith-Breaker in Mercia, did you know that?"

I said that I knew it, or I thought I said it. Sweat ran on me now, I was having trouble separating Ros's voice from the larger roar in the hall, my own voice from what I was thinking. I longed for a breath of night air, and sharper wits. But Ros was brooding over his jug, and he didn't seem to notice that it took me a while to speak again.

"None of this talk makes me happy," I said. "And I'll tell you this: I'm not happy to be lost in Welshlands, either. I hope someone can set me right and tell me how to find a village they call Eotenfeld. That's where I'm bound and it's supposed to be around here somewhere, if I haven't strayed too far and—"

Ros held up a hand for silence, took the jug from under his arm, filled my cup solemnly.

"Eotenfeld, y'say?" He shook his head, drink-sad. "I hope you've not got friends there."

I had a strange urge to laugh at that, Sif, either because I was thinking of the friend I'd left there, or because I was thinking of the friends who'd broken their bond there, or because I'd had too much to drink. I managed to hold the laugh, and I told him I didn't have friends there, said the village was just a way-mark for me.

"Well, that's good. You'll not find much more than a way-mark since our Osric and Peada Penda's son went through."

I whistled low. "They're running together now, those two?"

"Two? Skald, we're talking about the un-holy trinity."

"The un-holy what?"

"Trinity. It's a *Cristen* word, means some kind of three-headed god. Or sometimes it means three different gods who're all kin to each other—that Jesu you hear about all the time, his old father, and some bird-god." Broadly grinning at his own cleverness, Ros said: "*Cristens* say 'holy trinity' and I say un-holy trinity—Peada, Bran, and Osric, yes?"

"Yes," I said, my mind still in Eotenfeld. "The young bucks rattling horns with the stags."

He nodded. "Just so. Peada and Bran are tired of waiting for the old ones to fight each other to death. Year and year Cadwalla and the Panther have been coming against Eadwine. Year and year, they get nothing and lose nothing but the lives of their men. The boys've been getting tired of that this year."

Like a wolf grinning, him, and the whisky unbound his tongue, made him talk about some things his lord might have liked to keep private for a while.

"I'll tell you, skald, they won't be the un-holy three for long."

"Why's that?"

He didn't answer that at once, went talking on his own wandering way. And I listened, Sif, more or less, while he told some war-tales of how Peada and Osric had lately beaten back the sons of Eadwine from Ceastir and then gone raiding into Northumbria. Eotenfeld had been in their path.

"And Ceastir's where Peada's kin live," he said. "His mam's folk, and he's there now." He shook his head, grinning. "And Osric's got the use of this fine hall, some men at arms and a witch or two, while Bran's gone fighting the Panther's other boy, what's his name—?"

Merewal, I thought. Aloud I said that I didn't know the name, and I made a show of looking round the hall. "I'd like to see that Peada; I've heard some things about him. They say he's white and black, like Hel herself."

"Well, you'll not have long to wait. Our Osric's used those Welsh men-at-arms to go fetch something Peada wants—"

Ros shut his mouth then, and so suddenly I could hear his teeth click together. He looked around him, even over his shoulder, though there was not but a wooden wall there. He'd spilled out one secret too many and that brought me most of the way back to my senses. I pretended to have no interest in what he'd last said, pretended I didn't know that Peada would murder his young brother soon after he laid eyes on him, that he would know Hinthan and kill him gladly.

When I spoke, my heart was racketing hard in me, but my voice was steady. And yes, my Sif, if ever you tell anyone this tale, you may say that was a miracle because it surely wasn't magic.

"Ros, my friend, it sounds to me like a skald could find his life's worth of songs to be made right here where everyone's having a good share of the fighting—Bran battling Peada's brother, Osric and Peada fighting off Eadwine's sons. And so I guess those boys of Eadwine's learned a lesson, ay?"

Ros shook his head so hard he had to sit quiet for a moment before he could talk again.

"No, no, not at all. Eadwine's boys decided they'd like to try their luck in the south again, down by Powys way. They got whipped away from there once—all the way to Ceastir. But there'll be folk there to welcome them with good hard iron when they scramble back again."

Erich! The war-hawk *cyning* yet fought to defend the Marches.

Ros belched thoughtfully. "I'll tell you something, skald: Osric's got this much of his home back, and soon you'll see that he's not minded to share any of it with Peada and Bran."

I heard an old tale in Ros's words, of allies who fought beside each other, each looking for a chance to take all the winnings. Peada and Bran, these new war-friends, were tired of the long game their elders played, but they hadn't chosen a different one for themselves. Young and wild and sure they could have what they wanted, they didn't know how to see that Osric, him with his Scotland army, would reach right past them and snatch their prize away. Peada and Bran were fighting for a kingdom, but Osric was fighting to take back his home.

Ros said no more, fell suddenly silent. And a strangeness rippled through the hall, like the widening unease in a pool when a stone is tossed in.

"The lord's in the hall," he said. He got to his feet and nudged me to say I should stand.

I did that, tossed the rest of my meal, bones and crusts, to the hounds. I stood with the stone cup in hand, and I saw Outlawed Osric for the first time, him who was the nephew of Eadwine Faith-Breaker, him who'd been shamefully exiled when he was but a babe in his mother's arms on the day Eadwine killed his own brother Aelfric.

Well-grown now, the Outlaw was broad as an ox is, tall as a tree is, and—as Aescwine had said—not but a handful of years older than Hinthan. And maybe you're thinking, my Sif, that how a man looks is not always how he is, but I'll tell you now that this Osric had all the strength he seemed to.

He came in from one of the doors at the other end of the hall, parted the crowds of men. He looked not to the right or to the left, but strode down the length of Bran's high hall as though it were his own. From one man he accepted an offered cup, downed all that it held before he'd taken two strides. He drank whisky like it was water and never flinched from the fire. He shone as he walked, torch-light gleamed on his mail-shirt, spun along the gold arm-rings he wore.

"Folk will tell you he's *god-cynn*," Ros said, low and awed.

"He is." And, when he looked at me sideways, "I'm a skald, Ros. I know the kinship of the kings. *God-cynn*, him; and his faithless uncle, and the Golden Panther of Mercia, and Eadbald who is the King of Cent, and all their kin. Eadwine's trying to forget that, but forgetting a thing doesn't change it."

Then and suddenly, like distant thunder, we each felt the mother-earth speaking, her voice rising up even from the earthen floor of the hall, from the rushes under our feet, her news whispered in our own bones. Riders were coming.

Ros left me, but I didn't see where he went. Belly clenching tight, suddenly cold as though there were no fire to warm in the hall, as though I didn't have a bellyful of whisky, I edged along the wall. And I wasn't so easy on my feet. The whisky I'd had felt as addling as half a keg of ale. I only managed to make my way to the wide wooden doors unnoticed because all the hall-folk yet watched the Outlaw.

Hidden in shadows, I looked out on the fire-dazzling hall with whisky-blurred eyes and saw Bran's men bring their captives into the hall, Wulfhere and Hinthan. Mud-covered, those two, white-faced and weary. Both had their hands bound behind them, but only Hinthan was rope-leashed with a noose round his neck as though he were an ill-trained hound, or a murderer being brought to the gallows.

I went suddenly and coldly sober.

They shoved Hinthan, and they kicked him when he fell, laughing and yanking on that leash. And in me pride rose, like some thorny flower that is lovely and hurtful both, to see that blows or fear didn't cow my boy. Kicked to his knees, he snarled like a wolf, and he didn't stagger when he was yanked to his feet, but came up lunging, straining against his bonds, spitting curses.

Wulfhere followed and he struggled as best he could against his captors, but he was a small boy and he couldn't do much to trouble those who roughly urged him along. Few in the hall paid him much attention; all shouted and cried after Hinthan. I fell in behind the last of the Welshmen herding the two, only one of the many pressing close to see what could be seen. And so I was near enough to see the boys brought to Osric. Wulfhere they let stand, but Hinthan they felled to his knees. Two men held him there—it took two!—and kept him still before the Outlaw.

A tall Man shoved in front of me; a Dwarf followed, and he was Ros. I nudged him, and he turned. Wobbling and drunken, he grinned wide.

"Looking for a tale, skald? Might be one here—the boy's got some iron in him." He elbowed a path for us both, got us nearer just as Osric rumbled a question to one of the Welshmen, a short, lean man.

That one answered as swiftly as he would have his own lord. He was in Bran's hall, with Bran's ally. He didn't know that soon

Osric would show himself to be no friend to the witch-lord. He told the true tale of what befell last night, said how many were dead, and said a thing I'd not known. Two witches had gone out, and none survived. We who'd defended the ruined watch-tower had killed them both.

A woman's voice flew up in sudden woe, then fell to an aching moan. She'd heard the name of someone she knew among the dead. The chill light in Osric's eyes led me to guess that of Bran's folk now in the hall, none were witches.

The lean Welshman cocked a thumb at the boys. "But we got what we went for, what Peada wants."

He smiled, did Osric, very warm and friendly now, and he clapped the Welshman on the shoulder. "Looks like you got twice what you went for."

I moved only a step or two, till no one stood between me and Osric, and me a little behind him. I took a joint of mutton from the board, sliced some meat with my long-knife. I chewed and swallowed and tasted only bitter fear, but now I had my knife in hand. It was then Wulfhere saw me.

Eyes wide with suddenly dared hope, he drew breath to cry out. And because he realized in time that he'd be better off praying, the *aetheling* shouted: "Be thou, Lord God, a noble friend! Look, Lord, upon—"

Someone hit him in the back of the head and told him to stop his ranting. He did that, and he didn't look at me again. I was to him only another stranger. I praised him, but silently.

Osric waved away the two who held Hinthan. With only one meaty hand he kept my boy on his knees. With his other hand he took Wulfhere by the chin, lifted his head far back to see his face. White with terror, Wulfhere managed to stay standing, and Osric shifted his grip on Hinthan, grabbed a fistful of hair and yanked my boy's head back. Long he looked at them, Sif, but he found no way to know which one Peada would pay for.

"Tell me! Which of you is Wulfhere Gytha's son?"

Wulfhere tried to speak, but terror sucked all the words in him dry. And into the silence Hinthan cried:

"*I* am! I'm Wulfhere Gytha's son, you ball-less son of a bitch!"

Silence fell, like a pall over a dead man.

‹26›

Osric flung Wulfhere aside. The boy stumbled against a stocky, white-bearded Man who growled and pushed him roughly away— and right to me. I snarled to play the part, grabbed the *aetheling* by the shoulder and held him. He shook hard under my hand and I thought his knees were going to fold under him. When I let him go he edged away, but he didn't go far.

Osric grabbed Hinthan by the shirt and yanked him to his feet. They weren't far apart in age, but you wouldn't know it to see them—the Outlaw ox-broad, Hinthan whip-thin. Hinthan never moved, but I knew it looking at him that he had no idea how he'd get out of this.

And I saw, too, that he was ready to die. All the hall saw only a wildly defiant boy, maybe one worth remembering after he was dead. I saw what no one else did, because I knew him as no one else did. Hinthan was afraid right to the marrow. That fear made his white-lipped courage beautiful, and I swore—not knowing how I'd keep the vow—that I wouldn't let him die.

And Osric said to Hinthan, "You've got the look of the kin. Dark-headed like Peada. Black and white, like him; like Ice-Hel herself suckled the both of you. A *Cristen* boy, aren't you?"

"I am."

Out from the crowd someone called: "So's the other one to hear him rant."

Hinthan sneered. "So he is—and raised up on the pap they teach in Ireland and thereabout. Me, I know better."

He looked round the hall, head high, arrogantly, as though he were taking the count of Osric's men and sorting them. When he saw me, and Wulfhere standing near, his face twisted into an ugly hatred.

"And I was raised up with monks who taught me to have better sense than to welcome devil-kin under my roof, or ever feed one better than what my dog doesn't want." Then, like hissing, Hinthan said to me, "I've been taught about you *geldr*, ay?"

Wulfhere gasped, as you do when you see someone senselessly struck. I stood stunned and wordless. And I was so cold, Sif, it was like my blood was skinning to ice.

A serving woman cried "Shame on the boy!" and a great growling filled the hall, like the sea coming in, as Dwarfs and Men cried out against that worst of insults. And I shouted:

"Osric, hear me!"

I am a skald, I can silence a hall like that. Folk fell back, sure I was about to claim the right to beat Osric's prisoner senseless, or even to kill him. I didn't know what I was going to do or say then, but I stepped forward boldly.

Osric Outlaw eyed me narrowly; in the rise and fall of the firelight his face was a changeable thing. "*Dvergr,* I don't know you."

"And I don't know you, Osric, but I've heard of you. I'm Garroc, and sometimes they call me Ghosts-Skald. I came here for hospitality and ready to pay for that with song or tale. Till now your hospitality's been good."

I let that stand a moment, a stone in the silence.

"Now, I've heard enough here tonight to know that this boy's worth something to you, lord. I say don't damage your goods, for I've a right to claim a piece of the fee for him when it's paid. Give me that, and I'll be glad to tell all I meet that Osric Aelfric's son is a good and honorable lord, one any man must be proud to serve."

Not lord of the hall, but lord in it, Osric knew he owed me something, and he knew he'd better pay it if he didn't want folk to hear it from a skald's mouth—in words easy to remember—that he let a guest of his be mistreated while he looked the other way. People reckon it that a man who can't protect his guests can't protect his holdings.

Osric smiled, but carefully. Outlaws must always be careful. "Skald, welcome, and stay with us in peace—"

Like a storm-cry came a shout by the door. Dogs sprang up snarling and barking. Iron rang on iron outside. Someone screamed, dying. The hall filled up with the shouts of Dwarfs and Men running for weapons, and suddenly knowing they could get to none, would have only their long-knives. Good hall-guests don't bring weapons to the board.

Swords clashed outside the hall. Osric roared for silence, and roared against a storm. Another dying scream skirled up, the sound ravens love, and something heavy battered at the wooden door.

Wulfhere turned and turned again, wildly looking for me. I grabbed him by the shoulder, heard him hoarsely whispering his prayer again. *Be thou, Lord God, a noble friend. Look, Lord, upon me and shelter me . . .* ! But it was me he sought shelter with, me he clung to as he had in the river-rage.

Osric bellowed orders to panicked men who didn't hear him. He flung Hinthan away from him, shoved him to me, shouted: "Hold him for me, skald! Keep him—swear it on your life!"

I took hold of Hinthan and swore Osric the best oath I knew that I'd never be parted from the boy.

And the great wooden doors burst wide with a shattering crack, let in mounted men. One rode low over his horse's neck. Two followed close, and their swords gleamed red in the light of fire-pit and torch, thirsty for the blood of Bran Hel-Thane. The fire-witch flung balls of lightning behind him—blue-edged white, the size of my two clasped fists, spinning and crackling in the smoky air. I cut the rope from Hinthan's neck, snatched up a long-knife from the board, pressed it into his hand, gave my boy a weapon. But I'd no mind that he should have to use it. In the panic and the shouting I hustled him and Wulfhere away down the hall, to the back where the side doors were. Hinthan went stumbling ahead, bleeding from cuts, staggering against people fighting to get long-knives from the board, torches from the wall, anything to fight with.

It was hard going against the tide of them. Wulfhere trembled under my hand, his blue eyes wide as cups, his cheeks like snow, so white. I looked over my shoulder, saw we'd got more than halfway down the hall, and saw who'd chased Bran all the way home. Howling curses, wild laughter, Merewal Penda's son ducked a ball of spinning white fire. The man behind him wasn't so lucky. The fireball struck him full in the chest. Flesh burnt off bone, then bone itself burnt, and raw begging and screaming of fire-death followed us running.

Wulfhere stumbled and fell, Hinthan snatched him up from the rushes, ran holding onto him.

It was me saw that the door we wanted was warded, and the wards were Ros and Peada. Ros lunged for Hinthan, and Hinthan flung himself to the left, dragged Wulfhere with him, hauled the boy down to the rushes and covered the *aetheling* with his own body. And Ros, too full of the whisky, let himself be led, left himself unguarded. My blade went into him easily, and easily found the heart of him.

Behind us swift-flowing fire raced down the hall, raised a flaming prison for all within. And Peada filled the narrow doorway, legs wide-braced, arms folded tight across his chest. His father's throwing-axe, the rune-marked weapon, was thrust hilt-first through his broad leather belt. I snatched my knife from Ros's gut, ready to cut my way through Peada if that's what

I had to do. In the same moment Wulfhere wriggled out from under Hinthan, staggered to his feet, and tried to punch his way out of the burning hall.

Light and slender, the boy, and his brother towered over him, but sometimes it takes only one lucky blow to win a fight. Wulfhere struck that blow, punched Peada as hard as he could and right in the balls.

We got through the doorway only in time to get out of the way of a horseman thundering behind us—Bran of Gwynedd leaving home again.

There are things you hear in a battle, Sif, and things you don't know you're hearing till you've got time to notice. Bran's hall was burning from almost the moment he came fleeing home, but I didn't hear the sound of it till after I'd got into the cold night air. Then I heard fire roaring and gasping and roaring again as it won the walls and the thatched roof, crackling and cackling as trapped folk screamed in dread, shrieked in dire pain, dying. A sickening stench billowed out of that hall-pyre and into the night.

Battle roared outside the burning hall—Merewal's men and Bran's, what men of Osric's had gotten out the burning hall, Peada's men who'd never got inside. It was a collapsing battle, the four armies come together and not able to tell friend from foe in the rage and the night and the bloody glare. No fight is worse than that, for it's panicked fighting, and a panic-ridden man kills anyone who gets in his way.

I kept Hinthan and Wulfhere close to me, and all around us iron belled on iron, battle-curses flew like black-winged ravens shouting prophecy. The ground rang with the thunder of hoofs, the battle swirled and frothed like storm-whipped waters. The dark line of the wildwood was our only chance at haven and I didn't know how we'd get there with all the battle between.

Still, we must go. Peada was on his feet and raging. He wasn't going to do much walking for a while, nor much riding, but he still had the heights of his voice and he used that to shout orders. All black against the flaming hall, as though he were made of night and shadows, Peada jabbed a finger at Hinthan.

"Kill him!" he screamed. He pointed to Wulfhere. "Kill those boys!"

Hinthan, as rageful as Peada, lunged away from me. He didn't get but two steps away before I grabbed his arm, swiftly shifted grip, and held him with my arm round his neck. I reached for Wulfhere too late. As he were winged, the boy seemed to fly away from me, right up into the air. Hinthan's choked cursing turned to laughter.

"Merewal! Wulf, don't fight! He's a friend!"

Ay, Merewal, battle-wild, looking like red-bearded Thunor. He'd got out the burning hall somehow, and now he held tight to his young brother as he wheeled his big bay mare round and round Hinthan and me. Whirling his shining sword in the air, he made a small center in the battle-storm where no foeman could reach us. I knew by the laughing look of him that he knew well it was his brother he gripped tight before him on the saddle.

"Well met, Ghosts-Skald!" He looked behind him, then pointed to Hinthan. "Be ready!"

Merewal reined the bay mare sharply, turned her aside. Cynnere came riding, and he was golden as though he were riding right out of the fire. "Come on, Hinthan! Reach!" He gave Hinthan his good arm to grasp, lifted my boy up from the ground.

Again Merewal looked, then pointed to me. Came another rider; she was all silver and shining, like a Valkyrie reaching for me. Wrecker of Plans, her name. I grabbed her hand—warm and living, not icy like a Valkyrie's—and leaped up behind Reginleif, wrapped my arms round the *waecca*, held tight as we headed for the woods. We didn't ride alone, but went like the spear-point ahead of the shaft. Merewal's army came behind, some on horseback, most afoot, and there weren't very many of *mann-cynn* among them; the most were Dwarfs. These were the *waecca* of Northumbria, and many more than only Aescwine's small band. Among them I saw the Dwarfs I'd not seen when I'd left Merewal's Northumbrian hall, men I'd fought beside most of the summer.

"Reginleif! Where's Aescwine? Tell me about this *waecca* army!"

"What? Are you surprised? Didn't you tell Cynnere not to come knocking without an army?"

She laughed and said it was a shame if I'd thought she'd run off and left me. She told me that Aescwine was well and I'd see him soon enough. For the rest, she said, all my questions would have to wait till a quieter time. And then Aescwine's sword-girl said to hold tight, for she'd already pulled me out of the fire and she didn't want to have to come back with a rag and sop up what was left of me after all the army trampled me to pulp.

We went through the wildwood in single file, for the paths were narrow and no horseman could make better speed than thQse afoot.

The great glare of Bran's hall burning lighted up the sky; we heard eagles and ravens crying, wolves howling the deep of the wood, the hungry beasts of battle. Soon we lost the wails of the dying, the terrible screams, but the smoke of the burning followed after us for a long time. We went down steep trails, the great army of us, till we came to a broad racing river. That we followed south, along a barely seen path beside the bank, a deer track or hunter's trail.

After a while I slept, my head nodding on Reginleif's shoulder as if I was one of the weary boys who rode beside me. But soon I felt the horse stop, and dimly I heard Reginleif ask a question and get an answer. She heeled the horse, went a few paces forward.

"They're following," she said, low.

I woke then, and all at once, heart thudding hard as I reached for my long-knife. And my head felt like it was breaking apart; my belly was sick and sour.

"It's the whisky," Reginleif said when I leaned my head back down on her shoulder. "I hate the stuff."

Out the corner of my eye I saw two Dwarfs slip quietly into the wildwood. Behind me and around me the night breathed with faintly shifting shadows. Wulfhere, wild-eyed, looked all around him, saw that the shadows were men. The wildwood filled up with quiet-stepping *wraecca,* an army that seemed to me like all the Dwarfs that ever could have lived in this Northumbria.

"Easy, boy," Merewal whispered. "Whoever you see here is a friend." And to Reginleif he said, "Who follows?"

"Peada's men," Reginleif said. "Not too many, but enough to force a battle."

Merewal grunted and said it was too bad they all hadn't burnt up in the hall. Then he said that Peada wouldn't have to force a battle, he could come and get one any time he liked.

He put Wulfhere foot to ground, and Cynnere and Reginleif let Hinthan and me down. We waited only a moment till horses were brought for us. I gave the reins of my horse to Wulfhere and made a stirrup for Hinthan with my two clasped hands, gave him a boost onto his horse, and got up behind him to hold him.

Merewal said, "Cynnere will take you to a safe place to wait. And I ask that you do wait, *dvergr.* We've things to talk about, me and you." Swift, he glanced at Wulfhere and then away. "Garroc, I mean him no harm. My father's will is mine. I'm in your debt. Do you believe that?"

I believed that he meant his brother no harm. What sense to rescue the boy from those who'd murder him, only to do the murder himself? As for debts, we'd see.

"I'll wait," I said.

Like shadows retreating beneath the wildwood roof, Merewal and his *wraecca* army vanished away into the woods on either hand. Now we were only four riding, and we followed Cynnere, trusting.

I fell asleep again. Even so, I managed to keep hold of Hinthan, keep him straight with both my arms round him as we rode. But I didn't know about that till the stopping waked me again, the sudden stillness.

◄27►

A wide glade lay spread out before us, safe and secret in the embrace of a ring of tall oaks. A thin beck, a silver stream, ran through under the circling oaks, and smoke, smelling of meat roasting, drifted from a small cooking fire. Aescwine knelt there, tending the spit of fat grouses. Across from him Rowenna sat on the broad stump of an old oak. She coughed little when the wind shifted and sent blue smoke her way.

They were quiet when I saw them, Sif, and I didn't have the feeling they'd been talking before we arrived. Both came to greet us, and neither was surprised to see us.

Aescwine held my horse's bridle, steadied the beast when I helped Hinthan to dismount. Stunned with weariness, Hinthan staggered, but when Aescwine steadied him he said he wasn't hurt. No one listened to him. Aescwine kept hold of his shoulder and Rowenna took his arm. They led him away to the edge of the glade where the silver stream ran.

Wulfhere watched them; the *aetheling* stood at the fire and never took his eyes from Hinthan. In the space of a season all of Wulfhere's world had turned suddenly wild and frightening. There were no answers to his questions; each road taken had led to dreadful places and foes like devils and doomsmen roaring out of nightmare. Only one thing remained fixed—Hinthan Cenred's son was his friend, even to death.

And this is true of the kin of Penda, Sif: They hate fiercely and they love fiercely. If I'd never known the boy's fathering, I'd have seen it in the love blazing out of him as he watched his friend away.

• • •

I helped Hinthan to sit beside the stream near a tall broad oak. He didn't so much sit as fall. He'd not slept in more than a day and a night, nor eaten since then. The rope-burn round his neck was all raw skin and bruises. Rowenna left us with some strips of cloth torn from the hem of her gown and I soaked them in the beck. With the cold cloths I tried to ease the pain of skin rubbed bloody by the rope. I hated to see that mark, that red weal like a hangman's rune. His other hurts were a mounting-up of bruises, too many kicks, too much knocking around, more cuts than I'd seen at first.

"Youngling, I'd be interested to know which plans you passed over as too dangerous before you chose the one you acted on there in Bran's hall."

Hinthan drew a long, careful breath, let it out slowly. "I didn't know what else to do. I couldn't let them give Wulf to Peada—" He laughed, but from a cold and weary distance. "And I thought that when they handed me to Peada, I'd have a chance to fight."

"You didn't think Peada might kill you out of hand?"

He nodded. "I thought about it. And I was afraid they might kill Wulf when they decided he wasn't the one they wanted. But—" He shrugged again, and winced. "But I hoped there'd be time for me to find a way out."

He'd hoped for the best, Sif, counting every hour they were alive to the good. And maybe, in the end, he'd have managed only to sell his life and Wulfhere's at a high price. Was a look on him, a white-lipped weary look, that said he'd reckoned that would have to be enough if that's what was to be.

He slid me a sideways look. "And you? Did you have an idea how you'd get out of Bran's hall once you got into it?"

"Oh, yes," I said. "I had an idea or two."

Hinthan smiled then. "I'm sure they were as good as mine."

Suddenly his smile turned brittle, shattered and fell away. His breathing became ragged and he drew his knees up tight to his chest, rested his head on his arms. He was turned from me. I couldn't see his face.

"Garroc." He shivered, but not from cold. "In Saefast I said I hated it that you made me ride ahead of you and Aescwine like it was somehow shameful to ride beside you. And in Bran's hall—"

He looked at me, and he wouldn't say again what he'd said then.

"In Bran's hall you said 'shadow-kin.' " The word fell lifeless from my lips. I gave it no vigor, spoke it flatly. "And in Bran's hall you said *geldr*."

Not so lifeless, that word. I still flinched when I got near it. As I did, so did Hinthan.

"It's all right," I said.

He leaned back against the oak, tilted his head to see the last rosy mist rising up from the beck.

"*Geldr*," I said, deliberately poking at the wound to see how much it hurt. "Where'd you hear that?"

"Around." He smiled, but not for mirth. "From Wulfhere. He said it to one of Bran's men and got himself kicked so hard I think the word's been knocked right out of his head. Or it better be." He leaned back against the oak again, eyes closed. "He's tried it on you a few times, hasn't he?"

"A few."

"I guess you wanted to pound him for it."

"I'd have liked to."

In the glade Rowenna and Cynnere talked together, their voices low and soft and confiding. Aescwine said nothing, but I heard him walking watch, his step a restless one. Once he stopped where the horses were tethered, spoke softly to them. He was watching for Merewal and the *wraecca* army, watching for his Reginleif.

And Hinthan said, "I hate it here, Garroc. I hate this place and what it does to people."

He drew a breath, and that breath was very close to being a sob. I put my arm round his shoulders and held him close. He'd proved himself man-grown in Erich War Hawk's service, at Winwaed he'd left boyhood behind. In my cause—in our king's— he'd grown fast into his courage. But he wasn't yet fifteen, and he was still my boy. So he slept, like a boy in my arms.

A wandering breeze rattled through the dry oak leaves, sent some spinning down into the beck, little bronze boats skimming the silvery stream. A wood dove sighed, the low note I love best. The dove glided from one oak to another, her breast rosy grey in the brightening day.

I slept and I dreamed, but not of a dove. I dreamed of a kestrel, her sharp talons glinting in moonlight, her dark eye glittering, a baleful red light under her black-edged wings.

The kestrel flew over a burning war-field, a smoking battle-ground. She flew in the night, the stars shining down on her, the air under her wings a chancy thing, changing always, lifting her suddenly when she passed over a burning, dropping her with no warning when it turned cold again.

She flew over a blackened heath where funeral pyres burned like hearth-fires in a terrible hall. She flew over villages where houses and byres and smithies and grain-stores burned, the buildings all aflame as they were one massy pyre. Even in the starred heights a kestrel can see the smallest mouse afoot on the heath, and so she had no trouble seeing ravens quarreling with eagles over supper.

She saw bright-pelted wolves, the witch-beasts loping across the land. They howled and they snarled, and they killed as wolves kill, ripping the throats from foemen, tearing lifeless bodies till they were gutted. But these wolves didn't feast. That would be kind eating kind, and Dwarfs and Men don't do that. Even in the darkest battle-mood the ravening beast of battle never so far forgets what he really is, a witch in a wolf-shirt.

The kestrel flew over the wreckage and the ravaged land, the stars shining on her back. She flew over the heath, round the edge of the wildwood, the dark forest like fence round the deathland. In the center of the heath stood a tall stone cross, like a way-mark. Down she dropped, to rest on one of the arms. The stone cross was old, made by the heathland folk who'd had Dwarfs to help them. These Men had taken up new beliefs but they'd had the wisdom to keep old friends.

The kestrel was in her homeland now, but she wasn't home. The cross stood in Cadwalla's Gwynedd, the Welsh kingdom by the sea. All the burning marked Cadwalla's efforts to stop Eadwine's sons, them and their armies driven out of their own lands by Osric, beaten back to the Saxon Marches and out of there to Gwynedd. Beset by enemies, those raging sons had turned on Gwynedd, ramped up and down the coasts, burned and killed inland, and torn up the land till Cadwalla Witch-king came home to help his people.

The kestrel rose up again, and she didn't want to see what lay below now. She sailed away from the dead-grounds, away over the wildwood, over fen and marsh. She flew west till she had sight of the sea, and she went to ground again in a high place, on a dark crag where—a very long time ago—giants had stood to look out at the sea.

With a breath, a whispered word, Lydi shed her kestrel-shape, became a woman again. She walked to the edge of the land, where a pile of stones lay. Owain slept in the shadow of the rocks. No night-fog was abroad in the land, but here something like it gathered, a cold mist that smelled of the sea. It covered Owain as it were a blanket.

Owain was dreaming of home.

Out over the burned lands the moon rose, the Harvester with his grain-sack full on his back. The moon's light was pale, but not whiter than Owain's face. He looked like a dead man.

Lydi knelt beside him, reached through the mist of his cold dreams. She touched neck and wrist to find his pulse. It beat, but raggedly. He woke at her last touch. Gasping for breath, like a man with lung-sickness, Owain closed his hand round her wrist.

"I've got you, witch."

He was so weak he could hardly hold the grasp, so weak he could only just whisper. He tried to smile, as though he were joking. In her, Lydi's heart ached for him. Deeper in her, she was afraid.

Never forget what he is!

Lydi freed her hand, and she brushed his hair away from his forehead. His skin was dry, like that of a man who was burning all the strength out of him in fever.

"Owain, are you thirsty? There's a spring not far from here."

"Thirsty . . ." He closed his eyes. "No. I'm not thirsty."

Lydi got up and went to look out beyond the crag. Almost at the foot of the cliff lay the sea. They'd walk down the stony shore tomorrow, slowly. Owain was so weak, and she couldn't heal this sickness. They'd go till they got to the place where Owain would take the sea-road home, the road he'd try to make her take with him. And she might do that, even if she didn't want to. Owain lay weak and sick now; but he wouldn't always be. And she'd been shown only lately that there are stronger magics in the world than hers.

Moonlight shone on the old stone, silver on the crag where eagles had sharpened their beaks, where soldiers had honed arrow heads. Some of those marks, crossing forth and crossing back, looked like runes, and one looked like *gifu*, the rune that meant gift and partnership and a soldier's blood offering; the one that always meant Garroc to her.

Lydi put her back to the sea. She was safe yet; Owain was no danger to her, yet. And so she lay down to sleep and let herself be lulled by the sea-song and the unbroken wind. She would dream of her flight and all that she saw, comforted by hope.

She did dare hope. Though they'd been torn away from each other, she hoped that Garroc was still alive. She'd always believed, in the deepest heart of her where things didn't have to make sense, that if he were to die, she'd know it. She'd feel it, the emptiness, the loss, the never-healing wound that bleeds always when half the heart is stolen away.

Lydi was weary, and frightened, and she was sick for the sight of her Garroc. But there was no ever-aching wound in her. Her dream would find him when next he slept, and he would know she was alive.

"Come and find me," she whispered, on the very edge of sleeping. "Come and find me if you can. Oh, I need help now!"

Down on the stony shore the waves rushed in and ran out, waves like strong grey horses with silver manes tossing.

Skald! Find her if you want to keep her! Skald!

I woke suddenly, Sif. Gasping, I woke, jolted, like I'd fallen hard to earth. Hinthan woke in the same moment. He sat up, away from me, and it must have hurt him to, but he didn't wince now. And now he remembered what he'd seen when we came into the glade, and what he hadn't seen.

"Garroc, where's Lydi?"

"She's gone—"

"With Owain! When—?"

He stopped, suddenly, and he couldn't have known what dream I'd had, or heard the ghost speaking, but he knew me, and my every look.

"Skald, skald," he said. "I thought the ghost was gone."

"So did I. I know where Lydi is, Hinthan. Or at least what it looks like round about there. We're going to find her."

"But—"

I stilled him with a gesture. I heard Aescwine's glad *hael!* and Merewal's greeting, Reginleif's sudden laughter. Merewal had left his army elsewhere. He had only the sword-girl with him.

I got to my feet, gave Hinthan a hand up. I had an idea that was almost a plan. And better, I had a king's son in my debt.

Reginleif, the silver girl, was tarnished with weariness, with battle-grime and the blood of enemies. She slipped Hinthan's bow from her shoulder, took his quiver from her hip, and she said, "Thanks for these. I kept them for you, and they kept me well." She'd managed to retrieve some arrows from the battle-ground, but she thought they'd need mending.

She didn't say more, and Aescwine took her away. He covered her with his mantle and took her into his arms and let her sleep in peace. With no more need to keep watch, Cynnere stretched out before the fire and slept almost as soon as he lay down. And so it was only Rowenna and Wulfhere, Hinthan and me, awake to hear Merewal tell how his army drove off those who'd tried to force a battle.

"First it was only Peada coming at us, but Bran caught up with him, and Osric fought beside them for a while. He was first to leave. Last anyone saw of him was the back of him heading north."

Wulfhere sighed his relief, and Merewal roughed the boy's chin. "No one will be troubled by Osric anymore this year."

But the look he gave me said he understood that Osric wasn't going home; he was returning to exile. If Eadwine managed to hold Northumbria for another year, he'd have Osric to deal with again. If Penda won the kingdom, Osric would haunt the peace until he won his home back or died in the trying.

"After Osric left, Peada and Bran found themselves without enough of an army to fight. They ran west into Wales, with my army on their heels. Maybe they'll get chased right off the edge of the world and drown in the sea."

Hinthan looked up, eyes alight, alarmed. With only a glance I hushed him. I had no mind to give into fear now. I waited till Merewal finished eating, and when he was still licking his fingers I told him I'd be grateful if he'd come with me while I checked the horses.

"We've got some things to talk about," I said.

He nodded to agree.

The horses were picketed in the shady edge of the woods, near to where we'd entered the glade. We two went among them, checking hobbles and speaking quietly to the good beasts, making sure all was well with them. And Merewal said, "What's on your mind, Garroc?"

"This: Tell me again, is your father's will yours?"

He twisted a bitter smile. "It always has been. I'm not spending my life waiting for him to die so I can be king. And I'm not spending it working for his death so I can be fatherless. I'm his, Garroc; not my mother's."

I asked no more about that, not then, nor ever again. I saw the truth, and didn't misread him.

"Now," I said, "we'll talk about the debt you owe me."

He stroked his mare's broad flat cheek. The bay pushed him with her shoulder; he pushed back like it was an old game between them. "I'll pay you back however you wish."

He said that lightly, Sif, maybe thinking I'd ask for what he could easily give once we got home—a sackful of gold, a wide tract of land. I wanted none of that. I told him I wanted good horses, and I wanted Cynnere and Aescwine.

"I'm yet bound to take your brother to safety, Merewal, and I'll do that. But there's another thing I need to do on the way. I won't ignore it."

He smiled, but coldly. "What's calling you louder than your promise to my father?"

I let silence be my answer.

"A secret, ay? You're full of 'em, skald." He eyed me narrowly. "And you don't trust me yet, do you?"

"I trust you. If I didn't, I'd have borrowed the horses and the men and got out of here without a word to you."

He laughed. "While I'm sleeping."

"Oh, ay, while you're sleeping. I like you too much to hit you over the head and take what I want."

But I'd do it if I had to, and Merewal knew that. He leaned his arms on his bay's broad back, looked to the camp. I looked where he did, saw Rowenna and Wulfhere, the two sitting quietly together as he unloaded his scrip. Wulfhere took out the box that held quills and ink pots and the sheets of vellum he'd carried from Haligstane. He looked up to say something. As though to answer, Rowenna smiled and brushed the boy's hair back from his cheek. I saw a likeness between them, an expression, a gesture. But it couldn't have been more than a trick of light. The likeness vanished as soon as I became aware of it.

"Garroc, have you ever heard the old saying that there's nothing more powerful than a secret?"

"What I've heard is that there's no one more powerful than him who holds the secret you'd like to know. But I've not come here to talk about secrets. I'll take care of your brother. I've sworn to, and I don't break promises. Now I have to leave here soon, and I want Cynnere and Aescwine with me."

He frowned, tugging at his red beard like he was a miller haggling with a farmer over the grain-price. After some thinking, he said that I could have Cynnere.

"And I guess you'll get Rowenna along with him, but you can't have Aescwine. I need him, Garroc. His isn't the only *wraecca* band filling up my army, but there are precious few soldiers among all of 'em. Aescwine's worth any ten men to me."

I didn't argue. I would miss Aescwine, but I had a bigger thing to ask.

"Now I have one more thing to say to you, Merewal."

He nodded, but I let him wait a moment to hear. Not till he looked back to the center of the glade, to Wulfhere sitting cross-legged before the oak stump with his scrip emptied and quills and inks all around him, did I tell Merewal who I'd chosen to be Wulfhere's foster-father.

Very still and quiet, him. Horses snorted and shuffled and blew, but he had nothing to say. Then he laughed, suddenly and hard, as at a good joke. When I didn't laugh with him, he frowned, maybe thinking I'd gone off my head. But I insisted on what I wanted, and I told him in no unclear way why I wanted it.

"Your father gave me this choice to make. I've made it."

"Then I guess I can't argue. We'll just have to wait and see how well it works out. Are you going to tell him now?"

I said I wouldn't, and he tugged at his beard for a while again. Then he said he reckoned I knew what I was talking about.

"I do. And I know what I need—we're not finished talking about that. I want you to come with me, Merewal. You say Aescwine's worth ten men—he can take your place for a while."

"Oh, ay," he said. "And since I'm worth any dozen men, he won't have too hard a time of it." Then he laughed, a big booming sound that reminded me of Penda when he was in good humor. "I'll go with you, Garroc. As for my little brother, it's likely no more dangerous for him in Wales than anywhere else, the poor boy. We'll find your garden-girl for you."

In the woods, behind and above, a dove sighed. A quick clap of wings like small thunder, she flew, overhead, out of the shadows and into the sunny glade, gliding as on the sunlight.

And I said, "Merewal, who told you about her?"

"Reginleif."

"Have I no secrets left?"

"Not from me, unless her name is a secret."

"Lydi," I said, watching the dove lift and fly again.

"Well, you're all out of secrets now, skald."

So it seemed.

We talked for a while longer, there among the horses, and one of the things we talked about was the *wraecca* army. They were most of them Northumbrians, Dwarfs and a few Men cast out from their homes by *Cristens*. Merewal said that it used to be there were *Cristens* here in Northumbria, some few, and no one bothered about that. Then the queen brought the priests of Rome here. 'Fierce in faith,' Rowenna had said of the queen's priests. These people of Rome had talked against any of *mann-cynn* who didn't turn *Cristen*, and against Dwarfs altogether. It mattered what these Men of Rome said, for they spoke with Eadwine Faith-Breakers' authority. The *mann-cynn* who didn't feel like turning their backs on the old gods were outlawed.

"But the Dwarfs . . ." Merewal shook his head. "Them, they couldn't do anything to please the Roman folk. If they were inclined to turn *Cristen*—and none I've spoken with are!—they'd not have satisfied the Romans. But those *wraecca* aren't mine. They're only lent, and they lent themselves gladly. I only had to go out and gather them up, tell them one of Wotan's kinsmen needed their help."

"And you trust them, Merewal? People who'd have been happy to kill you if their king would have them in his army?"

He combed his fingers through his horse's mane, tugged a little, thinking. "I know what's true, Garroc—they're not mine because they love me. Those *wraecca* are mine because Eadwine threw them away, and they'll stay with me only as long as I can give them the vengeance they want." He smiled, cold and grim. "Don't worry about it, skald; they'll gladly be mine for a while yet."

We didn't have much more to say after that. I told him I'd learned that Cadwalla was back in Gwynedd, that he was chasing Eadwine's sons from his kingdom and didn't seem to be having much luck. These things I told him as though I'd learned them in Osric's hall, and he said he'd warn Aescwine of that, for he was sending the rest of his army south. He wanted them to keep a good eye on Ceastir where his mother lived.

"I haven't seen her in a while," he said, smiling darkly. "But I don't reckon she's changed much. If Peada gets tired of the sea air and takes a sudden longing for home I don't want him getting into Ceastir where our mother will happily stiffen his hatred and gladly arm him again."

He shook his head, but over private thoughts that didn't want me asking after them.

"We can ride with the army till Ceastir," he said. "If that fits your plan."

I told him it did, and I told him that I'd be grateful if he could manage it that Wulfhere didn't learn that they were both the sons of Penda.

"He's not been raised to love your kin, Merewal."

Merewal said he reckoned that was all right, but only for now.

"Soon or late, he'll have to know. But if you think later will be best, so be it, Ghosts-Skald."

• • •

Aescwine liked the hills ringing Ceastir and he set his *wraecca* army just below the crests, hid them where they could see in all directions and not be seen. We parted from them on a cold damp morning, said our farewells only briefly as is the soldier's habit. Aescwine and I parted peacefully, but there was yet no peace between him and Cynnere. The silence between them was a wound unhealed, and it hurt to see.

Last before I left the *wraecca* army I saw Reginleif. She came walking to say farewell to Cynnere, clasped his hand.

"Luck to you," she said. "Don't worry about our Aescwine."

"I don't worry about him," Cynnere growled.

She laughed, her sudden bursting glee. "Yes you do. People don't get over the habits of friendship so soon. But don't worry. And don't forget him, Cynnere."

Cynnere said nothing, but I saw his face, the small hope springing in him as he walked away.

Reginleif hooked her finger through the leather plait round my neck, caught the Ing-stone out of my shirt. "We're a little closer to the sea than last time I saw this on you, aren't we? Don't lose it." Then, soft, "I hope you find your garden-girl."

Hinthan watched her walk back to Aescwine and he said, "That is a very strange girl, Garroc."

She was a strange girl, and she was lovely like a sword is, keen and bright.

PART FIVE

Aelfen

Stane Saewulf's son said to me that few tales of the *aelfen* have come down to us.

"And we don't see alfs often, my youngling, but when we do, usually they are *niht-aelfen* we see, them in the sky at year's end, riding on horses that are black when seen in the dimming, white when seen at night, like they were clouds. These alfs are the Wild Hunters, and some people call them the Raging Host."

So said Stane Seawulf's son to me one dark night, a wild-wind night when all the leaves of the falling rattled and hissed and scratched at the door. The hearth-fire didn't seem bright enough, the flames weren't warm enough. I was man-grown then, but that night I felt like a boy who wasn't sure if he was hearing wind moaning or night-alfs laughing.

And Stane said that all the *aelfen* are soul-reft, but the night-alfs are fell hunters who spend no time mourning for what was taken from them, and no time searching. They steal what others have, sink sharp fangs into a man's neck, drink out his blood, hoping to drink out the soul of him.

I shivered to hear that, and my foster-father poured more of the honey-wine we'd been drinking, filled our cups with mead kept warm at the fire's edge. He said to me that of alfs other than night-alfs we know little. There are sea-alfs and wood-alfs and alfs who live only in stonelands. And too there are alfs who never left Aelfenheim. These stay home and mourn. They never go abroad, for they are ashamed.

"Youngling," said Stane above the wind's sad sobbing. "I have heard folk of your own kindred say that *dvergr* owe the *aelfen* a debt."

This was not a thing I'd heard. I moved closer to the fire, asked him to tell me about that.

Stane took a deep drink before he spoke again. The cups we used weren't richly made, only good kiln-craft, but that cup of Stane's—old and chipped and the color of red mud—shone like it was made of gold, gleamed in the firelight.

"My Garroc," Stane said, "there isn't much to tell about the making of *aelfen*. There isn't much we know. We know that they lived in Aelfheim, and we know that gods made them, but we don't know when or how. We know that they—like others— thought it would be good to have the long life of the gods."

Sorrowful the sighing of the wind, and Stane said that *aelfen* were the first to try and steal the golden apples from Idun's garden, the first to lust after long life. They had to face Wotan with guilty hands full of stolen apples.

"We can say that Wotan wasn't happy about that."

Rose the fire, leaped the flames, and light and shadow tangled round each other. Outside, branches clacked together in the wind. Deep, the chill in me; the dread was dark.

Stane said that Wotan wasn't one to brood on unhappiness. He liked to let people know how he felt. He called the *aelfen* to him, said that he would deal them theft for theft. With one word—it so dark that no one not a god dares to speak it or even think it—Wotan All-Father took the souls from the *aelfen,* flung those souls away through all the Nine Worlds, scattered them on the winds like leaves a-whirl when the year is ended.

It's the fate of alfs that they must search for those scattered souls, each for his own, and those souls went winging out to all the worlds. Some are in Jotunheim, some in fiery Muspellheim. Some are yet in Godsheim, and other souls flew all the way to Niefelheim, which is the cavern-world where—so it is said—some Dwarfs yet live. Some of those souls went flying to the Winter World, where Hel lives, and the alf can have his back who dares

go and take it. Some souls are in the great Deep, the wild and icy
sea, and others flew away to Vanaheim, where lives the race of
gods no mortal has ever seen. None are in Alfheim, the twilight
world of the Shamed.

"And some of the souls—" said Stane, my foster-father, watching me over the rim of his cup. "Some of those souls flew to this
middle-world of ours, and so there are *aelfen* here, searchers. And
not an alf has been born since the first were soul-reft, not an alf
will be born ever again. What alfs there are will live on till the
trolls come raging out from Muspellheim to end the world. Alfs
have lost their time, and they wander through ours only as doomed
searchers."

Came a tapping at the window, a scratching at the thin-scraped
horn pane. Crept a chill up my spine, and I reached for my long-
knife.

"Rest easy, youngling," Stane said. "It's but the wind and the
rain."

And I, not so happy to be seen afraid, put my knife aside and
said, "Foster-father, you haven't told me what debt Dwarfs owe
to the soul-reft *aelfen*."

"Ay, well, I don't know if it is a debt. Or at least, not one the
alfs claim. But here is what I heard, and this from more than one
of your *dvergr* kin: When Wotan scattered all those souls, it was
seen by other gods as a punishment too harsh. And he swore—
took an oath with strong words—that never would he deal so
with trespassers again. He would punish thieves, harm them to
the end of their days. But he wouldn't take away a soul, the one
thing that binds all kindreds together—Man and Dwarf, even trolls
and giants and, once, the alfs."

He was quiet for a while, and I watched the firelight on his
face, shadow and light playing. He was old, his hair and beard
very white, his blue eyes very pale, almost the color of water.
He was thinner lately than he'd been. Age had pared him. His
wrists were knobby, his large hands sinewy and strong, but so
gentle when he reached for mine and held them.

"Boy mine, maybe you will say it's not my place to judge
whether the fate of Dwarfs could be easier or harder, but I don't
know if someday one of *mann-cynn* will go climbing to Asgard
to see what he can steal from the gardens there, and it seems
to me that if he's so foolish as to do that and get caught, no
matter how Wotan takes revenge, all the race of *mann-cynn* will
be luckier than if *aelfen* hadn't been before him. So with Dwarfs,
ay?"

• • •

My Sif, I told that tale before the campfire on the night when the Harvest Moon rose. We'd left Aescwine and the *wraecca* army behind two days before, and tonight we camped on the crag where Lydi and Owain had been only a few nights gone. We yet smelled the stink of burning, the dark scent of Cadwall's defense against Eadwine Faith-Breaker's sons.

It was a wild night, windy and sea-roaring, and we passed the time with stories. Hinthan and Wulfhere asked first for a tale of Arthur, and Rowenna said she knew one. Speaking quietly, almost whispering the story of a like-named woman, she told of Rowenna Hengest's daughter. He was a pirate, that Hengest. People named him Sea-Raven, and he became the first King of Cent. To a Welsh king he gave his dearest treasure in honorable marriage, a peace-weaver between them. But King Vortigern treated Rowenna badly, harmed her deeply, and she bore more than she should before she told her father of her shameful treatment. Hengest Sea-Raven and all his war-band rose up in rage, killed that king in his hall, and it was Rowenna struck the first blow. She killed Vortigern and earned the name folk know her by even now, Rowenna Long-Knife.

"How is that tale of Arthur?" Hinthan asked.

The sea pounded at the shore; the fire rose high as if it wanted to reach up to the stars. Merewal answered.

"That's the tale of how Arthur got his kingdom. Uther Pendragon, who was his father, was two years dead, and Arthur was an un-tried boy in a time when everyone with ten soldiers and two horses called himself a king. Vortigern probably would have been king of all the Isle if he'd treated his wife well, for her father and his sea-wolves were content to tie his friends and had won nearly all for him in those two years. But Vortigern died, and Arthur claimed the kingdom. Of course Hengest and his Centishmen had things to say about that.

"Skald!" he'd said, laughing and abandoning that story suddenly. "Now it's your turn. Tell us a good and ghosty tale."

And so I told the tale of *aelfen* and, soft, through all the telling, I heard the scratching of quill on vellum, Wulfhere at his pen-craft, close to the fire and never looking up, never seeming to hear even one word of the story-telling.

So I thought until, all the tales told, Hinthan got up to walk a watch and Merewal went with him. Rowenna, very quiet, wrapped herself in her cloak and went to sleep. Cynnere lay down beside her, and soon they slept in each other's arms, way-found lovers.

Wulfhere yet sat close to the fading fire, and when all was still and quiet, he put his writing aside.

"Garroc Ghosts-Skald, what is the fate of Dwarfs?"

His eyes were wide and blue, intent on me; and he flushed a little, for he knew that others who'd heard the tale tonight didn't have to be told what the fate of Dwarfs is. But he didn't know; he'd never been taught. I told him, with lean words, about the child-reft, the Last. He listened, with his finger absently tracing one of the marks in stone Lydi had seen as *gifu*. When the tale was done he didn't say anything. I didn't think the news had touched him.

But after a while he said, "We have a tale about folk who stole apples from God and were cast out of their home for punishment."

I asked him who those folk were.

"The folk," he said, "are Men, and we are exiles all our lives and will never go home until we die. Even then—" He stopped, swallowed hard. "Even then, some will die and not go home; they'll go to Gehenna, for they have done evil in the world and they don't deserve Heofon."

So said the lorn little exile, him sent away to Haligstane when he was hardly more than a babe, kept there and taught to shoulder an unearned shame, bearing the ill name of bastard. And now he sat here, at the edge of the world, telling me this sad untruth, this tale of a great banishing that makes outlaws and exiles of Men all over the middle-world. I thought again that Penda should have taken better care of his treasure.

Wind blew suddenly, and the fire rose in a gasp of light. Wulfhere quickly caught his page from flying. This wasn't the emerald sheet, but a new one.

"Wulfhere, what is it you're writing?"

He was a moment answering, and then he said he wrote down all the things he mustn't forget.

Almost I asked him why he didn't just remember what he mustn't forget, but I didn't. We'd had a few peaceful words between us; I saw no sense in spoiling that.

"Wulfhere, we've got a long ride tomorrow. Go to sleep now."

He nodded, but absently. "You didn't say why there are only a few tales about alfs. Did your foster-father tell you?"

The wind moaned around the heights. The sea roared below.

"There are few tales because down all the countless ages folk have guarded themselves from *aelfen*, the souled afraid of the soul-reft. All we know about alfs comes from the time before the theft, and that's not much."

"What happens if an alf finds his soul? Does he go home again, or is this world now his home?"

"I don't know. I've never spoken to an alf and so I've never been able to ask."

He didn't say anything more, and he took up his page and began to write again.

Cynnere found a path down from the high crag to the sea, a winding way, a stony trail with walls so high we had to look up to see the sky, and it only a slender strip of blue. Sometimes gulls or curlews flew over, their wings bright as shining silver in the morning sun, but we didn't hear their cries. In that narrow passage the sea's roaring deafened. Our horses pulled back against the downward way and we must lead them slowly, for the path was slick with spray, the high-walled passage filled up with mist that soaked us through. And I heard again countless voices in the sea-roar, voices to remind me of Aescwine's tales of Ran, the sea-god's greedy wife. We'd stood together on another shore, him and me, and I'd thought I was standing at the edge of the world. There I'd heard the voices of all the drowned, and Aescwine said some of those voices belonged to sea-alfs and water-grimmings.

When we rounded the last bend in the passage we were near to deafened by bellowing. Ahead lay the sea and the strand, and the opening out to there was so narrow that our horses only just fit through. Light gleamed bitterly bright on wet stone walls. It flared to blinding brightness when we finally came out onto the shore.

There, between the cliff and the sea, the sky hung higher than I'd ever seen it before. Sea-surge soaked our horses to the knees, splashed against the man-high stones marching out into the frothing water like a line of folk gone to drown. When the tide was low, those stones—sea-shaped, twisted, crusted with salt—would be the tallest things on a rocky reef.

Rowenna caught her breath and held it, silent before the wild beauty. Wide-eyed, Wulfhere looked all around him, quivering with excitement, flushed with wonder. Hinthan didn't pretend to less, though this wasn't his first sight of the sea.

"All of it's alive," Merewal said, shouting to be heard above the sea. "Air and water and sky and even the light jumping."

It seemed so, and I felt like the earth was rocking under my feet, forth and back. It wasn't a good feeling, Sif. I glanced at Cynnere, who stood beside me. In him I found some fellow-feeling. He smiled, a game and grim kind of smile, and swallowed hard, once and then again. Green in face, he said the sea had gotten no easier to like since last he'd seen it.

"How far do you think Lydi's got?"

"She's two days ahead of us, but Owain's not well. I don't think they could be too far along the coast."

He drew breath to ask how I could know that, then let the question go unspoken. This was a witch we were speaking of, and Cynnere didn't like to ask too many questions about witches.

"North, or south?"

"South," I said. "Then west."

"So we're looking for a port?"

I said I didn't know.

We rode all the day long, Sif; south down the stony shore, south with the sea on our right and the tall stony heights on our left. The shore was narrow; sometimes we rode in the water. When the salt spray made us thirsty we stopped to drink from fresh and swift tumbling falls of water, thin ribbons of silver trailing down the cliff to the stony shore. As the day lengthened and chilled, we rode soaked and shivering and weary. When the sun set, a fiery ball of red sinking into the sea at the end of a golden sea-road, we made a camp in the shadow of the heights. We ate well; Hinthan remembered what he learned from Aescwine about catching fish in rock-pools.

In the night a wind came down from the north, whistling along the curving coast, moaning among the rocks and groaning in the fissures, the gaps in the cliff-face. It was hard to keep a fire, and the thin flames bent southward like arms stretched out in yearning.

Voices whispered in my dreaming, Sif. They were as many as the voices on Deorcdun, but I couldn't understand what they said. I heard no single word among the sighing. Once, dreaming, I thought these must be the voices of sand, for no one can make out what the countless grains of sand have to say. Their voices are too soft, and all together they are only a hissing even to Dwarfs. I tried to listen, to understand, and the voices hushed, drew away like the tide retreating from the shore.

Once—a sharp cry, high and bright—*kee-keee-keeee!*—I heard a kestrel crying among the gulls and the storm-petrels.

In my dream I got up from sleeping and walked away south down the shore, looking up into the sky and the great sweeps of stars, searching for the sparrow-hawk. The salted sand glittered under the starlight; the wet stones shone like burnished silver. In the tide-pools weedy kelp drifted forth and back among the

mossy rocks, the sea's green tresses. I tried to find the kestrel.
The dream-sky was empty of all but stars, and a thick fog came
rolling in from the sea, white and clammy, cold as ice and filled
with voices. The fog pressed all around me, shifting and swirling,
and trying to take a shape.

The kestrel cried again, but the thickness of the air made her
sound far away.

"Lydi!" I shouted. "Lydi!"

I couldn't hear my own voice, could only feel the force of it
in my chest. The fog pressed too close, too cold, too wet. Every
breath I took in was filled with it, and now fog and sea-spray
filled up my lungs, pooled there. I couldn't cough it up, couldn't
spit it out. I couldn't even gag on it, and I couldn't breathe. I was
drowning.

Came a shadow gliding over the fog, high in the sky.

Kee-keee-keeeee!

The kestrel flew over me and past me, and the fog found a
shape, became a thing tall and grey and looming. Not but the
bulk of it did I see, that thing of fog and night. The mother-earth
shuddered when it walked, each step a thunder. Small lightnings
leaped around its feet, hoof scraping stone, flint-fire flashing. It
rose up on hind legs, taller than the tallest of *mann-cynn*. Its voice,
a wild challenge, was like the sea roaring, and that wordless cry
filled me with fear. I had nowhere to flee. The sea was at my
back, the waves nipping at my heels.

Then all the boom and hush of the sea stilled. In the soundless,
breathless moment a familiar voice cried out.

Skald! Skald, find them!

And the fog-wight loomed tall in front of me, thunder and
lightning and a voice like the sea's. It rose up again, powerful
like the waves crashing, pitiless as any storm.

Skald—!

In the sky the kestrel screamed.

From behind me—where only the sea was—someone grabbed
me hard by the shoulder just as the Ing-stone fell from round
my neck.

Hinthan's hand was warm on my shoulder, his grip strong. And
he held me still till he could tie the leather plait again, make it safe
round my neck.

"It's all right," he said. He gave the charm a tug, tested the
strength of it, newly tied. "I guess the leather frayed. You almost
lost it, but it's safe on you now."

He whispered, for all around us folk slept, Cynnere near to Rowenna, Merewal within easy reach of Wulfhere. Stars shone down, sand on the shore of night. The curling waves, soft-voiced, quiet now, sighed.

"We'll find them tomorrow," I said.

Hinthan accepted that with a short nod, and we two sat in silence. The wind blew colder, right down the shore from the north, and Hinthan looked out at the sea, the waves' white manes glittering in starlight.

"I still can't hate him, Garroc."

"I'm still not asking you to."

He poked up the fallen fire and put more sea-wood into the ember-bed. But he kept one piece aside, one silvery length, and set to whittling, using the skill Owain had taught him, deftly shaping and carving.

After a time he said, "I can't hate him, but if he hurts Lydi, I will kill him."

In the rising firelight, his eyes shone darkly.

The wildest beauty there is can be found at the edge of the world, my Sif. There sea-birds sail the sky, kittiwakes and shearwaters and gulls wheeling and banking and diving down into the waves, plundering the sea for her silver, shining fish struggling and thrusting and gasping in the cruel air. Sanderlings run along the water's edge, hunting in the rock-pools; brown and white turnstones stalk the shore, flipping over shells and flat rocks with their long beaks, looking for something to eat. And the sea is never silent, but sings on endlessly, a voice that never stills.

Shortly after noon Wulfhere came to ride with me. We went on ahead, two scouts searching up the beach, and for a time we were silent company for each other, wordless by choice 'midst the sea-roar. But after a while he brought his horse closer till we were knee to knee.

"Garroc," he said, "will they care where you're taking me if I have no father to tell them about?"

He turned a face to me that I'd never seen before, Sif. His eyes were steady, and his jaw was stiff, and I knew that all of it would crumble if I spoke even a whisper of scorn for the bastard who wondered as he did. I'd seen that before, but never till now this new trust—maybe yet only a risked hope—that I wouldn't hurt him.

"You have a father, Wulfhere."

He looked back over his shoulder to our friends riding behind.

He was gauging distance, wanting to be sure no one could hear what next he'd say.

"In Haligstane they said that I'm *il bastardo,* the bastard. That means I'm no man's son."

"Boy, it makes no more sense to say you're the son of no one that it does to say that Dwarfs have no mothers and fathers."

He flinched a little then. He remembered another time we'd talked about Dwarfs this way. And I remembered something, too; I remembered what Raighne of Haligstane had said of him, that in pain, he gives pain.

"Wulfhere, tell me: If you have no father, where did you come from?"

Little waves splashed against our horses' legs. Wulfhere shrugged, but made no other answer.

"Did you come down with the rain?"

"No," he said, low.

"Maybe you blew in with the wind, and your mother said, 'Ah, look! A boy blew in through the window! I think I'll keep him.' "

He tried to swallow a smile.

"You have a father, Wulfhere. He's a good man. I know him, and I promise that's true."

Merewal came riding near just then, close to Wulfhere so that the *aetheling* was between us. "Garroc's right about your father, boy. There are men who would die for him if he even whispered that it was needed."

Wulfhere glanced at me, then away. He knew the last was true. Shyly, he said to Merewal, "Do you know my foster-father, too?"

"I've heard of him. He's not such a bad fellow."

"And my foster-mother?"

Merewal threw back his head and laughed; the sound of it rivaled the sea's voice. "He's not found the chance to marry yet, that foster-father of yours. Maybe you'll help him find a wife."

Wulfhere didn't answer, but he rode the rest of the way smiling. It was him and Merewal, the two sons of Penda riding ahead, who found the cove.

A wide beach lies within the cove Merewal and Wulfhere found. The beach is sandy and smooth and so broad that the tide could rise as high as it liked and still not trouble anyone. The beach was filled up with turnstones and sanderlings, shore-birds at supper in the last of the day's light. From the seaward side the cove gave no welcome. Its mouth was filled with teeth, man-high stones and taller, sea-shaped, wind-whittled, so close together that they might have once been part of the land till the sea broke them and ran in to delve behind and make the cove.

One arm of the cove was longer than the other and it made a stone road that reached all the way out into the water. You can walk it when the tide is low, Sif, and you can stand and look up at the headland. If you like, you can take that stone road right up to the hill, for the slope is easy and slow. Atop the headland a wall stretches, and it was old past counting on the day the first Roman saw it almost six hundred years before. You can camp up there, snug against the wind, and stand by the wall at night and watch the sea tossing, the stars shining down. You can watch the moon lay a path across the sea, a swath of silver between the waves.

Welshmen call the headland Caer Coblyn. In our language we'd say Alf's Watch.

The cove wasn't empty. Merewal pointed to the beach, to a campfire and someone standing north away from it.

Wulfhere cried, "Lydi!" and my heart lifted, rising hopeful. She stood face to the wind, her cropped hair tumbling round her cheeks and neck. She stood shading her eyes with her hand, looking north, and the wind hugged her boldly, shaped the green shirt to her, arm and breast and slender waist.

Merewal whistled low to see her. "Now, tell me, Ghosts-Skald, that this is your garden-girl and I'll tell you she's worth this wind-blown journey and any worse one the Norns can weave for you."

"She's worth it," I said.

Hinthan called out a question, but I left Merewal and Wulfhere to answer. I gave my horse the heel, forgot about everyone but my witch, my girl running down the strand to me.

Lydi greeted me fair, held my horse's bridle while I dismounted. With a glad cry she came into my arms. The wind blew cold behind me; I felt her shivering. I wrapped her up in my mantle, used the journey-stone to pin it close, and took her back into my arms.

"You found me," she whispered. Her heart beat, and so hard I could feel it running where she pressed against me.

"I've found you, my girl," I said, whispering against her neck. "Now come to the fire. We'll talk about things there. Come on, before you shake apart in the cold, ay?"

She let herself be led, and there at the fire I saw Owain. He lay huddled under his own cloak and Lydi's blue mantle, and his face

was white above his black beard; he shivered as though he lay
not near a fire and wrapped up warmly, but naked to the winds
of winter. A small fog drifted near him, like a dog come to sniff
at its fallen master.

He opened his eyes when I knelt beside him, and he reached for
his oaken staff, the one Hinthan had carved with the journey-runes,
the one marked with lifting lines like waves or a horse's mane in
the wind.

"Owain," I said. "Tell me. What are you?"

He drew one long breath, like the sea coming in. He let that
breath go, like the tide ebbing.

"Listen, poet. Listen . . ."

‹29›

Hear the tale of Owain Dwarf-Smith; Owain Woman-Thief; Owain
Earth-Deaf. These things happened a long time ago, Sif, before
storied Arthur was king, before the first Roman Man came to
the Isle, and soon after giants were driven from the land. In
those days Dwarfs were not cursed. In those days, in all lands,
we didn't look to live longer than any Man. Then, no hundred
years and a hundred for us. And in those days we knew the joy
of child-wealth.

Was a girl went walking in the cove at sunrise, under the shadow
of the headland and Caer Coblyn. She was *corres,* and that is how
the folk in Welshland say that she was a Dwarf. Sioned, her name,
and she was the daughter of Caerau ap Einion, a bard-witch famed
for his magic and his singing. Her eyes were blue, her lips red as
sun's setting; her arms and legs and all the soft skin of her was
golden. Sioned's father always said that the best song he ever
made was the song of her voice.

That morning Sioned was hunting the cove for what treasure the
sea had flung up in the night—cowrie shells and oyster shells, the
dark tooth of a shark, the gleaming white ivory of a walrus tusk.
Maybe, if she was lucky, she'd find a bit of amber, the sea-stone
colored like frozen fire and shining like a golden egg in a nest of
kelp. Small waves lapped at her ankles. She kilted her green gown
and she danced along the shore, kicking up sand and watching it

fall like gold dust, kicking up spray and watching it rain down like silver.

Once—or so her father had told her—a woman found a golden chain draped over a rock, the links as thick as her thumb. An amethyst the color of the twilight hung from the chain, and caught, the stone drifted back and forth with the flow and the ebb. No one had been that lucky in this cove since then, but Sioned, dancing down the shore, didn't see why no one could be as lucky again. And all the stones in that cove weren't right at the water's edge. Some lay farther out, only to be got to when the tide was low, as now. These were far enough away from the Teeth—those warding stones at the mouth of the cove—to make a look worth the risk. Who standing on the shore could tell what that glinting was on that broadest and roughest of the little rocks unless she went out to see?

Sioned stripped off her gown and her white shift, set them to warm in the sun, and walked down to the sea. Sleek as an otter, the bard-witch's daughter; lovely as gold. She saw no one but gulls and terns and petrels in the cove that day. She could play in the water and splash and swim, and lie out naked in the sunlight when all her play was done.

Yet though it seemed that she was alone, what seems isn't always so. Sioned had company. Someone saw her walking, someone watched her step into the sea, heard the hiss of her breath when the cold caught her. And he heard her sudden laughter when a strand of kelp swayed against her ankle. He watched from beyond the Teeth, and he was not Dwarf or Man. In shape and size, he seemed like a horse, tall and broad-chested, grey-coated and white-maned; but he wasn't that, either.

He was a sea-alf, and in Welshlands the word they have for his kind is 'kelpie.' His name was Ewyn, and in Welsh that means Foam.

Ewyn kept behind the ragged columns of sea-carved stone, and hidden there, he watched Sioned. He loved to see the splash and the spray try to dress her in shining. He loved to see her laugh and stretch her arms high as she reached up for the light and the sun to warm her. Then all of her, shoulder and breast and hip and thigh glimmered and glittered. Ewyn groaned with hunger.

An ages-old ache filled the kelpie, like a dimly remembered hope. Alfs know hunger and want as no other wight has ever known it. This alf, this Ewyn, this iron-grey horse of the sea, always told himself that he'd find his soul in the women he took. Sometimes he even believed it.

He believed on that long-ago morning, and when he heard Sioned laughing he knew that he could have her. Hers was no timid laughter, but bold and brave, and a note of wildness ran through it, like a bright bell ringing. That morning the sea-alf came out of the water secretly, and secretly he put on the shape of a young and handsome Dwarf. He walked down the beach and greeted Sioned. He told her his name was Owain.

Sioned was filled up with youth and sunlight and the coaxing song of the sea. Ewyn didn't have to take her; she gave herself, and did that laughing for the joy of it. Nor did she run or scream or cry when, after a time, he showed her another shape, the true form of him.

Sioned, the bard-witch's daughter, was as Ewyn knew she'd be—brave enough to ride with the kelpie to the sea, brave enough to let him work all his magics on her so that she could live under the water. She loved it there in that wonderful undersea, and soon stopped missing her kin and friends, stopped thinking about them at all. And Ewyn was Sioned's lover on the beach, in the coves, beneath the sea. He wore any shape that pleased her, and he never tired of her or the games they played. Sioned never wanted to leave him, and she didn't till she died, years after the bright morning when the kelpie found her.

It was her father found Sioned's body washed up with the tide; the kelpie had sent Caerau ap Einion's treasure back to him, empty and dead. Many years had passed, but Sioned seemed no older than the day she'd gone down from Alf's Watch to look for treasures at the waterside. And so, after all the weary time of mourning his daughter drowned, Caerau ap Einion knew at last that Sioned had gone away with a kelpie. And he knew what vengeance he would take.

The bard-witch climbed up to Caer Coblyn, the Alf's Watch, and he spoke powerful words, wove a commanding magic to force a tall grey horse up out of the water, him with a white mane like the waves of the sea, him with an eye like lightning, a voice like thunder. Ewyn had no choice in the matter; he'd met a magic stronger than his. And he raised his proud head. Like the sea surging, he rose up on his back legs, and his hoofs flashed and shone in the moonlight. He raged, but the kelpie couldn't fight the mighty word-woven curse. There in the cove, in the moonlight and the starlight, he changed—all unwilling—to the shape he'd taken to lure Caerau ap Einion's daughter.

Ewyn became Owain, and he looked like a Dwarf, a young man and handsome. But he was none of my kin.

Cursed, Owain was made sick by the sight of the sea. When waves came in to the shore, whispering or thundering, the sound staggered him. The withdrawing was like an ebbing of his own blood, his own life. He had to flee, up the stone-road, away from the sea. On Caer Coblyn the bard-witch told him his doom.

The sea and all its sounds and scents would be as poison to Owain. He learned that there was a way home, and he could know it for the asking. It was Caerau ap Einion he'd have to ask, and Owain could have asked then, right there, and gotten what he needed, but he was too proud.

Caerau ap Einion laughed at that ragged pride, his scorn a gale, a whipping storm.

"Come find me when you're ready to go home, thief. And it may be that you'll outlast me, but you won't outlast the curse. Take as long as you like, only remember that your road back begins on Tŵr Du, at the dark tower that rises up out of the heart of this Isle. You can take that road as soon as you ask me the way."

Proud Owain asked nothing; he took up his exile and he went away. He wandered for many years, and he listened always for news of his enemy. Came a time when he learned that Caerau ap Einion was dead on his high dark hill, Deorcdun, his Tŵr Du. But Owain didn't think he'd lost his chance to go home. He knew his foeman, knew that Caerau ap Einion would find a way to tell him what he must know. Blood-feuds and vengeance are things Welshmen hand down from father to son, like good old swords. In that they are no different than Saxons. Owain would go to the dark hill when he was ready.

At last came a day when Owain's wandering became wearisome, his exile a heavy burden. He heard in his journeying that in Seintwar valley was a healer-witch, and he found his way to Gardd Seren when Lydi's mother was witch there. He told his tale to Meredydd, then said: "Witch, can you heal me of this curse?"

They love to heal, the witches of Gardd Seren. They love that magic of theirs and they work it willingly. It's no easy thing for them to say, I can't heal you; you must heal yourself. Meredydd said that to Owain. She said that he must go to Tŵr Du, to Deorcdun, and learn what was there for him to learn. He must set down his burden and go home.

"I'll help you," Meredydd said, "if only that I stand by you when you learn your fate."

For a day or so that sounded like a good idea to Owain. But

soon that road to the dark tower looked like a hard one, and
Owain felt a little lightened just to have the tale told. And so
he left Gardd Seren, with the witch's promise, and it stayed him
for a while. But only a while.

He returned to Gardd Seren, looking for Meredydd, and he
found Lydi.

All this, my Sif, Owain told me in the cove where, many years
before, he'd found lovely Sioned dancing at the edge of the world.
He told his tale while he lay in Hinthan's arms, too weak to sit,
too sick, too close to the sea. Hinthan held him warmly against
weakness and cold, maybe the more so for the oath he'd taken
last night to kill him. There was no need of the oath now, and
if Hinthan must repent it, he repented in tenderness.

Above, on Caer Coblyn, firelight ran like gold on the stonework.
There I saw shadows against the light, Cynnere and Merewal in
close talk. A little away from them stood Rowenna and Wulfhere,
and the boy leaned over the wall to see the moon, the Harvester
sliding swiftly down the sky. The light lay like a path on the
rising sea.

I looked away from the Watch, and the light of the silver road
shone in my eyes. In me a ghost sighed. Caerau ap Einion drew
near, the grieving father come to see his vengeance done.

And Owain, his eyes closed in weary sickness, said, "Caerau
ap Einion spoke through you, poet. 'Leave as you entered,' he
said. What he meant was this: Owain must walk into the sea and
drown before Ewyn can live again."

The sea came in, sighed out, came in; the pulse of the night and
the sudden silence. And, an aching time later, Hinthan leaned over
his friend and whispered, "No, Owain. That's self-murder!"

Owain reached out, took my left hand, turned my wrist up to
the moonlight. His fingers felt dry and old and sapless as he traced
the blade-rune, the dark thin mark Caerau ap Einion had made on
me with my own knife and my own hand.

"It would be no more a self-murder than this would have been.
What seems isn't always what is, Hinthan."

Hinthan shuddered, and Lydi took his hands in hers, held them
to warm. They sat in silence, and I saw it that Lydi's sorrow was
no less than Hinthan's, though she'd known since Deorcdun what
Owain must do.

But I refused to be moved by the mourne tale.

"Owain, if you know what needs to be done, why are you still
here?"

He smiled, a mirthless smile for just him and me. "Because I can't do what needs doing."

And outside Eotenfeld, looking at the burnt waste, he'd said that he didn't know anyone who lies down to sleep thinking he's had enough of being alive. Not even the un-souled *aelfen*.

"I look sick and dying to you now," said the alf. "But it'll be a different thing once I get into the water. That's life, that water, for me. All the strength of this good body would come back, and I would be as strong as ever you've seen me at the forge." Like glittering ice, his eyes. "Could you do it? Could you walk out and die in the sea for the sake of what your enemy promised to you at the drowned end?"

It was a cold question, and each of us heard and asked ourselves. Hinthan and Lydi answered silently, if answer they found. I answered with words, and still bitterly, even cruelly.

"I don't know if I could. But it's not for me to do, is it, Owain?"

He closed his eyes. Between us we knew, even this dark tale of his hadn't moved me past hating him.

"No," he said. "It's for me to do. And I thought . . . I thought I could do it. I thought I could come here and have everything I wanted." He opened his eyes then, looked right into Lydi's. "Girl, I thought . . . that I could go and drown. And drowned—" His dark eyes flashed, maybe like the lightning Sioned had seen and loved. "Drowned, I'd be who I am, at last. Drowned, Owain would be Ewyn. And witch, there's a magic in Ewyn you'd never stand against."

"I know everything you planned," Lydi said, whispering.

"But you came here with me anyway. Why?"

Wind moaned down the beach, ruffled Lydi's dark curls. Her face was white as the cold moon, but her eyes shone with a warm and quiet light.

"Because I made a promise to my mother."

To Meredydd, and not to Owain. He smiled, but to mock himself and some over-burdened hope.

"And how if I'd been able to win home? How if I'd come back here to the cove again, changed? What then?"

"Then you would have tried to steal me, and I would have fought you. You think I'd lose that fight."

"And you think you'd win. Why? Because you'd have your soldier-poet to come back to?" Bitterly, he laughed. And he said, "Poet, I hate you for how much she loves you."

He spoke to me, but his eyes were on Lydi.

The moon touched the sea; the silver road widened, Owain's

way stretching out. And the sea-alf said, "Poet, do you think any of the *aelfen* can learn how to love?"

"No." To the thief I said, "You'd have to have a soul for that."

He smiled, the old crooked smile I hated, the taunting smile that warned 'Keep an eye on your woman. I'd like to steal her.'

"You, witch? Do you think—"

Lydi hushed him, with a word and a hand laid tenderly over his lips. She granted him what I wouldn't; without words, with silent tears, my Lydi said that she thought he could love.

I thought she was too generous.

Owain closed his eyes, took a long breath, another. He reached for his oaken staff, the one Hinthan carved with runes and the shapes of windy-wild manes lifting. He got to his feet, but not without Hinthan's help and Lydi's. He leaned heavily on the staff.

Skald! Drive him off!

"Poet, walk with me."

I did that, Sif; I went to the water with Owain, stood with him while he looked out on his homeland from the edge of exile. Each wave flung against us ran away with some of the sand, and my belly turned weak with the dizzying feeling that it was the land that moved, not the sea.

Ran's Hall, Aescwine called the great wide waters. The Whale's Road, poets say. Ymir's Blood. In all lands, Dwarfs know it as the Deep.

"*Sae-aelfen* call it Foam-Weaver," Owain said. He laughed to see my surprise. "Hinthan told me you said that. You're right."

He looked over his shoulder, at Caer Coblyn, tall and black against the starred sky, at the cove and Lydi standing there like a jewel in the dark.

"Was a time," Owain said, "when I'd have stolen her right out from your hand and you'd be left gawping on the shore."

Dark his eyes, like storm-threat. And in me, suddenly fierce, the ghost of Deorcdun thundered.

Drive him off!

Lydi got to her feet and took a step toward us. Hinthan quickly caught her hand and kept her. Owain laughed, that brittle, fated sound like glass breaking.

"Was a time when it didn't matter whether a woman came with me willing." Low, his voice; and soft like the withdrawing of the waves. "Was a time when I'd not have cared if I had her heart or didn't, as long as I had all the sweet rest of her. It matters now. Is that love?"

I didn't answer him. Soft and sad, he sounded. Like his heart was breaking. Maybe. Yet it was him said that what seems isn't always what is. He'd told a sad tale, but he hadn't done anything to make me trust him.

Owain laughed at my silence, and he said that he was tired of talking now. He said he'd like to get home, but he still needed help.

Drive him off!

To Owain, or to the ghost, I said, "What do I have to do?"

Owain shrugged, as we were speaking of a small matter. "Take me into the sea and make sure I drown." He grinned, again that crooked smile I hated. "Tell the truth, poet. You'd not mind doing that, ay?"

"Not at all," I said coldly. "But I'd mind it if I drowned out there with you."

None of his brittle laughter did I hear now. He wasn't looking at me. His eyes were on the sea, the curling waves, the great wide places beyond the Teeth. He pointed out, along the silvery road of moonlight.

"Take me home, Garroc Ghosts-Skald, and I swear on what I love that you'll see your Lydi again."

Take him home, to the icy sea where landsmen can't long live.

In me, the ghost of Deorcdun cried: *Drive him off!*

The waves rolled and curled and leaped out past the Teeth, and I took off the good ring-mail Merewal had given me. Lydi cried out, but I didn't heed. I took off my shirt. Raighne's gift, the Ing-stone, gleamed in the faint light, the graven limestone glistening against my skin.

"*Dia dhuit*, poet," the monk had said to me. "God to you, Garroc Ghosts-Skald." He'd blessed me in the *Cristen* god's name, but he'd given me the rune that is the mark of Ran's lover. What had he known? His one god, my several? Or had Raighne of Ireland, in wisdom, allowed all the gods there are, even to the one no one knows?

Hinthan shouted, ran down the beach to me. And he took my two hands in his, as if he'd hold me back from the sea.

"Foster-father—"

"It's all right, youngling. This is mine to do. Let me do it."

He let go my hands, and I put my weapons by, laid short-sword and long-knife at his feet. Owain lifted the rune-carved staff, sighted along the length of it, as to test its straightness.

"Don't take him from me, Owain," Hinthan said. "Don't—"

Owain handed the staff to Hinthan, and he smiled. I'd not seen a smile like that on him before now, Sif. I'd not seen bright and brittle Owain ever smile so warmly.

"And orphan you again? Trust me."

White, Hinthan's face, and white his knuckles when he grasped the staff. He clung to that oak as it were the promise Owain made. From me he asked the promise he always asked.

"Garroc, stay alive."

"I have no other plan," I said.

I dropped my belt-pouch to the sand, the one with the two halves of Gytha's arm-ring and the whole of Peada's silver wrist-bracer. I kicked off my boots, and Owain walked out from the land. He didn't stop until he stood in water up to his knees.

Waves leaped at him, over him, and spray shone all around him. Not so old and sick and weary did he seem now, and round his knees, across all the waters of the cove, a thick white fog drifted. He lifted up his face to the stars and the sky, stood against the leaping waves, laughing.

"Come on, poet! Do you dare?"

I dared. I ran for the water, into the surf and the pulling of the sea.

Hinthan shouted, in sudden wordless rage and fear.

I heard wings cut the air, hissing. Flew a kestrel, her sharp little talons glinting in the starlight. Lydi! I caught Owain's arm as, with a cutting cry, the kestrel banked and turned.

"Hold onto me, poet! Hold for your own life! Never let go— even when I'm drowned!"

I heard, and tried to heed. But Owain grew stronger the longer he was in the sea.

"Hold!" he cried, and made that hard to do.

Owain fought me, kicking and thrashing. I was near to blind in the stinging salt-spray, but when I could see his face I knew that he hated to fight. Wild, the waves—the tide was highest now, strongest, and the sea crashed into us with pounding force, tried to whelm us and drown us.

In the sky, starlight on her wings, the last moonlight on her white breast, the kestrel cried *Keee! Keeee!*

I know a warning when I hear one, Sif, but I didn't know, couldn't see, what Lydi warned against, for in that moment the sea caught me and held me. The waves rushing in fueled the undertow, water fleeing out to sea again. I couldn't stand against that pull, couldn't stop myself from being dragged down into the cold salt sea. I held onto Owain with white-knuckled grip while he twisted and turned and fought to free himself.

Choking on bitter brine, I came up dragging Owain with me. I didn't know the undertow had pulled us as far as the Teeth—the tall pillars of stone—until I hit one. Owain cried out, cursing. Blood ran down the stone, into the froth of spent waves. My blood or Owain's, I didn't know. Numb with the cold, I could have been bleeding all the life out of me and not felt it.

Roaring, the waves came in again, tall as the tallest of the stones, white-maned, galloping. They caught me in cold hands, flung me back to the Teeth again. Owain went suddenly limp in my grasp, dropped away and down. Held against the stone by the weight of the water, I shouted for him, cursed him, looked around, wildly searching for him.

Was that the corpse of him even now dragged out to sea by the tides? Above the Teeth, the kestrel cried again.

Keeeeeee!

Come back!

A hand shot up out of the water. Green kelp tangled in the fingers. Owain came up from the whelming sea, gagging on briny water, blind in the salt-spray, fighting me still.

Skald! cried the ghost, the bard-witch long dead. *Drown him!*

"Do it!" Owain cried. "Do it!"

His were the eyes of the exile, lost and lorn and anchorless. His was a desperate cry, and I felt it in the heart of me, felt it in the deep of me.

I grabbed his shoulders, thrust down, held him under the icy water, felt him drown and die. All the dead worlds filled up with Caerau ap Einion's triumphant shout, all of me filled up with the great roiling of that cry.

Then, silence. I was alone, clutching a dead man's hand, holding on for my own life's sake.

Owain's last breath was the kelpie's first. Long and strong and filled up with all the power of the sea, that *sae-aelf*. He was grey as storm-sky, his eyes like blue-edged iron, like god-Thunor's own lightning.

Keeeee! Keeeeeee! the kestrel shrilled, warning, searching; crying. Come back! She glided over the Teeth, and they were far away. Was it dawnlight I saw shining on those tall stones? Red dawnlight glinting on her wings?

But I'd not been so long in the sea—

Came another wave charging, roaring like an army in fierce battle-rush. I grabbed Ewyn's mane, held tight when he rose up into the moonlight, all of him a-light, shining.

Keeee! the kestrel cried. Her wings gleamed red in the new-come light that wasn't dawnlight. Come back!

Plunging, Ewyn dove down, deep into the sea, running home.

Where the kelpie went, I went; and I had no chance to fill up my lungs with air.

◄30►

Salt water burned my eyes, blinded me. Briny water filled up my lungs. Icy water numbed me as the kelpie took us down into the sea, into darkness ungraced by any light. Ewyn went laughing, wildly into the dark and the deep, a gale of gladness. He went, and I dared not let go his mane, Sif.

And so I heard what no one has heard and lived to tell about. I heard the sea-water hissing through a kelpie's mane, I heard his voice—just like thunder. I didn't hear him with my ears, nor in the bones of me as I hear the mother-earth, nor in the heart of me where I hear ghosts speaking. This voice came from the very waters of the sea, and it was in every part of me.

Afire, my lungs! Aching for a clean sweet breath.

Laughing, thundering, the kelpie said, "Poet! You'd better breathe soon!"

I didn't see how I could, and I clung to that burning breath as I clung to the kelpie's mane. Yet there are things your body does, whether or not you ask it to. Only so long could I hold my breath. Then it must burst out of my lungs, or burst my lungs.

Hopeless, I let go the breath I held.

I didn't have to take another.

And now I could see despite the inky darkness. Now the cold didn't numb me, and I could feel.

Ewyn said I'd die drowning, blind, deaf, hopeless, if even once I let go his wave-white mane. "But you'll be all right if you hold on and remember that you're Ing's friend. The god's friends don't have to worry here. Or not if they're careful."

I'd no mind to stop clutching that mane tight, and no wit to ask why he wouldn't take me back to land where I belonged. Ewyn laughed—storm and thunder—just as though he knew that. And he bade me enjoy the ride, for though a great many have been where he'd take me, none that he knew of had ever come back.

Down we went—me all unwilling!—into darkness that didn't blind, cold that didn't chill. He took me through fields of kelp, green and thick. Not empty, those fields. Fishes swam through, hunters and hunted, and the current shifted to show drowned men netted, rocking in the watery bed. Dressed in flesh like rags, bones gleaming through, the dead rolled and drifted with the rounding eddies. They stared at us from empty eye sockets, their faces twisting and writhing. Tide or will moved one to roll and twist, to reach past the waving sea-weed with a pale, half-fleshed hand.

Ghosts-Skald!—The dead hand touched me, the flesh shredding from finger-bones, the bones like claws—*Stay with us, skald!*

With his sudden might and magic, Ewyn took us away from that cold grasp, used the sea as birds use the sky. The water around us hissed with his speed.

Beyond the place of the netted dead wonderful plants grew—red and golden and green as emeralds, meadows of *sae-wort* as fair as jewels. Ewyn told me that these were not plants but tiny wights. Each was covered in countless spines, and each spine carried poison. No adder's brew is worse than what the least of these spines held. I didn't like this foul sea-meadow, and now I didn't think it was so lovely.

The kelpie took me away, out into deeper waters, to the country of sea-drakes. And those beasts had flanks of silver, Sif, and they are as long as dragonships. Wingless, armless, without legs, the drakes were in all ways like fishes. These too wore spines, a crest like spears and red as a dragonships's sails. Ewyn didn't take us too close, went away from there and into the land of the whales, where one-horned narwhals raced. He swam with these, thundering greeting. But it was too long since he'd been gone; these narwhals didn't know him. A little, the kelpie's joy ebbed.

A little more his home-coming dimmed when a whale we saw, a mighty beast wearing deep battle-scars. So long, so big, so wide the sea-beast that men have mistaken his back for an island, his head for a skerry. Deadly docking is found there. The kelpie said to me that whales are not fishes and they are not land-goers; they are some of each. Time and again they must rise up from the sea, spout water like rain, and dive down again.

My Sif, the song of that whale travelled through the water with the current, first a sweet high note of longing that lighted my heart and lifted, then a lower note that pulled me as it were the voice of the undertow.

"Whales don't know what they are," Ewyn said. "Too long in the sea and they will drown, too long in the air and they will smother. Whales aren't beasts, nor *aelfen*, nor fish. Whales don't know what they are."

In his voice I heard and felt the lowest note of the whale's song, the song of the undertow.

When the whale sounded, we went our own way. Ever downward Ewyn went, swimming strongly, and now flocks of fishes swam by, some small and grey, only their eyes shining. Some were not so small, and once we saw a shark. Then Ewyn showed me what speed he had. He didn't dare the ranks of dark gleaming teeth, the flat dead eyes. He didn't challenge the fish we know as Ran's Steed.

When we came at last to the sea-bed, the ever-moving bottom of the Deep, I put foot to the sandy floor and stood in a vast 'scape of wreckage and ruin.

Here was the doorstep of Ran's golden hall, and all around us lay the rotting hulks of once-proud dragonships. Now they lay broken-necked, sprawled on their sides, their flanks burst and battered as though a sea-drake had rammed them. And there were other ships than these, Sif—the galleys of the Roman folk, other ships of people I didn't know, had never heard of. In and out of the hulks, forth and back, went all kinds of fishes, large and small, silvery and bright-colored, as though each hulk were the hall of a king and they his folk. Weapons lay all around the ruins, knives and swords and broad-bladed war-axes. The blade of each was pitted with rust, the hilts of knife and sword bent and ruined, the iron hafts of axes pitted and sea-gnawed. From all, grips and hafts, the gemstones had been picked out, the gold and silver wire unbound.

Beyond this graveyard lay Ran's Hall, the hoar and horrible place. The high gables were draped with sea-weed. The weird and waving plants of the sea-meadows filled up her sandy garden, and the pave-stones of that garden-walk were the shining shields of every sea-farer drowned. Light shone from the hall's wide-flung doors, shone out from windows, a sickly, heatless green. Gold made the walls of that hall; gems studded doorways and windowsills, and the high roof was made of silver, but the green light turned these treasures foul and ugly.

Standing there, Sif, in the sea-woman's dooryard, I heard again all the ghosts of drowned men.

And from within the hall came other voices, the sharper voices of water-grimmings at feast—sea-trolls, grey-faced, scaled and hairless things born of the drowned. On bones they gnawed, on flesh they feasted, and I didn't dare ask Ewyn what meat these water-grimmings ate, for fear he'd tell me what I couldn't bear to know.

At the wide doorway a shadow lurked, like the drift of a drowned man's hair. Ewyn lifted his head, arched his neck proudly, and thundered greeting to Ran and to Aegor her sea-husband. He cried *hael!* to the two who are the lords of the sea-alfs, by sea-folk and land-goers no less feared than Hel herself.

The shadow came closer.

There were no fish to be seen here now, all the ship-dwellers were gone. There was no living thing but me and the kelpie and the plants in the poison garden.

The shadow took a shape. The sea-woman stood before us—Ran, whose breath is storm-wind, whose hands are death-grip, whose dead-pale skin is whiter than the adder's milky poison. Her dark eyes were like a shark's, flat and dead and pitiless. Her hair drifted with the current, reaching out and wandering away with the water's will.

Ran is Aesir, Sif. She is of the clan of the gods. Some say she's a shape-shifter, but she's not that. She wears many shapes at once, for she is to every man what is delightful to him. To me she seemed like the loveliest Dwarf woman, shaped so that the sight of her might break my heart with wanting. I longed to close my eyes, I tried to turn my head. Held by those pitiless eyes, I could do neither.

And I don't know what Ewyn saw, but in his eyes the shape of Ran was not so delightful as to chase away fear. Every muscle in him quivered, crying to flee and bound by his will to stay.

"You've changed, my Ewyn," Ran said. She laughed, a sound like the sea rising up. "You've found what none of the *aelfen* ever hope to find."

And she was another who saw what I refused to see. Ran knew that the sea-alf had found what Wotan had taken from him. Her laughter was the hiss of a dark fin through water, and Ewyn quivered to hear it.

"Now what, my Ewyn? You and your kind have been without a soul since soon after you were made. Who can count those years? All folk have stopped trying. Tell me, my Ewyn, where does the sea-alf go who has found his soul?"

"I don't know," he said.

And he spoke proudly, Sif, but I had my hand on him; I knew the question terrified him.

Ran laughed scornfully. "And you might not be happy to learn the answer."

Then she turned her glance on me. I had to clutch the kelpie's mane with both hands to keep dread from dragging me to my knees. Ran's were the eyes of all the dead, and the eyes of what killed them.

She stood suddenly close, and I felt cold coming from her, as you'd feel the warmth of a blooded land-goer. She is kin to Hel, both sister and mother of the Ice Woman. They are a lawless clan, the kin of god-Loki, and they get children across bounds no mortal wight would go.

Ran lifted the leather plait that held the rune-stone round my neck. Her finger brushed my skin, seared me with the coldness of her, left behind a scar like the feathered mark of frost. But when the Ing-stone, monk-Raighne's gift, touched her hand, she hissed and withdrew, sneered to hide a sudden, naked fear. Sea-Ing was once her lover, but he is no friend of hers.

Ran changed her voice into promises.

"Cut yourself free of the rune-stone, skald."

She drifted closer, her hair swirling gently. Hers was an old and dark magic, a pulling magic, a yearning magic, a magic to fill you up with wanting. But that wanting is like a drunkard's hollow dreams, a suicide's frozen hope.

"Stay here, Ghosts-Skald. There's no need to go back now." Her voice was like the tide, rushing in, sighing, withdrawing. "No one waits for you."

Like a doom spoken, her words, and I felt them as I'd feel a hand clutching at my throat, the grip tightening. In her flat dark eyes I saw a sudden image of fire, flames leaping, red and greedy tongues lapping. Fire filled the shore, the beach, the cove. Above the burning a kestrel flew, her wings shining, her beak and talons red as with blood. And the sky rocked with thunder, flared red with witch-light. A fire-wolf ran on the shore. A hundred men fought there, the battle-din louder than the booming sea.

Ran closed her terrible eyes, threw back her head. Her laughter was a gale screaming.

Only faintly did I hear Ewyn's cry as, swift, he turned and fled with me. Thrusting upward, the kelpie carried me with him. Not fast enough did we leave; too late did we start away from the sea-woman. Her voice followed us, called up laughing, the sound every drowning man hears.

"We know you, Ghosts-Skald! The gods of the dead know you!"

Ewyn took me up to the light, carried me away from the sea-woman and her dark visions, her words like to those Caerau ap Einion had spoken on Deorcdun. Up through all the weighty sea the kelpie took me, and he was strong, knew the currents and how to use the tide's ebb and flow.

But Ran only let him go so far before she cried out in magic and bade the seas fling us apart.

Come back to me, Ewyn!

I heard him roar protest even as we knew he'd not stand against the sea-woman. What his magic did to land-going women, Ran's magic did to him. And in Ran's magic was the bitter echo of what god-Ing had done to her. There was no resisting for the kelpie, only wanting to.

Separate from Ewyn, I couldn't see and I couldn't feel but numbing cold. I couldn't breathe and had no breath in me to hold.

I clutched the rune-stone in my two hands, put my faith in the god when I could put no faith in my lungs. And he saw me the rest of the way back to the light. Sea-Ing sent me back to land, back to the stone road, risen now that the tide had fallen.

I came up from the sea to fire, Sif. I came up from Ran's Hall to burning Muspellheim.

So seemed that battle I saw, Peada's men and Bran's witches, Aescwine's army of *wraecca*—like all the Dwarfs there are—standing against them. Above, in the smoking sky, the kestrel flew, crying mournfully, circling the battle. I came up from the sea with a weapon in my hand, Owain's rune-writ oak staff, the one Hinthan made. It came to my hand as if called, even as I reached for the stone road.

I'd not go into this battle, but I would try to go through. I came onto land staggering and clumsy, with only the quarter-staff for a weapon. Nothing about victory did the rune-marks say.

They were all *rad,* all the journey-rune.

Witch-light flashed, red lightning streaked the moon-reft sky over Caer Coblyn. The sea-froth changed to red, dyed by blood and baleful light. The armies fought on the stone road, and blood ran down that road like rain. They fought on the beach, black and faceless forms in the witch-light, the sweat on them like gold running, Dwarfs and Men shouting battle-songs, roaring curses to cover fear, screaming when they died.

They died, Sif. In numbers they died, arrow-shot, sword-gutted, by war-axes reft of limbs and screaming in their own blood. They died, friend and foeman.

Witch-light blazed, burning, and all the battle-magic stained the stars red. One witch wore the fire-cloak, dressed in blaze. A second went loping four-footed, a witch in a wolf-shirt, a wolf with a pelt of flame. That was Bran, and Cadwalla's nephew ran wild, snarling and foaming. Every step he took left little fires behind, small flames kindling on magic, burning in the sand, even at the water's edge. He ran howling and tearing at the bellies of horses, slashing at the legs of riders.

One of those riders was Reginleif, and she beat the fire-wolf off with the flat of her sword, wrenched back on the reins, forced her mount to rear up, slash at wolf-Bran with iron-shod hoofs. Burned, the horse screamed. Terrified, the beast turned, lashing and kicking. I swung at the wolf, hard with the oak staff, heard ribs crack, sent the wolf limping. Reginleif pulled me up behind her.

"Reginleif! Where—?"

She answered before I could ask. She pointed, showed me Cynnere sword to sword with a man of Peada's. And Aescwine fought steadfast at his back, iron gleaming in the light. Here on this war-ground they'd not forgot the old ways of friendship. She pointed, showed me the kestrel circling, wings red in the glare.

A woman screamed—Rowenna!—snatched up for booty by a dark-bearded Welshman riding. She was grabbed, but she wouldn't be stolen. In the witch-light iron flashed, blood red. Rowenna Brand's daughter might well have been Rowenna Long-Knife of legend. She killed the thief with his own iron.

Reginleif called, "Hold me tight, Garroc Ghosts-Skald!" and she kicked up the horse. She sent the beast plunging across the sand, cut a way through the battle. She knew where she was going, and I let her take me there. I beat off all comers with the oaken staff, broke heads, shattered limbs, while she guided the horse, took the brave beast past fire and through the dying.

I saw the fire-cloaked witch die, his head shaved from his shoulders by a long and bloody sword. I smelled the stench of burning flesh and hair. Peada's men had come into the fight outnumbered, but confident that their witches would make the difference. But now one witch was dead, and wolf-Bran was hurt. I saw the beginning of fear in their eyes, saw them reckoning numbers and knowing that now it mattered that they were fewer than their *wraecca* foes.

Beneath me, the horse screamed, staggered, twisting and hamstrung. I flung myself off, to the side, dragged Reginleif with me and away from the thrashing beast.

Out from the dark between fires Hinthan cried, "Garroc, stay down!" One arrow whistled past overhead. Behind me a Welshman screamed; his long-knife fell from his hand. The horse he'd ruined wailed, thrashing on the sand. Then it stilled, suddenly. Reginleif wiped her long-knife clean on her shirt.

Hinthan pulled me up from the sand. "Come with me!"

Reginleif staggered to her feet, blood-covered and cursing. Abruptly, the cursing stopped. She snatched up her sword, ran for the stone road, ran for Aescwine and Cynnere. Beset by foemen, those two, and wearying fast. I started after her, but Hinthan grabbed my arm, pulled me back.

"Peada's got Wulf!"

In the black sky, the kestrel circled; high above the beach, over Caer Coblyn where red witch-brands flashed, she cried, *keee! keeee!* Hinthan ran for the shadows under the headland, pulled me after him into the curve of the stone road.

Piercing, the cry of the kestrel now, like a scream as we ran up the stone road. Halfway up the hill we heard a voice raised in a wild victory cry. Other cries swelled after, the echoes bounding off the cliff-face. Over Caer Coblyn the red lightning pulsed, sullen in the cloudless sky like a dragon brooding.

On Caer Coblyn we found the sons of Penda.

The Watch was a round place, unroofed, naked to the wind. It was colder there than by the water. Nightwind blew in from the heath, the sweeping headland, and I shuddered before that wind with not but sea-soaked trews on me. The warding wall was made of stout stone built as high as a tall Man's shoulder. In that wall were two breaks, one to inland, one to the stone road. The one to the road was blocked, by a boy's body held.

Wulfhere lay still on the stone road. Blood ran down his face but he wasn't dead, only knocked from his senses. I lifted him up, carried him into the shadow of the wall, and he came to himself. When I put him down, he clung hard to my hand.

"Merewal tried . . ." He gasped, a shuddering sob. "He tried to defend me."

Iron belled, swords clashing. Hinthan hid himself on the other
side of the wall, slipped into the shadows as Peada laughed, high
and shrill.

"Peada is my brother!" Wulfhere's hand was like ice in mine.
"He said he's my brother! Garroc, why does my brother want to
kill me?"

Blades clashed, ringing, scraping sparks one from the other.
Hissing, Merewal cursed. Hinthan nocked an arrow, rose up to
shoot. He didn't let fly; he had no clear shot. The scent of blood lay
heavy on the air. Merewal groaned, cursing. Below, the battle-din
ebbed. I heard ghosts, their voices low under the thunder of two
brothers trying to kill each other over the life of a third.

Above the Watch the kestrel circled, lower and lower. I pressed
Wulfhere deeper into the shadows.

"Stay here," I said. "Don't run off."

Wide-eyed, wordless, he heard; but I wasn't sure he understood.
The stone at my back rang and shouted, sparks leaped when iron
struck the wall. And Wulfhere screamed, high in dread and terror.
I turned, saw the fire-wolf, Bran Hel-Thane, on the stone road.
Thin licks of flame ran from his mouth like slaver. He came
limping up the road, shambling, and his eyes shone red in the
blackness like the heart of hate.

Soft, a hissing. Hinthan checking an arrow's black and white
fletching. He nocked the arrow, drew to aim to kill the fire-wolf.
I heard the arrow in flight, the witch rage in pain.

The kestrel cried warning—*keee! keeeee!*—and I turned again,
saw Merewal fall hard to one knee. I heard the bones break, his
knee shatter. Peada shouted his glee. Merewal, reaching for a
sword he couldn't touch, looked up at me, his eyes a wasteland
of pain and fear. Not dead of his brother's sword, but soon to die,
he couldn't reach his fallen sword.

But I could reach it, and in my hand that sword was mine. And
so it was my iron Peada struck when it was his brother he meant
to kill.

Iron belled on iron; the sound and the thrill of it rang in my own
bones, in the deeps of me where the battle-lust is. I heard Hinthan's
arrows in flight, one and two and three. I heard a wolf screaming,
then roaring. I heard the kestrel cry, dread and warning, *Keeeee!*
But I heard these things only dimly.

Sparks leaped each time Peada hit my sword, each time I hit
his. Bits of iron flew up—so hard did we two strike. We wasted
no time taunting, no time trying to show each other how good we

were at battle-play. We hacked, tried to maim; thrust and tried to kill. He was good, Peada. He'd learned war-work from Penda, from Wotan's Blade.

Slick the stones, wet with Merewal's blood. We stepped wide round that, kept our footing. And, fighting, I saw that Merewal wasn't dead. He got himself to the side. Knee-broken, he managed to get to where Wulfhere could help him up and out of the Watch. I saw it all from the corners of sight, and that way did I see Hinthan leap atop the stone wall. Parrying a bladed thrust, I saw him brace wide and draw on Peada.

That way, past crossed swords ringing, did I see Bran Hel-Thane—blazing against the darkness, eyes like burning coals—leap high for Hinthan. Wulfhere cried warning, and Hinthan leaped nimbly aside, changed aim all in a heartbeat, and let fly his arrow. The arrow took the fire-wolf in the shoulder, dropped him inside the Watch.

And my foot slipped on slick blood, even as the witch fell.

Black and white, like Hel herself, cold as winter-ice, Peada laughed to see me stagger, and he lifted his red-blazing sword as it were an axe for chopping.

Keeeeeeee!

Between us, like a curtain fallen, a kestrel's sudden wing. Her cry rang across the night. Talons gleaming, she tore at Peada's face, marked him deeply, drew blood. He flung up an arm to protect his eyes, and dropped his sword to do it. But he wasn't weaponless; in his other hand he gripped his father's rune-writ throwing-axe.

Hissed an arrow past his ear in the very moment the kestrel veered off. Hinthan shouted, "Drop the axe! Drop it!"

Iron clattered on stone, ringing. In Peada's eyes the will to murder showed clearly. But he had nothing in hand to work his will, and he stood under Hinthan's arrow. The fight was over.

The kestrel's wings brushed me as she came to ground; a breath of magic touched me as she changed her shape, became Lydi, my witch standing on the battle-ground, standing beside me. Wulfhere cried out to see that changing—in dread I thought, till I saw the face of him. He was not afraid.

Wolf-Bran lay panting against the stone wall, trying not to die, trying not to give himself up to his own fire. Alive yet, he struggled to change from beast to man again before he lost control of his magic. And dark against the bloody sky, Hinthan stood atop the wall, above the fire-wolf, above Peada. Nocked to bow he held Peada's death.

Lydi cried, "Hinthan, don't!" But he drew to loose the bolt. Lydi whispered, "Stop him, Garroc."

I shook my head to say I'd not do that. Merewal, leaning on the wall, his hand on his young brother's shoulder, said nothing.

It was Wulfhere made Hinthan pause. "Let him go, Hinthan." Hinthan's eyes were like grey hard ice.

"Please." Wulfhere swallowed hard. He'd not ever expected to know a kinsman, and this one he knew was not what he'd ever hoped for. "Don't, Hinthan. Don't kill my brother."

In the sky the red lightning pulsed only faintly. On the stone floor, wolf-Bran sighed once, deeply. He changed, became again a man. Arrow-shot, his ribs broken, he didn't move but to breathe.

Nor did Peada move, and he wouldn't look away from Hinthan. My boy must look right into his eyes to kill him.

"Get out of here," Hinthan said.

Just a little, Peada tested Hinthan's will. He bent to retrieve the throwing-axe, his father's weapon.

"Leave that."

Under the arrow, Peada must do as Hinthan willed.

And this can be said for him, Sif: Peada didn't abandon Bran, didn't turn his back on the Welshman. He helped him to his feet, gave him his shoulder to lean on, and so he didn't leave the Watch shamed utterly. We watched them away, saw them walk out of Caer Coblyn, to the heath and down the road away inland. In the sky, the red witch-light faded, trailed only faintly after them, a spent storm.

Lightly, Hinthan jumped from the wall, snatched up the rune-marked axe and tossed it to me. I caught it, just as I'd caught it from the king. And he came and took me by the shoulders, held me at arm's length to see all he could see, if I was hurt and how badly. When he was satisfied, he looked east again, to the heath and the red light pulsing over it.

"I should have killed him, Garroc."

I thought he was right about that. I knew it—the knowledge cold in the belly of me—that things weren't finished between Peada and us. But it remained that the deed was done, the life not taken. Things would be what they'd be.

Her eyes dark as ever I'd seen them, Lydi went to help Merewal. He leaned heavily on the wall, his knee shattered, bleeding and weak. He took the hand she offered, and I saw the magic happen. Pain had etched hard lines into his face; they softened. Dread had darkened his eyes; it fled. Lydi's lightest touch can do that.

And Wulfhere, white-faced and shaking, came into the Watch, to me. I turned him right around again, sent him back to Merewal. "Wulfhere, go help your foster-father. Hurry now."

In the night, the sun shone. Or so you'd have thought to see the boy's face a-light. He'd found a brother who hated him, but that dread fell away before a wonder. All that Hinthan had said to him about foster-kin paled before what he knew now. Small boys worship men like red Merewal for heroes, and they often confuse them with gods.

◄31►

Dawn flushed the eastern sky only barely. I stood on Caer Coblyn with Lydi, our backs to the rising day. She'd been all the night at healer's work. The wounded weren't too many. Peada's army had taken away their injured, and the *wraecca* weren't even a dozen. Still they were enough to tax her, who'd already spent much of herself in magic. I stood behind her, wrapped her up in my mantle and held her close to me against the chill.

Maybe, though I wasn't thinking it, I held her against the pull of the sea.

"Garroc," she said now, her eyes on the sky and the water still dark. "Is he dead?"

"Owain is."

"And Ewyn?"

From out on the heath came the clatter of stone on stone, the song of barrow-crafting. Peada's dead were given to the sea, to Ran. The *wraecca* dead would rest in a long earth-hall, high on this headland. The ships going by would know that Dwarfs were barrowed here with all honor.

"Ewyn is home," I said.

Lydi turned up my wrist and saw that the blade-mark was gone, healed of itself.

"What happened to Caerau ap Einion, Garroc? How did he die, all those years ago?"

I gathered her closer, and a knot of pain loosened in me, one I'd not let myself feel till just then, tangled strands of dread and loathing and pity for the grief-driven bard-witch.

"He killed himself."

And then I told her what I hadn't thought to be able to tell anyone. There above the sea on the Alf's Watch, I told Lydi that I'd had speech with the sea-woman, and I said that I hoped never to see her again. I told her what Ran had cried after me, and she turned in my arms, away from the sea. She reached for the Ing-stone I yet wore. Reaching, she touched the feathered frost-scar and knew who'd marked me.

Wide and dark, Lydi's eyes shone like bluest sapphires. She tested the strength of the leather plait, and must tie it again to be sure of it. She touched the scar again, with fingertips, and then kissing the whitened skin, as though she could smooth the frost-burn away. She couldn't.

"This scar was got in my cause," she whispered.

"And in mine. That's what you'll always be, Lydi—my cause." I took her face in my two hands and kissed her. "May I always be yours."

One simple Welsh word she used to answer, *Cariad*.

Beloved, she said.

In the cove, on the beach, red Merewal went among the *wraecca* dead. He limped, with Owain's rune-writ staff for a crutch. His broken bones were not wholly healed. Lydi saw, and she shook her head over it.

"I wish he would listen to me and rest. He's risking lameness no one will be able to heal."

I said that Merewal, who had often risked his life in battle, was used to worrying about death, not lameness. "And, more, he's used to having his way. You can warn, Lydi, but you can't force."

She knew it, and it was a part of healer-craft that she didn't love, this about letting a man make his own choices.

"Lydi, I'm done with gods and alfs and the sea. But I'm not done my promise to Penda."

She said she knew that, too, and when I asked her if Merewal and Wulfhere could go with her to Gardd Seren, she told me that anyone who wanted to go there was welcome. "I wish you could be among them."

"I wish I could be too, girl dear."

"But you have to go away."

I always had to go away and I was mortally tired of saying good-bye to her, Sif.

I went down the stone road, and in the pouch at my belt two pieces of a golden arm-ring chimed against a silver wrist-bracer, tokens of Penda's kin. I took Merewal away from his work, and I told him that if he went with Lydi to Gardd Seren he'd be bringing Wulfhere to the safest place I knew.

"We're not all done with Peada," I said.

He leaned on his staff and asked me how I knew that.

"I feel it."

"Well, if you're looking for him, you'd better look where our father is. Peada runs to our mother when he's in need of men and gold. He runs to our father when he's got lies to tell."

Fear sprang, sudden and cold. "What lies?"

"You're not dead, Garroc. And he's not going to find Wulfhere again. He knows it. Now it's time for vengeance. Find my father, and you'll find Peada craving his forgiveness and telling lies."

The day spread rosy and blue over the sea now. Gulls hung in the sky, ever-hungry. At the end of the stone road Hinthan stood watching the water rising and falling beyond the Teeth, waves like white manes tossing.

"Merewal, I'm leaving. I want two of those good horses of yours for me and Hinthan."

"And you'll not be asking for Cynnere and Aescwine?"

"Not this time. And I want something else."

Merewal smiled, a lean grin, and shifted his weight a little off his good leg. "Have you got another foster-son for me?"

"Only this one. This is what I want: Sooner or later Wulfhere's going to hear it that he's Penda's son. I want him to hear it from me."

"Now?"

"Now."

He called out to Hinthan, waved my boy away from the water.

"Hinthan," said the king's son, "go fetch Wulf and bring him here. We have some things to say to him."

Hinthan glanced at me, and he knew what we'd be talking about. He ran and did what Merewal asked him to do, but before they came back, Rowenna came down the stone road. She was dressed in rusty rags, the rent gown Hinthan had found her in. She was thinner now, and she'd not been plump then.

One look—and very brief—passed between her and Merewal. She lifted her chin, as to defy. He shrugged as to say, Do as you will.

Gulls hung over the sea, motionless in the shining blue sky.

And Rowenna said, "Garroc, once I said that I might be of help to you. I know you didn't think that was but a politeness, but I can keep that promise now."

And me, I was restless to get away; the certainty that Peada was abroad and making trouble was growing in me. I was in no mind to be delayed.

"I don't know how you can help—"

"I know who Wulfhere is. And I am his kinswoman."

On the stone road Hinthan came walking with Wulfhere, down to the sea in the rosy morning. They stopped suddenly when they heard red Merewal's laughter. Merewal wasn't surprised. He'd known what I hadn't. It was me, standing and staring, dumb in the face of what I suddenly understood, that so amused him.

Merewal had recognized her for a kinswoman when first he saw her. Their eldest father was god-Wotan. Before that, Aescwine— who knew the kings of the Centish folk—had seen the shadow of Witta Wotan's son in this young woman's face. And the tale of Rowenna Long-Knife, the story she'd told a few nights ago, was the tale of one of her own kinswomen, Rowenna who was the daughter of the first King of Cent.

This Rowenna was Aethelburgh Aethelbriht's daughter, the sister of Eadbald who was that year the King of Cent. She was the wife of Eadwine Faith-Breaker, and I'd brought her safely out of Northumbria.

Aethelburgh smiled at me, and she said, "Garroc, I owe you a great deal, and what I do now is only a part payment."

I nodded, yet wordless, and I took the pouch from my belt. But I didn't spill out the small hoard it held, not yet.

Wulfhere stood close to Merewal, let his foster-father steady himself with a hand on his shoulder. He had a look on him like he could smell another change on the salty breeze.

"Garroc, Hinthan says you have something to tell me."

I looked from Merewal to Aethelburgh to Wulfhere. The Queen of Northumbria took the problem from me.

"Wulfhere, it's time for you to learn about your kin."

Wulfhere paled a little. High above us a sea-bird cried, a gull hanging on the wind.

Aethelburgh said, "Your mother and I were cousins."

Penda's young son let his breath go softly, like a sigh. Hinthan looked swiftly from Aethelburgh to Merewal to me; then he found himself a seat and settled to listen. He had a skald for a foster-father; he knew how to hear a tale.

"Wulfhere, I don't think you know much about your mother."

He didn't answer but to flinch. He knew only a little, and what he thought he knew had been most of the pain in his short life.

The sunlight shone down, gold on the water. The sea rose and fell, waves came in and went out.

"I know what they said of her in Haligstane," Aethelburgh said, very gently. "But Gytha was no whore. She was good and kind, and she came to live with me in Northumbria when I was just wed and lonesome in my new home. In those days . . ."

She looked away, out to sea, up to the sky, away.

"In those days, before my children were born, I longed for sight of a familiar face. Today I see Gytha's face in yours."

Nor ever would she look on her children's faces again, Sif. That much of Rowenna's tale was true. I saw it in Aethelburgh's eyes.

"And she was headstrong, my cousin. She met a man and loved him—"

Shaking, Wulfhere said, "Peada's father . . ."

Faint, the sound of barrow-crafting came down from the head-land.

"And yours," Aethelburgh said. "Gytha loved him at once, for he was strong and handsome. . . ." She smiled, sweetly and right into his blue eyes. She touched his cheek, brushed flaxen hair from his forehead. "But Gytha wouldn't marry him, though he wanted that badly. She wouldn't wed a man who refused to become *Cristen*. But I know this, Wulfhere: She loved him the more for his steadfastness—even as she turned him away. And she mourned him as dead, but when she bore him a son, Gytha sent to him and told him. He promised that no harm would ever come to you if it was in his power to make it so."

She stopped, silenced suddenly by wide and frightened eyes. And Wulfhere, as though he knew he stood on the brink of a bigger change than he'd imagined, turned and looked at me.

"Garroc Ghosts-Skald," he said, low, whispering.

"Listen, boy. Hear it all."

"Wulfhere," Aethelburgh said. "Your father has some power, and enough to see that you stayed safe where your mother had put you. He has enough power to send good men to fetch you away when he knew that you were in danger. Your father is Penda Pybba's son. To honor him, his folk call him Wotan's Blade. The Welsh folk name him Golden Panther."

White as snow, the boy.

"Wulfhere, you've been taught to see devils where there are none. You've been taught to believe ill of your mother, who deserves better. Now learn something else: Your father is no demon. You've seen two of his sons. One was terrible, and he wanted to kill you. One stands beside you now, and he loves you."

It is never silent near the sea. Birds cry, the water hisses and sighs, or roars. But it seemed silent to me then as I waited, not breathing, to see what Wulfhere would do.

He didn't look to his foster-father. He looked to me, his blue eyes wide, and I'd not seen him so lorn and lost since the day he and Hinthan stood watching Haligstane burn. Again and again, all the world kept changing around him. Now, of a sudden, he was no ill-gotten boy to be scorned and shamed. The word 'bastard' would have no meaning among his father's people, and he was a king's son. So it had been in all the tales of old Arthur, the tales he liked to hear. But Arthur of Wales hadn't been taught to fear and loathe the king who was his father.

Thin, his voice when he spoke. "Garroc, is all this true?"

"Put out your hands, boy."

He did, and I emptied the pouch into his cupped hands. Sun glinted on emeralds and etched gold, on the bracer's silver and dark onyx. Aethelburgh caught her breath to see the halved ring. She knew it. Wulfhere knew it, too.

And I said, with the best voice I could, "One half of the ring you know, Wulfhere. The other my king has kept all the years since you were a babe. And the bracer is Peada's, but now you can claim it for booty. You've earned it. What Aethelburgh says is true. You are my king's son."

Even as I said it, a look passed between Merewal and me. Aethelburgh had told Wulfhere all the tale of himself as she knew it, but one part yet remained. She didn't know that Wulfhere was Penda's heir.

We'll let that be for now, Merewal said silently.

As silently, I agreed that we would, and red Merewal sat down on the stone road so that he could take his foster-son into his arms, his young brother who would one day be his king.

I sent Hinthan to find two good horses for us, and I said to Aethelburgh that we two still had some things to talk about.

"Walk with me," I said.

We went quietly, and quietly she said, "Cynnere knows the truth of me. I told him, and . . ." She drew a long breath, let it out in a slow sigh. "And it doesn't matter to him. He doesn't care that I am Eadwine's wife; he doesn't care."

"He loves you."

"I know."

She bent to pick up a shell from the sand, a glittering cowrie new-washed in from the sea.

"Girl, what will you do about that?"

She laughed, but thinly. "Confess my sin, and sin again. It's not just him who loves."

We walked some more, along the shore, and the little waves lapped at her hem.

"Garroc, Rowenna said that the queen was wrong to bring her priests here. The best of the Roman-born. The finest speakers. The fiercest in faith . . . Rowenna was right. I didn't know what harm they'd do here. I didn't know that Eadwine would be so weak in his spirit, and let himself be turned away from friends. My father, and my brother, they never let the people of Rome talk against friends. They forbade it, and they banished every priest who wanted to talk against *dvergr*. But there's power to be had from those Romans. They ruled all the world once, as soldiers and kings. That kingdom fell apart. We see the ruins of it all over the Isle. But now as priests they've got back much of what they lost as soldiers. And now they're coming for the rest, offering God with one hand and power with the other. Eadwine wanted the power."

She looked up to the headland, to the barrow growing tall. Cynnere stood near the highest part. I didn't recognize him, but she did.

"In Cent we know who our friends are. I'm sorry to the heart of me for all the *wraecca* in Northumbria. I'm sorry to the heart of me for what happened at Eotenfeld to Aescwine and Cynnere."

"Aethelburgh," I said, and not gently or roughly, but flatly. I was tired of *Cristens* and the harm they'd done, the dark age they'd brought. "If you're sorry, make it better. You can't heal all of Northumbria, girl. But Aescwine and Cynnere have been friends for most of Cynnere's life. Maybe Cynnere had two bad choices that day at Eotenfeld. If that's so, there's no way he could have made a good one. If you want to heal something, heal the wound between these friends."

Her eyes on the barrow rising, she said, "I will. I want to ride down the coast till I find a port where I can take ship for home, for Cent. Ask Cynnere and Aescwine to ride with me."

"Cynnere is yours, Aethelburgh; you know it. I'll ask Aescwine, and if he agrees you must be prepared to get Reginleif as well."

The Queen of Northumbria said it suited her to have another friend for the way.

I went to the barrow when there was no one but Aescwine there.

I told him what Aethelburgh wanted, and I said, "Aescwine, will you go?"

He settled a stone more closely against its kin a-top the barrow, wiped sweat from his face, and leaned back against the earth-hall.

"With her," he said, flatly. "You want me to go back to Cent, with her?"

"And Cynnere."

He thought about it, and his face was turned from me so I couldn't see and reckon out what he was feeling. Out on the moor, silver Reginleif sat astride a black mare, and she leaned down to say something to Hinthan who stood beside her. I knew it that they were watching Aescwine and me.

"Garroc," Aescwine said, "I'll go because you want me to."

"No. If you go, go because you want to."

A gull cried overhead; inland, a hawk's whistling scream haunted the sky. Aescwine didn't say anything for a long time, and at last I decided that his silence was refusal. I took him by the shoulders and said that I must be going away.

"I wish you well, my old friend."

He hugged me, but he let me go without saying anything until I was well away from the barrow. Then he shouted:

"All right! I'll go!"

For whatever good it will do . . .

He didn't say that last, Sif, but the words hung in the air. I smiled, for I had better hopes than he did. Out on the moor, Reginleif leaned down to Hinthan again, and she kissed him lightly in farewell. To me, she raised up her sword in salute.

Grave and dark-eyed, Lydi pushed her hair away from her face and said that she would see me in Gardd Seren. Her hair wasn't so short as it had been. Soon she would have to decide to cut it again, or let it all grow. And she yet wore Hinthan's old green shirt, the trews that had stopped fitting him a while ago. She looked like no boy in that gear.

And I saw, too, that Lydi didn't look as homesick as she'd been. She didn't look at the starless day and sigh for what she didn't see. She'd got used to being away from home. An ache, like homesickness, tugged at me when I realized that.

"I love you," Lydi said, and said it suddenly and fiercely as though she feared someone would come and take me away from her.

I took her into my arms, held her tenderly, said that I'd go nowhere but home to her when I was free to go again.

She didn't watch me away, and it was Wulfhere Penda's son who held my horse while I mounted. He said he'd see me in Gardd Seren when I came back, and then his foster-father called him. He ran away with only a wave and a shouted farewell.

"Good-bye, Garroc Ghosts-Skald!"

Hinthan smiled to hear that. He said he reckoned things were getting better between the *aetheling* and me.

"It's about time," I said gruffly. "Don't you think?"

But I didn't fool him, Sif. He knew me, and so he knew I was pleased.

We put heels to horse and rode away across the headland, east and north. It was only us now, just Hinthan and me as it had been on the first day of spring, a long time ago when we left Gardd Seren, I not so eagerly as him. Now I rode eagerly. I wanted to get to Eoferwic and find the king.

Before we left Wales we learned from a goat-herd that Eadwine Faith-Breaker was dead.

"It was a hard dying," the boy said, but not with any sadness. "Our Cadwalla got him, killed him in a great battle at some place called Doncaster. They took him and cut off his head. They say the king brought that head back to Penda and those two hung it high on the walls at Eoferwic, all bloody and dead. . . ."

And so Cadwalla had killed his breast-brother, and in most places that's reckoned a kin-slaying. Later Hinthan said that he wondered how it would be when Aethelburgh heard about her husband's death.

"Did she ever say if she loved him, Garroc?"

She never did say, but I don't think she did. It hadn't been about loving, between her and Eadwine. It had been about power.

Me, I didn't wonder how I felt about the news. I'd helped lord and king hunt that death these long four years gone. I wished I'd been at Eoferwic to see the head of Eadwine Faith-Breaker hung up.

Now all the ways and roads we took were filled up with rumor. We heard from a farmer that Bran had gone fleeing by one night. We heard from a miller that he'd been alone and that he wasn't looking hard for Cadwalla, his uncle. We heard whispers and guesses about why that could be, and we didn't tell anyone what we knew.

Late on the third day away from Caer Coblyn Hinthan lagged behind, took his time walking along the road with a pretty farm girl. When I looked back to see them together, I felt the jolt of his growing as though he'd done it all between one moment and the next. He was taller than me now, if just. He'd soon be fifteen, and the next time he saw his face he'd be wanting to shave. He'd got him a soldier's swagger that only looked a little outsized, and he and the girl walked for a while together. When she ran away across the fields to home, Hinthan caught up with me and he told me that the farmer's girl said she'd heard it that Cadwalla would soon be home from Northumbria.

"And she heard that Eadwine's sons have fled to Cent, and that Penda's gone to rest at Hordstede in Rilling."

The king was waiting at Rilling for us, Sif. No rumor told us that. We heard it from two men we knew well, Eldgrim and Pearroc. Those two were my scouts. Dwarf and Man they'd been riding the roads looking for us.

"As friends," Eldgrim said. "But I'd be less than a friend, Garroc, if I didn't tell you there's trouble waiting for a welcome."

All the wildwood beyond the Rill blazed golden on the day we came home. The sky hung low and blue over the river, ducks paddled in the stills on either side of the current. Wood-smoke rose up from hearth-fires all around Rilling. Erich War Hawk waited for us at the gate.

"The king's waiting in the hall for you. Be careful of him. Peada's been here since last night."

"And has the boy poisoned him against me?"

Coldly I said that, Sif. I'd earned a better home-coming. But Erich let that go by.

"Garroc, just be careful."

He said no more to me, but when Hinthan made to follow me, Erich held him back. I went alone to Hordstede.

◄32►

All the hall was filled up with storm-feel; the hair rose prickling along my arms. The heart of that storm sat in Hordstede's high-seat, the place that was his by right in the hall of every *cyning* in his land. At the king's feet a black hound rose up, growling at the sound of my step. Penda stilled the beast with a word and came down the long hall to greet me.

"Welcome, *dvergr*. You're later back from the wars than the rest of us."

He wasn't poisoned against me. I heard it in his voice, the honest heart of him, and I felt a pang of shame that I'd ever thought he could be. He knew who his friends were, that king. Still, all was not well. I saw that, too. Something dark hung between Penda and me.

He cocked his thumb at the ale-keg, said we two would talk better for having something to drink. And he went and sat on the table, his feet on a bench. While I drew the ale he took up a sword from the board, a fine straight blade with a polished horn-grip. Crouched atop that grip was a golden dragon, brooding. For eyes, the little dragon had rubies.

When I offered him a filled cup, Penda laid that sword across his knees. The fire loved the rune-writ iron, caressed the grip and the crouching dragon.

"King," I said. "You've been waiting, and I'm here. Shall I tell you about Wulfhere?"

Very dark, his eyes when I spoke Wulfhere's name. He laid aside the sword and lifted the cup, drank half off in one swallow.

"Tell me."

I didn't tell him about Aethelburgh, nor that two men of his were taking Eadwine's widow down the coast of Wales to find a ship for Cent. But I did tell the king all the story of Wulfhere. I told him of the cruelty and kindnesses of his young years, of the good friend he'd found in Raighne of Ireland, of the friends he made along the way from Haligstane. And I told the king about the foster-father I'd chosen for his son, and how I felt it that Merewal would take good care of the boy.

"He's twice-bound to the *aetheling*, King—as brother, as foster-father."

Penda said nothing about that, nor said if he thought I'd made a good choice. He rapped his knuckles against the board, small thunder growling.

"Garroc, did you speak of me to the boy?"

"Yes," I said. "He's a boy of Northumbria. He hasn't been taught to love you."

Fire hissed in the hearth, the hound growled low, scenting something he didn't like.

"But he's young," I said, wanting to give Penda more. "And he has a good teacher now in his brother. He'll learn to love the folk he'll rule."

"All the folk? You said he's a *Cristen* boy."

The ruby-eyed dragon winked in the firelight, as though it were laughing.

"Some of us he'll have a harder time learning to love than others. King, you left him among *Cristens*. He'll have to learn to love *dvergr* one at a time—and only after we prove ourselves to him. That's not a good way to rule, but I think that's how it will be with him. I don't know if he'll ever love you. Is that what you wanted?"

He looked at me over the rim of his cup, and at last I saw laughter spark in his eyes. But it was a bitter glee.

"Ghosts-Skald, the sons I've had with me don't love me. I didn't reckon Wulfhere would be different."

He hadn't reckoned on it, but I saw it in his eyes that he'd hoped Gytha's son would love him. And that's not reasonable, but hope is no more reasonable than love.

"King, don't say Merewal doesn't love you. He's proved himself your man this year. No one will wonder about him again. And what the foster-father knows, he tries to teach his boy."

Yet the king watched me over the rim of his ale-cup, yet his eyes were filled with dark brooding. Torches flared, and fell, and flared again. Light ran down the walls, spun along the gold of the dragon-sword.

We'd not spoken of Peada. The king had asked nothing; I'd offered nothing.

"Garroc, the war's not over."

"I heard it that Eadwine's sons are still alive."

He dismissed those two with a wave of his hand. "They've gone flying to Eadbald in Cent, but I don't think that alliance will hold now that Aethelburgh's a widow."

Penda took up the dragon-sword, traced the blood-groove with his finger, and set the iron on his knees again.

"Osric is still prowling around the borderlands, and he's got a clear war-ground now. Tell me what you know about him."

I told him everything I'd learned in Bran's hall, even to the alliance Osric had struck with Bran and Peada. It was hard to talk to a father about what treachery his son had planned. The harder when I saw that Penda wasn't surprised.

"He's his mother's, always," the king said.

He had no more to say, and nothing more he wanted to hear. He sent me away with only a word of thanks.

"But come back in the morning, Garroc. We're not finished talking to each other yet."

Darkly he said that, and my belly tightened up with fear. Something was wrong here in Rilling, and that wrongness—like a storm a-brew—hung between the king and me.

Erich said to me, "Don't go to the hall to sleep tonight, Garroc. Bring Hinthan and come and sleep in my house. Gled's made everything ready."

So she had, and Golden-Hair opened her door to us and said we were welcome in her home always, welcome at her hearth, and welcome to the best she had to eat and drink. She knew me, did the *cyning's* wife, and we two got on well together. She liked to hear a tale or two after she'd settled her children to sleep, and I liked to sit by the fire and get the petting and praise and good honey-wine that is a hearth-skald's portion.

In the morning Erich woke me and Hinthan, and he told us to dress quickly and come with him to the hall. As we left I caught only a glimpse of Gled Golden-Hair, saw her standing by her children's bed, her hands clasped tight together as though she were hoping mightily for something.

The hall of a *cyning* is the home of his soldiers, their hearth, their board. So early had we come to Hordstede that the table was not set back in place, the benches were yet against the wall, and the hearth-fire only newly lighted. No sign of the men who'd slept there did we see; they'd got up and out already, and earlier than they'd have liked to. Still, the hall wasn't empty, and I knew at once that we'd walked in on something, knew by the hush in the place that we'd come too soon into there.

Penda sat again in the high-seat, and I remembered what Aescwine had said of him in the spring—that he looked like Wotan brooding, the Raven-god sitting dark-eyed over the problem of the war he was bound by fate to fight and lose. Before him stood his eldest son, Peada, who always made me think of Hel.

Beside me Hinthan stood stiff and still, head up, ready to fight. I touched his arm; he didn't heed. I gripped his wrist. He stood down, but his grey eyes were dark and cold as flint.

Said the king to his son, "The choice is yours. Exile or the rope."

He said it flatly, his voice parched of the anguish I'd heard after the battle at Winwaed, when he'd threatened Peada with outlawry. Then he'd been a father; now he was a king. Penda would dole out no forgiveness today. If Peada chose the rope, the king himself would see to the building of the gallows.

Peada knew that. He knew, too, that his father shouldn't have given him a choice.

"King," he said, his voice like a snake's hissing. "I choose exile."

The blood drained out of Penda's face, but I don't know if it was the force of a father's relief or a king's sudden, swift understanding that he'd done the wrong thing.

Peada picked up his gear—not much, bow and quiver, sword and long-knife—and turned his back on his father. Then he saw us, but he didn't let us know if he was surprised or not. He walked down the hall with an easy, careless stride. Only once did he stop, and that was to put himself in front of Hinthan.

Black and white, him, like the Ice-Woman. And he was deeply marked by a kestrel's talons. Low, he said, "It's not over between us, boy."

Hinthan looked into his eyes, his own wide and clear and steady. "It won't be over till I've killed you."

Peada laughed and he went away, strutting down the long hall as though he'd walk out the door to a kingdom waiting for him.

It was then the king said to me that charges of murder had been brought against Hinthan Cenred's son, who was my foster-son.

Have I said to you, Sif, that your father was beautiful? That he stood straight in courage, braced in defiance, most lovely when he was ready to do battle? Just so did he look that day, and my heart ran with dread when he lifted up his head and said, "Who brings the charge, King?"

Penda answered darkly.

"Daeltun Orahamm's son. And he's said that the murder happened in Wales, in Gwynedd by the sea. Hinthan, tell me true: Did you kill Orahamm?"

White and tight-drawn, Hinthan's face. The pulse beat wildly in his neck, his heart raced; you could see it. He knew what price must be paid for man-killing, knew that Daeltun could claim even his life if that's what he deemed would pay the blood-price on his father. Hinthan went to stand before the king.

"I don't know, King. I killed some men in battle. Maybe Orahamm was one of them."

"Peada claims it was murder, not battle. It's what he's told Daeltun, and Orahamm's son believes it."

Erich put a hand on my shoulder, brought me into the light and the warmth near the high-seat and the hearth. In the rafters a hunting hawk screamed. Erich lifted up his arm, offered his wrist, and the falcon stooped and took its place.

I went and stood behind Hinthan, put a hand one on each shoulder.

Into the silence, he said, "I murdered no one."

I'd never reckoned out Penda's age before then, Sif. I knew he was somewhat older than Erich's father, but not much. That day, in the pale slanting sun, he looked older than that, worn and torn and battle-weary.

"I know it, boy. But the story's gone all around Rilling, and farther than that. Peada's done his work against you well. Witnesses to the murder have sprung up all over the Marches and they are happy to swear to what they say they saw. Tell me this: How am I to excuse you without saying to all the kingdom that you killed the man in battle to defend Wulfhere? How am I to lay open that secret for all his enemies to study and find a way to him?"

Under my hands, Hinthan's shoulders tightened.

"You can't, King. Will you hang me?"

Penda laughed, and not so bitterly now. "How could I do that? No killing would be more unjust. And your foster-father would have reason to come after me and claim my life in payment. I think he'd do it, too. Then my kin would be bound to avenge my death. No, Peada can't have all that, and Daeltun will have to settle for the *wer-gild*."

Erich spoke up, my *cyning* who'd been silent till then. "Penda, I'll pay the *wer-gild*. And I'll pay whatever else is needed to take the name of murderer off Hinthan."

Grimly the king said, "Daeltun wants more than gold, Erich. He wants that fine farm by the Rill."

"Then I'll give him land, but not Hinthan's. Hinthan deserves better of you, King."

The hunting hawk lifted, went back to the rafters. Penda watched the flight, or seemed to. After a moment he said that Hinthan did indeed deserve better, but there was nothing else he could do.

"Boy," he said to Hinthan, "that farm's not the only good land in the kingdom. I'll double the acreage for you—when you return from outlawry."

That was an open-handed offer, Sif, a generous promise that would be kept. Any man would have taken it, but Hinthan had no such idea. Daeltun Orahamm's son would walk away from this false charge with all that remained to Hinthan of his kin, the good farm he'd had no interest in these four years gone. In the losing of it, Hinthan at last saw the value of the farm by the Rill.

"King, I don't want what's not mine. You'd better hang me, and barrow me by the river. Orahamm's son won't have my land unless he gets the ghost of me with it."

All the blood in me ran cold. Those are ill words, the kind that should never be spoken for fear that fate, or a king, will take them seriously. I turned Hinthan right around and put him into Erich's hands. And the *cyning* took him out of the hall, away from Penda, away from his own foolish words. He went, grimly, silently, and his footsteps felt like thunder in me.

We stood in silence, the king and me, and he wasn't too hardened against my boy.

"He's a handful, the boy, ay, Garroc?"

"Two handsful," I said.

"I don't reckon you think I should hang him, though."

A little I smiled. "I'd be happier if you didn't."

He left the high-seat, went walking down the hall to the board. The dragon-sword lay there, unsheathed. The ruby eyes gleamed in the pale sunlight spilling down from the high windows. Penda took it up, sighted along it, the soldier's habit of testing a blade's straightness.

"I don't feel good about this, Garroc. Hinthan does deserve better. And I know if I outlaw your boy, I'm going to have to do the same to you."

"For how long are we exiled?"

With that question, I accepted outlawry for Hinthan and me. And him, glad not to have to speak the words, he let go a sigh.

"Come home after five years, and you'll both come home welcome."

He said that comfortably, the matter already disposed. But I didn't know how well things would be if, after five years, Hinthan returned to find himself shut out from his home and living in sight of the one who'd stolen his father's farm.

"We'll leave now," I said. "You won't have to worry about Hinthan. I'll keep the reins tight till we're well away."

He nodded, and he took up the dragon-sword, came and gave it to me.

"I owe you better than you've got from me, Garroc. I'll pay it, and gladly, if in five years time you come to remind me. Until then, give this sword to Hinthan, when he can think calmly again. Fare well, Garroc Wand'ring Skald."

And so I left the hall, my Sif, and I left with two gifts. For Hinthan, a sword. For me, another name from my king.

Erich saw us away, stood outside his hall and bade us farewell. Folk who knew us lifted a hand to wave; a scout of mine called greeting. No one knew what had passed between us and the king; no one would know till we were gone. Erich wouldn't let us go stared at, like exiles driven from home. Nor did he let us go empty-handed. He gave us two of his finest horses and good gear.

Now he glanced from me to Hinthan, my boy sitting straight and tall on his horse, sitting in cold silence.

"Be careful of him, Garroc."

Was a grim look on him when he said that, Sif. He wasn't bidding me take care of Hinthan; he was warning me against him.

Taut as an overdrawn bow, my boy; with a white-knuckled fist he beat a restless rhythm against his knee. His eyes were on the road away from Rilling, the road that could take him to the farm where he'd been born, the one he'd not known how to love till he'd had it snatched from his hand.

"Erich, he's the one who's paying for the promises you and I made this summer past. Grant him the anger, ay?"

"I grant him that. But don't let the anger poison him, Garroc. Don't let him turn away from friends."

The wind blew chill off the river. All around us the song of the village rang—a young woman's laughter, a child's voice lifted in question. In the smithies iron rang on iron; a sword was being born on an anvil. Gruffly a smith said to his boy, "Easy, easy! Don't waste strength lifting the hammer. Hit the iron, and let the anvil throw the weight back. Ach! Will you never learn?"

He would learn. Or he'd find other work, with the cooper or in the ale-house. Maybe he'd go and be a soldier.

On the wind I smelled the falling of the year, leaves turning, the heady scent of crops being cut for harvest. Wheat and rye for bread, barley for ale.

Erich said, "I'll miss you, Father's friend. Good luck to you, and remember to come back to us when you can."

Swiftly I said good-bye to Rilling; silently I ended the farewell. I told my *cyning* I'd come back.

We did not ride out past Hinthan's farm, didn't take the road all lined with golden trees to there. I asked him if he wanted to, and he said that he didn't.

"There are plenty of farms that aren't mine along the way. I'll look at those."

We turned our horses west, to Gardd Seren, to Lydi, to where exiles go when they are in need of shelter and haven and home. Once Hinthan glanced at the new sword I wore, but he asked no question. Ours was a grim riding, and no word of mine, nor any silence, eased what hurt him.

At Gardd Seren we were greeted gladly, welcomed home first by Wulfhere. He saw us from the riverside, where he sat at fishing. Warily, I watched to see how Hinthan received the *aetheling's* greeting, afraid that some blame or grudge would fall like a shadow on their friendship.

I misjudged my boy to ever think so. I left him with his friend and the solace of welcome, and I went to find Lydi and Merewal to tell them how things had fallen out. I found them in the garden, they two sitting comfortably in the sun on the bench near the cottage door.

"It's a bitter wage for Hinthan's faithfulness," Merewal said when the tale was done. "My father owes him better."

"The king knows that, Merewal. His hands are tied, and he's done the best he can. That's how things are, for now."

He didn't like that answer, and he liked the truth of it even less. He went away, up the hill path to the oak grove that stood over the river. He went limping, for he'd have done better to heed Lydi's advice on Caer Coblyn.

And Lydi, watching him go, said, "I've told him that he and Wulfhere must stay here as long as they like, but I think they'll be going soon."

"Where?"

"To Cent. Aethelburgh knows the way here, and she knows that Merewal can't take the boy into his own homeland. 'Trust me,' she said. Merewal's trusting."

And then Lydi smiled and said that she was very glad to see me safe home at last, for she had a small chore for me to do. There was a blue pot on the table in the cottage, she said, and it was filled with seeds that must be planted now if we hoped to see the flowers of them in the spring.

Later that night, my Sif, when everyone in Gardd Seren was asleep, I took the dragon-sword, the rune-marked iron, and wrapped it up well. I put it away in the byre loft for the day Hinthan could accept it without bitterness.

Not that winter did I give the sword to him.

‹33›

On a chill day in the falling, when harvests were in and the people of Seintwar were starting to think of winter, Hinthan stood among the oaks at the top of the hill-path where Owain Dwarf-Smith used to go and look down at the river when he was thinking about going home. Brooding east, it was him saw Cynnere riding across the ford and it was him who cried the news.

Cynnere got himself a few good greetings from us in Gardd Seren, and one mighty surprise when he saw Aelfgar there. But Aelfgar, he greeted Cynnere with the same ease and pleasure he'd have done if years hadn't separated them, only days. Child-minded Aelfgar lived in a land of wonders; he lived in my Lydi's garden. What surprise then to see a friend come riding?

Cynnere was full hale and handsome as ever, and we soon learned that he had no need to name himself a kingsman any more. He was a queen's man now. I asked him what that meant, but he had nothing more to say than that I could think what I wished, and likely all of it would be true. He'd served her well in the summer, and Aethelburgh served him well now.

"She's sent a message for Merewal," Cynnere said. "She wants him and Wulfhere to come and stay for a while with her."

Here, at last was the summons Merewal was waiting for.

And Cynnere had other things to tell us after we brought him into the cottage, fed him and gave him to drink; good tales before the hearth-fire, stories of the doings in Cent, the doings in the Marches. He brought news of Peada's exile, but he didn't seem surprised when we knew about that already.

"Where is he?" Hinthan asked. "Do you know?"

Some other news Cynnere had heard on his ride through the Marches, Sif. He knew about other exiles, other outlaws, Hinthan and me. And he'd reckoned out the truth of the matter before ever I told him anything.

"I don't know," he said. "I didn't hear about that."

Hinthan smiled darkly over the lie, and Lydi took his arm, asked if he would walk her down the way to the village, for she needed someone to help carry her pots of salves.

"We'll be back for supper," she said. "Don't go riding away before then, Cynnere."

"Not till morning," he said. "Not till then."

When they were gone, when Merewal had taken Wulfhere to pack his small belongings and make ready to ride away, Cynnere said that he was sorry to see Hinthan so darkened. And he said that he'd heard word that Peada was seen around the borderlands between Scotland and Northumbria.

"Here and there, and some of the rumors must be true." He brooded quiet for a while, then, "Things don't always work out, ay? Aescwine and I went down the coast with Rowenna." He smiled. "With her. We got a ship—yes, it was a terrible trip— and she was welcomed home like she'd come back from the dead, by her brother who was still mourning her, and by the priest she'd fled Eoferwic with.

"And we stayed there in Cent, me and Old' un and Reginleif, but he couldn't be there long. He had to go back, he said. I thought he meant home to the Marches. But he said no, the Marches were no more home now than Cent. He's gone away, Garroc. He went north with his sword-girl; those two are with the *wraecca* in Northumbria. They're not Merewal's anymore. 'Just lent,' Old 'un said. 'Lent for the time, and back where we belong now.' "

"And so it's no better between you two?"

He was a while answering. Maybe he wasn't sure if what he'd say would be truth or hope.

"I don't think he hates me. It wasn't hate between us. It was hurt. Old 'un says we're all changed, and he's right. But Lydi made sure we both know the way here. 'I'll not go into Wales to be with witches,' he said to me. You know him. But he marked what I said. He knows there's friends here to welcome him."

And I thought, Maybe that's all he needs to know for now.

Cynnere left us in the morning, and the two sons of Penda went with him. Wulfhere and Hinthan sat all morning at farewell, and when the time to leave was come, the *aetheling* had fair thanks for Lydi but only a word's farewell for me.

Hinthan said he wished Wulfhere had said more to me, of thanks at least. But I'd not expected more. We'd not ever had much to say to each other, Wulfhere and me.

That night Lydi took a fat beeswax candle from her store and set it on the table. She lighted it, and when the flame was steady, she brought out the wooden box that Wulfhere had carried all the way from Haligstane.

"It's for you," she said, placing the box before me. "A gift from Wulfhere."

Hinthan put aside his whittling and came to see. I sat with my hands on the box for a long moment, not knowing why Wulfhere would leave his treasure behind for me.

"And you're not going to know," Hinthan said, "till you open it."

I said I reckoned he was right, and when I did no more than that, he took the box from my hands and opened it. The halved arm-ring and the silver bracer were gone. There was only one sheet of vellum, rolled and tied with a scrap of green cloth. It was the emerald-page, the last work Wulfhere had done in Haligstane. Then it had been only half-filled with his writing. Now it was covered front and back.

"All of that writing tells a story," Lydi said.

Hinthan nodded. "Wulf worked on it all summer long, every chance he had." He touched the edge of the page, gently. "We can't know what it says, though. He's not here to read it."

Lydi smiled, but with lowered eyes to hide some secret. She moved the candle a little closer to her, turned the page around so that the emerald was at the top. She began to read halfway down the sheet.

Soft, she said:

"Stane Saewulf's son said to me that few tales of the *aelfen* have come down to us. 'And we don't see alfs often, my youngling, but when we do, usually they are *niht-aelfen* we see, them in the sky at year's end, riding on horses that are black when seen in the dimming, white when seen at night, like they were clouds. These alfs are the Wild Hunters, and some people call them the Raging Host. . . . ' "

Almost I could hear the sea rushing in and sighing out, as it had on the night I'd told that tale.

"Garroc, he heard you," Hinthan said. His face brightened with the smile rarely seen these days. "You told that story the night before we went down to the sea. He heard and wrote it out."

With her finger following under each dark line, Lydi plucked words from the page and spoke them in a voice strong and clear and sure. On some nights in Northumbria, on other nights here, the king's son had taught her what red Raighne of Ireland had taught him. Now she read a tale I'd told, and one she'd never heard. And when she was done that old tale of Stane's, Lydi turned the sheet over and showed us more writing. She said that here was a poem Wulfhere had made, and she read it to us.

Wonderful this warding wall!

Then fate broke the *burgstede,*   battered giant's work.
Towers tumbled,   gable's targe split,
age stole stout gates.   Frost shines on lime,
chills the mother's breast,   breaks earth's bond.
Wyrd drove down   the wall-maker's dream,
earth-gripped, strong   a hundred seasons since
doom found the folk.   Of faith spoke this wall,
grey-cloaked, red-stained.   To king after king
hard oaths and hoar   gave this high-reaching friend
to stand stout under storm.

For memory men built,   bold stone-wrights binding,
fitting stone to stone.   Mead-halls soared.
High horns filled,   flowed the foam of poet's ale . . .

You know the rest, my Sif. It is a famous poem and even tonight someone may be singing it, a soldier at the campfire, a skald in his lord's hall, a traveller gone to sleep in the ruins of the forts the people of Rome built here long before the time when Arthur was King of the Isle.

"This is a boy's work," Lydi said, smoothing the page, touching the vellum as though it were the most fragile leaf in a waking garden. "What will the man's work be, I wonder?"

"Kingship," I said. "If his foster-father can keep him safe and teach him what he must know."

Clear light and shadow made currents on the written page, like a golden river running. Lydi reached across the table, and she took Hinthan's hand in hers.

"You gave a lot to his cause, Hinthan. Wulfhere won't forget."

Hinthan squeezed her hand once, in thanks for her care, and said nothing. The wound of his loss was still quick and bleeding. It would be a while at healing. And Lydi didn't press him. She rolled up the vellum sheet, carefully put it back into the box, and gave the whole to me. We have it still.

One afternoon, in the deeps of winter, Lydi said, "Garroc, the witches of Gardd Seren are not wanderers."

She said that as though she'd been having some private argument with herself. If she'd been arguing, she'd been doing it over the page of Wulfhere's writing. Through all the winter a day never passed that she didn't take the sheet from the box and read it, over and again.

Snow hissed at the window, wind ranged round the eaves, moaning low. Hinthan, sitting by the fire, looked up from his whittling. It was a horse he whittled, its neck long, stretched in running. He was thinking of Ewyn whom he'd never seen.

And I said, "I know one witch who wandered."

Aelfgar turned away from the window where he stood watching the snow, a small frown on his face. Branwen, sitting close to the fire, stroked red Werrehund's whitening muzzle. She said nothing, didn't look up. The honey-haired girl who came to Gardd Seren to learn wonder-craft from a witch only smiled as over some secret knowledge.

My words stayed unanswered, and Lydi said no more about whether the witches of Gardd Seren wandered or they didn't. But I remembered that she'd learned how to be under day skies without stars. She'd learned how to be away from Gardd Seren. Owain had taught her that. Still, I thought for a while that she wouldn't go away. I watched as she turned all her heart toward spring, toward planting and waiting for her garden to wake from winter.

But soon I saw that she was only waiting to say good-bye, for one frosty morning as I came up the hill from the river with a string of fishes for breakfast I heard her and Branwen in close talk as they walked around the garden beds.

"Branwen," Lydi said, "could you be the witch of Gardd Seren again for a while?"

I went the long way to the cottage, around the edge of the garden, didn't intrude on their talk. I wasn't surprised when, on the first day of spring, my Lydi woke me and said that she wanted to go away.

"And I want you to come with me, man dear. I want to go away up the coast and to Ireland, to where the monasteries are, to where there are books and writing. I want to see them, I want to learn about them."

She said that with tears on her cheeks, and she said it smiling. She wanted to go and she hated to leave, and I knew how she felt. We stayed late abed that morning, as was our habit on the day of the leave-taking.

Later I went to talk to Hinthan, and I found him standing among the oaks at the top of the hill-path, looking east to where the mist lay thickly on the hillside, east to where he couldn't go. He wasn't surprised to hear my news, and he agreed willingly to go. There was only one place he wanted to be now, and if he couldn't be there he didn't much care where he was. It was a poor reason for leaving, but I accepted it and gladly. His mood had got darker and darker through the winter as he brooded ever east, his loss unhealing.

I went to the loft above the byre and brought out the rune-marked dragon-sword. I unwrapped it and cleaned it, I put a keen edge on the good iron. But I didn't give the sword to Hinthan, Sif, not then.

The sea rose up, high waves curling. Loud as thunder, the voice of the Deep, roaring, surging, crying out with a hundred hundred voices. I heard them all from Caer Coblyn above the cove. The Watch had been washed of battle-marks, scrubbed by winter winds and storms come tearing in from the iron-grey sea. No blood stained the stone floor. The only mark of the battle was the barrow, the exiles' hall on the headland.

Faint, I heard a ghost whisper, a passer-by on his way to a dead-world and the gods waiting there.

Hinthan stood with his back to me, watching out to sea. In his hands, as ever, were knife and wood. He seemed to work by touch, hardly ever looked at what his knife was doing. It was another horse, and this one was of driftwood and so it would be silky grey.

I took the dragon-sword from its sheath. He knew the sound of iron waking and he turned, but he didn't put his work by. In silence he watched as I laid the weapon flat on my two hands, the long blued length of rune-marked iron.

"It's yours, Hinthan. From Penda."

He said, "I want no gift from the king."

But his hands yearned for that sword, Sif. How to resist the gold and the rubies? How to spurn the grace of the straight, clean blade? He couldn't help himself. He put wood and knife by and lifted the sword.

Gulls hung over the cove, white against the blue sky, crying and dropping down to the sea for fishes. Hinthan tested the sword's balance, its weight. He'd have to grow into it, but he would soon enough. He held it in his two hands, blade to the sky, followed the edge up with his eyes till he was looking right into the sun.

Then, slowly, he grounded the iron. Aching, forcing the words, Hinthan said, "Garroc, I've lost what my father left me. I have nothing of his anymore."

He looked at me with the eyes of shame, and I wouldn't let him wrongly shoulder that burden.

"Boy mine, the farm has been stolen from you. You didn't lose it. Lift your sword. Look at it."

He lifted the weapon, but he only looked at the dragon, the golden scales shining, the ruby eyes flashing challenge.

"Look at the blade," I said, gently.

And then he saw the rune-marks there. *Thorn,* and *thorn* and *thorn,* graven all along the length of the iron.

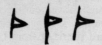

"Thunor's rune," he said. "The soldier's rune."

"That, but it means more. *Thorn* is a gateway, Hinthan. The mark of changes. What changes once, can change again. What's been taken, can be got back. We'll get your land back, youngling. Not now, but one day. I swear it."

He believed me, Sif. I saw it in him.

Out beyond the Teeth the stone road was sinking, the tide coming in. Lydi stood as close to the water as she dared without risking a cold soaking. She pulled my mantle tight around her, fastened it with the agate mantle-clasp, the journey-stone.

Came a gull sailing over the cove, crying once, and winging away. The wind kicked up, sent old leaves whirling around the Watch, scratching and scrabbling.

"Skald, skald," Hinthan said.

He pointed to the shore where Lydi stood, just then lifting her head. She turned to look away north where waves leaped and danced on the shore, white water splashing, grey breakers rolling away. Hinthan was a step ahead of me out of Caer Coblyn as Lydi shaded her eyes against the sun-glare.

On the beach a horse ran, grey as iron, white mane flying. Almost I could see the small lightnings where his hoofs struck stone, flint-fire flashing.

Then I saw only waves.

Maybe it was a trick of the sun and the glitter, Sif. Maybe it was Ewyn the pirate. I ran to catch up with Hinthan. We'd be a while going north, up the coast to find us a passage to Ireland. All that while I would keep near Lydi always, and watch carefully against any old friend who might want to come up from the sea and visit.

PART SIX

Sif

Ellisif sighed, soft for the story's ending, soft because the night was back, the war-dread, the witches ravaging fiery in the land. Arnulf stood by the window, watching. Like a dark flower blossoming, Ellisif's fear sprang. Iohann had been gone all night, and he wasn't back yet.

In the byre an early cock crowed. Chill air crept from beneath the door, from the window, and a thread of smoke-scent drifted, dark and damp. With dawn would come more fighting, King Aethelred's battle to keep the Welshmen from the rich farmlands by the Rill. The wounded one stirred, him with his golden beard, his golden hair. He drew a small breath, let it go raggedly. Ellisif took his hand and held it till he quieted.

"Iohann's all right, Sif," Garroc said.

Ellisif drew breath to ask how anyone could know that, but she stopped, even smiled, when Garroc touched his heart, the place where he heard ghosts.

The wounded man groaned again, and he opened his eyes. He saw her, truly for the first time, and he tried to smile at her. Garroc

fetched a dipper of water and Ellisif held the stranger while he
drank, then helped him to sit when he tried to do that. He was
heavy in her arms, a big and tall man who didn't yet have enough
strength to support himself. With Garroc's help, she brought him
closer to the fire, helped him to sit in the inglenook where the
hearth-stones warmed him like embracing arms.

Hoarsely, only just voiced, the stranger asked for his sword.
Garroc fetched the weapon, laid the naked iron across the man's
knees. With all tenderness, he closed the man's hands over the
hilt.

With all love the man said, "Skald, for whose benefit was that
tale of yours? Mine, to learn the manner of your foster-son's
outlawry—at least the first of the two exilings? Or was it for
the girl here who—"

"Hush," Garroc said, and swiftly. "Don't waste your strength.
Sit there and be warm and still."

Again, the early cock crowed, impatient for the day. Ellisif
went and stood by her husband, her Arnulf who looked more
a soldier than a farmer now. He put his arms round her, drew
her close, held her warmly. Even the smell of him had changed.
Gone was the warm scent of earth and the plough and the byre.
Now he smelled like a soldier, bitterly of iron and blood. So it
used to be with her father—times were Hinthan smelled like one
thing, times were he smelled like the other.

Arnulf's arms tightened round her. "Listen!"

Ellisif's heart raced with sudden terror. Came the sounds of
horses, a low whinny, a snuffling snort. Arnulf let her go, slipped
outside into the darkness at the end of the night.

And Garroc, suddenly standing near, said low, "That's Iohann.
All is well."

In the shadows Ellisif saw what no one else did, Garroc's eyes
tight-shut in grateful prayer.

"Who's with him, Eldfather?"

"No one. It's just our boy and some horses. Go dress the children, Sif. Make them ready for a ride, ay?"

"A ride—?"

His blue eyes glinted like iron's edge. "Go!"

She went. And she found that Arnulf had done some packing
in the night. Two scrips, filled up fat with clothing, lay near their
bed. She had only to rouse sleepy Blithe and Leofsunu, dress them
as quickly as she could. This she did with Garroc's help, for he
was but a step behind, and it was him lifted Blithe from the bed
and hushed her sudden fright with whispered words. Only when

the sobbing stopped, only when Blithe lay still on his shoulder, her thumb in her mouth, her eyes closing, did Garroc tell Leofsunu to take the scrips out to the yard.

"Your father wants your help, boy."

Leofsunu needed no more word than that to go scampering, at once too important for fear.

"It's time, my Sif. Come outside now. You've got to be well gone by sunrise."

And so she was going away after all, flying from the witches and the fire and the battle. In the hearth-room the stranger was on his feet, and he managed to walk as far as the table, where he leaned for support. He reached for Ellisif, touched her arm.

"Ellisif Hinthan's daughter, thank you. And remember what went unsaid in your eldfather's tale." When she looked at him, puzzled, he smiled. "Your father got his farm back, ay? So will you. I promise it."

Ellisif thanked him for his kind wish, and she bade him good luck. Garroc gave her no time to say more. He hustled her out into the night where all her kin stood gathered near a richness of horses, two sturdy beasts, high-headed and restless. Each bore a scrip across the saddle. Iohann reached a hand down, pulled his younger brother up behind him.

We're leaving . . .

And there was a swift embrace from Arnulf, not the less loving for the brevity of it, before he lifted her up to a seat on the second horse. Garroc handed Blithe up to her, saw the little one settled.

"Now go, my Sif. Iohann knows where to take you, and he can be trusted in all things."

"But where—?"

Garroc laughed, but softly. The sound of their talking mustn't carry.

"Where? Girl mine, you're bound for Gardd Seren, where else? Now hush you. Iohann knows a few ways to there, and all of them safe."

She sat mouth-agape, staring from her dark-haired handsome son to her eldfather. "Has Iohann been there?"

"Of course he has. Now go, and when you get safe there tell my Lydi how it is with me, ay? She'll like to know. And don't worry about the farm, child. You've had promise from the king himself that it'll be here waiting for you when you come home again."

And so, she knew who'd come hurt into her home, blown here by battle-storm. She knew the face of King Aethelred Penda's son, in the shape of it the shadow of an old god only Dwarfs honor now. A hundred questions pressed to be spoken, but Ellisif had no chance to voice them. Iohann kicked up his mount, and she must follow, away to a place she'd never been, away to a place she'd but heard of and dreamed. It was no easier to think of leaving now than it had been, but she had the promise of a king, the certainty of her eldfather, that she would have a home to return to.

Said ghost-Hinthan, her father speaking soft in the heart of her: *None could find better promises to trust.*

Ellisif looked back, to the light spilling golden from the open door, to her Arnulf just lifting his hand to say in silence that he loved her. She knew that what her father said was so.

AUTHOR'S NOTE

The Panther's Hoard is a fantasy that takes place in Britain during the Dark Ages. Garroc tells his tale to Ellisif in or around the year A.D. 693. At that time King Aethelred, the last of Penda's sons to rule Mercia, was striving to hold the kingdom against his traditional enemies—other Saxon kings, and Welshmen who weren't known for their fondness of any Saxon. The tale Garroc tells takes place some sixty or so years earlier.

There are threads of history woven into the fantasy and the myth in Garroc's tale. We read in *The Anglo-Saxon Chronicle* that Wulfhere was Penda's son. Little is known of his childhood but that he lived it much as Arthur of Wales is said to have done, in secret fosterage. We are told that the boy was kept safe from his brother Peada by a group of Penda's loyal *cynings* and thanes against the day when he would become King of Mercia. Gytha of Northumbria is a necessary invention for the sake of my story, for *The Chronicle* does not say that Wulfhere was Penda's son by a woman other than his wife. (Still, in light of such news of King Penda's doings as has survived, it wouldn't be surprising if this was the case.) It is believed that Wulfhere knew how to read and write. Some historians think it was Wulfhere who wrote out the genealogy of the Mercian kings that can still be read today, the names of his kinsmen reaching all the way back to Whitlaeg Wotan's son. It isn't known whether Wulfhere learned to read and write in a monastery, however, that's where one usually learned the skill.

The Chronicle doesn't have much to say about Merewal Penda's son, but an old legend whispers that he married a kinswoman of Aethelburgh and that, later in life, he embraced Christianity.

The Chronicle has quite a bit to say about Peada Penda's son, and most of it tells about a ruthless young man who was fonder of the idea of ruling Mercia than of his father the king.

Aethelburgh of Cent was in fact the Queen of Northumbria. It was she who brought Roman Christianity to Northumbria, with the result that most of England was converted and the non-Christian culture systematically obliterated. Aethelburgh did flee Eoferwic (York) at the time of Penda's siege, but she took a straighter road than I set her on. Her husband, Eadwine of Northumbria, met exactly the fate I describe here and he was regarded as a saint by the early English Church.

Finally, historians don't know who authored the poem Garroc attributes to Wulfhere. For the curious, here is all of the poem as it has come down to us:

Wonderful this warding wall!

Then fate broke the *burgstede,*   battered giant's work.
Towers tumbled,   gable's targe split,
age stole stout gates.   Frost shines on lime,
chills the mother's breast,   breaks earth's bond.
Wyrd drove down   the wall-maker's dream,
earth-gripped, strong   a hundred seasons since
doom found the folk.   Of faith spoke this wall,
grey-cloaked, red-stained.   To king after king
hard oaths and hoar   gave this high-reaching friend
to stand stout under storm.

For memory men built,   bold stone-wrights binding,
fitting stone to stone.   Mead-halls soared.
High horns filled,   flowed the foam of poet's ale.
Good gifts and gold   gorged treasure-halls.
None changes fate.   Chance and chant are stronger.

Great the sore sorrow   in days of sickness.
Hearts bleed courage.   Hard men are humbled
in wind-haunted streets,   wail weeping in high halls
as idols decay,   their dwellings drear temples
of midnight mourning,   murdered dream-craft.
And this red tile,   white-fingered roof-hoard riven,
falls on heaped howes.   Here sleep brave men,
glad-minded soldiers,   gold-gleaming kings.
War-wolves, sword-lovers!   Wild and wine-flushed,
they looked on sweet treasures,   on silver shining,
on chant-crafted gold-work   and gem-carver's cunning,
on power and pride   and precious wealth.

In this brave city,   the bold bright kingdom,
stone houses stood . . .

The rest of the poem is lost, the words forever vanished from
a crumbling manuscript page. Today we know the poem as *The
Ruin.* The translation in this novel is mine, and I hope the poet
knows that I made it humbly and with all respect.

CLASSIC SCIENCE FICTION AND FANTASY